DESERT DESIRE

Her face was only inches from his own. He could feel her sweet breath upon his face, smell the fragrant jasmine that perfumed her pale gold hair.

"I've wanted you from the moment you came riding across the desert to meet me. A fiery young woman on a camel, dizzy with brandy, ready to do battle. I wonder now why I didn't fling you over my own camel and ride off with you."

"I don't remember any of that meeting," she said breathlessly. "For all I know, you did just that."

His fingers moved to caress her chin, tilting her face toward him until their lips were almost touching. "Do you think I had my way with you in the desert?"

"Did you?" she whispered.

"Maybe. Maybe I carried you off and laid you down in the hollow of a sand dune. Perhaps I took off every stitch of clothing you had on, then stripped mine off as well," he continued. "And we made love in the bright sunlight, naked."

"Naked," she echoed in a tone of wonder.

"The dunes are softer than the pyramids, lass. You'd not shrink from loving me on a sand dune, would you?" He brushed her lips with his own.

CYNTHIA KIRK

THE LADY AND THE LION

LEISURE BOOKS NEW YORK CITY

For Melanie Bagil, Elena Lincoln,
Steve and Jaime Rodriguez
The members of my first—and best—archaeological team
And for all the archaeologists who work to bring the past
to life.

A LEISURE BOOK®

April 2001

Published by

Dorchester Publishing Co., Inc.
276 Fifth Avenue
New York, NY 10001

Cover art by John Ennis
www.ennisart.com

ISBN 0-8439-4856-6

Chapter One

1895

Charlotte Fairchild refused to scream. She even kept her hand steady as she poured out the coffee, the delicate porcelain cups tinkling slightly.

"I regret that I cannot offer you tea, but our foreman is from Constantinople and insists we drink Turkish coffee. He's much too fine a worker to cross, so coffee it is. Would you care for cinnamon or sugar, Lady Havers?"

The tiny woman sitting across the table shook her head. Her face showed beet red beneath her sashed bonnet.

"Sir Thomas?"

"Cinnamon, please."

She marveled that they dared drink hot coffee at all; it was beastly warm for an Egyptian January. The desert sun beat down on them like a blazing anvil.

Charlotte gestured toward a copper tray piled high with dates and candied fruit. Only Sir Thomas ventured to choose

11

one. Her duty as hostess completed, she carefully stood up.

"If you will both excuse me."

Backing up slowly into the tent behind her, Charlotte disappeared for a moment. When she emerged again, she held a large pistol in her hands. She stood ramrod straight, ignoring the startled gasps from her visitors. Taking aim at the hooded snake, she fired. The great cobra hissed once, spun about, then fell heavily onto the ground.

Charlotte lowered the gun. "I must say that was the boldest cobra I've seen in all the years I've been in Egypt. If he'd been a tad quicker, he would have quite spoiled our little repast."

She turned to face her two guests. Lady Havers had a hand poised as if about to take a sip, but her cup and its contents now lay spattered in her lap. Sir Thomas was choking on a date.

The gunshot had roused their foreman, who came running up from the supply tent. He arrived breathless, his dark eyes widening at the sight of the dead cobra.

"I think we'll need something stronger than coffee, Ahmed. The brandy, perhaps."

He frowned. "Mr. Fairchild will not like this. Shooting guns in the middle of the day, distracting the workmen. What a most dreadful occurrence for a European lady to be involving herself in."

"Thank you, Ahmed. Now could we have the brandy, please?"

Beneath his bristly mustache, his scowl grew deeper. "Strong spirits in the afternoon? That is why the beasts of the desert seek out this place. A curse has been brought upon us."

When he left, muttering all the while, Charlotte turned back to her guests. Lady Havers appeared rigid with shock.

Sir Thomas pulled out a handkerchief and mopped his forehead. "I can't imagine how you kept your hand steady, my dear."

"Father saw to it I had plenty of opportunity for target practice. Normally I need it only for the scorpions, although two seasons ago, I encountered the most contrary hyena." She tucked the pistol within the voluminous pocket of her skirt. Lady Havers still seemed far too pale. "Cobras, however, are always a nasty business. It was just fortunate I caught his reflection in that."

The Haverses turned their alarmed gazes upon the copper pitcher on the table.

Charlotte sat in the camp chair across from them. If she treated this as an ordinary occurrence, perhaps the elderly couple would look less petrified. "Come, that's all over. We don't want it to ruin our tea." She smiled. "Even if it is Turkish coffee."

Lady Havers retrieved her fallen cup with a trembling hand. "My memories of Egypt never included cobras."

Charlotte wasn't surprised. Although Sir Thomas had an excellent reputation as an Egyptologist, she suspected his corseted wife rarely left the confines of the first-class suites at Shepheard's English Hotel.

"No need to be alarmed, Lady Havers. I'm convinced we're far safer in the desert than on the streets of London. And it is quite the most beautiful place on earth, don't you agree?" Charlotte looked at the sandstone cliffs surrounding them. "London has such dreadful air to breathe, the morning sky thick with chimney smoke and factory fires. But here, the air is sweet as honey water."

She inhaled, then bit back a grimace. At that moment, all she could smell was camel dung.

"Not even Egyptologists should spend most of their lives in the desert, despite its unique charms." Sir Thomas cast a wary glance at the dead cobra a mere twenty feet away. "There comes a time to put down the shovel. I excavated far too many years, depriving myself of the company of Lady Havers. And depriving myself of professional opportunities as well."

13

"Working in the storerooms of the British Museum, or the dusty galleries of the Colville Collection, perhaps?" Charlotte sipped her coffee. "Hardly comparable to uncovering a Fifth Dynasty tomb."

"A man must spend time in the right circles back home if he wants his discoveries in Egypt to be appreciated. Knighthoods aren't won by obscure scholars, Mrs. Fairchild. No matter how many tombs they've stumbled upon."

"Sir Reginald, my father, would have disagreed with you," she said quietly.

From behind the tent came the sound of men running. A moment later, her husband appeared, out of breath, a rifle in his hands. Ahmed stood beside him, holding a bottle of brandy.

"Charlotte, are you killing cobras again?"

She pointed at the serpent, coiled lifelessly in the sun.

Ian's tanned face wore a weary expression. "I've asked you to call for one of the men in these circumstances."

Ahmed nodded. "It is not fitting for a European lady to concern herself with cobras."

"Well, I am most grateful we had a concerned European lady on hand this afternoon," Sir Thomas broke in. "Otherwise my good wife and I would now be as dead as the mummies of Thebes."

Ahmed placed the liquor bottle on the table with an air of disapproval, then stalked off.

Ian turned his attention to their visitors. "Sir Thomas, Lady Havers. So dreadfully sorry that I wasn't here when you arrived, but we've been busy erecting wall supports for the tunnels."

Despite the smile he wore, Charlotte knew that her husband was angry with her. She understood that his fury only demonstrated his concern for her welfare, yet she felt diminished by it. Married nearly a year, they'd known each other since he came to work for her father three years earlier. But he still wouldn't acknowledge how capable she was at handling not only the desert but his difficult moods.

"I did want to be here to greet you. You see, I have not yet told Charlotte about your offer."

She looked up from pouring brandy into Lady Havers's cup. "What offer?"

Ian ran his hand through his black hair, which was covered with dust from the tomb. "Sir Thomas has come to Egypt to offer me the position of director of the Colville Collection."

She stared openmouthed at both men.

"It is an opportunity not likely to come again for many years. Lord Barrington, who previously held the position, was killed last month in a carriage accident. And the gentleman who was his most logical successor has been found to be in the throes of a grievous addiction." Sir Thomas raised his eyebrows.

Lady Havers leaned over the table. "Opium," she whispered.

"Ian should be commended for carrying on your father's work in the Valley of Amun. But despite its glorious past, even you must admit there is little left to be uncovered here."

"Nonsense." Charlotte felt as if Sir Thomas was speaking ill of a dear friend. "At least a dozen tombs have not yet been opened. One of them may be the burial place of Princess Hatiri."

"Princess Hatiri?" Lady Havers asked.

"Actually she wasn't a real princess, although some legends claim she was." Charlotte ignored Sir Thomas's mocking smile. "She was the daughter of a high priest of Amun, and the favorite concubine of Rameses the Great. It is said that she was murdered by the jealous queen, but so great was Rameses's devotion to her that he had her buried in secret, surrounded with as much treasure as any pharaoh."

"Poppycock." Sir Thomas pointed to a mud-brick building that her father had erected years ago to house the artifacts. Inside were stacked dozens of crates, each filled with every object that had been excavated from the Valley of Amun.

"In there lies everything of value that this site has to offer. A respectable collection of funerary art, but nothing spectacular enough to warrant your husband passing up such a sterling opportunity. It is time for you and Ian to end your work here."

"You are mistaken, Sir Thomas. I am certain that when we at last deliver the material to the Cairo Museum, the director-general will be most impressed by our 'respectable' collection."

"I find the offer from the Colvilles to be far more impressive." Sir Thomas tapped Ian on the shoulder. "The Earl of Morley's son was pursuing the position most vigorously."

"Fine. If the Earl of Morley's son wants the job, let him have it."

"Don't be absurd, Charlotte. The fool never even finished university." Ian couldn't resist chuckling over the idea.

She thought a moment. "Well, that fellow Barnabas Hughes, then. He's an antiquities scholar, reasonably competent. And he's been working at the Collection for over ten years."

"I thought you hated Hughes."

Indeed, when Barnabas Hughes visited their site last year, she'd taken an immediate dislike to him.

"I do. He's arrogant and rude, but if it means we must give up the Valley, then I'd see Attila the Hun become director first." Charlotte grabbed her husband's arm. "Ian, please. I beg you."

"Ian will be the youngest director in the history of the Collection," Sir Thomas said after an awkward silence. "The Colville family have even agreed to postpone the opening of their new Egyptian galleries for another year, time enough for him to organize everything to his own tastes. But the offer is contingent upon the two of you leaving for London as soon as possible."

"I've made some sketches on how I'd like the galleries to be laid out," Ian said. "I'll show them to you this afternoon."

Charlotte felt suddenly light-headed, as though she had inhaled the hashish smoke of the coffeehouses in Cairo. "You speak as if you were going to accept their offer."

"I already have." Her husband brushed the specks of dust from his goatee.

She opened her mouth, but no words came out.

"Best thing in the world for both of you, Mrs. Fairchild. Sheer folly to stay out here." Lady Havers poured herself another cup of brandy. "Everyone knows the Valley of Amun is cursed. Your first foreman died most unfortunately, and then there was your poor father."

"I am not leaving." Her voice trembled with anger—and fear. "I made a promise to Father on his deathbed that I would finish his work. I can scarcely believe that you would even consider giving up the site. It would be criminal to leave the rest of the Valley unexcavated."

The two men exchanged glances.

She reached for the amulet that hung about her neck on a thin leather thong. "What haven't you told me?"

He sighed. "The director-general has agreed to transfer our *firman* to another archaeologist."

"You're transferring our permit to excavate?" She stared at her husband as if he were a complete stranger.

"Yes."

"To whom?"

Ian looked away, a guilty expression finally appearing on his face.

Sir Thomas cleared his throat. "Dylan Pierce."

"Pierce?" She sat back, stunned. "You dare call him an archaeologist? Why, he's a looter of temples, a libertine, a—a drunkard!"

"I believe he drinks no more than the average Irishman."

Ian cleared his throat. "He's Welsh."

"As though it matters whether he's Welsh *or* Irish!" Charlotte could not believe what she was hearing. "The man is a pornographer!"

17

"He translated a volume of Arabian poetry," Ian said.

"I hear it's quite erotic." Lady Havers frowned. "Sir Thomas won't allow me to read a single verse."

Sir Thomas shot his wife a warning glance. "I have it on the best authority that Dylan Pierce is no longer the wild man he once was."

"The idiot set the native quarter on fire six months ago. Ian and I were in Cairo at the time. The tentmakers' bazaar was ablaze for an entire night. And all because Pierce got into a drunken brawl over some belly dancer."

Lady Havers hiccupped. "Dreadful what strong drink can do."

"I've heard he has his drinking under control now, Mrs. Fairchild."

"Hang his drinking!" Charlotte banged her fist on the table, upsetting the cups. "Dylan Pierce loots the sites in the desert like a grave robber. Ripping away priceless artifacts without regard for scholarship or history, selling them off to the highest bidder—"

"Except for your father, Charlotte, that is how most of Egypt's artifacts have been uncovered until quite recently," Ian said. "You can hardly blame Pierce for using methods every other scholar employs."

"He's a treasure hunter, not a scholar. And a drunken one into the bargain. Do you know, he used dynamite to open up the tomb of Pharaoh Thutmose?" Even now the thought chilled her blood. "Think of all that he destroyed in his pursuit of gold!"

"He is an able, educated man." Ian sat back, crossing his arms in front of him. "And I wish to hear no more about it."

"Pierce is quite brave, too," Sir Thomas added. "Here in Africa, they call him 'The Lion.' It is said that a lion once attacked him."

Lady Havers hiccupped again. "I heard that it was a woman who dubbed him that. No doubt he's a jungle beast in the boudoir."

Sir Thomas removed the cup from his wife's hand. "I believe you've had enough 'coffee' for today, my dear."

"Well, I haven't." Charlotte poured a cup of brandy for herself and gulped it down. The fiery liquid made her gasp, but she needed something shocking to calm her growing despair.

"Charlotte, I've never seen you drink spirits." Ian frowned at her. "It's most unbecoming. And unwise in this heat."

"If I am unwise, then you are unkind." She reached for the bottle, but he snatched it away. "Unkind to make decisions that affect my whole life and not breathe a word to me about it. As if I were an infant in a pram."

"Well, you're behaving like one, and in front of guests, too. You're five and twenty, past the age when tantrums are acceptable. Instead of carrying on in this manner, you should be grateful that Pierce is willing to step in at such short notice."

"I should be grateful that you're turning over my father's life work to a drunken thief and pornographer?"

"Stop exaggerating." Ian sighed. "Pierce wanted to begin excavations at Deir el-Bahri this season, but the French got there first. Luckily, Sir Thomas dined with him three nights ago in Cairo and convinced him to visit the Valley this morning."

"Pierce is coming here now?" It was like hearing that a gang of brigands were en route to carry off her greatest treasure.

Sir Thomas nodded. "He should arrive before noon."

"I can scarcely believe what you've done!"

"This is no longer a topic for discussion. Now stop being so stubborn and selfish. We must be ready to leave for England within a fortnight, and you have a lot of packing to do."

"We are not leaving Egypt." She stood up abruptly, the camp chair falling over behind her.

"Don't expect me to indulge you at every turn. I am not your father, Charlotte."

Charlotte reached over and grabbed the brandy bottle out of his hands. "Indeed, you are not. My father and his work were not for sale, not even to the Colville family."

She hurried away from the table. In her haste, she stumbled over the dead snake and nearly fell. Ignoring the shouts behind her, she kept on walking into the desert.

To think that but a moment ago, the greatest threat to her life was a mere cobra. But with one unwise decision, Ian had put their future—and her love for him—in far greater danger.

Dylan Pierce hated camels.

Storm-tossed schooners rocked less than these rancid smelling beasts. To make matters worse, they attracted more flies than a dung heap and spent half their time trying to bite him on the leg.

Unfortunately he was riding one now. The rolling gait of his camel had already made him nauseous. He scanned the surrounding sand dunes, golden and silent in the sun. If he hadn't just recovered from another attack of malaria, he'd get off this beast and walk to the Valley of Amun. No doubt he'd be retching before he and the cursed camel reached their destination.

For the tenth time this morning, he wondered if he'd made a mistake in taking on the excavations. From all accounts, no real treasure lay in the Valley. And if there was one, it would have to be turned over to the Cairo Museum and kept out of his eager hands.

No, the Valley of Amun was a scholarly assignment: respectable, painstaking, poorly paid. It required a man of integrity and patience, qualities he was not even certain he possessed any longer. Yet it was the sort of undertaking he had been telling himself for years he should devote himself to, before his brawling and adventures destroyed any chance he might have of ever being taken seriously. But now that he had let his finer instincts get the better of him, he regretted it.

"I could tell them that my malaria has returned," he said aloud. "And hint that I've picked up cholera, too."

The camel twitched her ears at the sound of his voice.

"By the time I arrive, I'll probably look like a fellow on his deathbed. They'll take one glance and chase me off into the desert."

He was only half joking. He truly did not feel well. A week ago, he awoke in the throes of another bout of fever. Over a hundred and five, the doctor told him. Although he had learned to control his symptoms with quinine, malarial attacks still made him feel like the very devil. For weeks afterward, he was drained, weary. And too much sun sometimes brought on a wave of dizziness that sent him crashing to the ground.

He should have gone on that Nile cruise with Mademoiselle Eva. He could be lying on a deck chair aboard a river steamer right now, while a lovely Frenchwoman kept him cool with a palm frond fan. Instead he was bouncing on a camel and hoping the bloody creature didn't get bit by a sand viper. He wondered if a respectable career was worth so much aggravation.

A shape appeared on the horizon. He reined in his camel, who responded with a bellowing grunt.

He sat watching. Slowly, the shimmering image began to solidify. Someone on a camel was riding straight for him. This was no mirage. And if the sunlight wasn't playing tricks on him, the rider appeared to be female.

Probably one of those infernal tourists somehow lost her way from exploring the ruins at Luxor.

Dylan adjusted the sun visor on his cap with an exasperated sigh. It was bad enough he had agreed to visit the Valley of Amun; now he would have to waste even more time guiding some distraught woman back to safety.

But as the camel drew closer, he saw that the female rider did not seem distraught at all. In fact, beneath her wide-brimmed bonnet, her expression was as severe and controlled as a statue of Anubis, god of the underworld. She suddenly reined in her mount.

With a practiced air, she forced the animal to its knees and alighted from it as easily as if she were stepping from a brougham in Leiscester Square.

To his irritation, his own camel was not as tractable. When he at last got the maddening creature to sink to the desert floor, he jumped off and walked over to where the woman stood waiting.

"Are you lost, madame? If so, allow me to be of assistance."

"You can assist me by going back to Cairo." She swept off her hat. As soon as she did, he knew who she was.

Years ago, he had visited the Valley of Amun and spoken with the great Egyptologist Sir Reginald Grainger. He remembered being briefly introduced to his daughter, a young girl with hair as white as moonlight. "Moonfire," the native workers had called it. That same striking hair was now piled and twisted behind her head like a gleaming rope. Although close up, he could see it was not silver at all, but more like white gold. And a startling contrast beside her tanned skin and light gray eyes.

"You're Sir Reginald Grainger's daughter, aren't you? We met five years ago." Actually, they hadn't really met. When her father introduced them, she was so intent on removing a stele from the sand, she had barely spared him a glance.

"I am Mrs. Fairchild now. Charlotte Fairchild." Her voice was low and hoarse, a result of the parched desert air.

She unhooked the canvas water bag hanging from her belt and drank for several moments. When she was finished, her lips were moist from the water, drops still running down her chin. She didn't bother to wipe them away. Not the demeanor of a European gentlewoman at all. And with those

22

light eyes set against that nut-brown skin, she seemed a hybrid: part English maiden, part Egyptian queen.

"So you are Dylan Pierce."

He took offense at her tone.

"I am." Despite his irritation, he was curious. "I'd almost forgotten that you married the man who took over your father's site."

"Yes, I married the man whose excavation you are usurping." She tried to rehook the water bag to her belt but couldn't. With an angry mutter, she tossed it to the ground.

"I have just learned that you—you of all people!—will be taking over our work. Well, I've come to stop you."

The young woman seemed unsteady, weaving from side to side even though there wasn't a hint of a breeze.

"Are you all right. Mrs. Fairchild?"

"No, I am not all right. I am angry. I'm angry at you! You're a barbarian who destroys temples for a fistful of treasure." She shook her head as if to clear it. "You brigand from hell!"

Dylan shook his own head. At least he had malaria to blame for his dizziness. This woman was obviously suffering from heat exhaustion. She was already babbling in delirium.

Would these fool English never learn that the desert was no place for their overbred ladies? Although most English ladies didn't have white-gold hair or sit a camel like a Bedouin. Most of them weren't beautiful either, although he wasn't sure if this one was. She was striking, he decided, not beautiful. Slender, imposing—even majestic. But there was nothing delicate about her, or soft. He pitied the man who attempted to curb all that furious energy. Even he would be reluctant to take such a woman on, although she did have glorious hair and haunting eyes.

"I believe you need to sit down on the sand and rest for a moment. You're suffering from sunstroke."

"I never get sunstroke." Her chin lifted proudly. "I've spent every winter in the desert since I was thirteen. Only tourists get sunstroke. I belong here, unlike them. And you. That is why I want you to keep your brutish presence away from my site."

"*Your* site?"

"The Valley of Amun belonged to my father. Now it is mine."

"I don't think you can claim possession, lass. The last I heard, an archaeologist called Ian Fairchild was the official director of excavation."

"My husband is not an archaeologist." She leaned forward and nearly toppled to the ground. "My husband is a weasel."

Dylan caught a whiff of her breath. He waved a hand in front of his face, clearing away the fumes. "Didn't anyone ever warn you not to go riding off into the desert when you're drunk?"

Her eyes widened. "How dare you suggest that I—Charlene, Charlolo—that *I* cannot drink a little bit of brandy without becoming drunk." She pointed a finger at him. "You're the drunkard. They told me you were a drunken lion."

He groaned. Not that "lion" business again. "Who's been telling stories about me now?"

"Don't deny it, sir. You are a lion who loots. You—you sack temples as brutally as the ancient Hykasysos."

"Hyksos," he corrected softly.

"So you admit it." She straightened to her full height. "Well, I've ridden out here to warn you. No one, not even a lion, will be allowed to dynamite the tomb of Princess Hatiri."

He held out his hands. "Rest easy. I am traveling without explosives this morning."

"You're laughing at me." She hiccupped.

"If I were feeling better, I might be tempted to." He tried to take her arm, but she pushed him away. "Look, Mrs. Fairchild, neither of us is fit for a leisurely conversation under the desert sun. Why don't we get on our camels and ride to the Valley of Amun?"

"It is *my* valley. One I will never surrender to you, sir, not even if—" Her tanned face suddenly took on an unhealthy pallor. "Oh, dear."

"What's wrong?" He grabbed her arms.

"You were right." Her knees buckled. "I think I've had too much sun."

He lowered her to the sand.

"I don't feel well," she murmured.

That makes two of us, Dylan thought. But he dutifully clapped his own hat on her head, making certain to adjust the visor to shade her face. "Just sit here and rest."

Walking over to her camel, he opened up the saddle bag. The only thing in it was an empty brandy bottle.

"Don't tell me you drank the entire bottle, Mrs. Fairchild."

He turned around only to discover that she was now lying flat on the sand, spread-eagled.

She hiccupped again. "Sunstroke is a terrible thing."

At least she was still conscious.

He looked off into the distance. Not an oasis in sight, just hot sand as far as the eye could see. And it was an hour's ride to the Valley of Amun. He'd have to sling her over his camel and take her there before the sun rose any higher. He could just imagine the reception such a sight would elicit from her husband.

Unhooking his own water bag, he knelt beside her again and poured the water over her face. "Let's try and come out of this drunken stupor, Mrs. Fairchild."

"I'm not drunk, Mr. Lion. It's the sun's fault." She paused. "And Ian's."

He cradled her in his arms, coaxing her to take small sips of water. "My name is Dylan, not Mr. Lion."

She nodded, eyes closed. "All right, Dilly."

"Dilly!"

She opened her eyes and stared up at him. "Don't take

my site, Dilly. Please. It's my whole life. Don't steal it away. Be a nice lion." She touched his hand. "Father would want me to keep it. I must carry on his work."

"I was a great admirer of your father. I heard him lecture once at Cambridge. No one in the field had better instincts."

"My father was the greatest Egyptologist who ever lived." Tears filled her eyes. "He wanted me to marry an Egyptologist, too. But I married a weasel instead."

She burst into tears, great sobs racking her body.

"There, there." He patted her as though she were a child. With luck, the drunken crying jag wouldn't last too long. She pressed closer to him, and he felt the weight of a metal object against his leg.

"Excuse me, Mrs. Fairchild, but what in the world are you carrying in your skirt pocket?"

"A pistol," she sniffed.

With a swift movement, he fished out the gun from within the folds of her canvas skirt. He examined it, cursing aloud to see that it was loaded. "My dear woman, did you mean to use this on *me?*"

"Don't be silly. I needed it for the cobra." She gave another loud hiccup. "I would never shoot a lion. In fact, I— I should have married a lion. A lion would never leave Egypt."

Lions, weasels, cobras. The woman seemed to inhabit a veritable zoo.

He lay the pistol down on the sand, making certain it was safely out of Mrs. Fairchild's drunken reach. "When are you leaving Egypt?"

"Two weeks." That brought on another flood of tears. "I shall wither and die if I go back to England." Great sobs shook her. "Everything I love is here. Everything!"

He didn't bother to remind her that she would be returning to England with her husband. Apparently all was not well in the Fairchild marriage.

"You understand, don't you? You don't think I'm being selfish or stubborn?"

"Maybe just a bit." Dylan smiled. "But since I'm rarely anything but selfish and stubborn, I'll not hold it against you."

"Father was stubborn, too." She choked back another sob. "He searched his whole life for the resting place of Princess Hatiri; he died in the pursuit of it. Now when we are so close, Ian gives it all away."

A long silence followed, filled only with snorts from the camels.

"And it wasn't his to give," she whispered.

He felt sorry for both her and her husband. Ian Fairchild had clearly tired of Egypt, and such things being the way of the world, his wife would have to follow him no matter where he chose to go. Even if leaving meant breaking her heart. Looking into those clear gray eyes, Dylan felt certain that her heart *would* break when she left Africa. As his would, if circumstances demanded. For the thousandth time in his life, he thanked God he was born male and had control over his own destiny.

"Do not take the Valley of Amun away from me." She pushed herself into a sitting position. "It would be like losing my father a second time."

He sat back, thinking it over.

"But will your husband be willing to stay? According to Sir Thomas, he wants to leave Egypt as soon as possible."

The tears were still wet upon her cheeks, and he had to restrain himself from brushing them away.

"*I* want to stay." She rubbed at her forehead as if it throbbed, which no doubt it did. "I love Egypt. I love every drop of river mud and every grain of sand. I even love the snakes and mosquitoes. Can you understand that?"

He turned his gaze upon the shifting sand. "I first came here ten years ago. Within the first three weeks, I got bit by a mongoose, caught in a sandstorm, and nearly killed by the hippo who overturned our boat." He looked back at her. "I've refused to spend even a minute away ever since."

She smiled. He felt as though he had somehow coaxed the Sphinx at Giza to change her inscrutable expression.

"All right, Mrs. Fairchild. Your brandy-soaked pleas have moved me." He grinned. "As they would any decent Welshman."

"What?" Her eyes grew wide and excited.

"I'll leave you and your Valley of Amun alone."

She threw herself at him. "Thank you, Mr. Lion," she said, sobbing once more. "Thank you."

He wrapped his arms about her and held her while she cried. She felt sweet in his arms, proving that a soft, tempting woman lay hidden beneath the canvas skirt and practical boots. After a moment, he gently pushed her away. The feel of her body pressed to his was getting a shade too exciting. And who knew what she might propose next, awash as she was in both gratitude and brandy?

He noticed she wore a dark green amulet about her neck. It swung from a thin leather thong, nestling between her breasts, which were heaving in the heat. He needed a distraction.

"I've never seen an amulet like that before." He peered closer. "It's a lion, isn't it?"

"A lioness. The goddess Sekhmet." She closed her hand about it. "Green faience, Third Dynasty. It's my good-luck charm." Her eyes widened. "I'll give it to you, Mr. Lion. It's only fitting."

He stopped her from taking it off her neck. "Please keep it. I don't need good-luck amulets. I make my own luck, lass."

"But it works," she said with a loud hiccup.

"It certainly worked for you today, Mrs. Fairchild." He got to his feet, pulling her up after him. "Although when I tell your husband I've decided not to take over the site, I fear your good luck may desert you."

"Ian doesn't frighten me. Leaving Egypt does. Thanks to you, I won't have to." She flung wide her arms. "Mr. Lion, you've given the desert back to me. Let me embrace you once more."

She fell heavily against him.

"Drunk as a rum-running sailor," he muttered.

It took him a moment to realize she'd passed out.

With a grunt, he picked her up in his arms. "By the saints, I never knew England grew such strange young ladies."

She smiled like a sleeping child, oblivious to both him and the desert heat.

He brushed his cheek against her own. "Between you, me, and the camels," he whispered to the unconscious Charlotte, "I hope your husband appreciates what a fierce and amazing wife he has."

Then again, perhaps only a "lion" would know what to do with a woman like Charlotte Fairchild.

Chapter Two

The woman was beautiful, willing, and as carnal as Cleopatra.

Dylan watched her as she moved gracefully about the boat deck, humming to herself, casting an occasional flirtatious glance his way. The river breeze caressed him, while from the shore came the cries of the *fellaheen* urging their oxen through the dark Nile mud. He leaned back in his chair, sipping cold hibiscus tea. And wishing he felt happier.

The paddle-steamer was stocked with delicacies, books of poetry, even a Victrola. Surrounded by music, the Nile, and a beautiful Frenchwoman, Dylan should be as content as any pasha. Yet try as he might, he couldn't dismiss this absurd feeling of guilt about Mrs. Fairchild.

Why should he be feeling guilty because he gave an Englishwoman what she desperately wanted? Indeed, what she'd begged him for. But he couldn't forget how angry her husband had looked when he brought Charlotte Fairchild back to the Valley of Amun. She was still unconscious when he left an hour later, having added to Ian Fairchild's fury by telling him that he had decided not to take over the excavations.

Fairchild had been *too* angry about his refusal. That was what continued to bother Dylan a week later. Just because he had refused the site didn't mean Fairchild couldn't find another Egyptologist to take it on. Men with far better credentials than he boasted. His young wife had been correct: His methods up until now had been crude, brutal even. There were a half-dozen fellows in Lower Egypt who were more trustworthy and better qualified. Why then should the refusal of a rogue like him send Ian Fairchild into a cold rage?

"I hope he doesn't take it out on her," he murmured.

"What did you say, *cheri?*" His companion leaned against the boat railing. She smiled at him prettily.

Mademoiselle Eva not only possessed a beguiling—if practiced—smile, but some renown as an actress. Of course, she'd never performed anywhere but the French colonies, but he doubted there was a Parisian actress as skilled. Certainly few could be so charming.

"I was just wondering if Mrs. Fairchild's husband has forgiven her yet."

She made a face. "*Si vous plait,* let us not talk about the Englishwoman again."

He barely heard her. "I should have stayed until she recovered. She probably awoke with a whale of a hangover, only to find her husband ready to strangle her. He didn't look like the sort of fellow who would find a tipsy wife all that amusing."

"Oh, the English are so cold to their women. No wonder the silly lady took to drink."

He drained his glass of red tea. "According to Mrs. Fairchild, it was her husband and I who prompted her to get drunk."

"As you make me drunk, *cheri.*" Eva moved toward him,

her skirts billowing about her like a cloud of azure chiffon. "With pleasure."

He held out his hand and drew her down onto his lap. Why was he wasting even a moment worrying about the woman? Eventually Fairchild would make his way back to England, dragging his wife along with him, and he'd never see either of them again. Right now he had a two-week cruise up the Nile to look forward to. And the scandalous company of a lady who would demand only that he pay undivided attention to her. At least until she took up with the next handsome fellow she met on her travels.

Yet, while he stroked the Frenchwoman's auburn curls, he couldn't help but remember the white-gold hair of Charlotte Fairchild. And those wide gray eyes that seemed to hold as many secrets as the Sphinx.

Eva nestled against his chest with an exaggerated sigh.

"I should have remained at the camp longer," he said after a moment. "At least until Mrs. Fairchild woke up."

"Enough about this Englishman's drunken wife." Her dulcet voice held an edge.

"He was in a damned foul temper. How do I know he didn't beat her after I left?"

She pushed herself away from him. "And what if he did?"

"I don't take to men beating women. Never could stomach the idea." He shook his head. "Although she seemed bold enough to challenge the meanest Algerian pirate to a fight. And quite possibly win, too."

"*Mon Dieu,* you act as if the English lady were your mistress." Her lovely eyes narrowed. "Maybe you should take this Nile cruise with her instead of me."

Maybe I should, he thought. Charlotte Fairchild was unlike any woman he'd ever met. Perhaps she wouldn't entertain him in bed as readily as this mademoiselle, but he suspected every other moment with her would be unpredictable and challenging. It had been a long time since a woman had aroused his interest, and not merely his appetite.

"Now, Eva, you know I adore you." He caressed her shoulders.

She pushed him away and stood up. "You are acting with me. And not very well."

Before he could stop her, she was mincing her way down the deck, pushing past the steward, who dropped a tray of sweet bananas and pears. Dylan heard the door to her cabin slam, which woke up the green lizard asleep beneath one of the chairs.

He thought briefly of going after her, soothing her with a pretty lie or two. Instead he walked over to the railing and gazed out at the lush spectacle of the riverbank. A flock of flamingos suddenly flew past the steamer, their outstretched wings only a few feet from his face. Yet he barely blinked.

Nothing seemed to hold his interest these days. Not French actresses, not bottles of Irish whiskey, not even the prospect of hunting rhino in the wilds of Abyssinia. He was thirty-one, too young to feel this jaded and weary.

But he feared he was too old to still be playing about. Playing with women, playing at being a scholar. Yet he had never really tried to be a respectable scholar. Perhaps everything had come too easily to him: his facility for languages, his uncanny knack for finding just where an ancient tomb lay hidden, his ability to charm even the most reluctant and respectable of women.

Not that he'd ever had much interest in respectable women. At least until he met Charlotte Fairchild. He must be changing.

Egypt—and archaeology—were changing, too. There were excavation rules in place, and a man of integrity overseeing things in Cairo. It was no longer acceptable to go in and dynamite a 4000-year-old temple merely to get at the gold that might lay buried beneath it. He wasn't sad to see the old methods die out. He had destroyed more than he had recovered these past ten years, and the scholar within him regretted the loss. The truth was that he wanted to be remembered for more than a volume of erotic poetry, a few plundered sites, and too many clandestine adventures.

So why, when he was offered the chance to carry on the distinguished work of the late Sir Reginald Grainger, had he let the opportunity slip away?

"The lass wanted to stay," Dylan muttered. He told himself that was why he'd given the Valley of Amun up so easily. Or had he looked for any excuse, any flimsy reason to play the rootless adventurer once more?

It was too late now. All he could do was hope that Charlotte Fairchild was as strong and unafraid as she seemed. Damn it all, he already had enough on his conscience. He didn't need to feel guilty about the young Englishwoman as well. But if anything bad happened to Sir Reginald's daughter as a result of his decision, he knew he'd never forgive himself.

As the boat gently turned south, he looked back. He felt like a coward, a callow boy who couldn't accept responsibility and was running off to the next youthful escapade. A grown man would have reassured Mrs. Fairchild that the site was safe in his hands; he would have calmed her fears and stayed until he knew she was safe from both her husband and the desert sun.

Instead he was sailing up the Nile with a woman he barely liked, let alone desired. Dylan wasn't proud of his actions. He rarely was. If only he could figure out how to change the aimless direction of his life.

Maybe he needed Mrs. Fairchild's good-luck amulet far more than she did.

Charlotte hadn't spent such a miserable week in Egypt since the terrible death of her father. Each day threatened to bring forth a new disaster. Yesterday their supply tent caught fire; the day before, one of the water boys gashed his leg open on the jagged lid of a sarcophagus.

And today the workers were in an uproar. A sleeping kitten had been found curled up at the entrance to the newly opened tomb. The superstitious workers swore it was a bad omen. That, coupled with Charlotte's ignominious return to the site—slung unconscious over the back of a camel—had unsettled every man here. Especially Ian.

Outside the tent, she could hear Ian arguing with their foreman.

"Ahmed, I don't care what the damn fools think. It's a silly kitten. There are dozens of them running about the desert and the streets of Cairo. I need three men to come into the tomb with me today. The cat means nothing. We've had cats on site before."

"Not lying inside the entrance to a tomb." The foreman sounded even grimmer than usual. "This is a tomb protected by the Goddess Bastet, and we are about to defile it with our unholy presence. The Goddess has sent one of her own to warn us away. No one will enter the tomb under Her gaze." He paused. "And that includes me, Mr. Fairchild."

Charlotte tied on her sun hat, preparing herself for battle. She couldn't stay in this stifling tent all morning, although the prospect of facing Ian's ill humor was hardly more appealing.

When she emerged from the tent, her husband shot her a forbidding look. She sighed. It was going to be another endless, incriminating day.

"I hear the workers are upset about finding a kitten."

Both men ignored her, their attention focused on the little animal squirming in Ahmed's hands.

Ian snapped his fingers at the foreman. "Enough with this blasted nonsense. Give me the bloody cat."

Ahmed handed over the fluffy yellow creature as though it were a poisonous viper. The kitten swatted playfully at the Turk's sleeve.

"If I drown the thing in front of the workmen, will that satisfy them?"

Charlotte's cries of protest were echoed by Ahmed.

"Are you out of your mind? Kill a defenseless little kitten? Give me that cat!" She swept the kitten up into her arms and cradled it protectively. "Have you taken complete leave of your senses?"

Ian whirled around. "This from a woman who was hauled into camp stone-cold drunk. You're lucky I don't drown *you* in a bucket of water. Not many husbands would tolerate such heavy-handed interference from their wives."

She turned to the foreman. "Tell the workers that Sir Reginald's daughter will bear the brunt of any curse the Goddess wishes to inflict. And no harm will come to the kitten." She stared hard at Ian. "You have my word."

Ahmed walked away, shaking his head.

"Your bad temper is worrying the men far more than any cat. Why, you've behaved like a madman this past week. Screaming at everyone, throwing things about. If I hadn't stopped you last night, you would have broken that beautiful canopic jar." She stroked the kitten, who purred loudly in response. "You must try to control yourself."

"You're a fine one to give lectures on self-control. Galloping off into the desert with a bellyful of brandy in you! It's a wonder you didn't fall off the camel and break your stupid neck."

She felt her cheeks flush. "I told you. I only had a drop or two. It's just that I am not accustomed to strong drink."

"Do not even try to justify your shameful behavior." He held up his hand. "Go back to the tent, Charlotte. Get out of my sight before I do something I have never done before and strike you."

He was as tight-lipped and angry as she had ever seen him, and these past seven days, Ian had been very angry indeed.

"I've had quite enough of your threats and your temper." She had been contrite and patient this past week, but now her own anger won out. "If you insist on carrying on like this, we *will* come to blows. And I won't balk at flinging one or two canopic jars at your head either!"

Ian scowled. "You care for nothing but this bloody site. You're just like your father. Nothing matters to you except the next discovery, the next tomb, the next desert sarcophagus. It's a mummy you should have married, not a man."

"I thought I married an archaeologist." She suddenly found it preposterous that she had ever married him at all.

"So you did. I am the *only* archaeologist in this family; it's time you understood that. If I decide that my professional interests lie elsewhere, then we pack up and leave. And all your meddling won't stop me. As soon as I find another man to take on the site, we're sailing home to England."

The kitten licked her cheek, and Charlotte held the animal closer. Its loud purring was a comforting sound beside Ian's bitter words.

"You may change your mind about leaving Egypt after we've explored this latest tomb. Who knows what we may find inside?"

"We?" He shook his head. "From now on, I will be the only Fairchild doing the exploring. You'd best find a suite at a Cairo hotel. That's where you'll be staying for the remainder of the season."

"I know you want to hurt me, as I hurt you by convincing Mr. Pierce to refuse the site. But if this arguing continues, we shall become enemies. Don't you understand? I want what's best for us both. I'm sorry I stopped you—"

"You have not stopped me, Charlotte, only delayed me. Unfortunately I can't just pack up and leave. Not without another archaeologist willing to take over the site and pay all these bloody workers I've contracted for the season."

"But you left me no choice."

"Well, you've left me no choice either. As soon as I find a replacement, we shall leave Egypt. And we will not return." He paused for obvious effect. "Ever."

She stared after him as he stalked off. Had she done the

wrong thing by going to Dylan Pierce? Even worse, had she destroyed her marriage by her actions? Ian had been angry with her before, but not like this. He had never treated her with such unrelenting hard fury. It was as if he had never loved her. And heaven help her, there were times she wondered if she had ever loved him.

Soft paws tapped at her cheek. She looked down into the amber-colored eyes of the little desert cat. "I think he hates me now, kitty. Indeed he does."

The kitten mewed plaintively.

The proof of his hatred was not his shouting or his threats, but his refusal to allow her to accompany him inside the tomb today. Heretofore, she had always excavated alongside first her father, and then Ian. She had learned to read hieroglyphics before she was fifteen, and had discovered the mummy of a queen one season along the Nile. She was as fine an Egyptologist as any man, but it was a man who had to give her permission to work. And that Ian would no longer do. The fact that he was about to walk into an ancient tomb without her beside him showed how little he now cared for her feelings. And Ian had always told her that she brought him luck.

"Oh, no!" Charlotte dropped the kitten, who meowed in disapproval.

Clutching the amulet about her neck, she raced toward where the men were gathered. She caught sight of Ian just outside the entrance to the tomb.

"Ian, stop!" She pushed her way through the men. "Here, put this on."

She removed her necklace and draped it about his neck. "If you insist on going in there without me, then at least take my good luck with you."

For a moment, she thought Ian was going to rip the necklace off. Instead, he stroked the amulet, his expression sad and tired.

"Charlotte, what am I going to do with you?" he murmured.

"Be careful," she whispered back.

He looked up at her. For the first time in a week, anger wasn't the only thing she saw in his eyes.

"I do love you." At this moment, she believed she did.

He pulled her roughly into his arms. "I love you, too, Charlotte, despite your stubbornness and my temper. But your meddling has upset all of my plans." His embrace grew even tighter. "You must share the blame for what happens to both of us from now on."

She nodded. So it wasn't a complete truce yet, but at least Ian hadn't pushed her away. "Good luck, darling."

A moment later, he disappeared into the shadows of the tomb. Some part of her ached to walk along that dark passageway with him, but she also wanted to give Ian the pleasure and pride of first discovery.

She crouched down near the entrance, hugging her knees. The kitten thought she was ready to play and pounced upon her feet.

If Ian found anything of value inside the tomb—an ebony statue of Bastet, a wall painting still bright with color—surely then he would feel less angry about having to remain in Egypt.

He might even forgive her one day for having convinced Dylan Pierce to refuse the site. Although, to her shame, she couldn't remember a moment of their encounter in the desert. Had she tearfully begged the Welshman to turn down the site, or had she been angry and demanding? She might even have attempted to seduce him. No wonder Ian looked as if he wanted to throttle her. But how was she to know the damage brandy could do? Until a week ago, the strongest liquor she'd ever sampled was a thimbleful of rum punch on Boxing Day.

The kitten began chewing on the laces of her shoes, and Charlotte smiled at the effort the little cat put into the endeavor. Despite Ian's fury and her lack of memory, she didn't regret going off into the desert to confront Pierce. Whatever transpired between the two of them had the desired effect. The Valley of Amun was still hers, and no dynamiting treasure hunter could destroy it now.

A deep rumbling sounded from inside the passageway.

Ahmed looked up worriedly from his notebook.

"What was that?" She pushed the kitten away and stood up.

Ahmed, now visibly pale, stepped into the shadows of the tomb. He cried out something in Turkish before rushing out.

She tried to push past him, but he threw his burly arms about her. The other native workers ran over, yelling and shouting.

Another loud roar came from the tunnel.

"Ian will be trapped in there! Help him, Ahmed!"

Several men were needed to keep her from running into the tomb. Dust, rocks, and dirt now poured out of the entranceway.

She watched in horror as the roaring finally ceased and the last of the rocks cascaded out into the light. There was no way in now, not unless they dug for days, perhaps months.

"Ian?" Her voice came out in a broken whisper.

The men finally released her, and she slid to the ground. She was vaguely aware of the men rushing about, and heard their shouts in Arabic. No one could survive such a cave-in. No one.

The realization hit her like a blow and she crumpled over onto the ground. A high-pitched wailing broke through the noise. She didn't realize for the longest time that those unearthly sounds were coming from her.

What she did realize, however, was that she had killed her husband as surely as the rocks and sand of that accursed tomb.

Chapter Three

London, 1897

So this was what Dylan Pierce looked like.

Charlotte leaned forward in her seat, trying to see what color his eyes were. Although only two years had passed since she confronted him in the desert, she couldn't recall a single feature of his face. Of course, she had only herself to blame for that. Had she really been so ridiculous as to ride off into the desert while guzzling a bottle of brandy? She flushed at the very idea. It was a miracle she hadn't gotten lost.

Pierce's deep voice soared through the lecture hall like a great bell. The more she listened, the more she thought that perhaps she did retain a dim memory of that brogue-tinged voice.

"He may have translated some filthy Arab poetry, but you must admit he has the longest lashes ever seen on any male out of short pants."

41

High-pitched giggling followed this ridiculous comment.

Charlotte wished she had sat up front, even if it meant breathing in the fumes of lavender scent and barley water that permeated the first two rows of the auditorium. The infernal gossiping of the ladies behind her caused her to miss every other sentence of the lecture.

"Long lashes and a barrel chest form quite a potent combination. And with that mane of auburn hair, Mr. Pierce is the spitting image of a Viking warrior."

Charlotte shot a dark look behind her, but the two young women had eyes only for the speaker. She faced forward again. Since when did archaeologists elicit this sort of moon-faced reaction from London's female population? She had never heard of such a thing, and she was the daughter of the most renowned Egyptologist of his day. What next? Would young women swoon at the sight of geographers and pen love notes to Cambridge dons?

It wasn't as if Mr. Pierce were spectacularly handsome. Not that he was unattractive, not at all, but he possessed exaggerated features. Large eyes, a nose that seemed to have been broken a time or two, a wide mouth, and thick red-gold hair that hung unfashionably over his starched collar. He looked ill at ease on the lectern, like a man who couldn't wait to shed his gray broadcloth suit and patent leather oxfords.

Not that long lashes and a Celtic profile meant a tinker's dam to her. Men, no matter how handsome, were no longer of interest to her. With a sigh, she smoothed down her black skirt, prompting a purr from the cat napping within its folds. Because of her blind stubbornness, she had kept Ian at the site. Because of her, Ian was dead. She would have to live forever with the guilt. And the loneliness that accompanied it.

"Mama says that he is sure to be offered a knighthood within the next ten years."

"Not a bad catch, I'd say. A knighthood, family estates in

Wales. And think of all those shameless poems he's translated. Imagine what impossibly wicked acts he would demand from his wife. He might even require more than one partner at a time."

"No! Do you think so? How wonderfully sinful!"

She could stand no more of this. Charlotte swiveled around in her seat so quickly, the cat fell to the floor with a surprised growl.

"Could you please continue your nonsensical conversation outside? Some of us are interested in the kings of the Eighteenth Dynasty."

The two young women broke into another fit of giggles. Even worse, she could see that both of them were decked out as if for a yachting party at Cowes: white summer dresses, frilled parasols, and wide straw hats. Charlotte couldn't help but stare at the large stuffed dove that decorated the hat of the plumper girl. Its beady eyes peered at her through a spray of dyed yellow feathers.

"Excuse us, madame," the plump woman said with a mocking smile.

Charlotte faced forward again. She should never have come. She couldn't imagine what had possessed her. For over two years she had resolutely refused to attend an archaeological lecture or enter the Egyptian Galleries at the British Museum. After all, it was her obsession with Egypt that had led to Ian's death. Her punishment for being so selfish was to be deprived of anything remotely connected with the glories of that sun-drenched land.

As though to contradict her, Nefer pounced upon her lap and circled until she found a comfortable spot before settling down again. Her long brindled tail swept across Charlotte's face. Maybe she hadn't forsaken everything connected with Egypt. The desert kitten she had prevented Ian from destroying had become her most precious companion and a constant reminder of all that Charlotte had once loved. She might have sacrificed the sandstone valleys of the desert and the

43

smell of river mud along the Nile, but she would not be parted from Nefer.

She actually managed to hear Mr. Pierce expound for several moments about the funerary urns found at Nabesha before the giggles commenced once more behind her.

"I don't know why I allowed you to talk me into coming," Charlotte whispered to the woman sitting beside her. "By all rights, Mother should be here. After all, the Society is bestowing a posthumous honor on her late husband. Isn't that more important than yet another Votes for Women meeting?"

There was no response. She glanced over and saw that her sister was fast asleep.

"Do wake up, Catherine, before you fall right off the chair."

"What? Is the lecture over?" Catherine sat up straight, her bonnet slightly askew. "Is it time for Father's presentation?"

"No, it is not. And it may seem insulting if you are totally unconscious when they do ask us to come onstage."

Catherine laughed. "It would be rather funny, wouldn't it? Me snoring away and you marching up there in that ridiculous veil."

Charlotte touched the black tulle. "I see no reason why anyone should object to a widow wearing mourning clothes."

Her sister shot her a reproving look. "You're not the Queen, my dear," she whispered. "And not even she should be decked out in black bombazine for the rest of her life."

"I refuse to discuss my wardrobe with you. You know my views on this."

Catherine sneezed three times in rapid succession. "If you insist on looking like a black crow all your days, so be it, but I do wish you would refrain from taking that cat everywhere you go." She sneezed again. "Cats make me sneeze."

Charlotte scooped Nefer up in her arms. "Cats have nothing to do with it." She nodded toward the rain pelting the lecture hall windows. "You always sneeze when it rains."

Charlotte felt a tap on her shoulder. It was the plump young woman behind her. "Pardon me, but do you mind keeping quiet? We find your constant jabbering quite annoying."

Her friend smirked behind a gloved hand.

Muttering under her breath, Charlotte faced forward once more. She felt defeated by circumstances that had forced her to attend a lecture on the one subject she had sworn to avoid. Even worse, the scholar speaking so authoritatively on the pharaohs was the same man who had innocently played a role in her husband's demise. No, she should not be here, even if the Society did wish to honor her late father. In another moment, Catherine would be asleep again, while the two featherheads behind her were even now discussing the passionate, though degenerate, physiognomy of Dylan Pierce.

"Now I understand why Georgina told us to come. His thighs are the most impressive I've seen in London all season."

Charlotte groaned aloud.

"Absolutely. Any woman with blood in her veins would have to take care not to throw herself at him. Of course, the dried-up old crones here are barely aware that Mr. Pierce is a male, let alone an attractive one. Makes you pity their husbands." She cleared her throat. "Assuming they have a husband any longer."

"Seeing how disagreeable some of these ladies are, I wouldn't be surprised if their husbands found the afterlife far preferable to the married state."

Charlotte flung aside her widow's veil. Nefer looked up at her. She bent down to nuzzle the cat's upturned face and whispered in her ear.

"What *are* you doing?" Catherine asked between sneezes.

"Will those two crones never keep quiet?" a youthful voice trilled behind her. "In another moment, I'll ask to have them thrown out. Along with that ugly, flea-bitten cat."

Turning about, Charlotte faced the gossiping pair once more. She held Nefer up so that the cat's face was level with her own.

The two young women stared back at her, eyebrows raised defiantly.

"Do you want something?" one of them asked, snapping open her fan with a flourish.

Charlotte pointed to the stuffed bird atop the plump woman's hat. "Kill the bird," she commanded in Arabic.

The desert cat narrowed her eyes and crouched low. Then, with a fearsome growl, she pounced like a lion upon its prey.

They were making more noise that a crowd of Cairo water sellers. Dylan looked up from his notes. Who would have imagined that a lecture before the Greater London Society of Antiquarians would attract so many females? Perhaps it was the exotic nature of Egyptology that drew them, the legends of mummy curses and tales of golden treasure hidden in the sand. Clearly they didn't expect to hear a dry discourse on the funerary monuments of Nabesha.

Bored or not, the least they could do was keep quiet and pay attention while he spoke. At the moment, however, his own attention was diverted by the presence of a real-life cat. At least he assumed it was a cat; he swore he caught a glimpse of a long tail swishing behind a row of bonnets.

He stifled a groan. These London ladies and their plethora of pet spaniels, fat tabbies, and parakeets. They doted on their animal creatures as though they were devoted swains. But to bring one of them to a scholarly lecture seemed the height of lunacy.

Dylan gripped the lectern and told himself that he had only five minutes remaining. Then he could present Sir Reginald Grainger's widow with the Society's medal. After which he intended to run for the door, and heaven help any noisy lady who stood in his way. Oh, to be back in the desert with only jackals and grave robbers to worry about. At least jackals and grave robbers were quiet, unlike these fools who were raising a positive din.

He spied the worst offenders about twenty rows back. The dreadful thing was that one of them was dressed in widow's weeds, veil and all. He only hoped it wasn't Sir Reginald's widow.

"And so in conclusion, I would like to reiterate my findings." Even he heard the relief in his voice. "Unlike my distinguished colleague, Sir Ronald Petrie, I do not believe the—"

A horrendous scream went up from the audience.

"What the devil is that?" he shouted.

A woman in a large feathered hat stood up, screeching and fighting off something that looked like a small lion.

"I do believe a cat attacked that woman," whispered Mrs. Rumpelmin, who sat on the stage behind him.

Actually, it appeared as though the cat was eating the lady's bonnet. Another lady kept hitting the feline with her fan, while the widow batted that woman over the head with a drawstring bag. To add to the mayhem, yet another woman sat in the midst of all this female fury, laughing and sneezing uncontrollably.

"And so I conclude my talk on mortuary practices as evidenced at the site of Nabesha." He gathered up his papers. "Now, would someone like to prevent the cat from eating any more of that young woman's costume? Thank you."

The audience members were now on their feet, calling for someone to save the young lady from this murderous feline.

"It went rather well, considering," Mrs. Rumpelmin said.

"Considering what, madame?"

"Considering that most of the audience today does not even belong to the Society." The white-haired matron patted him on the shoulder. "I do believe the ladies thought you were going to talk about that disgraceful poetry you translated, Mr. Pierce." She leaned closer. "I have a copy in my bag, and if you wouldn't mind signing it for me . . ."

He was spared a response when yet another screech went up from the audience. Had these lunatic females descended to fisticuffs?

Storming down from the stage, he pushed his way through the crowd. Someone had to put an end to this circus, and apparently it would have to be him.

"There he goes! Grab him!"

Something ran past his feet. Dylan turned in time to see the cat race into the library just off the main hall. In order to prevent a mass lynching of the unfortunate feline, he hurried over to the room and shut the door behind him.

The small library held floor-to-ceiling bookcases, an enormous globe set on a pedestal, and a long mahogany table. Peeking from underneath one of the many spindle-back chairs, Dylan spied a pair of glowing eyes.

A chorus of shouts broke out from the other side of the door.

"I have the matter well in hand," he called out as he locked the door. In fact, he had half a mind to give the Society medal to the blasted cat.

He walked slowly toward the table. "Come now, you must trust me," he said in a soothing voice. "If you don't let me smuggle you out of here, you'll be cat stew for some unhappy lady."

A plaintive meow was the only reply.

Dylan sat down cross-legged on the floor. After a few moments, a tail swished out from beneath one of the chairs. He waited. Two minutes more, and the cat herself cautiously walked out. She stared at him with large orange-gold eyes, meowed once, then sat down a few feet away.

By thunder, if this cat wasn't a *feline chaus*, a direct descendant of the ancient desert felines prized by the pharaohs. She was large—too large for a domestic cat—and her fur was brindled. The nose was narrow, the neck sleek and long. The same breed of cat that archaeologists had seen staring back at them from the walls of Egyptian tombs. How did such an exotic cat get into this musty building in Euston Square? If the jeweled collar about the animal's neck was any indication, this was someone's cossetted pet.

"Come here, girl."

The cat only yawned, then opened her eyes wide. What a lovely clear amber they were.

He leaned forward. "Come here," he said in Arabic.

The cat meowed again, then sauntered over, rubbing herself against his legs.

He scratched her head, and the resulting purrs sounded like thunder in the quiet room.

This peaceful interlude was suddenly interrupted by someone beating against the locked door.

"Let me in! I insist you let me in. If you harm that cat, I'll have the constable cart you away!"

He looked at the cat. "Someone you know?"

The door groaned, as though something heavy had been flung against it. Dylan stood up. He'd better unbar the door before they resorted to battering rams.

"Cease and desist." Another loud thump was heard against the door. "I'm going to unlock it."

Apparently no one was listening to him, for as soon as he turned the key, the door flew open and a body went hurtling past.

The woman crashed to the floor, her black skirts and petticoat flying so that they landed nearly atop her head. She lay there, the breath knocked out of her, her black-stockinged legs exposed. Her widow's veil was gone, and her blond hair was in disarray, as if someone had tried to pull it out by its roots.

Dylan quickly bolted the door once more as the feminine screeches outside continued. The cat bounded over to the woman and began licking her face.

"Nefer, are you hurt?" the woman asked as she gasped for air.

"She's perfectly fine. Although she seems to be an audacious creature. Like her mistress." He walked over to her. "I had hoped you would attend the lecture, Mrs. Fairchild, but I had no idea you would bring it to such a rousing conclusion."

She frowned. "I didn't expect you to remember me, Mr. Pierce. It's been over two years."

"How could I forget a woman who rode across the desert alone to meet me?" Especially a woman who was roaring drunk, he thought to himself.

A slight blush rose to her cheeks. "I'm afraid I recall very little of the camel ride or our conversation."

"I'm not surprised."

He held out a hand. Only then did she seem to realize that she was sprawled on the floor with most of her legs exposed. She flung her skirt down, then attempted to stand up. Dylan grabbed her wrist and pulled her to her feet.

"Thank you, Mr. Pierce." She took a deep breath, busying herself with smoothing down her gown. "I apologize for bursting in like this, but I had to make certain no harm had come to Nefer."

"Nefer? So she *is* Egyptian."

"A rare breed of North African cat. I brought her with me when I left Egypt."

The cat rubbed against her mistress's skirts, amber eyes half shut with obvious delight.

"Well, I would not dare harm a denizen of the desert, Mrs. Fairchild. You, above all people, must know of the curses connected with such an iniquitous act."

He had meant to make her smile, but she only stared back at him. Her somber gaze was disconcerting.

On closer examination, Dylan was a bit amazed he *had* recognized her. Gone was the sun-bleached hair that had seemed so spectacular. Her hair was now a pale gold— lovely, but not remarkable—and her once tanned skin was as pale as ivory. He suspected she rarely ventured out into the sun. Beneath her plain black gown, she appeared delicate and thin, far less imposing than the woman who had confronted him in the desert two years ago.

But the greatest change was in her demeanor. The Charlotte Fairchild who accused him of stealing her father's site had been passionate, sure of herself, strong. The young woman standing before him now seemed diminished, weaker. No doubt she had become like all the other women he knew: querulous and discontented.

Then again, the poor woman had lost a husband. And on the very site she had begged him to refuse. Small wonder she seemed so changed. Wouldn't any sane person be altered by such tragedy? As Dylan could sadly attest, even he had been shaken—and changed—by the harm done to innocent people. Still, he couldn't help mourning the loss of that defiant woman he had glimpsed briefly in the desert.

She tried to brush her hair back from her face, but too many pins had been lost in the lecture hall fracas. With a sigh, she resigned herself instead to repinning her black shawl.

"I was overly impulsive then, Mr. Pierce. I should never have sampled the brandy, nor asked you to refuse the site." Her light gray eyes clouded over. They, at least, retained the unearthly beauty he remembered. "I regret my actions on that day more than I can ever say."

"I admired you. You simply fought for what you wanted."

She stiffened. "Unfortunately, it wasn't what my husband wanted."

For a moment, she grew so still and quiet that he feared she had turned to stone. Had these intervening years made her an emotional hysteric, subject to strange moods and fainting spells?

"I hope you will allow me to express my deepest regrets over Mr. Fairchild's untimely death. I was in Upper Egypt when I heard the news. I returned to the Valley of Amun immediately, but you had already left for England."

"Yes, I left as soon as I could." She took a deep breath,

her skin taking on an even paler hue. He prayed she wasn't about to faint. "They said it would take months to retrieve the body. I had to leave. I couldn't bear to remain in Egypt, knowing I'd forced Ian to stay. Knowing he'd be alive if not for me."

An awkward silence followed, broken only by the cat's purring. Mrs. Fairchild's expression softened. She scooped up the cat and held it close. With the fur framing her face, she took on a less severe aspect.

"I do want to thank you for the condolences you sent to my family's home, however. That was most kind of you."

Dylan nodded. "I admit to feeling some degree of guilt in the accident. If I had been there, I might have seen that the wall supports were weak. Perhaps I could have prevented the cave-in."

She held up a hand. "The accident was not your fault. I won't hear of it."

But you believe it was yours, he thought. So that was the reason behind the full mourning she still wore, the reason behind her pallor and stony expression. She was punishing herself with as much determination as a Hindu woman performing purdah.

"I'm glad at least to see that you haven't abandoned your interest in Egyptology."

"What do you mean?" she asked sharply. "Of course I have."

"Your attendance at my lecture this afternoon—"

"Has nothing to do with its topic, I assure you. My sister and I came only to receive the award the Society plans to bestow on my late father. I'm afraid Mother had a previous engagement and could not be present. But I haven't given a thought to mummies or dynastic tombs in years." Her large gray eyes dared him to deny this.

"It's a pity to give up something that you once felt so passionately about."

"There are worse things, Mr. Pierce. Now, if you will

excuse me, I believe both Nefer and I have overstayed our welcome."

He cocked a thumb toward the closed door. "The furor hasn't died down. I wouldn't recommend either of you venturing out there just yet, unless you want to see the fur fly again."

This time a small smile did appear. "It was turning into quite a brawl, wasn't it?"

"What *did* cause all the commotion?"

The smile grew wider, transforming her whole face. Really, she should do that more often. With a smile like that, he suspected her laughter could be positively bewitching. She seemed almost girlish now, wanting only a spot of color in her cheeks and a brighter gown. Perhaps grief and guilt hadn't yet crushed the life out of her.

"A young lady in the audience had the misfortune to be wearing a hat decorated with a stuffed bird." She gave her cat a quick hug. "Nefer does love to pounce on birds."

He grinned. "The cat thought it was real?"

Laughter burst out of her like a bubbling spring. What an intoxicating sound. "Nefer isn't such a fool as that." She pointed to a stuffed falcon on the mantel.

"Kill the bird," she commanded in perfect Arabic.

The cat sprang upon the mantel, claws jabbing into the dead bird. With a fearsome growl, she sunk her teeth deep into its lifeless feathers.

Dylan wiped tears of laughter from his eyes. "By thunder, you should be a lion tamer in the circus."

He looked over at her. She seemed as pleased with her trick as a young girl. No doubt she thought the proper pose was that of a grief-stricken widow. But there was a vibrant woman beneath the black bombazine.

"I know it was a dreadful thing to do, but the young lady wouldn't let me hear two words of your lecture."

"I see. So you set the cat on her and stopped the lecture cold."

"I am sorry about that. However, I did catch some inaccuracies in what I was able to hear, so perhaps it's for the best."

"You what?"

She cleared her throat. "I don't agree with your interpretation of the feldspar artifacts. You should read Sir Lionel Cole's recent monograph on his excavations at Thebes. You may trust my scholarship on this. Scarabs and amulets have long been my special field of interest."

He moved closer to her. There was a nice spring fragrance about her. Jasmine, he thought.

"For someone who has no interest in Egyptology, you seem to be keeping abreast of the latest theories."

She refused to back away, even though he was now close enough to stir her hair with his breath. "Although I no longer follow the discipline, I haven't forgotten all I have learned."

"Which was considerable."

"Yes, it was." She finally took a step back. "Now I really must leave."

He didn't want her to go. Suddenly she seemed like the most fascinating creature in all of London. "But there's an angry mob outside the door, clamoring for revenge. And these poor civilized Londoners don't know that you've trained your cat to kill on command."

"There's a great deal London does not know about my cat." She paused. "Or me."

Yes, he definitely did not want this unusual young woman to leave. But how long could he keep her locked up in this musty library? Any longer and gossip would start anew, this time regarding the Welshman and the widow.

He glanced over at Nefer, who had batted the bird onto the floor, then flung herself upon it.

"I suggest we remain here until the crowd loses its taste for blood and drifts away." He looked at his pocket watch. "Which I wager will be in approximately thirty minutes."

"That close to tea time, is it?"

He laughed. "Exactly. And we both know the English never miss their tea and scones."

"I'm loath to miss it myself." She looked behind her. "I see another door over there that I'm sure eventually leads out into the street. My sister is resourceful enough to find her own way back, so there's no reason to remain any longer. Thank you, however, for an interesting lecture."

"Will you allow me to call on you this week?" The words were out of his mouth before he realized it.

She looked alarmed by the suggestion.

"Absolutely not. I told you that I have no interest in archaeology any longer. I lead a very private life now, and have few visitors. Good afternoon, Mr. Pierce."

She walked over to the side door, the cat running after her.

"Hold on there. You can't leave before you've been given the medal for your father."

She stopped. "I'd forgotten about that."

"Stay here while I retrieve it from Mrs. Rumpelmin. The least you can do is linger a moment more, for your father's sake."

She picked up the purring cat. "I'm not a child you have to cajole into staying. Very well, then. I'll wait."

Dylan didn't know if he believed her. Apparently she was as unpredictable as a desert cat herself.

He walked over to the bolted door. The din seemed to have quieted, although he could hear a high-pitched voice wailing about a scratched cheek. "I shall return shortly, Mrs. Fairchild."

At that moment, the rain clouds outside dispersed, and a shaft of pale sunlight shot through the wide windows of the library. For a brief instant, the sunlight falling on her hair almost turned it into the silver fire he remembered. Garbed all in black, she stood straight and tall, stroking the sleek cat who stared back at him just as soberly. He felt as though he were gazing at an ancient statue. A statue of a mysterious goddess. Maybe even a dangerous one.

"I'll be right back."

She nodded.

Unfortunately, it took him at least ten minutes to find Mrs. Rumpelmin in the crowd. And an additional five minutes passed before she could recall where she had mislaid the medal.

"Has anyone seen my sister, Mrs. Fairchild?" someone asked loudly.

He couldn't see to whom the voice belonged, so he pushed his way back to the library. Turning the key in the lock, he slipped inside, feeling like a burglar who had pulled off a successful heist.

"Here now, Mrs. Fairchild. I've brought the medal as I said I would, although I'm sorry it took so—"

She was gone.

"Now I fear you will have to tolerate a visit from me, lass," he said aloud to the empty room.

Dylan Pierce was not a man who allowed anything to slip out of his grasp.

Least of all a woman as unpredictable—and intriguing—as Charlotte Fairchild promised to be.

Chapter Four

A French horn blasted overhead, rattling the windowpanes.

Charlotte looked up from her bath. Although it was only nine o'clock, her brother Michael was already engaged in his morning music lesson, which would be followed by a vigorous bout of exercise involving Indian clubs and bean bags. All this physical activity would occur on the first floor, right beside the parlor where Catherine tapped away on her new typewriting machine. Her sister had taken it into her head to become a crusading journalist for the *Free Women's Gazette*, and the house rang with her typing at all hours.

Another sour note sounded from above, making her cringe. A noisier household couldn't exist; even the maid-servants rattled the flatware and slammed doors. Thank heaven she wasn't engaged in scholarly research, for only a saint could concentrate in the chaos that existed at their Belgrave Square mansion.

The cat sat up as the music lesson continued. Ears laid back, Nefer jumped onto the windowsill to hide behind the cut-glass perfume bottles and geraniums. Charlotte sighed. To be fair, she supposed her brother was doing quite well for a twelve-year-old boy whose first love was cricket. But she couldn't tell if he was playing "Rule Britannia" or "Greensleeves."

Charlotte sank back down in the warm, soapy water, smiling as she recalled how Nefer had attacked that young woman's hat yesterday. Of course she was wrong to command the cat to do such a childish thing. She had to remember that she was no longer a carefree girl with her whole life spread out before her. But even decked out in black, seeing the world through her widow's veil, she sometimes found herself forgetting the terrible role she had played in Ian's death.

"I must never forget that," she said aloud. "As I must never forget my husband."

A familiar gloom descended on her, and she felt more at peace. This was how she should be: repentant and sorrowful. She certainly shouldn't be attending lectures on Egyptology, lectures given by the man who might have been the one killed in the cave-in if she hadn't interfered.

Of course, that was a dreadful thing to consider as well. Mr. Pierce no more deserved to die in a desert tomb than Ian did, even if he *had* once dynamited the resting place of Pharaoh Thutmose.

Why then did she feel like a fraud? Was she ready to part with her grief and her guilt after only two years and seven months? If so, she was even more wicked than she feared: headstrong, selfish, as shallow as those two chatterboxes at the lecture hall yesterday. And by goading Nefer to attack, she'd spoiled the very ceremony meant to honor her father.

Worse yet, she had enjoyed what little of the lecture she managed to hear. A keen pleasure soared through her as Pierce recited the names of the Eighteenth-Dynasty pharaohs; his descriptions of scarabs and soil composition sent her heart racing with excitement. To her ears, accounts of amulets and mummies were as seductive and alluring as *The Sonnets of the Portuguese*. Listening to Mr. Pierce's lecture had been like unlocking a treasure chest and viewing the secret splendor that lay within. Riches that she had once owned, but now no longer deserved.

Any more than she deserved to converse with the man who had given such a talk. To her shame, she'd enjoyed their conversation in the library. She saw so few young men now. Except for Michael's instructors and the clerics who presided over her charities, her world was dominated by women. But Dylan Pierce was unmistakably male. Still tanned from his field season in Egypt, he was virile, robust, and confident—as out of place in dreary, rain-sodden London as the obelisk erected on the Victoria Embankment, inaccurately dubbed Cleopatra's Needle.

She squeezed jasmine-scented water from her sponge, letting it trickle over her bare arm. Actually, she thought she liked his eyes best. She wasn't sure if they were blue or hazel, but they had been lively eyes. Vibrant and challenging—like the man himself.

"Father would have liked him," she murmured.

Sir Reginald would even have approved of his excavation methods now. According to all reports, Pierce had become quite the respectable scholar these past two years in Egypt: meticulous, sober, and as mindful of the ancient sites' historical value as he once was obsessed with their treasure. Certainly she was pleased that he had reformed; Egypt did not need more looters and treasure hunters. Yet she was mystified at what had brought on such a remarkable transformation.

The door to her bath banged open. Nefer jumped, knocking over a flowerpot. The cat shot past the freckled girl who entered, obviously seeking out a nook safe from French horns and maidservants.

"Sorry, ma'am, but Lady Margaret requires you down-

59

stairs," the maid said breathlessly. "And you're to be quick about it."

"Is something wrong, Lorrie?" Charlotte stepped out of the claw-footed bath, allowing the maid to wrap a towel about her. "Has Grandmama chained herself to Number Ten Downing Street again?"

"No, ma'am." She patted her shoulders dry with a smaller towel. "Something much more exciting. You've a visitor, a young man. Mr. Dylan Pierce."

Charlotte froze. "Who?"

"Mr. Pierce, a big red-haired fellow. Sounds like a Welsh-man, he does. He's downstairs in the front parlor. Seems he digs up mummies just like your late father. Lady Margaret and your sister are awful pleased to see him, even if he has come calling too early in the morning." Lorrie held out a cashmere wrapper. "Can't say as I blame them. It's been over two years since Mr. Fairchild died, and time for gen-tlemen to come round again, if you ask me."

"That's a most inappropriate thing to say."

She pushed Charlotte into the bedroom. "I'm only re-peating the sentiments of everyone in the household. Even Master Michael."

"Master Michael is barely out of short pants. He won't have sentiments worth listening to for at least five years. See here, Lorrie, you must go down and tell Mother that I cannot accept visitors today." She sat down on the bed. "Tell her I have a headache. In fact, I feel a terrible one coming on right now."

Lorrie threw open the doors to the armoire. "Sorry, ma'am, but Lady Margaret says that if you don't come down in ten minutes, she'll send Randall up to fetch you."

"She wouldn't dare."

Randall the footman was nearly seven feet tall; he was a silent, strong, but gentle member of the household, and com-pletely devoted to her mother. If Margaret Grainger told him to swim the English Channel, he'd jump off the cliffs of Dover without hesitation.

"You know she would, ma'am. She's been waiting for you to stop hiding from the world. And now that a young man has come to pay his respects, she's prepared to drag you downstairs herself."

Charlotte twisted the belt to her wrapper, thinking it over. To refuse to go down would seem strange, as if she were afraid of seeing Dylan Pierce. Certainly she wasn't afraid to see the man. Hadn't she been alone with him just yesterday?

And you enjoyed it immensely, she told herself. Much more than a proper widow should. Well, of course she enjoyed speaking with another Egyptologist; that was only natural. It had been over two years since she had allowed herself to converse about dynastic tombs and protective amulets.

The efficient maid hurried over, stockings and petticoats draped over her arm. "I heard Randall shuffling out there in the hallway, and if we don't get you dressed and downstairs in two winks, that big fellow is going to carry you to the parlor in little more than your camisole."

"Very well, then, if I must." She stood up and untied her wrapper. "I'll wear my black silk dress."

Lorrie frowned. "Wouldn't you like something a bit cheerier? I ironed your sprigged lilac gown just last week."

"The black silk, please."

"The gray tea gown, then. There's not a hint of color about the gray, ma'am."

Charlotte shook her head. "It's not proper for me to dress in anything but black. Remember Her Majesty the Queen."

"You're not the Queen," the girl muttered.

She might not be Queen Victoria, but she too was a widow. And if Her Majesty could wear black these forty years, then surely Charlotte could do likewise. At least the Queen was not responsible for Prince Albert's death. Charlotte would not be cajoled into forgetting that she had helped kill her husband. No one would make her forget that. Not well-meaning servants or hopeful mothers.

Or Welshmen with auburn gold hair.

The last time Dylan had felt this unsettled was four years ago, when he was attacked by street thieves in Port Said. Although grateful that Charlotte Fairchild had at last deigned to come downstairs, he was dismayed that her arrival hadn't been noticed by either her mother or her sister—who were questioning him with all the thoroughness of Scotland Yard.

Before he downed one cup of tea, Lady Margaret had gleaned his family history, educational background, and views on universal suffrage. And when she bothered to take a breath, her youngest daughter Catherine chimed in with her virulent opinion of the present House of Lords. Neither of them paid more than a moment's attention to the medal from the Antiquarian Society that he had delivered.

As their rapid-fire interrogation continued, he managed to sneak glances at Charlotte now and then. And there was a definite pleasure in gazing upon her.

She looked less wan and frail this morning; her cheeks were even slightly flushed. And though he sat clear across the spacious parlor from her, he could smell her intoxicating jasmine fragrance. The heady scent was at odds with her plain black gown—not a hint of jewelry or lace trim lightened its somber effect. He did, however, spy a stray curl and damp tendrils of hair along the nape of her neck. Had she been bathing just before coming down to see him? The image of Charlotte Fairchild lying naked in a steaming bath of jasmine-scented water brought a grin to his face.

"So why aren't you married, Mr. Pierce?" Lady Margaret asked.

He choked on his gooseberry tart. "I beg your pardon?"

"Mother, really." Charlotte shot the older woman a disapproving look. "Of all the impertinent questions to ask."

Lady Margaret ignored her. "It's a question that is asked

of every female on the far side of twenty. Why should Mr. Pierce be immune from the curiosity of a much older woman like myself?"

"Not that much older," he said, hoping to steer the conversation elsewhere.

Indeed, despite her salt-and-pepper hair and thickening waist, Lady Margaret was an attractive woman. Probably not yet fifty. Although he thought she'd look far more attractive if she wasn't wearing navy blue bloomers. In fact, he suspected she had looked just like her daughter Catherine when younger: buxom, brunette, and with large brown eyes. He wondered where Charlotte Fairchild got her strikingly different coloring.

"Save your gallantry for ladies who are susceptible to that sort of thing." Lady Margaret smiled. "And considering how much notoriety your poetry translations have brought you, I'm certain you have legions of susceptible London females trailing after you. Each one clamoring to be Mrs. Pierce."

"Not legions. Just a mere dozen or two." He winked at her. "And I rather doubt it's marriage they're after."

Both he and Lady Margaret laughed. Charlotte, however, didn't. He wondered if she was offended by the statement, or merely bored.

"I'm writing an article on marriage for the *Gazette*," Catherine announced. "A most disadvantageous state for both women and men. But then, men aren't subjected to the tyranny of endless childbearing." She sighed. "The insensitive brutes."

Maybe it was time to give the Graingers a taste of their own brash medicine.

"But Miss Grainger, what of the pleasure?"

"Pleasure?"

"Of procreation."

Catherine colored slightly. "I daresay there may be some physical satisfaction connected with the begetting of children."

"Yes, indeed." Her mother smiled at him. "In fact, Mr. Pierce is an authority on the subject."

He choked on his tart again. "I am?"

"I've read your translation of the *Songs of Rajya*. Unbridled licentiousness! I've been forced to keep it under lock and key in order to prevent young Michael from stealing it away."

"I didn't know that you owned a volume of the *Songs of Rajya.*" Catherine sounded offended.

"I'll lend it to you just before your wedding night, dear, assuming you ever decide to marry." Lady Margaret shook her head. "The things the Arabians came up with. And those amazing positions."

"Mother . . ." Charlotte warned again.

"I've no intention of marrying." Catherine said.

Her mother shrugged. "That's what Charlotte always said. I believed her, too, until I received a telegram from Egypt one day announcing that she'd become engaged to Mr. Fairchild." She sighed. "I didn't even have time to post the banns. They were married in Cairo by the end of the field season. A remarkably whirlwind courtship. A desert whirlwind, you might say."

He looked over at Charlotte, who gazed at the ceiling in obvious frustration. He could easily imagine Charlotte Fairchild falling headlong in love—or in lust. Would an innocent girl know the difference? He felt a pang of jealousy toward the young Egyptologist who had stolen her heart and introduced her to passion. Loving Charlotte might well feel as wild and hot as a desert whirlwind.

"So why have you never married, Mr. Pierce?" Lady Margaret was not to be deterred.

"Well, marriage has always seemed an acquired taste, like oatcakes or olives. And I find oatcakes and olives quite indigestible." He smiled to take the sting out of his words. "So I fear I'm destined to remain irresponsible."

"I've heard stories about your adventures in Egypt, Mr.

Pierce. *Irresponsible* would seem to be the least of it. I'm surprised the Egyptian authorities didn't arrest you."

"Mother, Mr. Pierce *is* our guest," Charlotte said.

"Whatever do you mean? I've admitted that I enjoy his poetry, and the gossip about his libertine past has entertained me for years. Especially those rumors about his romantic escapade atop the Great Pyramid." She leaned over and patted him on the knee. "I spend most of my time fighting for worthy causes, Mr. Pierce, so please excuse me for taking pleasure in idle gossip."

He grinned. "Take your pleasure wherever you can, Lady Margaret. Gossip for you, Irish whiskey for me."

"I don't think Mr. Pierce's disreputable past is the stuff of polite conversation."

He was struck by the scorn in Charlotte's voice. "Mrs. Fairchild, I suspect some of the tales told about me are exaggerated."

She stared at him accusingly. "So it isn't true that you dynamited the tomb of Pharaoh Thutmose?"

He was relieved she hadn't brought up a bawdy episode. "I was not the only archaeologist employing such methods."

"That is tragically true. But it hardly excuses such willful destruction." She sat back, arms folded across her chest.

Her sister fiddled with the green eyeshade on her lap. "Charlotte regards Egyptology as seriously as Mother and I regard politics."

"I can see that." Looking over at the inscrutable young widow, he wondered what had possessed him to call upon her. It wasn't as if she had shown the slightest interest in him. And he feared his dynamiting days would always loom between them. Still he found her attractive—and quite challenging.

"All Charlotte has ever cared about is archaeology," added Lady Margaret. "Just like her father. Mad for mummies, the pair of them. She spends hours upstairs reading every monograph published on Egypt."

"That's not true," Charlotte protested. "I'm far too busy with my charities to fritter away time reading about Egyptology. Now, perhaps we should ask why Mr. Pierce has come to call at such an unusual time in the morning."

"He brought the medal—" Catherine started to say.

"I came to see you, Mrs. Fairchild," he broke in. The past hour spent with the Grainger women had removed any desire to be oblique, or even polite.

Charlotte's eyes widened.

"I told you, Mother," Catherine said in a loud stage whisper. "The medal was just an excuse."

Dylan fought not to laugh at Charlotte's expression. "Our conversation was too brief yesterday, Mrs. Fairchild. And your comment about the inaccuracies in my lecture was most interesting."

"That was rude of me. I shouldn't have said anything."

"Don't take offense," her sister said. "Charlotte even corrected Father's papers."

"On the contrary, I want to hear more. I regard you as an expert on amulets and dynastic scarabs, Mrs. Fairchild."

A deafening screech thundered through the house. Dylan looked up at the ceiling in alarm.

"Michael's music lesson is over." Lady Margaret smiled proudly. "My son is down from school and spends every morning practicing his French horn."

"He seems to have no discernible talent," Catherine said. "But his music master claims that the energy he expends playing the horn will control his awakening male urges. After all, he's only twelve and couldn't express those urges anyway." She glanced over at her mother. "At least I don't think he could."

Charlotte sat back in her chair, one hand covering her eyes.

Dylan felt as if he were watching some bewildering circus being performed in a mahogany-paneled parlor filled with opulent furniture, fringed pillows, and Oriental rugs. And the principal performers were a respectable matron in bloomers, a young brunette with ink-stained fingers, and a gray-eyed lady garbed in black. He again doubted his reason for visiting the household. Especially when he caught a glimpse of what looked like a giant skulking past the parlor doorway.

Catherine sneezed. "The cat must be in the parlor."

"Perhaps I've come at a bad time." He looked about but didn't see the desert creature.

"You are a respected Egyptologist, young man," Lady Margaret said. "That means you are always welcome in the household of Sir Reginald Grainger. If for no other reason than that a conversation about archaeology will bring happiness to Charlotte. Don't believe my daughter when she says she's given up her interest in Egypt. Her bedchamber is filled with monographs and the dessicated remains of ancient creatures."

Catherine sneezed again. "One of them is the mummy of a rat. The maid fainted dead away when she found it."

Charlotte stood up. "Mr. Pierce, I suggest you take your leave." She gestured toward the hallway. "Even now I hear my brother racing downstairs. If you stay, you will be dragooned into juggling Indian clubs for two or three endless hours."

Lady Margaret got to her feet as well. "I'm glad you reminded me, dear. I don't want to miss my morning exercise with Michael." She held out a hand to Dylan. "That's why I'm wearing this costume, Mr. Pierce. I wouldn't want you to think we were a radical family with no sense of social niceties."

"Certainly not." He bowed over her hand, reminding himself that Margaret Grainger was not only the widow of a respected scholar, but the daughter of an earl.

Catherine stood up. "I've stayed away from my writing long enough. A great pleasure to meet you, Mr. Pierce. Come again."

Before he could straighten up from his bow, the two

women were gone. In the distance, he heard the shouts of a young boy. Then, a moment later, the tapping of typewriter keys.

"You have an unusual family, Mrs. Fairchild," he said finally.

"Consider yourself lucky that Aunt Hazel and Uncle Louis weren't here." Her expression told him the experience would have proved hair-raising.

"Perhaps we could save them for some other visit." He cleared his throat. "Look here, I apologize for calling at such an early hour, but I've a busy day ahead of me at the Collection."

"Yes, I heard that you'd been placed in charge of the upcoming exhibit. I was surprised the Colvilles asked you to mount the Valley of Amun show."

"To be honest, I was rather aggressive in pursuing the position. It's a fascinating site, and long overdue for a public exhibition." And it was one way to assuage his own guilt over Ian Fairchild's death. Nearly three years later, and he still regretted turning down the site.

"I agree." She paused. "Still your appointment was a surprise."

"A surprise or a shock?" Dylan felt hurt by her obviously low opinion of his abilities.

"You seem an able man. I meant no insult." She took a deep breath. "But the Colvilles haven't yet appointed an overall museum director. If the exhibit goes well, it's possible that you will be offered the position."

He laughed. "So you think I had ulterior motives?"

"I couldn't care less about your motives. All I care about is that the exhibit does justice to my father's memory." Her steady gaze was unnerving. "Since Ian's death, the site has been shut down; the artifacts we worked so long to recover lie gathering dust in Egypt, packed away."

"Not anymore. We've already received four shipments from Cairo, with more due within the month."

"I'm glad. Very glad." Her eyes filled with tears. "The past belongs to us as much as the future. It shouldn't remain hidden. I only wish that . . ." Her voice faded away.

"That archaeologists were still working in the Valley of Amun?" he finished for her. He was moved by her unexpected show of emotion.

She nodded.

"Maybe they will one day." He stepped closer. Another inch and he could reach up and stroke that stray tendril of hair. If he dared.

"Maybe that archaeologist will be you," she said softly.

"You wouldn't mind?"

"I honestly don't know." A small smile appeared.

He loved to see her smile; it was like watching the sun rise over the desert.

"I'm really not that disreputable any longer. No more escapades atop the Great Pyramid, no more dynamiting. I've become as responsible as the Archbishop of Canterbury." He couldn't resist, and gently tucked that silky strand of hair beneath one of her pins.

Charlotte stepped back. "Did you really call on me in order to discuss scarabs?"

"Of course." Actually, the thought hadn't even occurred to him until five minutes earlier, but it gave him an excuse to come calling occasionally. "Dr. Rogers, our scarabs specialist, has decided to accept a job with the Berlin Museum. He's left us in a bit of a lurch."

"I see." She walked over to the sideboard and rang one of the brass bells ranged along its polished surface.

A freckled maid appeared at the doorway.

"The rain has nearly stopped, Lorrie. Bring my hat and the leash." She turned to Dylan. "I thought we'd walk about the square. The fresh air will give you a chance to regain your equilibrium. Spending thirty minutes with my family is comparable to rounding Cape Horn in a hurricane."

He looked about the parlor. "You've a dog?"

"Oh, no. Ever since a terrier ate Michael's pet mouse, he refuses to let a dog anywhere near the house, or his other mice."

"Then why do you require a leash?"

"For my cat, of course. I never go out without Nefer. She would be quite distressed to be left behind."

Several discordant notes from the parlor piano punctuated this statement. Swiveling around, Dylan was in time to see the desert cat mince her way across the keyboard. With a purr rumbling from her sleek chest, Nefer crossed the piano, leaped onto the back of the sofa, then jumped right onto his left shoulder.

He staggered under her weight. "Doesn't the cat try to eat your brother's pet mice?"

"Certainly not." She looked at him as if he had just suggested Nefer was the Whitechapel murderer.

The cat crooked her head around and stared at him accusingly.

"By thunder, Mrs. Fairchild, I think I am in need of a little fresh air."

Chapter Five

The Englishwoman and the desert cat made an oddly attractive pair.

Dylan kept glancing over at his two walking companions. Both cat and mistress seemed indifferent to the drizzling rain. And aside from a brief comment about the cool July weather, Charlotte had remained silent, more interested in the hydrangea bushes they passed than in his company.

"Do you not mind the rain?" he said finally, wiping his wet cheeks. "I wish one of us had thought to bring an umbrella."

"It's not the rain I mind. It's this." She gestured to the neat rows of stuccoed houses.

"Excuse me?" Dylan's puzzled gaze swept over the pristine loveliness of Belgrave Square.

"A hundred years ago we would have been in danger." She frowned. "Belgravia has become so safe, so orderly."

"And this bothers you?"

"Certainly. Imagine how thrilling a walk through the

square would have been in the last century. Cockfighting, bull baiting, duellists fighting each other to the death on the green. Highwaymen and footpads hiding out in the market gardens. And over there stood the Bloody Bridge."

He looked in the direction she pointed.

"In 1728 a fellow was found murdered on the bridge, five fingers cut off, not to mention half his face. And his throat was slashed as well."

He thought she said this with far too much relish.

"Now Belgravia is as safe as the tinned foods section at Fortnum and Mason," she continued. "London has grown too tame."

"I assure you there are haunts in this city exciting enough for the most bloodthirsty Englishwoman."

"Don't misunderstand me. I've no wish to be accosted by knife-wielding ruffians. It's just that I wouldn't mind an unpredictable moment or two."

"Does my visit this morning count?" He grinned at her and was gratified that she smiled back.

"It does at that. Thank you."

They walked companionably for a moment.

"After spending so many years in Africa, you must understand my feelings." She sighed. "No blinding sandstorms, no flooding rivers. Not a scorpion or cobra in sight. It's all quite ordinary."

He looked down at the cat trotting alongside them, serene in her jeweled collar. "I don't think a desert cat who wears rubies is an ordinary sight in London. And I've seen spaniels that didn't tolerate a leash as well."

Nefer stopped, waiting for an omnibus to rattle past.

Charlotte shrugged. "I met a pasha in Cairo who kept two full-grown leopards on a leash."

"That's Egypt. On the streets of Belgravia, your cat is as out of place as a camel or sand viper." He paused. "As are you."

"I hope you're not comparing me to a sand viper."

"No, but I suspect you could be as troublesome as one."

He meant it as a joke, but her smile faded. "I've been told that before."

She quickened her pace, her sensible black shoes splashing through the puddles. He hurried to keep up with her.

"Why do you say I'm out of place here?" she asked.

He thought briefly of replying with a careless witticism but saw that she was serious.

"Maybe because you remind me of a potted date palm I saw years ago in a Brighton conservatory. From a distance, the tree looked as if it was thriving in its new home, protected by a glass roof, watered and fed on schedule. Up close, however, you could see that the trunk was dangerously brittle, the fronds thin and pale. The date palm was dying by inches, like a person going to sleep in the snow."

She stopped.

"Date palms belong in the desert, Mrs. Fairchild." He touched her shoulder. "I believe you do as well."

When she turned her gaze upon him, he was struck anew by how beautiful her eyes were. And how sad.

"I miss the desert. There are times I can hardly bear it." Her voice broke, and she took a deep breath before continuing. "I miss the Nile. The Thames is a poor substitute."

"Then go back. There are a dozen Cook's tours leaving England every month."

"I'm no tourist," she said sharply.

He shrugged. "Write the Egyptian Antiquities Service. Ask the director-general if you can work at the Cairo Museum. With your experience, I'm sure he'd welcome your assistance. But don't stay in a place where you're not suited, where you find no joy. If it's Egypt you crave, then go, lass. Before you waste away like that date palm."

"I can never return, Mr. Pierce. That part of my life is over. I'm only grateful that I enjoyed as many years in Egypt as I did."

She looked as forlorn as the drab sparrows that fluttered

among the wet branches overhead. She did seem out of place here, with her unearthly eyes, her confident stride, her longing for the forbidden and the dangerous. Like him, she would always feel a stranger in the country of her birth. For Wales could never touch his heart or stir his passion as Africa did.

"Your life in Egypt may be over, Mrs. Fairchild, but not your life here. You're too young to retire from the world. Besides, your husband would not wish you to grieve this long. Not if he cared for you and wanted you to be happy."

She seemed upset by the turn the conversation had taken. "I don't even know why we're speaking of such things. I thought you had questions about the scarabs in the exhibit."

"Aye, the exhibit. Well, the Cairo Museum has been very generous. The Egyptian authorities retained very little from the Valley of Amun, so most of the artifacts you and your father recovered will be on display when the exhibit opens in October."

"If only it hadn't taken so long." They began walking again; Nefer trotted ahead on her leash.

"It seemed bad form to mount an exhibit earlier."

She brushed away a large raindrop that spattered her nose. "You can be blunt. People believe the site is cursed. First Father died, then Ian. And there was that nasty accident involving our first foreman."

He nodded. "And since Mr. and Mrs. Colville are as superstitious as gypsies, I'm sure tales of an ancient curse put them off. I've heard it was their astrologer who finally convinced them to mount the Valley of Amun exhibit. And recommended hiring me as well." He laughed. "Apparently I'm a Capricorn with Aries rising. The Colvilles liked that, whatever it means."

"Actually, it was their palm reader who convinced them."

"Really? How do you know that?"

She smiled. "Aunt Hazel reads the palms—and sometimes the horoscopes—of all the best families in Mayfair."

"I should have known. And has Uncle Louis had a hand in this, too?"

"Not yet, but I'm sure he will. Uncle Louis can't bear to be left out of any enterprise." She took a deep breath as they passed a fragrant rosebush. "I'm glad now that you were the one appointed to oversee the exhibit."

"I thought you regarded me as a dynamiting treasure hunter."

"I did. But the reports from Egypt these past two and a half years seem to indicate you've reformed." She gave him a shrewd look. "You have, haven't you? Or are you still carousing at all hours and drinking to excess?"

"I don't answer those questions even when they come from my mother."

"I have a right to know how fit you are for this assignment."

"The last I heard, you were neither a curator nor a benefactor of the Colville Collection."

"No, but I am responsible for the material the Collection—and you—will be exhibiting this fall. We worked hard for many years recovering those artifacts. If your drinking threatens to detract from the exhibit, then—"

"Mrs. Fairchild, I've drunk only in moderation these past three years." He raised an eyebrow in her direction. "Which is more than can be said for you."

Her mouth fell open. "I beg your pardon?"

"I've done a lot of mad things in my life," he went on, "but riding off alone into the desert at high noon—drunker than Toby Belch—has not been one of them."

"I wasn't that drunk," she said primly.

"You passed out, lass. If I hadn't been there to haul you back to the Valley, you'd be buried under a sand dune right now."

"I can't believe I'm being lectured on sobriety by a skirt-chasing, drunken thief."

"Another endearment like that and I might take offense."

"I don't see how you *can* take offense. You looted over a dozen sites in Egypt, debauching females right and left while you were at it. The Emperor Nero was less decadent."

He couldn't help laughing. "If only half those stories were true."

"You *are* the man who did something immoral with a woman on top of the Great Pyramid, aren't you?"

"At least she was sober." He lowered his voice to a stage whisper. "I hope your excessive drinking is now confined behind closed doors, Charlotte. The English take a dim view of brandy-soaked widows."

"That's enough." She looked as if she were fighting not to laugh. "And I don't remember giving you permission to use my Christian name."

"You didn't, but we skirt-chasing, drunken thieves aren't known for our manners."

She finally did burst into laughter. "Now that we've both reformed, I suppose we can trust each other."

"*Do* you trust me?" He was amazed at how much he desired her trust and confidence.

She stared at him for a long moment. "Yes, I do."

But she apparently didn't trust herself to hold his gaze for more than a moment. He wondered if she sensed his avid interest in her. She was a contrary, blunt, intriguing creature. Conversing with Charlotte Fairchild was like stumbling across an undiscovered landscape; she seemed fraught with danger and possibility. A pity she wasn't dizzy with brandy now. He would have welcomed the chance to carry her off to his camel once more, or a waiting brougham.

Thunder suddenly rolled overhead and the breeze picked up, rustling the shrubbery.

He turned up his collar. "Are you sure you don't want to return to the house? Seeing as how we don't have an umbrella . . ."

"I never carry an umbrella." She lifted her face. "I love thunderstorms. They're so dark and thrilling."

A sizzling flash lit up the ominous morning sky.

"And lightning—I suppose you don't mind that."

She closed her eyes, obviously reveling in the danger that had descended upon them. "My, yes, lightning is lovely, too."

"What is your opinion of fried desert cats?"

Nefer shook her wet fur with a mournful meow.

"Oh, I'd forgotten about Nefer. I don't want *her* to get struck by lightning."

The rain poured down from the black clouds overhead. She pointed to a canopy that hung over the stuccoed entrance of a nearby residence.

Pierce scooped up the cat with one hand and grabbed her arm with the other. "Run," he said.

As soon as they were safe beneath the awning, Charlotte said happily, "Like the Nile overflowing its banks."

"You and I seem fated to meet in extreme circumstances. Two years ago we were knee-deep in sand dunes. Now it's likely we'll be drowned in the middle of Belgravia. I wouldn't be surprised if we end up in a raging inferno the next time we meet."

She snapped her fingers. "I called you *Dilly,* didn't I?"

"What?"

"Something about the way you spoke just now brought back our conversation in the desert. I still don't remember most of it—"

"That doesn't surprise me."

She ignored him. "I called you *Dilly.* And *Mr. Lion.* Why did I do that?"

He leaned closer. "You were drunk."

Lightning lit up the square, setting Nefer to growling at their feet. "A gentleman wouldn't keep reminding me of that."

"That's true. But *I* would. I'll probably remind you of it three or four times before I take you home."

Her expression turned thoughtful. "I do remember that Sir

77

Thomas Havers said you were called *The Lion* by the Egyptians."

"I'm sure he has several other names for me as well. He's never forgiven me for finding the tomb of Pharaoh Dozier first."

"But why do they call you *The Lion?*"

"You must leave me my secrets, Charlotte."

Those stunning gray eyes looked searchingly into his. She nodded finally, like a woman who had decided to surrender something. "I don't mind if you call me *Charlotte*. Colleagues should be straightforward with each other. Since we'll be working together, it's best to be informal."

"Working together?"

She didn't hear his question. Instead her attention had turned to a drenched figure hurrying past. "I don't believe it. It can't be."

Charlotte stepped out from beneath the awning. "Ahmed, is that you? Whatever are you doing in London?"

The man flinched, then spun about. "So there you are. Well, you have saved me the trouble of going further, Mrs. Fairchild. I was on my way to the house of your mother, to prevent you from causing more trouble before it is too late."

"But why are you here?"

Instead of answering, he pointed to the cat rubbing against her wet skirt. "So it is true, then. You have brought the cat with you." He closed his eyes. "And the curse."

Charlotte couldn't help but smile. Even after two and a half years, the dour foreman still spread gloom and doom like an Old Testament prophet. Although he was dressed in European clothes, his mustache was as bristly as ever. As was his manner. The familiarity of it all was tremendously reassuring. He reminded her of happier, freer times. He reminded her of Egypt.

"Come now, Ahmed. You're an educated man. There are no such things as curses."

Pierce came out into the rain to stand beside her. "I wouldn't say that. Has he ever sampled English cooking?"

"Quiet," she said, stifling a giggle.

"So now you find the curse cause for laughter?" Ahmed shook his head. "If I had lost a father and husband as you have, I would dare not laugh."

She sobered immediately. "Why were you on the way to see me?"

"I left for England as soon as I heard the dreadful news. I have come because no matter how many warnings you Europeans are given, you refuse to listen. And you will bring disaster upon us all. Again."

"Who is this person?" Pierce stepped in front of her, but she pushed him aside, She needed no protection, not from Ahmed.

"Dylan Pierce, this is Ahmed Vartan. He was our foreman in the Valley. Ahmed, this is—"

"I know who Pierce is. He is yet another European who wishes to loot and desecrate the Valley of Amun."

"Sorry to disappoint you," said Dylan, "but I've never sunk so much as a trowel into the Valley. I've been hired only to display the material that was recovered there."

"Yes. You expose the dead and their hidden burial goods for unbelievers to see. Or do you think they want to have their secrets laid bare before the mighty British public? The deaths in the Valley prove that they wish to be left in peace. Bah! You are a fool." Ahmed waved him away.

"Ahmed, how long have you been in London?"

The proud Turk only stared at her, his dark eyes showing disapproval beneath his thick eyebrows.

"If you can't be civil, Mr. Vartan, then I suggest you move on." This time she heard a hard note in Pierce's voice.

Ahmed peered over the side of his umbrella as thunder rumbled directly overhead. "You are cursed, Mrs. Fairchild. Cursed as your father was, and your husband."

She felt her heart begin to race. "My father died of a fever. You know that."

"He was cursed with the fever because he violated what does not belong to him or any European. I know that now. None of us should have dared set foot in the Valley."

"That's enough, Vartan," Pierce said.

"She knows the truth." He pointed at Charlotte. "She was there when her man was crushed in the tomb. She knows that the Goddess Bastet sent her emissary to warn her and Mr. Fairchild away. I tell you that if you proceed with this exhibit, not even the desert creature she keeps so close will save her this time."

As though knowing she was being referred to, Nefer hissed.

"Please go, Ahmed," Charlotte said. "You're upsetting Nefer, and she could pounce at any moment."

Ahmed took a step back, his eyes widening when the cat bared her fangs. "I have done my best to warn you, Mrs. Fairchild. I have tried to keep you from harm. I can do no more."

He turned on his heel and hurried off.

"You employed that rascal as your foreman?" Pierce led her back to the shelter of the canopy, although since they were soaking wet, it hardly mattered. "I would have set the jackals on him."

"Ahmed was a fine foreman, at least while we were only excavating steles and papyrus scrolls. He didn't become agitated until we discovered a tomb under the protection of the feline goddess Bastet."

"Well, don't let his ravings upset you."

"I grew accustomed to his grumbling years ago, but it's always painful to be reminded of the deaths of Father and Ian."

Indeed, she felt a sudden surge of dread. But she wouldn't give in to her fear as Ahmed had. She didn't want to be afraid any longer: she didn't want to be afraid to talk about

Egypt and the past—either her past or the past of the pharaohs. She didn't want to be afraid of life any longer. Even
if she was.

"I'm glad you visited me today, Dylan."

He looked over at her. No doubt he was surprised she
used his Christian name as freely as he did hers.

"And I agree to serve as consultant on the amulets and
scarabs. In fact, I can work at the Collection six days a week
until the exhibit opens."

"Excuse me." He shook his head. "I don't understand."

Maybe the thunder was drowning her out. "You agreed
that I was an expert on amulets and scarabs," she said loudly,
"and that your scarab specialist has gone off to Berlin. Since
you need help in identifying the artifacts from the Valley of
Amun, it only makes sense that I help you."

When he still didn't answer, she leaned closer. "That is
why you came to visit me this morning, isn't it?"

"Ah, yes. Yes, it was. But see here, there's no need for
you to come to the museum. No need at all. I can call on
you at your home whenever I have a question."

"Nonsense. One must never do anything in archaeology
by half-measures. And I want to be part of this. After all,
what better way to honor my father's memory—and Ian's—
than by working on this exhibit?"

Her decision felt like a risk, but for the first time in two
and a half years, she experienced no guilt. In fact, she felt
exhilarated, like those moments right before the sun rose
over the desert. This must be the right thing to do.

He seemed to be having difficulty believing her. "But you
were so adamant about retiring from Egyptology. I never
dreamed you would agree—"

"I want to do this," she said. "I need to."

With an audible sigh, he led her out into the street, apparently forgetting that the storm was still raging. She didn't
say a word, but only tucked Nefer safely under her arm. If

lightning did choose to strike, then it would strike both of them.

She touched his arm, and he looked over at her. "This is the second time you've been kind to me. The first was back in Egypt, when I begged you to give the Valley of Amun back to me. And now you've given me the opportunity to honor my father and Ian. You've given me the chance to immerse myself in Egypt once more. I feel like a sinner running toward temptation."

"If you'd rather not be tempted . . ." he said.

She shook her head. "I'm a lost soul. I know that now. Where Egypt is concerned, I have no conscience at all. Do you think that's so terrible?"

Even in the driving rain, she could see his eyes. They were midnight blue and as bold a sight as his thick auburn hair.

"I am not celebrated for my conscience either, Charlotte. So it seems we are well-matched."

He squeezed her hand. The sudden pressure—and the heat that shot through her—made her gasp.

They began walking again, as if nothing had passed between them but polite conversation. He clung onto her arm, though, like a man holding on to a lifeline. It didn't occur to her to pull away.

Why should she? She liked Dylan Pierce. Even more amazing, she trusted him. And he smelled of some exotic tonic water, a scent that evoked oranges and warm summer mornings. She imagined that they were walking along the cliffs surrounding the Valley of Amun instead of Belgravia, that the sun burned through their thin cottons, turning their flesh to golden brown. She could see them together, arm in arm, striding toward the pillars of a temple, laughing, talking, excited. Two acolytes of the desert, alike in their passion for the glorious past. In her vision, she gazed up into his bright blue eyes, eyes that would never accuse her as Ian's had.

A lover's eyes.

Her feet sank into the mud and she stumbled. But she was barely aware of the quagmire at her feet. Had she taken leave of her senses? A brief stroll around a rainy London street and she was mooning over Dylan like those ninnies at the lecture hall yesterday. Perhaps this was the price she paid for avoiding the company of young men these two and a half years. The result was an overheated imagination and a tendency to blush.

With an ear-splitting scream, lightning struck a nearby tree. Branches crashed down only yards from where they stood.

Dylan flung his arm about Charlotte's waist and jumped back. Pressed tight against him, she found it difficult to breathe. Nefer leaped to the ground with a frightened howl.

Charlotte and Dylan stared at the charred tree.

"It appears that Belgravia can still prove to be exciting," he said finally.

Charlotte agreed with him. But her growing excitement had nothing to do with lightning.

Chapter Six

Charlotte stroked the phallus.

She was pleased by its smoothness, its perfect condition. Composed of hard serpentine, it was easy to date. She held the amulet up to the sun, recalling the day that her father had unearthed it from the desert.

Smiling, she laid the piece back down on the tray. She wondered if this particular amulet had blessed its ancient owner. Probably not nearly enough, knowing men as she did. Then again, she'd only known intimacy with one man, and Ian had never been doubtful of his potency or his ability to please his wife in bed.

In fact, the only thing Ian had ever seemed unsure of was his feelings for her.

The day was too fine to waste on such unhappy thoughts, she decided. Since that lovely thunderstorm five weeks earlier, the weather had been amazingly un-English. Bright golden mornings followed by warm afternoons, soft breezes, and a sky filled with lazy, sumptuous clouds.

To take advantage of the remarkable weather, Dylan had suggested she spend part of each day in the garden courtyard of the Collection. He insisted that the light was better there, and she had to agree that sitting on the cool paving stones— trays of Egyptian amulets scattered about her, a summer sun blazing overhead—was as close to paradise as she had ever known in Britain.

It was so warm this afternoon that she felt smothered in her black costume. She'd already rolled up the sleeves as far as the silk would allow, but she longed to yank up her skirt and remove a petticoat or two. If her father were alive, he would have ordered her to leave off wearing black when working in the sun; it made a person beastly hot and ill-tempered.

But she hadn't known an ill-tempered moment since she began working with Dylan at the Colville Collection.

"I'm shameless," she murmured. And she was, putting aside her grief to play with such exquisite things.

Charlotte picked up another amulet, a stunning amethyst falcon. She brushed it against her cheek.

"Asking the god Osiris for help in identifying all this?"

Dylan stood beside the courtyard's fountain, his trousers and shirt covered with dust from the basement workrooms. She was surprised she hadn't heard him enter the enclosed courtyard, or somehow sensed his presence. The Welshman had a way of disturbing the air, like a stormy seawind blowing inland.

"This is Horus, the falcon god," she corrected. "And he grants protection from evil, in this life and the next."

He raised an eyebrow. "No doubt you're thinking of tucking a few of these away in your bodice. Keepsakes to remind you of the pleasures of working with me, not to mention the good luck you'd be looting from the Collection."

She gazed down at the gleaming display. "I don't believe one person has ever been surrounded by so many magical charms."

"And there's your own good-luck amulet, too. I remember you wearing a green faience charm about your neck in Egypt. Whatever happened to it?"

A chill ran through her, even though her neck was damp from the heat. "I gave it to someone."

He whistled. "Gave away your good luck, did you? This person must have been in a bad way."

His expression was good-humored; he seemed relaxed and happy. There was no reason to tell him that she'd draped the amulet about her husband's neck minutes before he met his death.

"I don't believe in good-luck charms any longer." She placed the amethyst falcon back on the tray.

"Sacrilege! Have a care, Charlotte, or this fellow here might be tempted to work some mischief in your life." He squatted beside her and picked up a solid-cast gold hippopotamus. "The Egyptians feared hippos, you know. Dreaded them more than snakes or scorpions. So don't anger him more than you must."

She took the amulet from Dylan, whose own neck glistened with perspiration. "This is Thoeris, a *female* deity, which you would be able to tell if you gave amulets half as much attention as you give those dusty papyrus scrolls."

"You're just jealous because I translate hieroglyphics quicker than you do."

"And the ancient Egyptians attributed evil qualities to their *male* animal gods," she went on, ignoring his teasing laughter. "The females were regarded as good and just, as indeed we are."

Nefer woke up from her nap just then and meowed. They looked over to where she lay stretched out beneath the sundial.

"Even Nefer agrees with me."

"She would." He gestured to the trays of amulets. "You must be nearly finished identifying them."

She nodded. "Most of the material Father and I excavated

has been cataloged. I only wish the last crates from Egypt would arrive. Nothing that Ian and I recovered has been properly identified yet."

Dylan began picking up the amulets, turning them over in his hand, holding them up to the sunlight. "It's only two seasons' worth of artifacts. Besides, the crates should arrive any day now, and I'm sure my team of experts will more than rise to the occasion. After all, I possess a secret weapon."

"Me?" she asked, only half joking.

He pointed to Nefer, asleep once more. "Her. The sacred cat who protects us all with her benevolent female presence."

Charlotte nodded. "There are times when I think she is watching over us. Maybe I spent too much of my youth in the desert. You begin to believe all manner of things out there in that vastness. Magic didn't seem beyond the realm of possibility. But back here in London . . ." Her voice trailed off.

"Maybe our memories are the real magic," he said quietly.

He squeezed her shoulder, and she remembered when he'd put his arm about her during the storm. She told herself it had been the fury of the thunder, the thrill of the lightning strike, or the prospect of working as an Egyptologist again that had excited her so. But when Dylan stood close, when he touched her without warning, when he looked at her with a certain, bold expression, she felt that sharp excitement again. The excitement of a woman responding to a fascinating man.

Yet it was more than physical attraction. She liked how he treated her mother and sister with such good humor whenever he came to Belgrave Square to visit. He'd even survived a bout of morning exercise with Michael. She liked how gently he spoke to Nefer, and how his laugh came rumbling out of his broad chest. And she liked that he listened to her with respect, as if she had something of value to say. Ian— God rest his soul—had too often been impatient with her.

And on occasion even seemed threatened by her. She doubted Dylan Pierce felt threatened by any woman. Or man.

"Mrs. Fairchild, is that you?"

Charlotte turned around, startled to see Sir Thomas Havers standing at the entrance to the courtyard.

"Sir Thomas?" She made an attempt to rise, and was quickly assisted by Dylan. "I thought you were in Egypt."

He frowned, twisting his hat in his hands. "I crossed the Channel yesterday and made my way here posthaste."

Charlotte and Dylan exchanged glances. The elderly gentleman seemed agitated: His bald head was shiny with perspiration, his lined face sallow and drawn. She could almost imagine she heard his heart pounding beneath the linen jacket.

"Is something wrong, Sir Thomas?" Dylan asked.

"Yes, something is wrong. I'm having second thoughts about the upcoming exhibition. I should never have suggested it to the Colvilles last year." He pulled out a handkerchief and mopped his forehead. "Too many people have died in the Valley of Amun. Exhibiting all this material so soon after their deaths shows a lack of respect. It's unseemly and crass." His voice shook.

"There was no need for both you and Barnabas Hughes to go to Egypt." Dylan led him over to a cast-iron bench. "Hughes and the curators at the Cairo Museum could have handled everything."

"As if I'd leave it to a bunch of foreigners to pack off the artifacts. And Hughes has spent most of his career in England. The poor fellow doesn't even speak Arabic. If I hadn't been there to help him, the customs people in Alexandria would have delayed him for weeks. No, I had to go. I owed it to Sir Reginald." The old man shot an accusing look at Charlotte. "And your late husband."

Was her interest in Dylan so obvious? She looked down at her black gown. She was a widow, her husband dead less than three years. Yet here she was, sprawled on the ground with another archaeologist—a man with a reputation for womanizing—happily playing with amulets and scarabs, preparing to display the very material for which her husband had died.

Her head began to reel. Ian would not have died had she not prevented Dylan from taking over the site. She had killed her husband as surely as if she'd run him through with a sword. And now she was ready to reap the benefits of his tragic efforts.

"What's wrong, Charlotte?" Dylan left Sir Thomas to attend to her now. "You look like you're about to faint."

"No, no, it's just that I've been working out here for hours. I haven't had this much sun in years. Besides, I'm almost done cataloging the amulets." She managed a smile. "I'll just go inside and sit down. The Assyrian Gallery, perhaps. It's darker than twilight in there."

Sir Thomas wore a forbidding expression as she walked past.

"I hope to see you later, Sir Thomas," she murmured, glad to make her escape to the cool shadows of the museum.

Once she left the courtyard, however, she paused.

"What in the world is that woman doing here?" Sir Thomas asked.

She held her breath, stunned by the fury in his voice.

"Charlotte Fairchild is a highly knowledgeable Egyptologist." Dylan's voice was just as angry. "Why shouldn't she be here?"

"Because if it were not for her, my friend and colleague would still be alive!"

Charlotte gasped aloud.

"Don't say such things again, or you'll strain my patience."

"Then strain it I must. I will not have Mrs. Fairchild mucking about in this museum. She's responsible for her husband's death and that's the end of the discussion."

She didn't hear Dylan's reply. She couldn't. Covering her

ears, she ran wildly through the galleries, away from Sir Thomas's stern voice.

And away from the terrible truth.

Dylan hadn't been so angry in years. And the pathetic sight of Charlotte running through the adjacent gallery—Nefer trotting after her—only increased his ire.

"Ian Fairchild died in a cave-in. He obviously didn't secure the tunnels before he went exploring. He had only himself to blame for what happened."

"How dare you!" The old man's voice shook. "Ian was a fine archaeologist, fine enough to take every precaution. No, the tomb would have collapsed regardless of how many supports had been erected. And Ian would not have been there when it did if not for his interfering wife."

"If you're looking for someone to blame, you might as well blame me. I was the one who turned down the assignment, after all."

"Yes, but only after that stubborn female turned you against the idea. What *did* she do to convince you? Did she employ tears, or simply offer herself up like one of your Cairo dancing girls?"

"Have a care, old man."

"You've led too checkered a past to pretend at being a gentleman now. She did try to seduce you, didn't she? After all, it was just the two of you out there on the desert. And she was drunk, too."

"Well, I wasn't!" Dylan had to remind himself that Sir Thomas was nearly seventy. If any other man were to speak that way about Charlotte, he would have had him by the throat.

"Are you certain of that?"

"Not that it's any of your bloody business, but I've not swigged back more than a glass or two of liquor in three years. And if you believe otherwise, then you're as wrong about me as you are about Charlotte."

Sir Thomas' scowl grew deeper. "*Charlotte*, is it? And I noticed she called you *Dylan*. I can only imagine what other endearments you fling at each other when people aren't around."

"I'd say you have too much imagination. Give that overheated brain of yours a rest."

"Only when I have your word that Mrs. Fairchild will not set foot in this museum again."

Dylan crossed his arms. "She comes every day and will continue to do so."

"I'll go to the Colvilles to complain. And I'll advise them to cancel this show."

He shrugged. "Do as you like. But the Colvilles are superstitious souls, and take to heart everything their palm reader tells them. They won't make a move without her approval."

"So?"

"So the palm reader is Charlotte's aunt." He couldn't resist grinning. "And Aunt Hazel has assured the Colvilles that her favorite niece and I are the keys to success for the Valley of Amun show."

"Palm reader!" The old man pursed his lips, looking suddenly like a frustrated badger. "So that's how you finagled your appointment. I couldn't believe it when I got the telegram in Cairo informing me that *you* were going to direct the exhibit. Poor Hughes nearly had a stroke. He had every reason to think that this exhibit was to be his responsibility."

"Oh, hang Hughes." Dylan had only worked with Barnabas Hughes for a couple of weeks before the assistant curator left for Cairo, but it was more than enough time for the two men to develop a strong mutual dislike. "Obviously my credentials in archaeology impressed the Colvilles more."

"But first you set out to impress that palm-reading aunt. Did you seduce both her and her niece to get the job? Have you no shame, man?"

91

"I'll leave the shame to you, Sir Thomas."

"The real shame belongs to Charlotte Fairchild. First she kills her husband, and now she—"

"I said that's enough!"

He stood up. "She'll lead you and this Collection to ruin."

"If ten years of womanizing and brawling didn't lead to my ruin, I doubt one scholarly widow will be able to do it."

"You may fool the Colvilles with this new respectable pose you've taken up, but not me. I remember the days you cared for nothing but gold, whiskey, and whores. I wouldn't be surprised if you've figured out a way to sell the Collection's artifacts on the black market while you entertain yourself with my late friend's wife."

Dylan shook his head. "You must have picked up dengue fever on this last trip. Only someone in the throes of delirium would say such idiotic things."

"Don't patronize me. I was uncovering dynastic tombs when you were still a Welsh brat wallowing in sheep dung and beer."

"I'm not a Welsh brat now. I'm the appointed director of the Valley of Amun exhibit. Please don't forget it."

Sir Thomas looked as though he had just swallowed something bitter. "You're not fit to sweep the back corridors of a museum."

"Then why did you come to me two years ago and beg me to take over the Valley of Amun site? I've always wondered about that."

"I was fool enough to try and help you. I was hoping such an assignment would make a respectable scholar out of a man who prefers diddling about with lewd poetry and Berber native girls. Obviously I was wrong."

Dylan would not let the old man goad him into fighting.

"Where are the crates from Egypt?" A change of subject might prevent the two of them from behaving like dim-witted schoolboys.

Sir Thomas glared at him. "At Victoria Station."

"I'll arrange to have them delivered safely to the Collection." He glanced down at the trays of amulets, their polished surfaces gleaming in the afternoon light.

Once Sir Thomas left, he must find Charlotte. He didn't believe she had had too much sun, not someone who spent most of her life in the African desert. The old fool had upset her.

"I warn you again: Don't let that woman near the Valley of Amun material. She has no right to touch any of it."

Dylan walked toward the courtyard exit. "You can find your own way out."

"I'll tell the Colvilles that Charlotte Fairchild is cursed."

Dylan turned around slowly. "You're the one who is cursed—with stupidity."

"Imagine how I could tell the tale." Sir Thomas's eyes brightened beneath his beetle brows. "A young woman whose father died mysteriously of a fever, a fever she never caught. Their first foreman was found dead one morning from a scorpion bite, right outside her tent. Then, a year later, her husband dies in a cave-in, the one time that she herself was not permitted to go inside. Yes, Mrs. Fairchild does seem unlucky—at least for those who surround her. I don't believe that either Mr. or Mrs. Colville would fancy all that bad luck being in such close proximity. I wager that will trump whatever Aunt Hazel, the palm reader, says."

"Go back to Egypt, Thomas. And stay there." He marched through the Roman Antiquities gallery without looking back.

"I'll be back!" Sir Thomas shouted. "And when I do, your drunken widow will be on her way out."

Charlotte wasn't in the Assyrian galleries, nor was she hiding behind the Persian statues. Luckily it was Monday, and the Collection was closed to the public. There was no one around to stare as Dylan hurried from one exhibition hall to another.

He stopped for breath at the door to the Egyptian galleries, which were roped off in preparation for the upcoming Valley of Amun exhibit.

The large skylight overhead lent the huge sarcophagi and basalt statues a chilling glow. Most impressive, however, was the exhibit's centerpiece: a reconstruction of an ancient tomb. Dylan walked closer to the crypt that once held the mummy of a priest of Amun-Ra. When the exhibit opened, this tomb would garner most of the attention, and rightfully so. After reconstruction was complete, visitors would be able to walk through the narrow corridor and into the heart of the tomb itself—where a mummy in a gilt coffin lay waiting. It was a sight designed to induce both dread and awe.

Such an exhibit could bring him considerable renown in the field of Egyptology. He hoped so. He had no wish to forever be regarded as a treasure-hunting drunkard who loved erotic poetry.

A few feet from the tomb entrance stood two limestone posts, an inscribed stone slab resting atop them.

Dylan read aloud the hieroglyphic inscription carved into the polished limestone: " 'Beware to the greedy man who trespasses upon the priestly dead. Let the crocodile chase him on the waters, and the serpent pursue him on the land. A thousand tortures he will suffer before his spirit is crushed beneath his iniquity and guilt. And his doomed spirit will forever be denied the blessings of Amun-Ra.' "

Of course he didn't believe in curses, at least not those invoked by long-dead pharaohs and priests who sought to protect their grave goods. But Egyptologists *were* cursed. Cursed with the need to understand the past, to uncover what might lay hidden and unknown forever.

And Charlotte Fairchild seemed more cursed than most. She had proved a tireless worker these past five weeks, and seemed to come alive among the canopic jars, faience figurines, and mummies. Her pallor was long gone, and she moved about with such energy that he sometimes feared she'd knock over a display case in her enthusiasm. But her obvious happiness made him happy, while her scholarship continued to amaze him.

He was glad she had agreed to spend part of each day working in the open courtyard. The sun had already lightened her hair and put color in her cheeks. Like the basalt statues and lotus jewelry, Charlotte didn't belong here. She belonged in Egypt. She was a desert creature who needed sun and hot sand to flourish.

"I don't belong here either," he said aloud.

"Yes, you do." Charlotte's voice echoed in the cavernous gallery. Nefer darted out of the shadows, then disappeared again behind a statue of Thoth.

"Where are you, Charlotte?"

She peeked around the side of a gilt-painted mummy case.

"I should have known you'd choose to huddle by Queen Dendera." He walked over to where she sat leaning against the sarcophagus. "The scribes say she was an intrepid woman who built temples to the sun god Amun-Ra."

Even though her eyes were red from crying, she managed a weak smile. "Dendera died at age twelve, just a month after her marriage to Pharaoh. The poor child probably didn't have time to even visit a temple to Amun, let alone build one."

"See how much I need you here. Without you to catch my mistakes, I'd get my dynasties totally confused."

"Your only mistake was letting me come here."

Dylan sat down beside her. "Don't get upset about anything Sir Thomas may have said. How much did you hear, anyway?"

"Enough." Her gray eyes were back to that sad somber cast.

She looked so forlorn that he couldn't help but put his arm around her. After a slight hesitation, he felt Charlotte relax. He drew her close, amazed at how perfectly she fit against him; he realized with a start that he had been wanting to hold her for weeks.

"I've never seen him act so foolish as he did today."

She took a deep breath. "He said only what I've said to myself repeatedly these past two and a half years. Ian would be alive if not for me."

"That's ridiculous, lass." The scent of her jasmine perfume filled his senses, and he leaned his head against hers. Her hair felt as smooth as silk. "It was no one's fault."

"Dylan, if I hadn't convinced you to refuse the site, Ian would have been on a ship bound for Portsmouth when the tomb collapsed." Her voice grew even more stricken. "And you would have been the one buried alive."

The emotion in her voice made his breathing quicken. So the idea of his death was as painful for Charlotte to contemplate as that of her late husband.

"I would not have been buried alive."

"Yes, you would. The cave would have collapsed on you just as it did on Ian." She shuddered, and he held her even closer. "It was so terrible. You don't know."

"Shhh, lass, don't think on it." He gently kissed the top of her head. "There's no changing the past. If you can't learn from it, then you must put it behind you."

He put his hand beneath her chin and tipped her head back so that he could look at her face. The sight of those sad, glorious eyes staring back at him so trustfully made him tremble. He had to stop himself from crushing her against him, devouring that luscious mouth with his own, caressing her arms. Another Dylan in another time would have done just that. But he couldn't just heartlessly take his pleasure with Charlotte, as if she were a belly dancer or Cairo street girl.

She trusted him; she considered herself his friend and colleague. He looked down at her, liking the way she nestled against him. Few women trusted Dylan, or had reason to. And only a coldhearted scoundrel would take advantage of her guilt or her sadness at this moment.

He kissed her forehead.

"You're a good friend, Dylan," she whispered, which only intensified his own guilty feelings.

He pulled away, forcing Charlotte to sit up. If he was to remain a good friend, he had to put some distance between them.

"Then as a friend, please believe me. Had I been there that terrible day, I would not have died in the cave-in."

She started to protest, but he held up his hand. "A skilled archaeologist knows when a tunnel is secured properly, lass. From all accounts, the walls collapsed within minutes of him entering the tomb. That means that your husband's work there was slapdash and incomplete from the moment he began organizing the digging. The entrance wasn't even supported."

Charlotte leaned forward and put her face in her hands. "It doesn't help to put the blame on Ian. He can't defend himself or explain. The poor man is dead."

"He's dead, but you aren't." Dylan paused. "I do understand how you feel, though. I understand all too well."

She raised her head, her expression even more stricken. "Please don't feel guilty over Ian. I was the one who begged you to turn down the site."

He was uncertain whether to continue. "I wasn't speaking about the cave-in, even if I do think I could have prevented it had I been there. But I do bear the blame for a terrible accident that happened while I was in Egypt."

"On one of the sites?"

"No, in Cairo three years ago." He took a deep breath. "The fire that burned down the tentmakers' bazaar."

For a painful moment, he could see the flames and smell the smoke. And, as always, he could still hear the agonized screams of the people trapped in the blaze.

"Ian and I were in the city at the time. I remember." She looked down at the floor, as if reluctant to meet his eyes. "People said the fire started when you got into a drunken fight over a belly dancer."

"I was not drunk!"

Charlotte jumped, obviously startled.

"I was not drunk," he repeated in a quieter voice. "In fact, I wasn't even in the bazaar when the fire started. I don't care what sort of lurid tales you've been told. Nonsense about drunken brawls and belly dancers! The fire had nothing to do with that."

"Then—then why do you feel guilty?"

"I feel guilty because three merchants died in the blaze; I feel guilty because a young Egyptian boy was so badly burned that he'll never walk again." He heard his voice begin to shake and stopped until he could gain control of himself.

"I feel guilty because no matter how much money I've sent to the boy's family, no matter how many of his doctor bills I pay, that child will always be crippled." He closed his eyes. "And horribly disfigured."

Nefer appeared suddenly and rubbed herself against his ankles, as though trying to console him.

"And I feel guilty because that fire was meant to kill me. It was deliberately set by a man who wanted me dead."

"But who would want to kill you?"

"Someone very much like myself," he said grimly. "A treasure hunter, a greedy man seeking gold. A man who was jealous of my success at finding rich archaeological sites and was willing to do anything to destroy me. He almost did, too. I was on my way to the bazaar to meet with a seller of antiquities when my carriage driver ran right into a camel. Delayed me by nearly an hour." He gave a short laugh. "That bloody creature ended up saving my life."

"What happened to the man who wanted to kill you? Who is he?"

"I don't know. I could never find out his real name." Dylan forced a smile. He'd only meant to sympathize with Charlotte, not cause her further worry. "But that was three years ago on another continent. I'm just a poorly paid archaeologist now, and of no interest to treasure hunters in Egypt."

She gave him a long, searching look. "That's why you turned respectable, isn't it? Because of your guilt over those men who died in the fire, and that poor injured boy."

"Let's just say I learned there are some things that not even gold can make right again." He squeezed her shoulder. "I understand how terrible it is to live with guilt, Charlotte. I understand how it can change everything. But don't let it destroy your future; don't let it take away any hope of happiness."

"You don't understand. I feel guilty because I *do* want to live again, without regret, without recriminations. I want to go back to Egypt, back to the Valley of Amun. I want to pick up a shovel and dig into the very tomb that killed my husband." She sighed. "And if Sir Thomas ever guessed that, he would fling me on a funeral pyre himself."

She stood up, and he quickly got to his own feet as well.

"You've been working in the museum too much. Without the desert sun, these statues and mummies would strike gloom in the cheeriest soul." He gestured toward the tomb standing beneath the skylight. "And seeing an Egyptian tomb every day can't be easy for you."

She shook her head. "I don't need ancient tombs or steles to remind me of my guilt. My memories are more than sufficient."

"Then you need a few fun and frivolous memories. I should take you off to the operetta one night, followed by dinner in a dockside saloon."

"So you think a plate of fried fish and some Gilbert and Sullivan will help put everything in perspective, do you?" She managed a tiny smile. "I don't remember the last time I went to the theater, and I've not read anything but monographs in years."

He raised his eyebrows in mock horror. "Do you mean to say you've not read my scandalous poetry?"

"It's not for lack of trying. Catherine found Mother's copy of the *Songs of Rajya* but refuses to part with it."

"I'll have to bring you an autographed copy. Wrapped in brown paper, of course. Wouldn't want them to start whispering about the scholarly Mrs. Fairchild."

"I fear they're already whispering about me." She glanced up at the darkening skylight. "It's late. I must be getting home."

"You will come back tomorrow, won't you?"

"I'll be back. The least I can do for Ian and Father is to make this exhibit worthy of them. A dozen doubting Thomases won't stop me from doing that. Nor will my guilt."

Dylan stood there long after her footsteps died away down the empty galleries. He feared he wasn't cursed only with his hunger for Egypt and her treasures.

He was also cursed with his growing desire for Charlotte Fairchild.

Sir Thomas couldn't believe that Ian's wife was being allowed to take part in the exhibit. In his day, young widows stayed at home and tended to their needlepoint and church charities. Of course, he'd forgotten just what sort of eccentric women the Graingers bred: rabble-rousers, journalists, palm readers. And worst of all, a woman who fancied herself an Egyptologist.

It was a wonder he hadn't had an apoplectic fit, seeing that brash female at the Collection, knee-deep in precious amulets. Laughing at close quarters with that bloody scoundrel Pierce, for pity's sake.

And Pierce had looked as happy as she had. Resembling in no way the brawling, drunken, coarse fellow with a taste for native girls that Sir Thomas had been led to expect. Well, it didn't matter how much Pierce wanted to moon over that infuriating, meddlesome woman. She would be gone soon enough.

He got into the waiting carriage. "Charlotte is working on

the exhibit," he said to the passenger waiting inside.

"What!"

"She's there now, her and Pierce as cozy as can be, playing with their scarabs and amulets. He's letting her catalog the material from the Valley of Amun."

"Of all the rotten luck! What will happen to us if—"

"Nothing will happen to us. It is Charlotte who is going to discover just how foul her own luck is."

He tapped on the roof of the carriage to signal that they were ready to leave. "And soon, too."

Chapter Seven

A gang of pirates crept up behind the lovely young girls who sang of rain and a warm July. Without warning, the pirates pounced upon the unsuspecting females, setting off a wave of laughter in the audience.

But Dylan's attention was on Charlotte, not the stage. Her face was aglow with excitement and pleasure. He was glad he'd been able to get tickets for tonight's performance, even if it had cost an indecent amount of money to buy the tickets from a Dean Street scalper.

On the other side of him, Michael burst out laughing.

"I thought you didn't fancy an evening at the operetta," he whispered to the boy.

"I say, you didn't tell me Gilbert and Sullivan were such jolly fun to watch." The twelve-year-old laughed again, thoroughly enjoying the rousing first act of *The Pirates of Penzance.*

Dylan sat back, feeling like a dutiful patriarch who'd taken his children out for an evening at the theater. It was an odd sensation, but not unpleasant. And if he somewhat regretted extending the invitation to Charlotte's family as well, he was gratified that it brought so much obvious pleasure to her.

He looked over at Charlotte once again. The woman had a delicious profile, like one of those ladies carved on sixteenth-century Italian cameos. And she had dared to liven up her mourning dress tonight with pearl ear bobs and an elaborate filigree comb that held her smooth mass of hair in place. In the flickering gaslight, her hair resembled that glorious moonfire he'd glimpsed two years ago in Egypt.

His gaze slowly traveled down the rest of her body. Although she was still dressed in black, the gown's expensive silk clung suggestively to her curves. And while her arms were primly encased in tight sleeves, only a panel of sheer black material covered her shoulders and neck. If he angled his head the right way, he could glimpse the swell of her breasts beneath the transparent chiffon. He'd seen half-naked belly dancers who looked less enticing.

Closing his eyes, he took a deep breath. He knew that for the rest of his life, the scent of jasmine would remind him of the young widow. Although in the closeness of the theater, her tempting fragrance was nearly lost among the dozens of competing perfumes and the gas fumes from the stagelights.

"This is delightful, Dylan. I'm so glad you bought tickets for all of us. I've never seen an operetta before."

He opened his eyes. Charlotte leaned toward him, allowing him a clear view of those sweetly rounded breasts. She looked as pleased as a child presented with a day at Astley's Circus.

"I thought it was raucous enough to suit the Grainger family," he whispered back.

She smiled.

Heretofore, he'd only seen Charlotte truly happy when she was discussing the Ramessid pharaohs, or the expert artwork decorating a papyrus scroll. The woman spent too much of her life immersed in Egypt and her glories. Not that he didn't understand the obsession, but life held other joys aside from mummies and scarab beetles. Or hadn't her late husband bothered to teach her that?

He recalled his only encounter with Ian Fairchild. To be fair, his memory was colored by the fact that Fairchild had been in a foul mood when he'd brought his wife back to the desert camp. Still, the fellow had seemed like a prig, the sort who wouldn't care if his young wife ever indulged herself in silly pleasures. Indeed, he wondered why Charlotte had married Ian Fairchild in the first place. Had she fallen desperately in love with him? Like a desert whirlwind, her mother said. If so, it was odd that whenever she had cause to mention Ian, it was in guilt-stricken tones. Remorse seemed the only emotion she associated with her late husband.

Dylan straightened up, trying to concentrate on the finale to Act One. He wanted to believe that she hadn't loved her husband, at least not passionately. The embarrassing truth was that he was jealous of Ian Fairchild, jealous that Fairchild had shared her bed and introduced her to desire. Even more frustrating, his death had sent her into a lengthy—almost melodramatic—mourning.

Despite all of the women he had known, Dylan doubted any of them would mourn his passing with more than a few crocodile tears, and a glass of wine to drown their short-lived sorrow. He laughed at himself. Self-pity never sat well with him, and he wouldn't allow more than a moment of it now.

He liked Charlotte Fairchild. She was an attractive, intelligent, fascinating woman. They'd spent every day of the last five weeks in each other's company. Small wonder she occupied so much of his thoughts. She was his only distraction aside from the Valley of Amun collection. And it was clear that she needed a distraction even more than he did.

It was just two days ago that Sir Thomas had stormed into the museum, accusing Charlotte of having been responsible for her husband's death. Luckily, his favorite Gilbert and Sullivan was playing at the New Royalty Operetta House. Pirate apprentice Frederic, General Stanley's daughters, and the wily pirate maid Ruth were just the thing for raising the spirits and making the world seem a less somber place. As if to prove his point, the unruly actors onstage broke into a comical dance, while the Pirate-King brandished an enormous skull-and-crossbones flag. The entire company sang about a certain "doctor of divinity" as the curtain rang down amid a chorus of cheers and warm applause.

Lady Margaret shouted "Bravi" as the houselights came on.

"That was delightful," Catherine said, looking like a schoolgirl in her ivory embroidered blouse and skirt. "Especially in how it demonstrated the absurdity of excessive female modesty."

"Yes, indeed," Dylan agreed with a straight face.

Lady Margaret got to her feet, smoothing down the folds of her own surprisingly fashionable blue gown. "I haven't seen an operetta in years. We really must attend more Gilbert and Sullivan productions." She squeezed Dylan's shoulder. "Thank you again for providing us with this rare treat."

"Mother, may I run downstairs and buy a lemon ice?" Michael swung open the door to their loge box.

"Make certain to be back in time for Act Two."

He raced out.

"I think Catherine and I need to step out for a few moments ourselves." She pointed to the loge box closest to the stage.

An older man boasting a white walrus mustache sat there alone. With his arms crossed over his stomach and his head bowed down, it was obvious that he had nodded off during Act One.

Dylan laughed. "The gentleman is apparently not a fan of Gilbert and Sullivan. Although I'm amazed the last chorus didn't wake him up."

"Well, Catherine and I will do our best to rouse him," Lady Margaret said. "It is most fortuitous that Lord Hamilton is here tonight. He has stubbornly refused to meet with us to discuss women's suffrage. Now that he's alone in his theater box, however, we have an excellent opportunity to put forth our case."

Catherine rose quickly. "Let us hurry, Mother. We don't have much time, and Lord Hamilton is renowned for his obstinacy."

"Ladies, are you certain you wish to do this?" Dylan blocked the doorway. "I mean, there's a time and a place for political debate, but a theater may not be—"

"Political debate should occur wherever there is injustice to be fought." Lady Margaret tapped him on the shoulder with her fan. "Stand aside, young man."

Against his better judgment, he let the two Grainger women march past. He sat down beside Charlotte, who was nonchalantly reading her program.

"You don't think they'll cause a scene, do you?"

"Perhaps." She thought a moment. "It depends on how disagreeable Lord Hamilton is."

He wondered if he should go after them. "What does that mean?"

"If he refuses to listen to their defense of women's suffrage, then they'll raise their voices, make a short speech." She looked over at the sleeping Lord Hamilton. "I don't think they'll do anything more. They didn't come prepared. At least I didn't see either Catherine or Mother bring along a pot of paint."

"Paint?"

"Sometimes they paint 'Votes for Women' on walls and doorways. Throw a little paint on people as well."

"But not in a theater, surely."

"Oh, yes. The Savoy won't even allow Mother into the lobby."

He sat back with a grunt. "I really do think you should

have warned me before I brought your family to the theater."

She laughed. "I can't believe you're the same Dylan Pierce who was expelled from Cambridge for gambling."

"I was nineteen. You can hardly expect a nineteen-year-old to be mature or responsible."

"Catherine is nineteen."

"Yes, and she's about to throw paint pots at some old man who only wants to take a nap."

"I told you, she didn't bring any paint." Charlotte seemed far too amused at his discomfiture. "I didn't realize how conventional a gentleman you really are."

"I don't see the need to be insulting."

"No, really. Back in Egypt, I heard a different tale told about you every month. Being tossed into jail for stealing a lady from a harem, racing camels around the Sphinx on a wager—"

"Who told you that? I hate camels. I raced stallions."

"And weren't you the man who was almost stoned to death for trying to enter a mosque naked?"

"I had my breeches on," he protested, not liking the sound of his idiotic escapades repeated back to him. "And I was too drunk to know what I was doing."

She raised an eyebrow. "Exactly."

"I admit my drinking was a problem," he said quietly.

She leaned closer. A stray tendril of her hair brushed across his face, and he felt an unaccountable thrill of pleasure run through him.

"And of course, there was your celebrated tryst atop the Great Pyramid," she whispered.

He breathed in her delicious fragrance, reveling in her closeness, the brush of her hair against his cheek, the sight of those lovely breasts beneath the black chiffon. "I don't know how celebrated the tryst was, but I assure you it was both scorching and wild."

Even in the shadowy box, he could see her smooth cheeks flush.

"You *are* a rogue." But there was humor in her voice, and she did not move away.

"You like rogues, don't you?" His own voice grew husky at her nearness, at the sensuous invitation he thought he glimpsed in her eyes.

"I like all archaeologists." She smiled. "Even roguish ones."

Was it possible that she was as attracted to him as he was to her? After all, just two days ago at the museum, she had nestled in his embrace without a hint of protest or disapproval. But Sir Thomas had brought her to tears that day; Charlotte had been upset, vulnerable, and he had comforted her in the most gentlemanly—even brotherly—manner. He didn't want to let his desire for Charlotte get out of control, at least not until he was more certain of her response.

He forced himself to sit back. "So, does your affection for archaeologists extend to our Mr. Hughes?"

She gave a mock shiver. "I stand corrected. There are some men who not even archaeology can make likable."

Indeed, in the two days since the assistant curator returned from Egypt, he had been not only openly scornful of both Dylan and Charlotte, but downright insulting.

Out of the corner of his eye, Dylan could see that Lady Margaret and Catherine had entered the old gentleman's loge box. "Your mother looks very angry. And determined."

Charlotte merely shrugged.

"Aren't you worried that they're sure to create a scene? I'm amazed this doesn't bother you."

"And I'm amazed that a man who flouted society's rules for most of his life should be taken aback by a mere political protest. You should be accustomed to public scrutiny."

He looked back to where the two women stood. Lord Hamilton was decidedly awake now, and staring at the two women planted in front of him as if they were footpads about to make off with his wallet and gold watch chain. "Well, I fear public scrutiny is about to be focused on your mother and sister."

Dylan leaned forward and put his arms on the loge box railing. Even though the theater was bustling with people—all chattering loudly—he clearly discerned Lady Margaret's voice. He prayed she didn't have a pot of paint hidden somewhere on her person.

But knowing the Grainger women as he did, he feared anything was possible.

Charlotte tried not to laugh, but the sight of the notorious Dylan Pierce nervously watching her mother and Catherine was too amusing. Why, despite his drinking, she now doubted if even half the tales told about him were true. And in five weeks she hadn't seen him touch a drop of alcohol, not even an after-dinner port.

He was quite a learned gentleman as well. She had never met anyone with such a gift for languages. He translated hieroglyphics, hieratic, and Arabic script so quickly, it left her breathless. And he spoke six other languages, including Kiswahili, like a native.

To be sure, she felt ashamed of herself for creating such a scene two years ago when she learned Pierce was going to take over the Valley of Amun excavations. Having observed how he worked at the Collection, she realized he *was* a better Egyptologist than her late husband. Dylan was more thorough, yet he also possessed uncanny instincts about the provenance of an artifact. She felt a twinge of guilt for comparing him favorably to Ian. Yet it would be dishonest to say that Dylan was not the better scholar.

And was he the better man? Heaven help her, but she believed so. She sighed and gazed down at her program.

The Pirates of Penzance was subtitled "The Slave of Duty." The words were a sharp reminder of how she'd viewed herself these past two and a half years: the dutiful, remorseful widow, denying herself pleasure, life, Egypt. Denying herself the company of a virile and appealing man. Until Dylan Pierce came calling one rainy morning and brought the glory and promise of Egypt with him.

She once thought it was her duty to remain closeted forever with her sad memories, apart from other men, and exiled from the land she loved. But her dutiful role wouldn't bring Ian back to life, nor give her a moment's happiness. And she did want to be happy again, if only she dared.

Dylan's broad shoulders seemed tense beneath his gray cutaway frock coat. She fought back the urge to stroke his shoulders, wanting to feel his strength beneath her fingers. She'd been wanting so many things these past five weeks, all involving the kind Welshman. For that was the most appealing thing about Dylan—his kindness to her and to her unconventional family.

It had been a sweet gesture to include her family in his theater invitation, but she wished the invitation had been for her alone. But maybe Dylan didn't regard her romantically. Sometimes she thought he did; but then again, she was cursed with an overactive imagination. Yet it wasn't her imagination two days ago when he took her in his arms. Admittedly, she'd been upset and needed consolation, but Dylan had held her so close, stroked her arms even. And, as soft as it was, Charlotte had felt his lips brush the top of her head. Innocent or not, that tender kiss had taken her breath away.

Feminine laughter trilled from the loge box beside theirs, where two young women posed provocatively along the box's railing. Fans fluttering, faces turned expectantly toward Dylan, they were obviously vying for his attention.

She didn't blame them, nor those two featherheads at the lecture hall all those weeks ago. Dylan Pierce *was* an attractive male. His less-than-perfect profile—with a nose probably broken in a drunken brawl—seemed irresistibly rugged and male. As did his wide mouth and unruly mane of auburn hair. And how many times in this past month had she delighted to see those dark blue eyes looking at her? It was small wonder half of London's female population seemed to trail in his wake.

And to think the man could discuss mummies and Theban burial rituals as well. It was a surprise she hadn't fallen head over heels in love with him already, but guilt about Ian had prevented any impulsive rush into romance. She had to admit, however, that Dylan did move her. Enough so that she found herself exchanging flirtatious banter with him, making innuendos that no respectable widow should. Then again, who was she to pretend at being respectable?

And looking at those two avid ladies did make her uneasy.

Maybe guilt could keep her from falling in love, but it couldn't stop her from being jealous.

"They're getting louder." Dylan sat back with a frown. "And Lord Hamilton shook his cane a couple of times. Maybe I should go over there before fisticuffs break out."

"Mother would create an even bigger scene if you tried to restrain her."

"There must be a better way to get their point across."

"But it's a noble cause. Why shouldn't women have the right to vote? If the government wishes to behave in such an unreasonable fashion, politicians must be prepared for a public outcry and a few embarrassing scenes. Even at a performance of Gilbert and Sullivan."

He looked surprised. "I'd no idea you were such a political animal, Charlotte."

"I'm not. As Mother said, I've only one obsession: Egypt." She nodded. "But I hope they're successful. I fear, however, that a lot of paint pots will have to be thrown first."

"Lord Hamilton has turned beet red," he muttered. "I hope he doesn't up and die while they're in there."

"Are any of the women in your family politically minded?"

"My youngest sister is a Welsh nationalist." After a moment, he turned toward her again. "You remind me of her. Morgana has always cared more for books and history than needlepoint and parties. And she's brave as a highlander, too."

"I'd like to meet her. In fact, I'd be interested in meeting all of your family."

"Bite your tongue. There are thirteen of us, and only Morgana is even remotely civilized. The Pierces are a reckless and disagreeable tribe."

She found her gaze drawn to his distinctive profile. For a scandalous moment, she wondered what it would feel like to kiss that broken nose, or stroke that unruly auburn mane of his.

"The one Pierce I have had the pleasure of knowing may be reckless," she said softly, "but certainly not disagreeable."

Dylan chuckled. "You haven't seen me in a stormy mood, lass."

"I might find your stormy moods exciting. After all, I love thunderstorms, the wilder the better."

"Yes, that's right. You aren't afraid of storms." His smile slowly faded. "But I've my own brand of lightning, lass. And you might get burned."

"I see." She returned his intense gaze, which seemed to hold as much electricity as a real bolt of lightning. "Is it as hot as that lightning that nearly struck us in Belgrave Square?"

"Hotter, Charlotte," he said in a low voice that made her tremble. "Hotter, and just as dangerous."

"But I'm the woman who finds London too tame." She was finding it difficult to keep her voice steady. "The woman who longs not only for storms, but for the burning desert."

"So is it the heat you crave?" He leaned closer. His face was now inches away, and she knew he was about to kiss her. "Or the danger?"

"Both," she whispered.

The door to their loge box suddenly swung open. Startled, they jumped to their feet.

"Mr. Pierce, how exquisite that we find ourselves at the same performance." A tall woman wearing a brightly colored apricot gown swept in, followed by a stout older gentleman.

"Lady Beatrice." Dylan bowed over her gloved hand.

Charlotte immediately stiffened.

The woman's bearing was regal, befitting the Ottoman silk dress she wore. Although its corselet left her arms bare, every inch of the gown was covered in delicate lace. And even though Lady Beatrice looked to be at least forty years old, standing next to the alluring woman Charlotte felt like the dowdy matron in her severe black costume. Pinned charmingly into the lady's upswept chestnut curls were two white ostrich plumes. A pity, Charlotte thought, that she had not brought Nefer with her tonight. The cat would have made short work of those feathers.

But even that silly image did not lift her spirits.

Dylan gestured toward her. "Lady Beatrice, Jeremy Brooke, may I present Mrs. Fairchild."

"Sir Reginald's daughter. Yes, I remember. Fine chap, your father. Beastly how he died in Egypt." Mr. Brooke gave her a curt bow.

"Thank you," she murmured.

"Didn't your husband also die in North Africa? Or perhaps I'm thinking of the wrong Fairchild." Lady Beatrice stared at her curiously, as if she were a strange bird that she had discovered nesting in a corner of the theater.

She nodded. "Two years ago."

"Ah, I also know the pain of losing a husband." The lady assumed a sad expression, then quickly turned to Dylan with a gay smile. "Where have you been hiding yourself? I hear you've been back from Egypt nearly three months."

"We've been preparing an exhibit for the Colville Collection." Dylan reached out and drew Charlotte closer.

Lady Beatrice's smile turned hard.

"Sir Robert Utteridge, Lady Beatrice's late husband, was my publisher for *The Songs of Rajya*," he explained to Charlotte.

"Yes, and you can't imagine the stir those poems caused

in England." She hit him playfully with her gauze fan. "Church groups demonstrating outside our door, the occasional tomato thrown at the booksellers. And all the while, this rascal was safe in Egypt."

"Ah, but one is never safe in Egypt. Especially from exotic and beautiful women." Dylan winked at Lady Beatrice.

Charlotte frowned as she watched how the light bounced off Lady Beatrice's diamond necklace and earrings, so that she glittered with her slightest movement.

"Here, here." Jeremy Brooke slapped his side, chuckling. "Deuced if I wouldn't like to tarry an hour or two with one of those harem girls."

"Why don't we discuss your Egyptian adventures at my house after the performance? I've a small dinner planned, and it will be no trouble to set another place." She smiled. "Nothing elaborate, only a bit of soup and marrow pâtès. Although Cook has promised meringues à la crème and sherbets for dessert."

"Sounds charming, but as you can see, I am otherwise engaged." He nodded toward Charlotte, who tried not to smile at his refusal.

"Oh, but of course Mrs. Fairchild is invited as well." She nodded graciously in her direction, but her brown eyes held no warmth. "Your old schoolmate Samson Pope will be there."

"Sam Pope? Why, I haven't seen him since Cambridge. Is it true he's an inspector for Scotland Yard now?"

"You must come and ask him yourself." Lady Beatrice looked victorious.

"I would like to see Sam again." Dylan turned to Charlotte. "What do you think? Would you care to accompany me to the dinner? If not, I'll drop you and your family off home, then continue on myself."

Charlotte stared back at the chestnut-haired beauty. She wasn't about to let Dylan wander into the lair of that vixen draped in apricot silk and plumes.

"I'd be delighted to accompany you."

She bowed her head in Lady Beatrice's direction, and the woman bowed back.

"We'd best get back," Jeremy Brooke said. "The houselights are dimming."

Lady Beatrice held out her hand, and Dylan brushed his lips over it. "After the performance, then."

She swept out of the loge box, Mr. Brooke trailing after her like a footman.

"Do you think your mother and sister would like to come?" Dylan asked as they took their seats again.

"Heavens no. They're not at all the sort who would enjoy dining with Lady Beatrice and her friends. And Michael will insist on going to Hawthornes afterwards for beefsteak pudding."

"Where is that boy, by the way? I hope he hasn't gotten into mischief down in the lobby."

"Would you look at that?" Charlotte shook her head in amazement. "So they did have a paint pot with them after all."

An angry Lord Hamilton stood in his loge box, waving a cane at the two departing ladies. His black frock coat was spattered with red paint.

The curtain rung up at that moment, and the orchestra began to play. Luckily it drowned out most of Lord Hamilton's curses.

She sighed and opened up her program once more. "If they keep this up, there won't be a theater in London that will have them."

"By thunder, I think your family could make the Borgias quail in fear."

Charlotte smiled. "And you haven't even met Uncle Louis."

Chapter Eight

They were as disagreeable as hungry hyenas. These hyenas, however, were dressed in glacè silks, court shoes of white kid, and extravagantly expensive lace. To make matters worse, Lady Beatrice's light after-theater fare consisted of more courses than a state dinner.

A snob's pomp and circumstance, Charlotte thought to herself, as she stared at the heavy candelabrum that had been placed right in front of her. The gleaming silver was festooned with vines and white flowers, while its multitude of candles gave off more heat than a hunting lodge fire. Indeed, every time she reached for her water goblet, a drop of hot wax managed to fall upon her outstretched hand.

Lady Beatrice's late husband had obviously risen far in the world, and she was now loath to have anyone forget it. She even decked out her servants in livery, as if this were Balmoral Castle and not the Mayfair home of a publisher's widow.

"Don't you care for green goose, Mrs. Fairchild?" Lady

Beatrice had not let a gesture or word of Charlotte's go unremarked. "You've barely touched your plate."

"I'm quite fond of it, but the soup and turtle more than satisfied my appetite." Not to mention the marrow pâtés and plovers' eggs in aspic jelly. She couldn't imagine what the next half-dozen courses would bring.

"A far sight better than whatever swill you were forced to eat in Egypt, I daresay." This comment came from the elderly viscount who sat beside Charlotte. He had taken an immediate dislike to her, and seemed affronted that he had not been placed next to a more appropriate female guest.

"On the contrary, the food of North Africa is delicate and flavorful," Charlotte said with a polite smile. "Cucumbers stuffed with meat, yellow pilaf, kebobs with plum sauce."

Even though he was partially obscured by the candelabrum, she noticed Dylan watching her. "Lamb, pistachio nuts, date pastry, ruby pomegranates," she went on.

"Not a bite of it fit for civilized palates," the viscount shot back.

"And how often have you tasted Egyptian cuisine, Lord Walburn?" Dylan asked.

"One doesn't need to sample heathen food to know it's disgusting. You don't have to eat mud to know it turns the stomach." The old man took a bite of goose and chewed it defiantly. "And I don't have to swallow a grasshopper to know it tastes dreadful."

Charlotte couldn't resist. "Actually I ate grasshoppers when I visited Abbyssinia. They were rather tasty, if a trifle crisp."

A wave of gasps went around the table. She peeked over at Dylan, who smiled at her so warmly, she felt as if sunlight had just dappled her face.

"Never cared for grasshoppers myself," he said. "But I did develop a fondness for snake meat."

"Too bland for me, but did you ever eat crocodile?"

"Many times. If the croc's young enough, it's better than

fresh game hen." Dylan's eyes sparkled with pleasure. "Now, have you ever eaten monkey? I was in the Congo one year and had—"

"I told you." Lord Walburn thumped the linen tablecloth, nearly upsetting his glass of claret. "Heathen swill."

"I don't think this is a proper topic for dinner conversation." Although Dylan sat at her elbow, Lady Beatrice directed her comments to Charlotte. "Mrs. Fairchild, I realize that you spent your youth in Egypt and are accustomed to all manner of wild things. But describing such crude behavior upsets polite society."

Charlotte choked on the water she was sipping.

"Yes, stop it, you scandalous woman." Dylan sat back laughing.

With a sigh, Charlotte put her goblet down on the table, once again getting seared by the dripping wax. She suspected Lady Beatrice had deliberately arranged for her place setting to be in dangerous proximity to the candelabrum. She was probably hoping it would topple during the meal and set her on fire like Joan of Arc.

She knew now why she so rarely went out in Lady Beatrice's "polite society." The after-dinner supper had been marked by anything but politeness. These people could learn a thing or two about hospitality from the Bedouin tribes of the desert.

"Now that I've met you, Mrs. Fairchild, I begin to understand where your mother and sister find the nerve to make such spectacles of themselves." The hawk-nosed woman who sat on the other side of the candelabrum leaned to the right, trying to catch Charlotte's attention.

"Since my mother and sister are not here to defend themselves, Mrs. Beardsley, I would prefer not to discuss them."

"I cannot imagine how they have avoided arrest," she continued, as if Charlotte had not spoken at all. "Throwing paint at gentlemen, shouting political slogans—"

"I'm sure we can find another topic of conversation."

But except for the brief foray into "heathen cuisine," the company had spoken of little else since dinner began. Apparently every guest here had witnessed the paint throwing at the theater.

"You must admit that it is rare to see such brashness displayed in public, particularly from the daughter of an earl." Lady Beatrice smiled at Charlotte. It was like watching a cobra bare her fangs. "Was your mother always so impetuous?"

"I never thought her impetuous. Only exceedingly brave and determined."

Lord Walburn snorted. "Determined to act like a fool."

Charlotte muttered to herself as she dabbed the hot wax from her hand with a damask napkin.

From down the table, she heard Dylan's deep voice. "Be careful, sir. I am proud to enjoy the friendship and esteem of Lady Margaret. I will not hear her maligned in my presence."

She caught his eye and smiled. If a long expanse of table and endless platters did not separate them, Charlotte might have pressed her cheek against his in gratitude.

"I'm sure Lord Walburn meant no offense." Lady Beatrice patted Dylan's arm.

"I believe he did." Dylan stared hard at the fellow, who nervously turned his attention back to his food.

The hawk-nosed lady was not so easily subdued, however. "All this nonsense about votes for women. As though any real lady wishes to be dragged into the voting booth."

"No ladies will be dragged into the voting booth, but they shouldn't be dragged away from it either," Charlotte said.

"So, you believe in women's suffrage, Mrs. Fairchild?" This question came from Dylan's old university roommate, Samson Pope. He was the only stranger here who had not treated her with disdain.

"Certainly. Voting should be the right of every adult, regardless of whether they wear trousers or petticoats."

"Never met a woman whom I would trust to run this government," said Jeremy Brooke from the other end of the table.

"Not even the Queen?" Samson asked in a tone so intimidating that it silenced any reply.

"So you *would* trust a woman to run the government?" Charlotte asked.

Samson reached for his water goblet. "I trust no one, least of all politicians."

"So speaks a policeman," Dylan said.

"Detective Inspector to you." Samson raised his eyebrows and the corner of his mouth turned upward as he insolently corrected his friend. "And don't you wish you had a title that sounded half as impressive."

Dylan raised his wineglass in mock salute. "To my humble school chum and his newfound success, may we all be as lucky."

The two men grinned companionably across the table at one another.

Charlotte could easily see how the two had been such fast friends at Cambridge. In fact, even with his dark beard and mustache, Samson Pope still looked like a university student. But his eyes were shrewd and knowing, and she suspected he made an excellent inspector for Scotland Yard.

Mrs. Beardsley cleared her throat. "As a policeman, surely you agree that Lady Margaret should have been arrested for her shenanigans tonight."

"Not again," Charlotte said with a groan.

"After all, she disturbed the peace," the meddlesome gossip continued. "Throwing paint at poor Lord Hamilton. She should have been hauled away in irons."

"Cease and desist, woman," Dylan said with a growl.

Samson Pope's expression turned solemn. "If you continue in this vein, Mrs. Beardsley, I fear I might have to arrest *you.*"

The older woman blanched, while Lady Beatrice asked, "Whatever for, Inspector?"

"For killing any hope of us enjoying a decent dinner conversation. It's quite criminal."

Charlotte, Dylan, and Samson burst into laughter.

"You must pay us a visit one day, Inspector. My mother would enjoy speaking with you." Charlotte smiled. "I only warn you that Grandmama might be there as well, and she's the most radical of the Grainger women."

"They're all wild and out of control," Dylan said in mock horror.

"Out of control indeed," muttered Mrs. Beardsley. "Vulgar is more like it."

"Well, vulgar or not, women should be able to participate in the political process. Even if some of them clearly have less intelligence than a spaniel." Charlotte smiled. "No offense, Mrs. Beardsley."

Dylan ducked his head, clearly, trying not to laugh out loud, while Samson took a well-timed bite of pâtè, clearly hiding his reaction behind a forkful of food.

"It seems you are no stranger to vulgarity yourself, Mrs. Fairchild," the offended woman sniffed with great disdain.

"If that were true, I would be throwing paint pots at several of you right this moment."

Lady Beatrice shot her a look that would freeze fire. It was all too apparent that irreverent remarks would be tolerated from both Dylan and Pope; they were young, attractive, successful men. Such men are forgiven much at Mayfair dinner tables. The same tolerance would not be extended to her. In fact, the guests kept throwing her nervous glances, as if expecting her to break into song or start dancing about the room. She actually had a mad impulse to do just that but was stilled by Dylan's expression.

Although he wore a wide grin, she thought she saw something else in his face, something she hadn't glimpsed before.

121

Admiration, perhaps. Whatever it was, she was grateful that he was there.

She didn't think she could ever feel afraid in his presence, or unwelcome. If the entire assembly of Lady Beatrice's friends decided to turn her out on the street—which she was half hoping they'd do—she knew that Dylan would be right beside her. What did it matter if a hundred snobs treated her and her family with contempt? She enjoyed Dylan Pierce's company and friendship. The devil with everyone else.

"You see now why Mrs. Fairchild and I work together so well at the Collection," Dylan said proudly. "She's bolder than me, and twice as daring."

"Oh, I cannot believe that." Lady Beatrice obviously caught the note of approval in Dylan's voice and didn't like it. "Not from the man who brought a blush to every London lady with his scandalous poems."

"Translations only," he reminded her. "I regret to say I am many things, but a poet is not one of them."

She reached over and squeezed his wrist. "I have read *The Songs of Rajya*, my dear man, and recognized your touch alongside all that Arabian fluff."

"Pretty explicit material to be called *fluff*," snorted Lord Walburn.

"Explicit, you say?" Samson swigged back the rest of his claret. "Why, that's the only sort of poetry worth reading."

Lady Beatrice stroked Dylan's wrist once more. Charlotte felt a strong urge to yank all those ostrich plumes out of the cloying woman's hair—and maybe some of her chestnut locks as well.

"Yes, indeed. Very explicit." Her vixenish smile deepened. Charlotte was certain that Lady Beatrice knew her smile displayed the most attractive dimples. "Which is why I am sure that the Arabians alone could not have produced such intense sentiments."

To Charlotte's relief, Dylan at last pulled his arm away. Lady Beatrice seemed nonplussed by his withdrawal.

"What do you think, Mrs. Fairchild? Has our Mr. Pierce not infused the poems with his own sensuality and experience? You *do* know him well enough to judge, don't you?"

Charlotte heard someone titter on the other side of the candelabrum. She longed more than ever to be back in Egypt, with only sand vipers and scorpions to trouble her. But if she were in Egypt, she wouldn't be sitting here tonight with Dylan Pierce.

"I haven't had the time to read *The Songs of Rajya.* I've been too busy working at the Collection. But if it's as scandalous as you say, I may ask him to recite a few poems to me." She looked over at Dylan, who gave her a devilish grin. "Perhaps even demonstrate several of the more erotic verses, assuming he's still athletic enough."

Lord Walburn leaned away from her. "You are an impossible woman."

"Thoroughly impossible," Dylan agreed. "Maybe Samson should arrest her instead of her mother."

Samson shook his head. "I left my leg irons at home."

"How droll the three of you are," Lady Beatrice said with an exaggerated sigh. "I do believe you're more entertaining tonight than the Gilbert and Sullivan."

"And we're less expensive, too." Dylan leaned toward Samson. "You won't believe how much this scalper charged me for the tickets."

Samson shrugged. "Tell me where he is, and I'll arrest him, too."

While the two men laughed, Lady Beatrice turned her attention back to Charlotte. "I can't believe you haven't read *The Songs of Rajya* yet. But then I forget, you fancy yourself an Egyptologist. No doubt nothing but decaying mummies and dusty pyramids really excites you."

"No doubt." Charlotte was suddenly tired of this venomous game and these brittle people. She wished now the evening had ended with Dylan joining her and her family at Hawthornes for beefsteak pudding.

But she couldn't have let him come here alone, not with the hungry Lady Beatrice lying in wait.

Charlotte noticed how imperiously Lady Beatrice sat at the head of the table, like a czarina or duchess. The publisher's widow looked as vibrant as she herself looked dull. Her costly apricot silk rustled with every graceful movement and diamonds shimmered about her ears, neck, and wrist. Even the ostrich plumes waving above her coiffure added to the older woman's allure. For the first time in two and a half years, Charlotte thought that it was time to put away her mourning dress.

"Did you really spend most of your youth excavating with your father in Egypt, Mrs. Fairchild?" Samson asked.

"Yes. Father worked in Egypt every winter. When I was thirteen, he brought Mother and me along for the season. Mother was upset by the Moslem view of women, so she refused to return. I, on the other hand, refused to stay in England."

"If I were your mother, I would never have allowed you to dig in the dirt all those years. And surrounded by those filthy natives, too." Mrs. Beardsley shuddered. "What a wasted youth."

Charlotte stared at the woman. "I assure you, there is no finer way to spend your youth. I was surrounded by Egypt and her glory. Britain will have to endure for several more millennia before we boast of a past as rich and wondrous."

"Well said." Dylan had grown as solemn as she. "It is no small thing to go out into the desert and retrieve the past, to rescue it from oblivion."

She nodded. "We help the dead come to life again."

"Aye, lass, I sometimes wonder if it's archaeology we practice, or resurrection."

They looked at each other. Dylan leaned to the side, the better to see past the flowers and burning candles. He raised his water glass to her in private salute.

Perhaps it was merely the flames from the candelabrum,

124

but she felt her cheeks grow hot. The thrill she received from his obvious regard and approval shot through her veins like fire. Dylan had the same effect on her as the desert. He need only smile at her in a certain way or nod his agreement, and she felt as giddy as when she watched the Nile thundering over the cataracts.

Lady Beatrice cleared her throat. "It seems that Egyptologists are the real romantics, not the poets."

"Are we romantics, Charlotte?" he asked her, as if ten other people weren't sitting at the table with them.

But Lady Beatrice was not going to let the conversation drift Charlotte's way again. "Enough about the past, Dylan. How much longer are we to enjoy the pleasure of your company? Or have you decided to remain in England now?"

"I leave for Egypt in November."

"You're going back this year?" Charlotte heard the dismay in her voice.

He turned back to her. "Yes. I'll be supervising the excavations at Nabesha again."

Someone else asked him a question, but Charlotte didn't hear the answer. Of course he was leaving England. He was an Egyptologist. Egyptologists spent half of the year in Egypt. Hadn't she done just that for twelve years? Isn't that what she expected her life would be when she married Ian Fairchild?

So why had her hands grown clammy, and the heavy food threatened to rise in her throat? Because Dylan was leaving. He was leaving her, leaving her for the sandstone cliffs, the Nile, the desert winds. He was leaving her behind on a gray, damp island, leaving her with the cold climate and even colder people. She wanted to howl at the injustice of it all.

She could sit at the table no longer. Without thinking, she pushed her chair back and got to her feet.

Everyone stopped eating and stared at her.

"Charlotte?" Dylan asked. "Is anything wrong?"

For a moment, she could think of nothing to say, but then

she caught sight of Lady Beatrice's malicious expression.

"Why no, nothing's wrong. On the contrary, I've enjoyed this meal so much, I'm off to the kitchen to compliment the cook." She tossed her napkin on the table. "I especially loved those marrow pâtés."

She forced herself to smile at the assembled company. "They tasted just like crocodile."

He shouldn't have brought Charlotte to the supper, even if he did want to see his old friend Sam Pope. It was maddening to have to sit through that endless meal, listening to a collection of aging snobs try to embarrass Charlotte. Although it would take a lot more brains and wit than any of Lady Beatrice's set could muster to give that extraordinary lady pause.

Dylan sat back in their closed brougham, relieved to hear the coachman shut the door. Relieved to at last be alone with her.

She sat across from him, her head down. Maybe the evening's activities had finally tired her. He didn't blame her. Having to fend off Lady Beatrice's relentless efforts to seduce him had driven him to exhaustion—and boredom.

"You'll be home in twenty minutes," he said softly. "It's been a long night. No wonder you're tired."

Charlotte looked up. The coach's lamplight showed her surprised expression. "I'm not at all tired. In fact, now that we've left the party, I feel quite invigorated." She glanced down again. "But my hand is still smarting from all the wax that dripped on it."

"The infernal candelabrum *was* treacherously close to you." He kept his voice light, even though he resented Lady Beatrice's obvious attempt to block his view of Charlotte at the table tonight. "But I didn't think it was near enough to cause real harm."

She rubbed her gloved hand again. "A couple of drops did sting a bit."

"You should have told me you were hurt." Dylan reached for her hand, but she pulled away.

"It's nothing, really. When I get home, I'll ask Lorrie for some bee balm."

"Let me see, lass." This time he took her hand firmly. "And I promise I'll have your glove off so gentle and soft, you won't feel the silk leave your skin."

"I'd forgotten," she said in an amused voice. "You have a lot of practice removing articles of clothing from women."

He peeked up to see her smile at him. "Ah, more fanciful stories about my wicked ways." He unrolled the black silk from her wrist. "I think they tell fewer tales of the Little People in Ireland than they do of me."

"The Little People haven't been caught atop the Great Pyramid with a naked woman."

"You do have a fondness for that story." He held her hand, liking the elegant shape of it, then slipped his thumb under the material and gently tugged.

"Not a fondness." Her voice had dropped to a near whisper. "It's just that I wonder what it would be like to—to indulge oneself at the top of the world like that."

His thumb slid over her palm, her mound of Venus full as a ripe pomegranate. He pressed his finger against it, and heard Charlotte's sharp intake of breath.

"Why don't you ask me what it was like, then?"

For a moment all was silent, save for the horses' hooves along the street. He cradled her fingers with his other hand, then slowly, by inches, slid the glove off entirely.

"Ask me," he repeated.

"What was it like?" she said, sounding out of breath.

"Exciting, coarse, shameless. Like animals rutting near the edge of a cliff."

"It couldn't have been comfortable. All those rocks."

He smiled to himself. "Don't be so English. Or haven't you ever loved a man beneath the open sky?"

"Never." She sounded wistful.

"A pity we didn't know each other better when we were in Egypt."

She tried to pull her hand away, but he wouldn't let her.

He gently blew on the top of her flesh as if to soothe it. "You and I are alike, lass. More than I ever would have thought. We're not afraid of Africa or mystery."

She was silent.

He pressed his cheek against her hand. "Or danger."

"Dylan, please."

He looked up at her. It was too shadowy to see her face. "You wanted to know what it was like to make love on the Great Pyramid. I'm trying to tell you."

"That's not what you're doing." Even though her voice sounded alarmed, she did not pull her hand away.

"Aye, but I am. I'm trying to describe the wildness, the hot madness of loving someone at the top of the world. I thought you wanted to know."

They stared at each other through the darkness. Occasionally they passed a streetlamp and light spilled in, revealing her wide eyes, her surprised, expectant expression. What did the light reveal of him? he wondered. His desire for Charlotte, perhaps.

He had felt this longing slowly grow over the weeks until now it surged through him like a torrential rain. It was new, this type of hunger. Never before had he lusted after a woman whom he also liked so damnably much. A woman he respected, admired. But then, he had never met anyone— man or woman—quite like Charlotte Fairchild.

He bent over her hand once more, ministering to the exposed flesh with little puffs of air. "I haven't told you of the wind," he said between breaths. "It was windy up there, as it always is near twilight. A hot desert wind."

"The *khamseen,*" she whispered.

"Aye, the *khamseen* wind." If he closed his eyes, he could feel the scorching power of the *khamseen.*

"I love the desert wind." Her voice sounded dreamy now,

relaxed. "Ian said it drove him to distraction, whistling across the sand. But it seemed like birdsong to me. Or music."

He nodded, sliding two of his fingers down her wrist. Her pulse beat feverishly.

"Who was she?" she asked in a ragged voice. "This woman you took to the pyramid?"

"I don't remember." He pressed his cheek to her hand again, and she shivered.

"I don't believe you."

"But you want to believe me." This time, he bent over her hand, and pressed his lips against it.

She cried out. He liked the sound. The sound of a woman's surrender. He had heard it many times, but never had it given him so much pleasure. Or so much trepidation.

"You want to believe I'm reckless and savage, don't you? You want me to have bedded a hundred women, and left them all hungry for more."

"Why should I care about the women you've known?"

"For the same reason I'm jealous of your Mr. Fairchild." She fell back against the cushioned seat. "Jealous?"

"I'm jealous of the man you married. Nothing strange in that. You took him to your bed, loved him right readily, I warrant. Why wouldn't I be jealous? I like you, Charlotte. I like you very much. You must have guessed that by now."

"But you've been a complete gentleman all these weeks."

He couldn't help but laugh, even if he did feel a growing nervousness. Had he miscalculated? Maybe the daring Mrs. Fairchild was not as bold as she seemed. With a sigh, he released her hand.

"I regard most gentlemen as weak and dishonest. I'd be disappointed if you thought me one of them."

"But you are a gentleman. A fine one, too."

He sighed. "It seems my baser instincts must be dull from lack of whiskey. I thought you fancied me as well. Forgive me."

She took a deep breath. "No need to ask for forgiveness."

"What is it you want, Charlotte?"

He suddenly felt as insecure as an untried boy. He liked this uncertainty; it made him feel young once more, unsophisticated, with the world spread before him, filled with possibilities. Charlotte now seemed one of those possibilities.

"I like you, Dylan. There are times when I like you more than any man I have ever known."

What that implied hung in the air between them as palpably as the evening mist.

He reached for her hand once more. Her fingers trembled in his grasp, and he caressed them, enjoying her smooth flesh—and her trembling. Once more, he pressed his lips to her hand, this time trailing his mouth along her fingers. When he reached her ring finger, he stopped. With a sudden swift motion, he pulled her wedding band off.

"My ring! Give it back to me."

He tucked the ring into his suit pocket.

"That's my wedding band! You can't keep it."

"I'll only keep it for a few minutes. I need to know what it is we both feel for each other, lass. And I don't want anything reminding us of your late husband."

"But taking off my ring won't make me forget Ian."

This time he took both her hands gently in his. "I know something of women. A few of those stories you love to hear about are indeed true. But for all that, I don't know you. Not like I should." He kissed her hands. "Not like I want to."

Thankfully she didn't shrink back from his caress. "I'm a widow. It's not proper that I—"

"Hang the manners and pretty speeches. You've not done a proper thing in your life, except for this endless mourning you've put yourself through." He pulled her closer.

Her face was only inches from his own. He could feel her

sweet breath upon his face, smell the fragrant jasmine that perfumed her pale gold hair.

"I've wanted you from the moment you came riding over a sand dune to meet me." He raised her hand and turned it over. When he covered her palm with his mouth, it was to nip lightly, not kiss it. She shivered but did not move away.

"A fiery young woman on a camel, dizzy with brandy, ready to do battle. I wonder now I didn't fling you over my own camel and ride off with you."

"I don't remember any of that meeting," she said breathlessly. "For all I know, you did just that."

His fingers moved to caress her chin, tilting her face toward him until their lips were almost touching. "So you think I had my way with you in the desert?"

"Did you?" she whispered.

"Maybe. Maybe I carried you off and laid you down in the hollow of a sand dune. Maybe I slipped off your boots, pressed my mouth to your bare feet."

She let out a nervous laugh. "You didn't!"

"How do you know?" He leaned over and kissed her cheek. As he did, she let out an achingly sweet sigh. "Maybe you let me pull your riding skirt off, and that damp blouse you wore. Then you let me unfasten your corset."

He kissed her other cheek.

"I never wore corsets in the desert." She stroked his cheek this time. He felt himself shiver. No woman had ever made him tremble.

"You were drunk that day, lass. You could have put ten corsets on and not remembered."

She laughed, then pressed her cheek against his. She felt fragile to him suddenly, like a woman who was more gentle than he knew. More vulnerable. And as desirable as buried treasure in the hot sand.

"Perhaps I took off every stitch of clothing you had on, then stripped mine off as well," he continued. "And we made love on the sand dunes, in the bright sunlight, naked."

"Naked," she echoed in a tone of wonder.

"The dunes are softer than the pyramids, lass. You'd not shrink from loving me on a sand dune, would you?" He brushed her lips with his own.

Damn it all, but he had to taste her. He had to learn what it was she did feel for him, and he for her.

The first kiss startled him with the raw power behind it, the desire they were unable to disguise. And by the saints, she had a sinful mouth, soft, moist, and eager. He barely took a breath before pressing his mouth against hers again. At almost the same instant, he felt her own mouth open beneath his, welcoming him. Inviting him.

He had had no idea that he was this hungry, this close to losing control. These months in Britain must have dulled his instincts so that he wasn't even aware when his desire for a woman was about to overwhelm him. Holding her close, it was all he could do to prevent himself from ripping off her black silk gown and burying himself within her thighs.

He'd been entranced by her from the moment he glimpsed her riding over the sand dunes toward him. And the weeks here in Britain had worked their insidious magic on him, he who usually disdained European ladies and their well-bred sensibilities.

But Charlotte Fairchild was different. No woman—European or otherwise—was like her. She was obsessed with Egypt, and shamelessly blind to everything else. As he was. That she'd stayed within society's strictures these past two and a half years was nothing short of a miracle—or a testament to her stubbornness.

But he knew the lioness within was only waiting for the chance to leap out.

He lifted her toward him, crushing her in his arms. She made no protest. Indeed, she flung her arms about his neck and drew him ever nearer. He liked the feel of her against him. The swell of her breasts, the pounding of her heart, the soft pressure of her arms about him.

His tongue darted into her mouth, and he moaned to feel her own tongue meeting his. She tasted of the cherry sherbet they'd had for dessert. How had he resisted taking her before this? The Dylan of just five years ago would have had his way with her long ago. Ravishing her on the floor of the Assyrian gallery or undressing her in the middle of the museum courtyard, so that the afternoon sunlight would show him every delectable inch of her willing flesh.

"Dylan," she moaned.

He grew harder, hotter. More insistent. Beneath the widow's weeds was a woman on fire for a man's touch. His touch. And he had been much too long without a woman. Too many months hard at work in the desert, and then busy with the Collection here. But no longer.

He bent his face to her neck, unfastening the tiny buttons that ran down the back of her gown. Amazed by his own self-control, Dylan carefully pulled open the sheer black material, coaxing it down over her shoulders. Once her smooth skin was bared, he kissed the damp, soft expanse repeatedly. She tasted of salt and perfume. It was all he could do to prevent himself from biting her, hungry now for both the taste and the feel of her.

"You shouldn't undress me," she whispered.

Yet, after a moment, she reached up and helped him lower her dress even more.

Her breathing was coming short and fast, and he grew harder with each urgent sound she made. Beneath the open gown, he glimpsed the swell of flesh above her corset. He let himself enjoy the luscious sight before caressing first one breast, then the other. She shivered, and he nearly climaxed.

Touching Charlotte was like scaling the Pyramid of Cheops or seeing the mighty statues at Abu Simbel for the first time. Momentous, extraordinary, thrilling. He bent over and kissed that luscious swell. Her flesh felt like warm satin.

"You're splendor itself," he murmured, his mouth pressed against her. "Such splendor."

He felt her hands plunge into his hair, tightening as if she were straining for control too.

At that moment the coach abruptly jerked to a halt, sending them rocking to one side.

In the suddenly motionless brougham, all he could hear was the sound of their labored breathing.

"We're home." With a pang of disappointment, he watched as Charlotte hurriedly pulled up her sleeves, then began working the buttons behind her neck. In a haze of interrupted desire, he was aware that his own clothing was wildly askew and tried to smooth things down—no small matter when he was as aroused as he was.

They had no more than a moment to recover before the door to the carriage was flung open.

"I was hoping it was you, Charlotte." Catherine stood by the open door. "Something dreadful has happened!"

Charlotte pushed her way past Catherine. "Is it Mother? Has something happened to Michael?" She was halfway up the steps to their Belgrave Square mansion when Catherine pulled her back.

"Mother and Michael are fine," her sister reassured her.

Dylan jumped down from the carriage. "Then what the devil is this all about?"

"It's Nefer. She's gone." Catherine grabbed Charlotte's hand. "I do believe someone has quite stolen her away."

Chapter Nine

"You've come to Scotland Yard because someone stole a *cat?*" Detective Inspector Samson Pope looked as if he didn't know whether to laugh or throw Dylan out of his office.

"I know it seems a damned funny request, but the feline means an awful lot to her mistress." Dylan squirmed under his friend's disbelieving gaze.

"So who does the cat belong to?"

"Charlotte Fairchild."

To Dylan's further embarrassment, the police inspector shot him a mocking smile. "So the pretty young widow lost her tabby, and she's sent you to Scotland Yard to track it down."

"Don't be ridiculous. Charlotte has no idea I'm here."

"Oh, I don't blame you for wanting to please her. Mrs. Fairchild seems a charming woman, and she has the most marvelous white-gold hair."

Dylan didn't like the turn this conversation was taking.

"Excuse me, but we were discussing Charlotte's cat, not Charlotte."

"Go ahead then."

Dylan sat forward in his chair. "She brought the cat back with her from the Valley of Amun. I believe Nefer reminds her of Egypt, and she's rarely out of her sight. It was only with great effort that I convinced her not to take the cat along to *The Pirates of Penzance*." He frowned. "I feel awful about the whole thing, and I was already feeling guilty."

"Why guilty? If I remember correctly, she said that she'd been a widow two years or more. I mean, if you're worried about disrupting her official mourning."

"No, I feel guilty about other things."

Samson raised his eyebrows.

"Not that, Sam. Let's just say that I bear some responsibility for her widowed state."

"Maybe I should be investigating you." He pointed to the stacks of files lining the shelves of his office. "I've solved a half-dozen cases in which the wife and her lover did away with the husband. If you're ready to confess, you'll save me a lot of paperwork."

"Very funny." Dylan sipped his tea, then grimaced. It was some strange green brew with a bitter, metallic taste.

"How do you know the cat didn't simply get out on her own?"

"Nefer never leaves the house except on a leash. And she's devoted to Charlotte; she wouldn't wander off willingly. Anyway, there's clear proof of an intruder. The window near the pantry had been forced open."

"Then we can assume someone broke into the house before you both returned at midnight." Samson drained his own cup of tea. "But why didn't the servants hear anything?"

"The house in Belgravia was empty last night, except for the cat. Since Lady Margaret and her family planned to spend the evening at the theater, she gave her servants the night off." Dylan shrugged. "Anyone could have broken into the house while we were gone."

Samson got up to pour himself another cup of tea. "Well, I'll see what I can do." He pointed to a pile of papers on his desk. "But I'm in the midst of investigating the Waterloo Road murders, so I can't vouch for how much time I can devote to this dastardly crime."

Dylan felt even more foolish but pressed on. "I'll appreciate whatever time you or your men can devote to it."

"I think I'll handle this one myself. I wouldn't dare ask one of the veteran Yarders to work on it. If I sent them to chase after some calico cat, it would spell the end of my meteoric rise to the top." Samson chuckled.

"She's not calico. Nefer is a very large, tawny cat with amber eyes. And she was wearing a ruby collar about her neck."

"Real rubies?" Samson asked quickly.

Dylan nodded.

"Then perhaps we have a jewel theft here, and not a mere catnapping."

"If it will persuade you to make a greater effort to find the cat, then treat it as such." Dylan sat back with a sigh. "Just do what you can. Charlotte's quite upset. If anything happens to Nefer, she'll be inconsolable."

"I always thought you had a lot of experience consoling women."

"You don't understand." Dylan stood up and put his cup on the desk. "I've got a funny feeling about all this."

"Probably just the tea I served you," Samson joked, although his shrewd eyes appraised his agitated friend. "It takes a stint in India to fully appreciate it. Can't get enough of the stuff myself."

"It's not your awful tea. I believe I know who stole the cat."

"Then you've solved your case. You don't need me."

"I wish that were true." He shook his head. "Everything has turned into such a bloody mess."

"Look here, Dylan, it's just a missing cat. I know the lady loves it dearly, but this month alone we've dragged ninety-three bodies from the Thames, most of them with their throats slit." He walked over to the open window that looked out upon the fast-moving river. "Next to that, a lost kitty loses some of its importance."

Dylan moved to stand next to him. It was a cloudy day, but warm. A gentle breeze swept through the small office, bringing the smell of fish and offal, and the sounds of river traffic and gulls.

"If it were just the cat, Sam, I'd handle it on my own. There's a Turk in London right now, a fellow by the name of Ahmed Vartan. I've a pretty good idea that he's the cat-napper. But there's something else." Dylan reached into his pocket. "I took this off Charlotte's finger last night and forgot to give it back."

He opened his hand. A gold ring lay nestled against his palm.

"Dare I ask why you took it off?"

"That's not important. Go ahead. Examine it."

Samson took it from him, holding it up to the window, running his finger over the engraving that circled the band.

"Looks antique."

"I guess a ring that's over four thousand years old might be considered antique."

"Egyptian?"

Dylan nodded. "Taken from the site of Sekkara four years ago. I was directing excavations there at the time."

"So this was stolen."

"And I'm afraid I know who stole it," Dylan said grimly.

"You said the ring belonged to Mrs. Fairchild?"

"It's her wedding ring."

"I see." Samson frowned. "Well, perhaps the husband stole it."

"I doubt Ian Fairchild snuck into our camp one night and made off with it himself, but I think he was responsible for its theft. That and a lot more."

Samson studied the piece of jewelry again. "I'm no expert on Egyptian artifacts, but I daresay there are a fair number of gold rings lying out there in the desert, along with all those mummies. Could be this just resembles a ring from your site."

"The inscription says 'Beloved Wife, Beloved Dove, Beloved Nahepsut.' This came from the tomb of Queen Nahepsut. I know because I unsealed the tomb. I found this ring." He took it back from Samson. "Nahepsut was the wife of Pharaoh Akerbad III, who died only seven months after she did. She was his first and last wife. There are no other rings like this lying in the desert. This was looted."

Samson sat back against the window ledge. The river wind ruffled his hair against his collar. "I'd heard that while you were in Egypt, you were quite involved in this looting business yourself."

Dylan stiffened. "Where did you hear that?"

"You forget, my friend, that I've been a professional policeman since I left Cambridge. And serving seven years with the police force in India brought all sorts of gossip my way."

Dylan pocketed the gold band. "Here I am, trying to be as secretive as possible all these years, and the whole blasted Service probably knew what I was up to in Egypt."

"No, only those of us who are as smart and clever as you. Of course, some of us are even smarter."

"Some time we need to have a long dinner together and swap stories."

"I look forward to it." Samson seemed puzzled. "But I don't know what you think this ring means. Ian Fairchild is dead, so even if he did mastermind the theft, what can you do now?"

"He didn't work alone. To loot a site such as Sekkara

required far more than one man." Dylan walked over to the desk and picked up his hat. "What I need from you is information."

"Information about looters and treasure hunters in Egypt? That's a job you're better suited for."

"It's information about the looters and treasure hunters in London that I require." He smoothed back his hair and slipped on his hat. "I had hoped to be done with all this. I am trying to be a respectable scholar now, you know."

"I'd heard," Samson said quietly. "Seems like you're doing a good job of it too."

"Not good enough. When you've lived a certain way for a long time, it's bloody difficult to change course." Dylan touched the piece of paper in his pocket and hesitated. "I feel terrible."

"You do look awful this morning. Malaria again?"

"No. I didn't get any sleep last night." He took a deep breath. After all he had been through in Egypt, he wouldn't allow himself to falter now. "You think I've gone mad, don't you?"

"Just a little. But I attribute that to all those years you spent in the desert sun."

"And too many years spent with scoundrels and thieves. I fear some of those criminals have followed me here."

"You think they're involved in a black market operation in London?"

He nodded. "I'm hoping this catnapping is just Ahmed's attempt to scare us away from mounting the Valley of Amun exhibit, but it could be more than that. I don't like the fact that Charlotte is wearing a stolen ring. I don't like it at all. And I don't like the feeling that an old enemy is circling about me once more. . . ." Dylan's voice trailed off as the memory of the Cairo fire swept over him again.

"You probably thought the life of a respectable scholar would be easy," Samson said with a rueful smile.

"Funny the way things turns out. Just when you decide to

change your life, the past looms before you like a deadly jungle cat." He paused. "A lion."

"So who are these people you want me to investigate?"

Dylan pulled a slip of paper from his jacket pocket. "I've drawn up a list of names. Vartan is on it. So is Ian Fairchild, Barnabas Hughes, Sir Thomas Havers." He took a deep breath. "Sir Reginald Grainger."

"Grainger? But wasn't he Mrs. Fairchild's father?"

"Dealing in antiquities requires experts. Few men were more expert than Sir Reginald."

Samson took the paper from him. He suddenly looked as somber as Dylan felt. And Dylan felt as grim and dark as death itself.

At times like this, Dylan wished he were as disreputable and immoral as he had been painted. Then he could look the other way while priceless works of art were stolen and sold to private collectors on the black market, lost forever to posterity. But he wasn't such an irresponsible cad. In fact, he feared he was even a dreaded gentleman.

If only he hadn't let things spin out of control last night in the carriage. And why in blazes had he pulled off her ring? If he hadn't, his conscience would be clear right now. But he was so tired of having to see past that elaborate mourning costume, so frustrated with her steadfast refusal to be anything but Ian Fairchild's widow. He couldn't rip away that infuriating black gown—although he'd longed to—so he'd done the next best thing and removed her wedding ring.

In all the excitement over the missing cat, he'd completely forgotten that her gold band was still in his coat pocket until he retired to his rented rooms in Russell Square.

Unfortunately, finding the ring had led him to Scotland Yard.

"If stolen antiquities are being smuggled into London," Dylan said, "Sir Thomas or Vartan would be the perfect conduit. And I have suspicions about Barnabas Hughes; he's an assistant curator at the museum. I need to know who their past associates were, living *or* dead."

Dylan opened the office door. The sound of footsteps and voices from the stairway drifted in.

"I'll see what I can do, Dylan. It may not be murder, but theft on this scale is a serious crime. I'll even spend some time tracking down that cat."

"Thank you. One more thing, though. I want your word that whatever information you find on these individuals, you first come to me before taking any official police action."

Samson gave him a long, shrewd look. "Agreed. But once I inform you as a friend, I shall then do whatever I feel is necessary—as a policeman."

"Fair enough." The two men shook hands.

Dylan was almost out the door when he turned back. "And Sam, I need every name on that list investigated."

"I'll handle it. If there's anything criminal going on, I'll discover it."

"Yes, I believe you will." That was exactly what Dylan hoped for. And feared.

After Dylan left, Samson walked back to the window. He loved the view from his office. His boss, who worked on the second floor, didn't have such a fine view of the boats and the clear, cold water. Maybe when Sam got promoted, he'd move the commissioner's office upstairs. But first he had murders on Waterloo Road to solve. Not to mention a cat-napping and a black market operation to uncover.

Actually, this catnapping might prove interesting. Dylan Pierce, once dubbed the "Don Juan of Trinity College" by his Cambridge mates, apparently had been ensnared by a pretty blond widow with a fondness for cats. Samson couldn't help chuckling at his infatuated friend. It was not a position Samson had ever found himself in—nor one he ever expected to experience.

Chimes announced the hour from the floor below. It was

the grandfather clock belonging to the commissioner, a gift from Her Majesty for solving the case involving her murdered footman. Even though Samson had been the detective responsible for tracking down the killer, the recognition—and the clock—had gone to the commissioner. He vowed it would not always be that way. If he solved the Waterloo Road murders, that office in the second-floor turret—whether he chose to move there or not—might be his one day. No, Samson Pope didn't need a woman to moon over. Ambition was far more exciting than love.

His smile faded when he remembered the list of names that Dylan had given him. A bad move, he thought, to include Mrs. Fairchild's father among the suspects. Dylan obviously cared deeply for Mrs. Fairchild. He'd even go so far as to say the man was besotted. Last night, he'd watched as Dylan hung on every word the young widow uttered, how his face lit up whenever she glanced his way.

Now here he was asking Scotland Yard to investigate not only her dead husband but her dead father as well. He felt a wave of pity for both Dylan and Charlotte. Clearly their relationship was not as blissful as he thought.

Samson looked down at the list of suspects and let out a long, surprised whistle.

The last name Dylan had written on the list was Charlotte Fairchild.

He shook his head.

Samson hoped neither of them had fallen in love. For he feared their romance had no future at all.

Charlotte hadn't been this upset since Ian died in the cave-in. In fact, there had been shameful moments since last night when she suspected she was even more heartbroken about Nefer's disappearance. It just confirmed her worst fears about herself. She was a fraud, a liar. A calculating, self-serving hypocrite.

She kicked at a rosebush, then bent down to look underneath the heavy blooms. Perhaps Nefer was still somewhere in Belgravia Square. Maybe she bit and scratched her abductor; she might have escaped but injured herself in the attempt and now lay bleeding and hurt somewhere close by.

But beneath the bush were only pebbles, dirt, a discarded page from the *Daily Mail*. She straightened once more, feeling helpless, infuriated—and bitter. All that she loved best had been taken from her: Father, Egypt, Nefer. And Ian.

Even worse, Ian's death was her fault. No one would convince her otherwise. She was a terrible, selfish person for forcing him to remain in Egypt. Sir Thomas was right: She'd killed her husband as surely as if she'd arranged for the tomb to cave in. Adding to her disgust was the damning fact that while she grieved for her father, she did not grieve for Ian. Not really.

Oh, she dutifully visited the Fairchild family plot in Lincolnshire, where Ian now lay buried, every three months. She brought flowers, wept, and said a heartfelt prayer or two. But she did not long for his presence; she did not harbor tender memories of their short marriage. Not that their brief months as husband and wife had been unpleasant, but she knew now it had left her heart untouched.

"I didn't love him," she whispered. It was time to say it aloud. She had been saying it to herself for nearly three years.

Charlotte loved Egypt. She loved her father. And she loved Nefer.

With Nefer gone, she had now lost everything that made her life rich and full. Everything that made her happy.

A figure turning into the square caught her eye. It took only a second to recognize Dylan. Even with his head down and a bowler covering that auburn mane of his, she would have known his walk anywhere. He covered the ground like the lion he was named after: sure, confident, and graceful.

Maybe she hadn't lost everything. These past five weeks had brought her more joy than she'd known in years. But it was not only the hours spent working with Egyptian artifacts again. It was Dylan who helped bring this trembling happiness into her life—happiness and desire.

Last night in the carriage her flesh had seemed to grow damp and heated with each word of his. And when he caressed her shoulders, pressed his strong mouth against her palm, she'd felt shocking waves of delight. Then there were his kisses. Heaven help her, but kissing Dylan felt as hot and dangerous as the desert sun beating down upon her.

No wonder so many women had given themselves to him. But they didn't love Egypt as she did, so they would never know the real splendor—and mystery—of loving Dylan.

She caught her breath. Had she really said *love?*

It was desire and affection she felt for this man. And admiration. What did she know of love, she who once thought she loved Ian Fairchild? She had to be careful before she bandied such a word about. She would have to be very sure she *did* love before she would admit it to herself, or to Dylan.

"Charlotte, what are you doing here?" Dylan was out of breath, as if he'd been impatient to see her.

"Searching for Nefer, of course." She pointed at the surrounding gates and gardens. "There's a chance she somehow got away and is hurt and hiding." The very thought made her stomach tense with fear, and she bent down to look under the next bush.

He pulled her up. "You look terrible, lass. Have you slept at all since last night?"

If she could have managed a smile, she would have. Dylan looked as exhausted and drawn as she felt. "How could I sleep when some filthy swine has made off with Nefer? When I find out who stole her, it will take ten draymen to get my hands from his throat!"

He brushed his lips against her forehead and she felt some of the tension leave her body. "I daresay it will."

"No one in the household slept. Mother and Catherine are

combing the parks right now. Michael is off asking the street vendors if they've seen a stray cat. I sent the servants in every direction this morning to look for her. And I asked Randall to track down Ahmed."

"So you think Ahmed took her?"

She nodded. "I hope Ahmed is the one who took her. At least I know he won't harm her. It would bring bad luck, you see." Her gaze swept over the square. "But if he didn't take her, then I don't know who did."

A breeze blew through the grass, rustling the flowers, filling the air with the heavy scent of roses. Charlotte shivered even though it was warm. In the distance she heard the bell of the muffin man. Nefer loved to nibble on warm muffins. If she found her—no, *when* she found her again—Charlotte swore she would feed her cat muffins morning, noon, and night.

Dylan reached over and tucked a stray lock of hair behind her ear. Instinctively she bent her head, leaning for a moment against his hand. She imagined she looked like a cat herself, begging to be stroked and petted.

"I went to see Samson Pope at Scotland Yard this morning."

She straightened immediately. "You asked him about Nefer?"

"I know catnapping is a little unusual for the Yard, but hang it all, it's still a crime."

"He agreed to search for her?"

"Said he'll look into it himself. In fact, I think Sam will probably—"

He didn't get to finish the sentence as Charlotte flung herself at him. She hugged him close. "Thank you, Dylan. If Scotland Yard investigates, Nefer is as good as found. Thank you so much."

His arms encircled her. Leaning her head against his shoulder, she nestled there. For the first time since Nefer vanished, Charlotte felt unafraid. With Dylan championing her cause, nothing was impossible. Between the two of them—and Scotland Yard—Nefer would be found.

"They'll find her," she whispered, shutting her eyes. "They'll find Nefer."

"Aye. Sam served seven years with the Bengal Police in India, and two years in South Africa before that. He's a good man."

"*You're* a good man," she replied softly.

Raising her head, she looked into his eyes. He looked sad this morning, drained and exhausted. Poor man, to worry as much as she about the lost Nefer.

He seemed embarrassed by her praise. "You're probably wondering what a police inspector was doing with Lady Beatrice's set last night. Sam's father was physician to the Queen; he was knighted a dozen years ago. Ever since then, the Popes have had entree to more rarefied circles." He frowned. "Not that I consider Lady Beatrice and her friends all that rarefied."

She put her hand against his mouth. "You're babbling. I think Nefer being taken like this has upset you nearly as much as it has me."

He stepped back and reached into his pocket. "Here, I forgot to give this back to you last night."

Startled, she glanced down at the ring he held out, then looked at her own hand. Merciful heaven, she had completely forgotten that her wedding band was gone. The fact that he'd pocketed her ring had gotten lost in the heated excitement of their first kiss. But surely she should have noticed that it was gone sometime in the past twelve hours, even if she was upset about Nefer's disappearance.

After a slight hesitation, she took it from him. Beneath the shifting clouds, the gold seemed duller than usual. Even the hieroglyphs engraved around its band seemed less legible. It could almost be jewelry belonging to a stranger.

"Thank you," she murmured, slipping it on.

"I was worried that you might have thought I'd lost it."

"Oh, no." She wondered if she would ever have the courage to take the ring off again. Perhaps not. She wished suddenly that he had never returned it.

"I noticed the inscription," he said.

She nodded. *Beloved wife, Beloved dove*, it read. When Ian gave it to her, she had been moved by the sentiments. Yet, remembering his frequent impatience with her, his indifference, she doubted now that he ever regarded her as his "beloved." Were both of them liars, then?

"I was wondering where Fairchild found it. It clearly dates from the reign of Pharaoh Akerbad III."

Surprised, she looked up at him. "It's a fake. Ian bought it at a village near Luxor. One of the locals claimed it was genuine, but Ian said the man had a pouch filled with rings, all with the same inscription." She shrugged. "Ian bought it for me because he knew I'd prefer even a fake Egyptian ring to an ordinary wedding band."

"I see." Dylan looked a little less agitated now but just as weary.

"Go home." She leaned over and kissed him lightly on the mouth. "I want you to rest."

He gripped her by the shoulders. "Charlotte, about last night. . . . Perhaps I was too bold. I care for you, lass. And I've no wish to hurt you."

"You won't." Despite the short time they'd known each other, she trusted him. And if she'd learned nothing else in her twenty-seven years, it was that her own actions brought her the greatest grief and harm. "I trust you, Dylan."

He groaned and pulled her to him. "I wish you didn't."

She wanted to ask what he meant by that, but a second later he was hurrying across the square, like a man trying to find shelter before an impending storm.

Chapter Ten

"Don't drop the mummy!"

Dylan cringed as his assistants shakily lowered the gilt sarcophagus onto the workroom floor.

"Be careful," he warned again. "Set it down too hard and you'll crack one of the painted corners."

Once the sarcophagus was safely down, the men mopped their foreheads. He could hear them muttering among themselves.

"We've handled mummies before, Pierce," Barnabas Hughes said. "No need to be railing at us like we were little parlormaids about to upset the tea tray."

The other men gave him disapproving looks as well. It was obvious they took their lead from Hughes, a burly antiquities scholar who had worked at the Collection for years. Dylan didn't blame them. It was only natural their first loyalty was to Hughes. Nor was it odd that Hughes so openly resented Pierce's appointment as director of the upcoming exhibit. Still, Dylan couldn't bring himself to feel much sympathy for the assistant curator. He was a belligerent, disagreeable fellow whom Dylan neither liked—nor trusted.

Then again, Dylan didn't completely trust anyone. Not even Charlotte. He wasn't proud of his suspicions, but he wouldn't lie to himself either.

He ran a hand over the surface of the sarcophagus. "It's just that we've very little time left to get the exhibit ready. The tomb of Amun-Ra still isn't properly braced, nor are the posts and lintels."

"So why aren't you in the gallery overseeing that?" Hughes asked. "Instead you come here to yell at my men, getting us so agitated that no one can properly concentrate on their work."

"Well, we've already had more accidents than I care to think of."

Hughes shot him an accusing look. "That's true enough."

Although Dylan busied himself with inspecting the sarcophagus, he was embarrassed. Several of those *accidents* had been his fault. He still couldn't believe he'd actually stepped on a pharaonic scarab beetle and crushed it beneath his heel. Then there was that statue of Hathor that he'd knocked over. Luckily it fell on one of his assistants and didn't break, but it did give the poor lad a concussion.

"I don't mean to imply that you and your men can't handle things, but remember it's my responsibility to see that everything is proceeding on schedule."

Hughes pulled out a handkerchief and blew his nose. "Well, unsealing sarcophagi and readying mummies for public display has been *my* responsibility for over a decade. If you think you can do a better job, then be my guest. Of course, it will set back the exhibit opening at least six months."

Several of the men snickered. And one or two of the assistants stared at him with outright hostility. He didn't blame them. He'd been a bear these past three days, shouting at anyone who crossed his path. Stamping around, angry at the world, a hazard to everything within his reach, man or mummy. But standing here while his workmen made fun of him wouldn't help either his humor or getting the exhibit ready in time.

He gave a last affectionate stroke to the sarcophagus. "Then I'd best take my disruptive presence out of here and let you get down to work."

Outside in the corridor, however, he paused. He really should see how Charlotte's research was progressing in the basement workrooms. Since Nefer was stolen three days earlier, he'd spent as little time as possible alone with Charlotte. Outside the museum, she was so preoccupied with finding her cat, he was certain she didn't miss his presence, but here it was difficult to avoid her. And foolish.

She was the only one in London who had worked with this material before. She and her late husband had excavated these artifacts, as she and her father had recovered everything already upstairs in the unfinished exhibit hall. Before Nefer was taken, he'd spent part of each hour by her side, discussing the artwork, the jewelry, the papyri. Now he looked for any excuse to busy himself elsewhere.

Their encounter in the carriage had changed something between them. Charlotte now seemed accessible, a woman who was willing—and ready—to love again. But he had ruined such a scenario with his visit to Scotland Yard.

Including Charlotte's name on that list of suspects had brought a vile taste to his mouth. He didn't want to believe that she was involved in looting these treasures. Hadn't she accosted him in the desert two years ago, merely because she believed such scandalous tales about him? But perhaps that had been a ruse. She and her husband might have conspired to keep him away from the Valley of Amun. A valley where he now suspected much more than mere excavation had been conducted.

What foul luck. After a lifetime filled with meaningless romantic adventures, Dylan had finally met a woman who gave him pause. He liked Charlotte right well, as his Welsh grandmother would say, right well indeed. In thirty-three years, he had never once considered the possibility of a long-lasting relationship with a woman. Until now.

But what if she *were* involved with a treacherous ring of thieves?

Of course, he had been telling himself for days that Charlotte could not be a thief. She was a dedicated Egyptologist. She could no more rob Egypt of its rightful treasures than she could forget her departed husband. But she'd forgotten about Ian the other night in the carriage. She'd returned his kiss eagerly, hungrily. She'd helped him pull her dress off, willingly exposing her flesh—and her desire. Who knows what further liberties she would have allowed had the brougham not come to a halt?

Dylan swore aloud. He knew better than to let his heart get the better of him. His years in Egypt had taught him that no one could be trusted. Not even someone as seemingly innocent as Charlotte. Improbable as it seemed, Charlotte might be guilty. It was a chilling and painful thought, but one he could not dismiss.

Yet what chilled him even more was that if she was not among his enemies, then she was in danger from them.

He paused once more in the corridor outside the work-rooms. No, he didn't have the courage to face her alone today. Maybe at tea time, surrounded by the rest of the staff, maybe then he could bring himself to look into those stunning gray eyes and make polite chatter. For now, he preferred to play the coward.

He made his way through the spacious galleries of the Colville Collection, nodding at the patrons who were wandering about, guidebooks in hand. More than one lady asked him about the upcoming Valley of Amun exhibit. One dowager wanted to know if it was indeed true that the site was cursed. Although he reassured her it was not, he wondered if it *was* blighted by bad luck.

As he entered the roped-off area of the exhibit, his gaze fell upon a fearsome statue of Horus. Its black basalt profile gleamed in the sunshine pouring through the skylight. The site had certainly been bad luck for Sir Reginald, dead of a fever at fifty. Bad luck, too, for that first foreman killed by a scorpion, and Ian Fairchild crushed to death in the tomb. Now the bad luck seemed to be touching him.

He wandered through the gallery, glancing at a row of canopic jars. No, he could not imagine Charlotte stealing such treasures. He'd watched how lovingly she handled the artifacts, as if each dusty fragment of pottery was as precious as diamonds. But if she was innocent, then it was likely that her dead husband and her beloved father were involved. Dylan stopped in his tracks. She would never forgive him for exposing them. He might not forgive himself.

"Oh, Dylan, I'm so glad you're here. I've been trying to track you down all day, but we keep missing each other."

He spun about to see Charlotte standing by a display case of terra-cotta figures.

"What are you doing in here? I thought you were in one of the basement workrooms."

She held up a sheaf of papers. "I've been going over the manifest that was sent from Cairo. Two boxes have been mislabeled, and there are specimens here that I've never seen. Nothing valuable, but clearly belonging to another site." She laid the papers down with a sigh. "Then again, I could be mistaken. I've hardly slept since Nefer's gone missing."

But Dylan didn't hear a word she said. He was too stunned by the change in her appearance.

"Charlotte!" He pointed to her gown. "You're—you're not wearing black."

The devil take him, but she was dressed in gray. Not even a dark, drab gray, but a soft, luminous gray like sea mist at dawn. He felt his mouth fall open.

A slight blush rose to her cheeks. She looked down at her

dress, lifting the skirt with one hand, as if to model it for him.

"Do you think it too shocking?" she asked shyly.

Dylan would have laughed had he not been so thoroughly delighted. After weeks of seeing Charlotte in her black widow's weeds, he had longed for a glimpse of her in bright colors, bold sashes, plumes even. The summer gown she wore now boasted no such lavish trimmings, but her silvery-gray blouse did sport sheer, billowing sleeves that displayed her arms most charmingly. And while her gray silk skirt was stark in its simplicity, tiny rhinestone buttons winked at him from around her belt. Even more amazing, she wore her hair down today, tied behind her neck with a silver sateen ribbon.

It was like viewing a winter garden beginning to bloom with color and life.

"You look beautiful, Charlotte," he said when he at last found his voice. "Not that you didn't look lovely in black, but I believe gray might be a better color for you." Indeed, the color deepened the unearthly hue of her eyes.

"It was time to put away my mourning dress." She took a deep breath. "Time, perhaps, to put away my mourning as well."

Dylan stood very still. Part of him was pleased that she was done playing the widow, but he felt uneasy at what it might signify.

"I'm glad that you're ready to move forward with your life." He sounded as prissy as a governess. "But I hope your decision had nothing to do with—with the other night."

She looked about the empty gallery before speaking again. "Do you mean the kiss?"

"Of course I mean the kiss, and everything that went before it. Maybe I was wrong to take such liberties." He raked his hand through his hair. Damn, but the lady had him babbling again. If only those silvery-gray eyes didn't stare at him so.

"Are you certain you're the scandalous Dylan Pierce?

There have been times these past three days, I'd swear a pale impostor has taken your place." She took a step closer. "In another moment, you'll have an attack of the vapors."

"Lass, you keep insisting I'm a gentleman. Well, I'm only trying to act like one."

She moved closer, and he couldn't help but glance at those bare, rounded arms beneath the billowing silver sleeves.

"I'm fond of gentlemen, Dylan, as long as they don't turn into timid little schoolmasters."

"Timid!" He reached out and pulled her toward him. At last he could grasp those enticing arms, stroke their softness. "Have a care or I'll show you how coarse and ungentlemanly I can be. Or have you forgotten how I behaved in the carriage the other night?"

She looked up at him, her expression now serious. "You behaved like a man who desired me. I find nothing coarse or ungentlemanly in that."

When she was this close, he found it easy to forget about stolen treasure, missing cats, and Scotland Yard. He was right: Since their kiss three nights ago, their relationship had changed.

"I do desire you, Charlotte. And I like you too much."

"Too much?"

"Too much to treat you as I have other women."

"Then don't."

He squeezed her arms gently, trying to restrain himself from crushing her against him. "If we let things continue as they started, lass, then I'll do more than simply *talk* about what it's like to make love on a sand dune or on top of a pyramid."

"I never cared for men who do nothing but talk," she said in a husky voice. "Nor women either."

"I don't want to hurt you. I respect you. Hang it all, I like you more than I've ever liked any female. So I'm trying to not fling you over my shoulder and ravish you behind the statue of Horus." He gazed down at her. "And you're not making this easy. Or do you really think you can go from being a grieving widow to my mistress without suffering any consequences?"

"I'm no schoolgirl, Dylan. I'll accept the consequences."

He felt the nearness of her very womanly body. He knew she was no innocent schoolgirl, but she was innocent enough to not understand what he was willing to offer.

"I agree you've stayed in those widow's weeds far too long, but you deserve something better than a few months sharing my bed. I've a notorious reputation where women are concerned. When you wish to marry again, a past liaison with me will make that difficult, no matter how discreet we try to be."

"Marry?" She stepped back from him. "I've no wish to marry again. What an impossible thought."

This woman never tired of keeping him off-balance. "You can't think you'll remain alone."

She shrugged. "I don't mind being alone. Besides, I have Mother, and Catherine and Michael. And one day I shall return to Egypt. I know that now. Once I do, I'll have my work to engage me. I don't see why I must marry."

"I know you well enough, lass, to be able to say you're a passionate woman. You'll want a man's company at some point."

"You may be right. But as your own life has shown, I needn't marry to indulge my appetites." She returned his gaze without blinking.

"Blast, but if you aren't the strangest young English-woman I've ever met." Sometimes he wondered how Charlotte had ever been tolerated in respectable British circles at all. He'd met gypsy girls from the Atlas Mountains who had a greater sense of propriety.

"And if you aren't the most conventional rogue and adventurer I've met." Those lovely gray eyes were bright with amusement.

"Well, no matter what you say now, you'll wish to marry

again one day, and you don't need scandal attached to your name."

"Dylan, I've had one husband already," she said quietly. "I have no desire for another."

So that was it. She might have taken off her black bombazine and crepe, but she still mourned the loss of Ian Fairchild.

"Of course, you were probably so happy in your first marriage, you can't imagine anyone taking your late husband's place," he said politely, fighting to conceal his resentment of Fairchild.

"Happy memories have nothing to do with my decision." She paused. "But looking back, I can see that it was wrong of me to marry. Ian thought he was getting a dutiful wife, someone willing to compromise and put aside her own dreams so that he could pursue his. But I couldn't give up my dreams, my passion for Egypt, for the past. And he died because of it."

She ran her fingers along the glass display case. "Do you see these figures of Bastet and Isis? I found them only an hour after Ian proposed marriage. He wanted to leave for Cairo that day, make a proper celebration of it at Shepheard's Hotel. But all I wanted was to get back to the digging, to the glory that I knew was buried beneath the sand."

He moved closer to her, drawn as much by her words as by her defiant spirit.

"I will never marry again," she said, turning back to him.

"Not even if *I* ask you?" The ridiculous words were out of his mouth before he realized it.

Those glorious eyes turned a deep gray. "No, Mr. Pierce. You are even less suited to the married state than I am."

"Ah, but what if I said I was falling in love with you?" He smiled to show he was not serious. Yet he suddenly needed to hear her say it would matter.

"Then I would tell you to be on your guard." She reached over and adjusted his collar. "For I would choose Egypt and the desert over the promise of the happiest marriage in the world. It's not a nice thing to admit, but I'm tired of pretending." She glanced up at him. "I thought you were a man with no taste for pretense as well. It seems I was wrong."

She had literally turned him speechless. He wasn't sure what he felt. Relief that she didn't expect marriage from him, excitement that she was willing to become his mistress, regret that she might hate him one day if he discovered her father and Ian were involved in the black market?

When he didn't answer, she picked up the sheaf of papers once more and walked over to the next display case.

Her glorious hair spilled down her back, like a river of white gold. He wished now he had ridden off with her in the desert two years ago. They should have run away together, found a place filled with sand, Egyptian temples, and heat-searing sun. Instead he had carried her back to the Valley of Amun where death and grief lay waiting.

He had deceived so many others in the past, including himself. Suddenly he had no stomach for deceiving Charlotte. He hadn't heard a thing from Samson since he visited him at Scotland Yard three days earlier. He'd planned to wait to see what information his friend had been able to uncover about Fairchild and the others, but the waiting was putting a strain on his relationship with Charlotte. And now that she had actually shown she was willing to become his mistress . . .

His blood pounded at the thought of finally possessing her.

No, Charlotte could not be guilty. And God help him, if she was guilty, he didn't want to know.

"Charlotte, I have reason to believe that Ian may have trafficked in stolen goods." His voice rang out in the cavernous gallery.

She turned around. "Don't be absurd."

He pointed to her hand. "That ring you're wearing. It's not a fake. It's real."

"Need I remind you again that your specialty is translating papyri?" Really, the man never knew when to be serious. "Leave me to accessing the jewelry."

"I don't want to lie to you. It wouldn't be fair if we became lovers, and all the while I suspected certain people of trafficking on the black market in antiquities." He paused. "People who may be close to you."

"Like who?" She genuinely didn't know whether to laugh or become angry. "Surely not Ian, who died without a shilling to his name. If he had been selling stolen goods, then where in the world is the money he earned so dishonestly?"

"I've seen your ring before, Charlotte. It was stolen."

She shook her head. "If memory serves me correctly, you were the one with a reputation for looting."

He winced. "I see how I would deserve such a charge. But that should only prove that I recognize a stolen artifact when I see one."

Clearly she had unsettled him with her boldness today— and three days ago in the carriage. This normally confident man now appeared hesitant, reluctant. This should teach her not to listen to tall tales or scandalous gossip. If she could rattle the adventurous Dylan Pierce with a few heated kisses and a refusal to marry, then he was not the immoral renegade he had been painted. But she knew that after the weeks spent working together. Indeed, she wondered if she knew him better than he knew himself.

That was why she wasn't angry at his silly statement about Ian stealing the ring. Dylan had already admitted being jealous of her late husband. Why should it be surprising that he would try to find a way to discredit him further? It wasn't particularly noble, but passion rarely was. And Charlotte knew now that the two of them shared not only a passion for Egypt, but for each other.

"I am quite certain this ring is a well-crafted fake."

"You don't believe me, then?"

"I believe you think you are correct," she said carefully. "But I *know* that you are not."

He frowned. "I shouldn't have said anything. Not yet. I—I don't want to hurt you."

"Stop saying that. It makes it sound as if you know some horrible secret about me that even I'm unaware of."

He looked at her with an expression she couldn't read. His eyes were filled with emotions that seemed to shift with each passing second.

"But I'd rather you not accuse Ian again," she continued in a softer voice. "I did not do right by him while he was alive. The least I can do is defend his name now that he's dead."

Dylan stepped nearer. He murmured something to himself.

"What did you say?"

"When I find myself at a loss for words, I start muttering in Welsh." He held out his hand.

She took it without hesitation. "And what were you muttering about?"

"That if either of us *was* suitable for marriage, I'd marry you in a moment."

Charlotte could hardly breathe.

Standing there in his rolled-up shirtsleeves, a magnifying glass peeking out of his pocket, his thick auburn hair looking like a mane, Dylan suddenly seemed not like a fearsome jungle beast, but an overgrown lion cub. Only mummies, desert tombs, and amulets had ever taken her breath away before, but now—at this very moment—Dylan Pierce seemed as moving and impressive as any pyramid or obsidian scarab.

Was she in love with him? She couldn't be. They'd been working together less than six weeks. No one fell in love in so short a time, especially a guilt-stricken widow. But, merciful heaven, if she ever did fall in love, she hoped it was not more intense than this. She would not be able to bear it.

"So we've agreed not to marry." Her voice trembled. "But does that mean we must not kiss?"

He cupped her face with his hand. "Oh, I believe we must kiss. We must."

Their kiss this time was not fevered or desperate. But one kiss turned into another, and yet another. Slow, caressing kisses. They'd been out of control in the carriage; now they were achingly aware of each other, now they gave themselves time to be tender and soft. She felt his hand slide about her shoulders, drawing her against him. She wrapped her arms about his back, resting her head against his broad chest. The magnifying glass poked at her, but she only pressed closer.

He broke away at last and gazed into her eyes. "I think it's time to ravish you behind the statue of Horus."

She laughed. "What if one of the museum visitors should ignore the signs and wander in unannounced?"

Dylan smoothed back her hair, his hand playing with the ribbon that kept it tied back. "I daresay the ensuing gossip will increase attendance when the exhibit does open."

"It's not a very big statue. Anyone strolling by could spy us." She gestured toward the basalt statue of Horus that stood near the corner. "Now, if we had an Apis lion, that might—" She froze.

"What is it?"

"Don't move," she whispered.

"Look, Charlotte, I was only joking. I'm not going to take you here like this, not with—"

"Quiet!" She wanted to hit herself for shouting.

"What's the matter with you?"

She grabbed his sleeve. "Look near the base of the statue."

A scorpion crawled slowly over the marble floor.

"Damn my eyes," he said hoarsely. "How the devil did a scorpion get in here?"

"There are two of them. The other is on the amphora."

She pointed toward a motionless creature perched on the neck of an ancient wine vessel.

Taking a deep breath, she started to move away from Dylan.

"What do you think you're doing?" he hissed at her.

She took another step toward a display table holding bronze oil lamps. "If I can get close enough, I'll crush it with one of the lamps."

"Are you out of your mind?" Dylan grabbed her arm. "Those things are poisonous!"

She raised her eyebrows. "No? Really?"

"This is no time for sarcasm."

Charlotte shook off his grip. "You're right. It's time for killing scorpions."

When she moved over to the table, Dylan was right beside her. He snatched the bronze lamp out of her hand.

"Let me handle this," he whispered.

Hands on her hips, she watched in exasperation as he crept closer to the statue. "Remember there are two of them, Dylan."

He waved at her to be quiet.

Shaking her head, she grabbed another lamp and tiptoed after him. "Mind your back, Dylan."

"Would you keep your voice down?" He jumped as she brought the bronzed artifact down on the scorpion that was nearly atop his foot.

"What in the world!" He stared as Charlotte lifted up her makeshift weapon, revealing a dead scorpion underneath. "How did he move so fast?"

"My mistake. There were three of them, not two." She pushed him aside. Without a wasted motion, she knocked the other scorpion off the amphora, then smashed it too.

Dylan looked at her in disbelief. "I wish you'd been with me when a hippo tried to overturn my *felucca*."

She barely heard him, intent on watching the remaining scorpion crawl closer to the statue. "Excuse me."

"Wait." He grabbed her arm. "I'll take care of this one."

But when he brought the lamp down, only the sound of metal ringing on the floor answered. "Bloody thing is moving too fast. Watch it, Charlotte."

She looked to see where it had gone. "Here it is."

After she'd crushed the last scorpion, she straightened up with a sigh. "First time I've had to use a lamp. In the desert, I usually just shot them."

Dylan squatted down on the floor, looking at the dead poisonous creatures, then at her. "Have you no fear at all, lass?"

"Of course. That's why I had to kill them. As you said, they can be deadly." She held the brass lamp up to the skylight. "Oh, no!"

"What's the matter now?"

"I've nicked the lamp. I knew I hit that last scorpion too hard."

Dylan fell back on the floor, laughing until tears ran from his eyes.

"I don't know what's so funny. After all, you knew that I spent years in the desert." She shrugged. "Everyone who lives in the desert ends up killing a few scorpions. Cobras too."

This only made him howl louder. "Oh, Charlotte. There's no one like you. Neither woman nor man." He looked up at her. "Are you sure you won't marry me?"

"As if I'd marry a man who couldn't manage to kill one little scorpion," she said.

This made him laugh even harder, but Charlotte thought his amusement now had a regretful quality to it.

Or perhaps she was the one with the regrets.

Chapter Eleven

Samson Pope felt his excitement growing.

It was one thing to search after a cat, even if she was wearing a collar of precious gems. And as interesting as sniffing out a den of thieves might be, such crimes didn't compare to murder. But with this latest incident at the Colville Collection, Samson was certain he was looking at attempted murder.

When Dylan had summoned him to the museum earlier today, he'd had three dead scorpions to show him. Although the other curators insisted that the scorpions had probably gotten into the packing crates in Africa—such a thing happened last year with a tarantula—Samson wasn't buying any of it. He had a policeman's nose for murder, and this one smelled glorious indeed.

Dylan's sharp instincts apparently told him the same thing. In fact, Dylan had wanted to rush over to confront Sir Thomas Havers, whom he insisted was responsible. Mrs. Fairchild had managed to persuade him to accompany her home

A Special Offer For Leisure Historical Romance Readers Only!

Get Four FREE* Romance Novels

A $21.96 Value!

Thrill to the most sensual, adventure-filled Historical Romances on the market today...

FROM 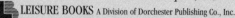 LEISURE BOOKS

As a home subscriber to the Leisure Historical Romance Book Club, you'll enjoy the best in today's BRAND-NEW Historical Romance fiction. For over twenty-five years, Leisure Books has brought you the award-winning, high-quality authors you know and love to read. Each Leisure Historical Romance will sweep you away to a world of high adventure...and intimate romance. Discover for yourself all the passion and excitement millions of readers thrill to each and every month.

SAVE AT LEAST *$5.00* EACH TIME YOU BUY!

Each month, the Leisure Historical Romance Book Club brings you four brand-new titles from Leisure Books, America's foremost publisher of Historical Romances. EACH PACKAGE WILL SAVE YOU AT LEAST $5.00 FROM THE BOOKSTORE PRICE! And you'll never miss a new title with our convenient home delivery service.

Here's how we do it. Each package will carry a 10-DAY EXAMINATION privilege. At the end of that time, if you decide to keep your books, simply pay the low invoice price of $16.96 ($17.75 US in Canada), no shipping or handling charges added*. HOME DELIVERY IS ALWAYS FREE*. With today's top Historical Romance novels selling for $5.99 and higher, our price SAVES YOU AT LEAST $5.00 with each shipment.

AND YOUR FIRST FOUR-BOOK SHIPMENT IS TOTALLY FREE!*

IT'S A BARGAIN YOU CAN'T BEAT! A Super $21.96 Value!

LEISURE BOOKS A Division of Dorchester Publishing Co., Inc.

GET YOUR 4 FREE* BOOKS NOW— A $21.96 VALUE!

Mail the Free* Book
Certificate
Today!

4 FREE* BOOKS ❧ A $21.96 VALUE

Free Books Certificate

YES! I want to subscribe to the Leisure Historical Romance Book Club. Please send me my 4 FREE* BOOKS. Then each month I'll receive the four newest Leisure Historical Romance selections to Preview for 10 days. If I decide to keep them, I will pay the Special Member's Only discounted price of just $4.24 each, a total of $16.96 ($17.75 US in Canada). This is a SAVINGS OF AT LEAST $5.00 off the bookstore price. There are no shipping, handling, or other charges*. There is no minimum number of books I must buy and I may cancel the program at any time. In any case, the 4 FREE* BOOKS are mine to keep—A BIG $21.96 Value!

*In Canada, add $5.00 shipping and handling per order for first shipment. For all subsequent shipments to Canada, the cost of membership is $17.75 US, which includes $7.75 shipping and handling per month.[All payments must be made in US dollars]

*Name*_____

*Address*_____

*City*_____

*State*_____ *Country*_____ *Zip*_____

*Telephone*_____

*Signature*_____

If under 18, Parent or Guardian must sign. Terms, prices and conditions subject to change. Subscription subject to acceptance. Leisure Books reserves the right to reject any order or cancel any subscription.

(Tear Here and Mail Your FREE* Book Card Today!)

Get Four Books Totally
F R E E* —
A $21.96 Value!

(Tear Here and Mail Your FREE* Book Card Today!)

PLEASE RUSH
MY FOUR FREE*
BOOKS TO ME
RIGHT AWAY!

Leisure Historical Romance Book Club
P.O. Box 6613
Edison, NJ 08818-6613

instead; Samson suspected she did not really require a chaperone, but simply wanted to prevent Dylan from creating an angry scene. Visibly concerned for her safety, Dylan had gone off to play protector and escort. And Samson had breathed a sigh of relief.

Interrogating suspects was a tricky proposition; he didn't need lovesick men blundering in and making a mess of things. Until he had clear proof of Sir Thomas's involvement, he was only prepared to go so far. With his notorious reputation, Dylan Pierce had very little to lose. Samson had a great deal.

The police inspector looked up at the imposing facade of the Mayfair mansion. Giving a last tug to his suit coat, he lifted the brass knocker, and banged it a few times.

The door swung open and a pale man in a butler's uniform peered out. "May I help you?"

"I'm here to see Sir Thomas Havers."

The butler had apparently spent enough time working in Mayfair households to ascertain that Pope didn't deserve undue consideration. "Concerning what?" he sniffed.

"Murder."

The man grew even paler. "Murder?"

"Tell Sir Thomas that Detective Inspector Samson Pope would like to speak with him."

A moment later, he found himself in the front parlor.

Samson slowly turned about, taking in the florid decor. He squinted at a naked statue, which was contorted in some strange sexual position.

"Good lord," he muttered.

He'd seen pawnshops with fewer items on display. Most of this bric-a-brac seemed quite costly, though. Each carved table held a bronze or porcelain figurine, as well as a vase of flowers, candles, Venetian glass, and enameled boxes. And he'd never seen so much pink fringe. It decorated every pillow, lamp shade, and ottoman. Even the pale green draperies were trimmed in pink fringe. He supposed he could tolerate that if he had to, but not the embossed pink-and-green wallpaper, or the bright rose fabric that covered the overstuffed sofas and chairs.

"New money," he murmured.

The Havers clearly had the coin to buy Murano glass, Oriental rugs, and eighteenth-century French landscapes. Unfortunately, they also used it to buy hulking statues of naked men, feathered fans, and a bewildering number of little porcelain cats.

It was like visiting the boudoir of a West End showgirl.

Just then, Samson caught sight of a bald man in the mirror over the mantel. The fellow was dressed in a dark blue suit, an embroidered vest visible against his ivory shirt. Obviously not a servant.

He turned around just as the older man entered the parlor. "Sir Thomas, I presume?" He bowed his head slightly. "I'm Detective Inspector Samson Pope from Scotland Yard."

Havers sat down, not bothering to acknowledge him with a greeting.

"My man told me where you were from. I haven't the faintest idea what business you may have that could possibly concern me."

Samson remained standing. "I've been asked to look into the disappearance of a stolen cat."

Havers looked at him as though he had suggested something lewd. "What in blazes has that to do with me?"

"I'm questioning every person who might have reason to wish the cat's owner ill."

"Cat? What cat? And who's this owner?"

"Mrs. Charlotte Fairchild." Samson watched Havers carefully. At the mere mention of her name, the old man's eyes narrowed, and every muscle of his face tightened.

"Mrs. Fairchild accused me of stealing her cat?" He pushed himself up from his chair. "That woman should be horsewhipped!"

"No one has been accused of anything. But Mrs. Fairchild's house was broken into last week, and only her cat was taken. I have been told that anyone with even a passing acquaintance with the young woman knows of her attachment to the animal. So it seems probable that the theft of her cat was meant to cause Mrs. Fairchild injury."

"I can't believe that Scotland Yard spends its time chasing after lost tabbies." Havers shook his head. "No wonder the Empire is crumbling."

"Sir Thomas, as I have said—"

"No, you have said quite enough. I don't give a hang if Mrs. Fairchild has lost twenty cats and her idiotic mother and sister in the bargain. She's been nothing but trouble since she married my friend, and here she is still creating mischief. Well, I'll not be a party to her disgusting shenanigans any longer."

He buttoned his jacket and started walking toward the door.

"Excuse me, Sir Thomas, but I have not finished questioning you."

He turned, his jowled cheeks growing red. "You dare to waste my time with this—this nonsense!"

"Sit down, sir, or I will have to take you to headquarters."

The old man's jaw dropped open. "For a cat? Has all of London gone mad? I tell you, that Fairchild woman is a menace. I wouldn't put it past her to have hidden her own cat away just so she can point the finger at me."

"Now why would she do that?"

Havers tried to collect himself. He straightened his vest before answering. "Two and a half years ago she prevented her husband—and my friend and protégé—from leaving Egypt. Within the month he was dead, buried in a cave-in, all because that meddlesome woman insisted on having her own way."

Samson nodded. "That explains your antipathy toward her, but not why she should wish you harm."

"Because I am the only person who knows her true character. Everyone else may succumb to that grieving-widow charade she puts on, but I know the truth of it. And she can't abide the fact that there is one person in London who knows her for the little hypocrite she is. I tell you, I could shake that woman senseless."

A movement caught his eye, and Samson looked up.

A handsome, silver-haired lady had entered the room while they were talking. She was a tiny woman and dressed in rose satin, the exact color of the upholstered divan. For a brief moment, Samson took her for yet another odd parlor decoration.

"Lady Havers?" Samson bowed from the waist. "Detective Inspector Pope at your service."

Sir Thomas spun around. "My dear, I thought you were still napping."

She walked farther into the parlor, daintily sitting down on a velvet love seat. "Now who is this woman my husband wants to shake senseless?"

Samson noticed that Lady Havers held a small crystal goblet filled with dark burgundy liquid.

Sir Thomas went to sit beside her. "No need for you to worry about any of this."

"Mrs. Charlotte Fairchild," Samson said in answer to her question.

"Ah, Charlotte again. Poor girl. Ian's death disrupted her life so." She sipped from her glass. "And I don't believe she has yet recovered from her father's death. Life in Egypt can be hard on a woman."

"Life in London too," Samson said softly.

Sir Thomas scowled. "Oh, yes, her little kitty is lost. Goes sending for Scotland Yard to find the blasted thing, if you can believe it."

"Kitty?" She turned toward her husband with a mystified expression. "What in the world are you talking about?"

He waved his hand. "I'll explain later, after this *person*

has left. Suffice it to say that Charlotte can't find her cat. And she thinks I, of all people, stole it."

"Is this true? How dreadful. I hope no one has harmed the poor thing." Lady Havers seemed genuinely upset by the news.

"It's true her cat was taken but no has been accused of anything." Samson paused. "Yet."

"I can't abide the thought of anyone hurting a little cat. As you can see, I've a great fondness for them." She gestured toward the dozens of porcelain felines that decorated the parlor. "If Sir Thomas did not cough and wheeze in their presence, I'd gladly share my house with three or four of the lovely creatures."

Her husband rolled his eyes at the ceiling. "Thank heaven for that," he muttered.

"Well, I'm afraid that things have escalated since Mrs. Fairchild's cat disappeared."

The couple looked at him with wary expressions.

"Three poisonous scorpions were found today at the Colville Collection."

Lady Havers swigged down the rest of her drink.

"Scorpions?" Sir Thomas sat up straighter. "Was anyone hurt?"

"No, luckily Mrs. Fairchild was the one who found them. She crushed them all with a heavy object. It was most fortunate that Mrs. Fairchild didn't lose her head. I don't know many women who would be able to kill off scorpions one by one as if she was swatting flies."

The old man only snorted.

"I'm not surprised at all." Lady Havers leaned forward. He caught a whiff of sherry and wondered just how many little goblets she had drunk so far today. "I've seen Charlotte shoot the head off a cobra at twenty paces."

"Really?" Samson's estimation of the young widow was growing by the minute.

"Oh, yes," Sir Thomas said impatiently. "In fact, I expect

her to trot off to Scotland one day and wrestle with the Loch Ness Monster. Infernal woman would probably win too. But I still don't see how any of this concerns me. I don't like Mrs. Fairchild; I've made that plain enough. But if you think I'm running about London stealing cats and letting scorpions loose, then you're as mad as that Uncle Louis of hers."

"I merely suspect that someone is trying to frighten Mrs. Fairchild. Perhaps even—"

A furious banging interrupted Samson in midsentence.

"What is going on now?" Sir Thomas threw up his hands.

Loud voices erupted from the foyer; an instant later Dylan Pierce stalked into the room, followed by a distraught butler.

Samson swore under his breath. He should have known that Dylan would show up sooner or later.

"I couldn't keep him out, Sir Thomas," the trembling butler said.

"Indeed you could not." Dylan stood in the middle of the parlor, hands on hips, as if waiting for someone to throw the first punch.

"You!" Sir Thomas turned even redder. "How dare you barge into my house like this!"

"And how dare *you* put Mrs. Fairchild's life in danger!" Dylan looked even angrier than Sir Thomas. "Do you hate her so much that you'll stoop to anything to harm her? Stealing her cat, setting loose scorpions. You vindictive old coward!"

"You're not only a drunkard, you're a mad drunkard." Sir Thomas pointed at Dylan. "I want this man arrested. He has no right to break into my house and level these ridiculous charges!"

Samson stepped between the two men. "Dylan, I told you that I would handle things. This is official police business."

"Anything that concerns Charlotte Fairchild is my business." Dylan glared at Sir Thomas. "Especially attempted murder."

170

"Oh, dear," Lady Havers gasped. "I believe I need another sherry."

"Murder?" Sir Thomas looked at Samson in obvious disbelief. "Inspector, I don't know what this scoundrel is talking about, but I do know he has no business in my house." His expression grew even more belligerent. "Nor do you, for that matter."

Dylan started to speak, but Samson clapped a hand on his shoulder. "Let me handle this," he warned in a low voice.

"Go on then," Dylan muttered.

Samson turned his attention back to Sir Thomas. "As I was trying to explain before we were interrupted, I suspect that someone is trying to frighten Mrs. Fairchild. Perhaps even murder her."

"So?" the old man asked impatiently.

"So you are the most likely suspect," Samson said.

Sir Thomas stepped back. "You insufferable bounders! How dare you both come here and accuse me of theft and attempted murder! I'll have your job, Inspector, I swear I will. As soon as you leave, I'm going straight to the commissioner and have you sacked."

"As you wish. But before you do, I have to know your whereabouts on the night of August the thirty-first."

The old man stared back at him, his face now ashen.

Lady Havers tugged at her husband's sleeve. "Dear, could you ring for my maid? I need more sherry. And have her bring my medicine too. I think I'm going to need it."

"I don't understand." Dylan was so restless, he could barely keep still in the hansom cab. "Why didn't you arrest him?"

"You're just lucky I don't arrest *you.*" Samson sat back with a stern expression. "What in the world were you thinking of? Barging in like that. This isn't some hashish-filled coffeehouse in Cairo where you can say what you like. This is London. Mayfair, I might add. And the Haverses have influential friends. You don't make wild accusations at people like that without some bloody proof."

He snorted. "I thought policemen were supposed to put justice ahead of their ambition."

"Don't push me too far, Dylan. You had no right to interfere." Samson shook his head. "You could have given poor Lady Havers a stroke with your carrying on."

"Well, I've no wish to harm the old woman. But I had to make certain that Sir Thomas understood he couldn't get away with it."

"With what? We've no proof. I don't care how much he hates Mrs. Fairchild, until I have evidence that shows he was involved in the catnapping and the scorpions, I can do very little." He sighed. "Except make him nervous. If he is guilty, he knows he's being watched now."

"Oh, I'll watch him." Dylan leaned back.

As restless as he was, he also felt exhausted. It had been a long day. He'd gone from worrying about mummies to discussing marriage with Charlotte to stalking scorpions. He felt better knowing that she was safely home. Although he didn't know why he worried about a woman who killed deadly prey without batting an eye.

But after he returned her to Belgrave Square, he couldn't resist the impulse to go to Sir Thomas's home. Perhaps Samson was right. Perhaps he should leave it to Scotland Yard to officially investigate the scorpion incident. Unofficially, however, he intended to do whatever he could. Because he knew this afternoon's events were no accident—it had been attempted murder. Charlotte could have died.

At least Samson had assigned two policemen to help guard the museum tonight. Damn decent thing for his friend to do, even if none of the other curators thought it necessary.

"Do you think two policemen are enough?" he asked.

"Two policemen and four security guards are more than enough. After all I've done on your behalf, you owe me a damn fine pot of tea when we get to your house."

172

"Never fear. I may not have that vile green brew you love, but I've a stash of Chinese tea I keep for special occasions." He gave Sam a rueful smile. "Especially when I want to thank a good friend for doing me a favor. I do appreciate everything you've done, even if I am too bullheaded to show it."

Samson chuckled. "You are a wild man, Dylan. Indeed you are. You scared Havers and his wife half to death today."

"Not knowing who to trust is making me jumpy." He leaned toward Samson, lowering his voice. "Look here, have you come up with any information about those names I gave you?"

"Yes." Samson leaned his head back and closed his eyes.

"Well, man, tell me what you've learned."

"Tomorrow." He yawned. "I've got a few things to finish looking into."

"You can tell me something, can't you?"

"Meet me at Rules Restaurant tomorrow at three. I'll have all the information for you then."

"Blast you, Sam—"

"Tomorrow." His friend settled farther down in the comfortable seat, as if getting ready to drop off to sleep.

Sam was as stubborn as he was. No use trying to pry anything out of him tonight. Dylan sat back with a sigh.

He was glad that it was an open cab. The evening air was still, and any breeze was welcome. As they wound through the crowded streets, Dylan found himself relaxing for the first time all day.

After a few minutes, the clopping of the horse's hooves started to make him drowsy, and he closed his eyes. Nearby a boy hawked the news, while a woman sang out, "Strawberries ripe, and apples on the rise."

Strawberries should be out of season, he thought as he drifted off to sleep.

"Look out there! Watch it!"

173

Dylan sat up with a start. "What's wrong?"

"Some bloke with more muscle than brain ran right out in front of us." The hansom driver pointed down the street.

"Probably running away from something," Samson said quietly. "Or someone."

It was twilight, and most of the gaslights had not been illuminated yet. Dylan couldn't make out much more than a figure running through the shadows.

"Good thing my Cassie here don't start at every little thing." The driver clucked to his white mare. "If she'd been young and skittish, that fool would have been like suet in a pudding bag under her hooves."

"Look, you can stop here." Dylan handed the driver the fare. "We'll walk the rest of the way. My rooms are only down the street."

"I guess we're not meant to relax today," Samson grunted as he climbed down from the cab.

Once on solid ground, Dylan felt strangely uneasy.

He looked about him. There was nothing unusual occurring on the street. Men in bowler hats walked briskly home; women hurried up the front steps of their houses, clutching parcels. The Cockney woman sat at her accustomed corner, surrounded by the caged nightingales she sold when the weather was good. He could even smell the steak-and-kidney pie from the open windows of Mrs. Rehman's boarding-house. He swore at himself for being on edge. Those damn scorpions had rattled him more than he wanted to admit.

"Why are we going so fast?" Samson asked as he hurried to catch up with him.

"Thought you wanted that tea." Dylan glanced over his shoulder. Someone was watching him from the shadows across the square. He knew it. He'd been in danger many times in the desert and had been forced to learn when he was being watched. Someone was watching him now.

Thank heaven Charlotte had not gone home by herself.

What if someone were outside her Belgravia house, waiting for her. Watching. But for what? And why?

"I like tea, but not enough to sprint down the street for it." Sam stood next to him, slightly out of breath, as Dylan pulled out his keys.

Looking over his shoulder one more time, Dylan put the key into the lock. There was no resistance. Surprised, he twisted the doorknob. The door opened easily.

"Who unlocked my door?"

Samson looked instantly alert.

Dylan opened the door farther. Both men stood in the foyer, listening.

All Dylan could hear was a mouse squeaking from the kitchen. For the first time, he regretted not hiring a manservant when he'd rented the house. Four times a week, a housekeeper came to clean and make dinner, but today was Mrs. Kelsingham's day off.

Sam lit the gaslights in the foyer, while Dylan quickly went into the parlor and sitting room to do the same. In the flickering light, everything looked normal, books and papers scattered every which way, his shirt from yesterday still flung over the mahogany rocker.

Dylan picked up the iron poker from beside the fireplace.

"Let's see if anyone is keeping the mouse company in the kitchen," he whispered to Sam.

He walked carefully over the hardwood floor, already knowing the house well enough to avoid the spots where the floor creaked the loudest. Pushing open the kitchen door, he stood brandishing the poker with one hand, daring anyone to attack him. He felt Sam standing just a step or two behind him.

Nothing. He didn't even hear the mouse. After putting the lights on in the kitchen and searching the pantry, he still found no trace of an intruder.

He lowered the poker. "Ah, I'm becoming daft in my old age."

Sam shook his head. "If you didn't leave your door unlocked, then you've had a visitor."

Dylan thought a moment. "Maybe our guest was that fellow who ran in front of our cab just now."

"Or maybe he's still here somewhere, hiding."

Dylan looked up at the ceiling. "To the second floor, then."

After the men crept upstairs, Dylan gestured to the nearest room. "You take the second-floor sitting room, I'll look in my bedroom."

Sam cautiously opened up the door to the sitting room and disappeared inside. He heard his friend move about the room, turning on gaslights. Obviously no intruder in there.

Dylan was about to open the door to his bedroom when he heard a loud thump from inside.

He froze. A moment later he heard another sound, like something heavy dropping.

With one hand on the doorknob, he pressed his ear against the closed door. Yes, someone was definitely moving about in there.

"Sam, we've got him!"

Samson instantly appeared in the hall. "In there?" he whispered.

Dylan nodded, then kicked open the door. "Fine, you bastard! We'll see how much you like sneaking about my house once I've stuck this poker up your arse!"

Something came flying out of the darkness at him.

Instinctively he threw up his hands to protect his face. He stumbled and fell back as a heavy object landed on his chest. A loud screech echoed through the house as he hit the floor.

"Where are you, you bloody devil?"

But it wasn't the devil who sat on his chest.

It was Nefer.

Chapter Twelve

Dylan felt just like Father Christmas.

"Hurry and ring the bell," he told Samson. "I don't know how much longer I can control this beast."

Samson kept a wary eye on Nefer. "Are you sure she isn't a small cougar or lion cub? I've never seen a cat so big."

"She's a desert cat." He struggled to keep a grip on the squirming feline. "The same breed of cat that the pharaohs kept."

Nefer must have recognized that she was home, but Dylan was not about to let her go. He had no idea how long the animal had been closeted in his bedroom, but it was enough time to allow her to scratch the newel bedposts, scatter every monograph, and knock over his collection of *ushapti* reproductions. Thankfully, Nefer had been calm on the carriage ride, but as soon as she caught sight of her own front stoop, she'd become positively feral.

"Well, I think I'd choose an Irish wolfhound over this kitty," Samson said.

Nefer turned her amber eyes in Samson's direction and hissed.

"Does she bite?"

Dylan shook his head. "No."

With lightning speed, the cat whipped out her paw and raked the top of the police inspector's hand.

"But she does scratch," he added.

"I see that." Samson rubbed his hand.

"You can't blame the poor creature. Who knows what was done with her these past few days?" Dylan murmured soothing words to her in Arabic and felt the cat relax.

Samson shook his head. "And to think I've been running all over London looking for this ungrateful animal."

Nefer only closed her enormous eyes.

The door finally opened.

Randall stood there, one hand still buttoning up his coat. "Mr. Pierce," he said breathlessly. "The family's gone to bed already. They've an early train to catch tomorrow. Lady Margaret has arranged a speaking tour in the Midlands, and Michael's to be brought to stay with his cousins before he starts at Eton."

"Yes, yes, I know." Dylan and Samson pushed their way inside. "But as you can see, we've brought—"

"Bless my soul, you've found Nefer." The footman grabbed the cat right out of Dylan's arms.

Nefer's purring sounded like a Charing Cross locomotive.

"Miss Charlotte, Lady Margaret!" Randall shouted so loud, Dylan feared the windowpanes would shatter. "Nefer is home! Hurry! Get down here quick!"

"This is a servant?" Samson whispered, obviously unnerved by Randall's unservile manner.

"It's not a very formal household," Dylan explained, although he thought the least Randall could have done was change out of his carpet slippers before answering the door.

Cries sounded overhead, and he could hear doors being flung open and people shouting. A young, barefoot woman ran out of the kitchen, wearing only a calico robe and curling papers in her hair.

"Merciful heaven, it's our little Nefer." She rubbed her forehead against the cat, who now looked to be in a state of bliss.

"Lorrie the parlormaid," Dylan whispered to his friend.

Then sheer bedlam broke loose. Charlotte raced down the stairs, followed by her family, all in various stages of undress. Screaming, yelling at the tops of their lungs, it was a wonder the cat's fur didn't stand on end with all the noise. Dylan certainly felt as if his own hair was.

"Not a sedate family, I see," Samson muttered.

Indeed, Dylan doubted if a returning soldier from the Napoleonic Wars had ever received such a thunderous welcome. Charlotte looked positively exultant as she cradled Nefer, crooning to her in Arabic. Nefer seemed to have entered a euphoric feline state, eyes half shut and long tail swishing lazily. Everyone clustered around, each of them stroking the animal or bestowing kisses on the cat's soft ears. Even Catherine managed a few kisses between sneezes.

The two men could do little else but wait for the furor to die down. When it seemed as though it wasn't likely to occur anytime soon, he and Samson wandered into the front parlor. Dylan picked up a copy of *The Free Womens' Gazette* and settled down to read.

Lady Margaret finally appeared, her colored lawn robe swirling about her. "What a glorious surprise. Glorious, I tell you. We must celebrate." She snapped her fingers. "We've cake in the pantry. I was going to serve it for breakfast as a farewell treat, but we'll have it now. And I'll tell Randall to break the seal off one of our best wines in the cellar."

She rushed over to Dylan and gave him a quick hug. "Thank you, my dear, for bringing Nefer back to us. You must tell us how you found her."

He opened his mouth to speak, but she had darted away.

"Now let me just see about that cake and wine. This will

179

make my daughter so happy. I can't thank you enough. Both of you." Lady Margaret finally noticed Samson. "Who are you, sir?"

"Detective Inspector Samson Pope, ma'am."

But she was already gone. Dylan could hear her telling Nefer what a fine and noble cat she was.

Samson nodded. "Interesting household. Titled ladies who throw paint pots, a cat who apparently is revered, and I heard today that Mrs. Fairchild once shot a cobra at twenty paces."

"Where Mrs. Fairchild is concerned, I've learned that anything is possible." Dylan looked over at him. "Who told you she killed a cobra?"

But he never heard the answer. Charlotte ran into the parlor, and Dylan's heart stopped.

Like Lorrie, she was barefoot, and her white-gold hair was loose, tumbling about her shoulders and down her back. She wore only a nightdress made of some creamy soft material, and when she stood in the light just so, he could see her long legs outlined. If Nefer hadn't been crushed to her chest, he was certain he would also glimpse a great deal more. But she was already the most tempting sight he'd seen since he'd stumbled upon Pharaoh Akerbad's treasure house.

"Detective Pope, I don't know how to express my thanks," she said to Samson in a trembling voice. "You can't possibly know how much this means to me."

His friend seemed to be almost as moved by Charlotte in her current state of undress as he was. "Thank you, Mrs. Fairchild. I'm glad I could be of assistance."

Dylan didn't like the expression on Samson's face, nor the sudden warmth in his smile.

"Excuse me." He cleared his throat loudly, and both Charlotte and Samson turned in his direction. "I do believe I was the one who found Nefer."

"Technically that is true," Samson said, "but I am certain that my investigations these past few days caused the cat-napper to grow uneasy."

Dylan gave his friend a warning look. "*I* found her."

Charlotte came over to him. This close, she seemed even more exquisite. He already knew there wasn't a woman in Britain who could match her in intelligence or spirit. Now he knew none of them could compare to her in beauty either. She suddenly seemed utterly irresistible.

"So you're the one responsible for bringing her back to me." Her eyes shone with happiness. "How can I ever thank you?"

Although Nefer lay curled contentedly in her arms, Charlotte reached up and hugged him. Even with the cat between them, purring like distant thunder, the embrace made Dylan weak.

She stepped back. "I may not have Egypt," she said quietly, "but I have you."

Emotion flooded over him so that he couldn't speak.

It was Charlotte who at last broke off their gaze. "I'd best fetch Nefer something to eat. The poor darling is probably half-starved." She brushed her chin against Nefer's tawny head. "This calls for a celebration that lasts until dawn. Michael will just have to sleep on the train tomorrow, for I vow no one will sleep tonight. And you must tell everyone exactly how you found Nefer. I can't wait to hear."

She was almost out the door when she turned back. "You, too, Inspector. We want to hear everything you have done to try to find my cat." She looked over at Dylan once more, and her expression grew softer. "But it is Dylan who is the real hero."

After she left, neither man spoke. From the other part of the house came excited voices, cutlery rattling, doors being slammed. Yet even from here, Dylan could hear Charlotte's distinctive, sweet laughter.

"I love her," he said finally, amazed.

Samson threw himself down in the nearest armchair. "I know."

* * *

181

Charlotte was wrong. Everyone managed to catch a brief nap at some point during the long, raucous night, although she suspected that had more to do with the wine than the late hour.

She shivered in her robe, trying to make as little noise as possible as she lit the coal grates downstairs. Randall had returned but an hour earlier from taking Mother, Catherine, and Michael to the train station. She had planned to see them off at Victoria Station, but that was before Nefer returned. She couldn't possibly leave her cat, and she wouldn't risk somehow losing her again during the carriage ride.

Indeed, every time she moved, Nefer trotted after her. Just now the cat sat at her feet, blinking and giving a great yawn.

After such an exhausting night, all of the servants were asleep. Randall could be heard snoring loudly from his rocker in the kitchen. She suspected no one would rouse themselves until tea time.

She turned as another snore sounded behind her.

Dylan lay sprawled on the sitting room divan, one stock-inged foot on the floor, the other slung over the armrest. He'd fallen asleep long before her family left for the station. Samson Pope had departed as well. She liked the Scotland Yard inspector; he had a dry wit and a way of listening that made a person nervous. It kept things from ever getting dull around him, not that life had been at all mundane lately.

Dylan let out another ear-splitting snore. Stifling a giggle, she walked over to the divan and covered him up once more with the blanket Lorrie had fetched earlier. The early morning light shone weakly through the windows, and she marveled at how long his auburn lashes were. Funny she had never noticed that before.

She knelt down beside the divan, one hand resting on the blanket, liking the feel of his chest rising and falling with every breath. After six weeks, she already knew every tiny mark and blemish on his remarkable face. She knew that his thick hair turned russet in certain light, that his nose was broken in two places, and that a small scar ran across his upper lip. She also knew that he was intelligent, kind, brave, and funny. But she didn't know until these past twenty-four hours that her feelings for him ran so deep. Whatever she had once felt for Ian, it was nothing like this.

Nefer leaned against her, her large paws moving up and down in a kneading motion.

"I haven't forgotten you, beauty," she whispered, stroking the cat with her free hand. She left her other hand, however, on Dylan's chest, reluctant to relinquish her physical contact with him.

"Aren't you glad we found you?" She bent down to Nefer and kissed her ears.

"What do you mean, 'we'? *I* found her."

Charlotte looked over in surprise. Dylan's eyes were wide open and staring at her with amusement.

"Why is it everyone wants to take credit for finding that cat?" he asked with a mock scowl.

She laughed and began to move away from him, but he quickly captured her fingers with his own. Under her palm she could feel his heart beating.

"As grateful as I am, it seems that you couldn't help but stumble upon Nefer. According to you, she was locked up in your bedroom. So I do believe you had a little help."

"From the catnapper?"

"Who else?" She liked holding his hand, liked being this close to him. They'd never been together in the early morning hours. She could almost pretend they lived together and were waking up in their own house, the servants still in their beds, leaving only the two of them to speak in hushed tones, huddled close for warmth.

"Well, finding the catnapper is Sam's job, if he ever wakes up."

"Inspector Pope left about an hour ago. He tried to say good-bye to you, but you were snoring too loud to hear."

"Am I the last one to leave?"

He pushed himself into a sitting position and looked about the empty sitting room. His shirtsleeves were unbuttoned and rolled up. She had to force herself not to run her fingers over the fine auburn hairs that covered his muscled forearms.

She nodded. "The servants have gone to bed. And Mother, Catherine, and Michael went to catch their train around the same time Inspector Pope said his good-byes."

"I see." His eyes seemed to turn a more intense shade of blue. "So we're the only ones awake in the house."

"Yes," she said softly.

He squeezed her hand. "We'll probably have the place to ourselves for hours."

Her breathing quickened. "I—I was actually planning to go to bed myself. But I wanted to light the grates first." She shivered again, but it wasn't from the morning chill. "I'm quite cold."

He pulled her onto his lap. "No, you're not."

Nefer yowled in disapproval at being abandoned on the floor.

"I'm not?" She closed her eyes as he kissed the nape of her neck.

"No, there's nothing cold about you, lass." He planted soft kisses all about her neck. She leaned her head back, inviting each one. "You give off more heat than the desert."

She smiled. "Have a care you don't get burned."

He gripped her shoulders and brought her so close against him, she could feel his heart pounding. "I've lived in the desert a long time. It can never grow too hot for me."

"Yes," she breathed, stunned at how her own heart started racing.

Suddenly, as though she could no longer control her actions, she kissed him. Kissed him with such ferocity that she wondered one of them didn't cry out in pain.

When they finally broke apart, both of them were fighting to breathe. "Yes," she said again and kissed him once more, just as fiercely, just as hard.

184

She needed to caress his shoulders, his arms, and feel his hardness against her. She needed to open her mouth beneath his, needed his taste on her tongue, his hands on her body. She needed him as she had needed no one before. After nearly three years of guilt and loneliness, she needed to feel a man inside her. She needed to feel desired and out of control—and wild. Even if she shocked Dylan with her need.

But she had no reason to fear that Dylan would find her too rough or bold. Instead, he groaned aloud, running his hands along her back, pulling off her robe. One moment he was clutching her hair in one hand, kissing her throat. Seconds later, he had unfastened her nightgown. Gripping her about the waist, he placed his mouth on her naked breasts, kissing, sucking, biting until she thought she'd grow dizzy with wanting him.

She cried out as he ran his tongue along her nipple.

His own chest heaving, Dylan sat back. His face was flushed, his hair tousled and wild. "We have to go upstairs," he said between ragged breaths. "I don't want anyone disturbing us."

She was too excited to reply. Her nightdress hanging open, she steadied herself on the divan and tried to stand up. But her legs were shaky and she felt herself wobble.

"You've made me go weak in the knees," she said with a wondering laugh.

He was beside her instantly, caressing her face. "Then I'll do what I should have done back in the desert, lass."

With a sudden strong movement, he picked her up in his arms. "I'm going to carry you off, and the devil take anyone who tries to stop me."

She threw her arms about his neck. "I think I'm going to like this carrying-off business. It's quite thrilling."

His arms tightened about her as she kissed his neck. A deep groan of longing rumbled in his throat.

He squeezed her, his hands feeling hot and urgent on her body.

She looked up at him.

"If you think this is thrilling," he said in a low voice, "wait until I get you upstairs."

It was a wonder that he managed to carry her up the stairs without his own legs giving out from under him. Once in her bedroom, he kicked the door shut behind him, barely missing Nefer, who scooted past with a startled growl. The woman had sent him reeling, and not just from desire.

After a hungry, lingering kiss, Charlotte whispered for him to put her down. Dazed, he obeyed.

Moving back from him, she slowly stepped out of her nightgown. He hardly dared breathe as first one long leg, then the other was bared. When she was naked, however, she didn't toss the cloth aside, but instead held it in front of her so that he could see only tantalizing glimpses of bare flesh. A rounded hip, a smooth shoulder. He ached with longing.

Her smoky gray eyes gazed at him with the calm allure of a bust of Nefertiti. In another moment he expected to smell the aroma of cardamom seeds and hear the splashing of the *feluccas* from the Nile.

She *was* Egypt to him: dazzling, mysterious, exotic. No one was like Charlotte Fairchild, no other woman possessed her unique charm, her fire, her unpredictable nature. And what he felt for her was unlike anything he had ever felt for any female before. It was like his love for the desert—its majesty, its danger, its wild beauty.

Nefer noisily jumped atop the dresser. His attention was distracted from Charlotte for a second, allowing him to take in his surroundings. At first glance the room might pass for any belonging to a privileged woman in Belgravia: pale gold wallpaper decorated with vines and white petals, oak furnishings, and a large, tempting bed piled high with gold and green tapestried pillows.

But every square inch of free space was taken up with

monographs, books, and journals. Next to the open window hung a reproduction of a wall painting from Luxor, its colors marvelously bright and African in the London gloom. And scattered among the piles of reading material were faience figurines, clay statues, reproductions of scarab beetles, blue hippopotami, gilt crocodiles. Lying on the dressing table— next to her silver-backed brush—was the mummy of a rat.

He turned his attention back to Charlotte, who stood watching him intently.

"I love you, lass."

She might be taken aback by such a confession, from him of all people, yet how could he not say it? She was all that filled his mind and his heart. For the first time in his life, something besides Egypt and her treasures sent his blood racing and made him weak with desire and need.

But she only nodded. "And I you," she said softly. "You would not be here now if I didn't."

Still watching him, Charlotte let the nightgown fall to the ground so that she finally stood before him naked. There was no shame in her stance, nor boldness either. She was about to give herself to him, and the moment felt as right, as natural, as when the wind swirled through the desert, sending heat and sand to fill the air. Such heat filled him now. Damn, but he felt as hot as a man wandering lost on the Sahara at high noon.

He wasn't lost, though. He had been heading for this mo- ment—with Charlotte willing and naked before him—since he saw her alight from her camel two and a half years earlier. And he knew that this woman had been waiting for him too. They were meant for each other. And she loved *him* as well. What had he done in his turbulent, stumbling past to warrant such a confession or such a woman?

Like someone waking from a delirious sleep, Dylan sud- denly moved to her, needing to feel her in his arms, wanting to run his hands along her flesh and explore her smooth, warm body with his fingers and his tongue.

187

She felt good to him. Her body seemed to burn through his own clothes, which he could not be rid of fast enough. She helped him undress, her fingers trembling when they unbuttoned his shirt, but then his hands shook too, so that he tore his trousers in his haste.

He didn't think he could wait long enough to get her onto that plush bed. It seemed he had waited so long already, an entire lifetime. And now that the woman he loved was here, he could barely think through a haze of desire. But then he felt her hands on his body, sure, more expert than he had ever imagined. A hot flash of jealousy tore through him as he remembered that Ian Fairchild had claimed this woman first. Yet when he felt her cup his manhood in her hands—knowing just how to press and rub and stroke him—he forgot his jealousy and felt only gratitude at her knowing hands, her fearless lovemaking.

She leaned down and kissed his chest, her long hair brushing his flesh so that his nerve endings felt as though they were on fire. He gripped her by the shoulders when she licked his nipples, which were suddenly as hard and erect as his manhood.

"Charlotte, don't." He fought to keep from flinging her down onto the carpet and pushing himself into her until he lost complete control. "I don't want it to be over so soon."

Instead she only covered his nipple with her mouth, sucking, pulling him into her in a gentle parody of love.

"Lass, you'll drive me mad." He tried to get her to look at him, his hands clutching her buttocks. He squeezed her firm flesh and pressed her against his hardness. "Let me take you to the bed."

"Bed?" She sank to the floor, her hands trailing down his body until he thought his knees would buckle from the effort of standing.

Smiling up at him, Charlotte stretched out on the bright red-and-gold rug that looked as if it had once decorated a Bedouin tent. "Who needs a four-poster bed in the desert?"

He threw himself down on top of her, not even wondering if his weight would be too much for her to bear, not thinking clearly any longer.

He rubbed himself against her, then bent down to suckle her own hard pink nipple.

She gasped. "Let's pretend it's that sand dune you told me about in the carriage. Let's pretend we're back in Egypt."

"No pretense, lass." He could barely get the words out, and nudged her legs apart with his knee. "I don't want to pretend with you. I can't pretend."

He couldn't wait. He wanted to take his time with her, slowly explore her body, but claiming her took on an urgency that swept over him. He wouldn't feel safe or secure about Charlotte until he was at last within her, until he felt her final surrender to him—and he to her.

As though she too needed to claim his flesh and his heart, she wrapped her long legs about his back, pulling him toward her.

With a great groan, he sank himself into her, the electrifying sensation making him shudder. She felt wild, hot, and wet—and he had to remain still for a long second, reveling in the wonder of being in her, her breasts pressed against his chest, her heart pounding, her arms and legs about him.

"No pretense," he gasped, and began the sensuous dance.

Charlotte rocked with him, murmuring in Arabic one minute, English the next. He heard himself answer back in he knew not what language.

The smell of jasmine filled his nostrils, as did the pungent smell of sex. He suddenly felt surrounded by all the warmth and color of Africa. Eyes closed, moving urgently within the woman he adored, he could pretend they were back in Egypt. Back in that baking desert, sand dunes on the horizon, the *khamseen* wind turning the very air to fire.

He opened his eyes, thrilled to see Charlotte gazing up at him. She was the glory of Egypt now too. He pulled her tighter against him, as if he would consume her whole, take

her into his body so that she would always be with him, her
scent, her flesh, her spirit. She was as exciting and rare as a
secret chamber filled with treasure. But he need never surrender this treasure or see it stolen from him. She was his.

The thought drove him over the edge and he cried out,
climaxing so strongly that he felt like a man who had survived a desert sandstorm: exhausted, on fire, and miracu-
lously alive.

She barely knew where she was. On the floor, surely, for she
felt the weaving of the carpet beneath her bare back. But she
could just as well be lost in the delirium of malarial fever,
or the throes of opium. In all her twenty-seven years, she
had never felt so sated, so physically thrilled. Or emotionally
complete.

Dylan lay upon her chest, slick with perspiration,
breathing like a horse run to ground. She stroked his back,
smiling as he moaned in response. She had enjoyed a healthy
physical life with Ian, but in the few months of their marriage she'd never been this frenzied or bold. Never had Ian
climaxed as wildly as Dylan, who yelled so loudly and long
that it was a wonder Randall hadn't come running up with
a London Bobbie in tow.

She laughed to herself. She had been pretty vocal herself
when her own pleasure came. And such trembling, fierce
pleasure it was. She kissed the top of Dylan's head, his thick
auburn hair damp beneath her lips.

To think that this romantic rogue had confessed he loved
her.

It seemed the most natural thing in the world to confess
that she loved him too. Loved him as she had loved no one
and nothing before, except for Egypt. Most staggering of all
was the thought that she did not love Egypt *more* than this
man.

If she never saw the sun rise over the Sahara again; if,
God help her, she could never trail her hand in the waters

of the Nile or climb through the valley of Abu Simbel, she would still know the thrill of such wonders by gazing into his eyes.

"I love you," she whispered in Arabic.

He raised his head at last. Those dark blue eyes gazed into hers now. "How did I live these thirty-three years without you, lass?"

She swept the hair back from his face. "You had Egypt to keep you company."

He nodded. "Aye. But I mean to have both now."

They kissed with great tenderness, as if amazed by their mutual good fortune.

"When I leave for Egypt this fall, you're coming with me."

Tears welled up in her eyes. Although she had promised herself she would return one day, she had not thought when or how that day would occur. Suddenly she found herself lying on a Bedouin rug with a naked Welshman, and every glorious dream she had ever entertained was about to come true.

"I am?" she whispered.

His expression was serious, almost grave. "I'll not be parted from you. I've spent too much of my time alone, or with women who left me nothing but regrets. I want to spend the rest of my life with you, if you'll have me." He kissed the tips of her fingers. "I want you for my wife."

She sat up, gently pushing him aside. The idea of marriage, even marriage to this extraordinary man, made her uneasy. "I—I don't see the need to marry. I'll stay with you just as readily without a marriage license. In fact, I'd prefer it."

"Do you not love me enough, Charlotte? Is that why? I understand that you probably still love Ian. I don't fancy the idea, and I don't know how to compete with a dead man. But if you'll just trust your feelings. If you'll just trust *me.*"

"I do trust you." She leaned over and kissed him. "And I

191

love you. But I thought I loved Ian once too. I pledged to honor and obey him like a dutiful wife should. Yet ten months later I refused to leave Egypt. I refused to leave even though it was what he most wanted. I refused, and he's dead now. He's dead because I cannot play the loyal and obedient wife." She stroked his cheek. "Not even for you."

He tried to speak, but she covered his mouth with her hand. "I don't give a fig for what society thinks. All that matters is what you and I think—and feel. Let's go back to Egypt and spend the rest of our days exploring the desert." She paused. "And our nights exploring each other."

Dylan pulled her tight against him. "Wife, mistress, concubine," he said in a husky voice. "You can be anything you want, Charlotte, as long as it means we're together."

For a long moment she couldn't speak, relief flooding through her so that she had to fight back a sob. For nearly three years she believed that life was closed to her: happiness, love, passion done. She had buried herself in guilt as surely as Ian had been buried by desert rock. But these past few weeks with Dylan had made her dare to hope again. She had dared so much that she'd let her guard down, confessed her love, allowed herself to be vulnerable to a man once more—something she had sworn never to do.

Yet Dylan made her feel safe, protected, needed. And she no longer wanted to be the guilt-ridden widow. She wanted to be done with regrets, with guilt and grief.

"I promise not to leave you, Dylan," she said solemnly. "I'll stay by your side for as long as we love each other."

His expression softened. "Even if I take you all the way to Egypt?" He smiled.

"If I have to make the sacrifice . . ."

They both laughed.

She nestled against him again. "Every time I'm with you, it feels like I'm in the desert once more. Life suddenly seems hot and bright and filled with adventure."

"Aye." He bent down for her kiss. "And I have a hot adventure in mind for us just now, lass."

She laughed as he began to caress her shoulders. But she could just as easily have wept with joy. After so long a time, both the man she loved and Egypt were now within her eager grasp.

Too much good fortune often tempted the gods, but for now, Charlotte was happier than she had ever been or might ever be again.

Surely nothing could harm her now.

Chapter Thirteen

Dylan wasn't certain he would ever walk again.

Exhausted, he lay back, dimly aware of pans rattling downstairs and the aroma of cooked sausages. How many hours had they been up here making love? Three? Four?

As much as he feared his legs wouldn't support his wobbly weight, he pushed himself out of bed. This might be an unconventional household, but servants—even eccentric ones—were prone to gossip. He didn't want Charlotte to become a scandalous figure even if she did claim not to care about society's opinion. She was too fine a person to be the target of vicious lies and cruel insults.

He pulled his trousers on, noticing that the buttons were missing.

Charlotte laughed. "If you don't want to clutch your trousers all the way home, you'll have to borrow a pair of suspenders from Randall."

"It's your fault." He sat on the edge of the bed and pulled

on his shirt. "If you weren't so desirable, I wouldn't have been ripping my clothes off."

"For a man called the Lion, you certainly seem abashed by normal jungle behavior."

"Very funny." He straightened his sleeves, wondering where his gold cufflinks had gotten to. "And at the risk of disappointing you, I assure you that I am not the man they call the Lion."

"Of course you are." Charlotte sat up, one hand clutching the bedclothes, although it still offered him a tantalizing look at her bare shoulders and the swell of her breasts.

Dylan thought she was more tempting than a chest of gold from Rameses the Third's treasure house. "No, lass, I'm not."

"Well, if you're not the Lion, who is?"

"I don't know."

She gave him a skeptical look.

"I'm telling you the truth."

He wanted to be truthful with this woman, he *needed* to be truthful. No more subterfuge, no more evasions. He'd spent so many years playing a role that he hardly knew who was the real Dylan Pierce and who was the creation of gossip and necessity. But he no longer needed to wait until Samson gave him the results of his investigation. Ian Fairchild, Sir Thomas, Ahmed, Hughes, even Sir Reginald Grainger: all of them might be dishonest and unethical. But not Charlotte. On this he was going on instinct alone—and the searing memory of the past few hours spent in her arms.

She smiled at him, lowering the sheet so that both her sweetly rounded breasts were exposed to view. "I think you're afraid that I disapprove of your past. You're wrong. I don't hold those scandalous escapades against you. In fact, I rather like them."

He frowned. Except for those who knew the truth—like Samson—everyone else regarded him as the Dylan Pierce of scurrilous legend. Once or twice over the years he had met a woman who moved him, a woman who made him painfully aware of just how solitary and lonely he was. But then he realized it wasn't the Welshman with a gift for linguistics she fancied, it was the fellow who reputedly set a Cairo market on fire. It wasn't the man who loved poetry and dynastic wall paintings that women craved, it was the daring rake who kidnapped harem girls and romanced belly dancers.

Even more thrilling was the belief that he used his legendary skill and knowledge to uncover hidden tombs and temples, only to strip them of their treasure like a desert pirate. Women seemed to like the idea of a man who plundered, yet was scholarly: an unscrupulous ruffian with a civilized mind.

Regarded as a rogue who refused to give his heart, Dylan had had dozens of females vying for his attention and his touch. In that regard, the scandalous stories were correct. But he had not given his heart or his love to anything but Egypt . . . until now.

"Charlotte, the Lion is a thief. A man who loots archaeological sites, then sells the antiquities on the black market, where most of them are lost forever to the rest of the world." He looked at her for a long moment. "We've worked closely together every day for the past six weeks. Do you really believe I'm capable of such things?"

Her smile faded. She reached out her hand, and he took it.

"I know of your work these past two and a half years in Egypt. Clearly you've had a change of heart. No one could have worked as conscientiously as you have done at Nabesha, and here at the Collection." She squeezed his hand. "I don't hold your past against you."

"So you're not troubled by a man who loots temples and tombs?" he said quietly.

Her gray eyes seemed darker now, wary. "But you don't do that any longer."

"Charlotte." He took her by the shoulders. "I never did."

"If that's what you want me to believe, I won't argue with you."

"No need for argument. In fact, I can prove I never stole so much as a glass amulet from Egypt."

She looked puzzled. "How could you prove such a thing?"

"By taking you to see Hiram Tennant. He's retired now and lives in Scotland. But if it's proof you need, then he'll provide it."

"Hiram Tennant? Didn't he have something to do with investigating the illegal trade in antiquities?"

"He had everything to do with it, as did I." He paused. "Hiram was chief of the Antiquities Service here in London. I worked for him."

She sat back against the headboard, her long, tousled hair looking far more glorious than the polished brass behind it. "I don't understand."

"I was quite the boy wonder in school, able to translate fifteen languages. Some people can play the piano at three without so much as a single lesson, or sit a horse like a cavalry officer the first time they ride. Prodigies, they're called. I was a linguistic prodigy, and it did not go unnoticed."

"By the Antiquities Service?"

He nodded. "They approached me in my third year at Cambridge. I had already declared my intention of being an Egyptologist; they told me about an even better way to serve the past. Why excavate the artifacts when I could work to expose the men who plundered and looted them? I agreed. So I joined the Service as a clandestine agent, and they arranged for me to be expelled. I suggested a romantic escapade, but Hiram decided gambling in the lecture halls would suffice."

"Why would they want you to leave Cambridge in disgrace?"

"To better convince certain unscrupulous elements in archaeology to trust me. If I was to discover who ran the smuggling rings, I would have to seem as ambitious and disreputable as they were. Being expelled from Cambridge was just the first step."

"But that's terrible. It's a stain on your past, and totally unearned."

"Oh, the devil with university life. I was eager to leave Cambridge. Most of the dons knew less about their morning kippers than they knew of Egypt. Being asked to take on such an assignment was more thrilling than a dozen university degrees." Indeed, he could still feel the excitement of setting off at last on his great adventure.

"So the Antiquities Service sent you to Egypt."

"I went to Asia Minor and Syria first, trying to track down a gang of grave robbers along the Euphrates. That's where I first read *The Songs of Rajya* in Arabic." He gave her a stern look. "Which you still haven't bothered to read. I'll think you don't care for poetry if this keeps up, and that won't do at all."

"And why is that?" The serious expression in her eyes lightened somewhat.

"Because I refuse to spend the rest of my life with a woman who doesn't love poetry." He was not entirely joking.

"I started to read them last night. Then someone banged on the door at an ungodly hour, carrying Nefer in his arms."

The cat heard her name and lifted up her head from where she lay curled atop the dressing table. Dangling from her mouth was his cufflink, its three rose diamonds twinkling.

"Maybe I should read the poems aloud to you." He moved over to her side, needing to feel her in his arms once more, needing her warmth and softness, needing her own sexual hunger, which he now knew burned as hotly as his own. "Especially the one that speaks of soft thighs and their secret honey."

He ran his hands down her bare hip, until his fingertips

touched the pale golden curls between her legs.

Charlotte placed her own hand over his, stopping him from exploring further. "Poetry later. First tell me where you went after Asia Minor."

He lay back with a sigh. "I went to Egypt and made it known that I was an ambitious, greedy fellow eager to get my hands on a rich archaeological site. I promised collectors that I could get them anything from Cleopatra's death mask to marble statues of Rameses. Told them I cared little for scholarship but everything for gold."

He looked over at her. She watched him with a solemn expression. "In order to carry out my role, I sometimes had to resort to ugly methods, brutal ones."

"Is that why you dynamited the tomb of Pharaoh Thutmose?"

"Aye. Having to be a party to that nearly made me quit the Service, but at least I was able to expose the smuggling ring's contact in Alexandria. And that led to the recovery of a huge shipment of statues bound for the Continent."

"So all those stories about you, the drinking, the women . . . they were all fabrications."

He caught a note of wistfulness in her voice. "I admit I once had too great a fondness for whiskey, but since coming down with malaria, I've had to curb it. Alcohol can bring on an attack."

"Father had malaria too," she said, almost to herself.

Dylan leaned over and kissed her forehead.

She smiled at him. "And the stories about the women? Are any of them true?"

He had to laugh. "They're true."

"So you did make love on top of a pyramid?" She propped herself on one elbow.

"Never fear, Charlotte, I did. And a great many other places too."

"Did you really romance all those belly dancers?"

"I do admire a woman who knows how to move her body."

She cocked an amused eyebrow. "Harem girls?"

"Now there I drew the line. Any male familiar with the Moslem world knows you don't play about in a harem—unless you're willing to have your manhood lopped off." He grew serious. "But I never let myself get too close to any of the women, Charlotte. It wouldn't have been fair to bring someone into my life, which by necessity was one of deception and danger."

"But not now. You can't still be working for the Service?"

"No. When I met you back in Egypt, I had just quit. I was supposed to excavate at Deir el-Bahri, but the French had better funding and got the *firman* before I did. So when Sir Thomas offered me the Valley of Amun, I jumped at it. I looked on it as an opportunity to gain an honest reputation as an Egyptologist."

She sighed. "I shouldn't have asked you to turn it down. If you had taken over, you might have found the tomb of Princess Hatiri."

He looked at her in surprise. "Charlotte, you don't really believe the legend about Rameses's favorite concubine?"

Now it was her turn to look at him in surprise. "Of course I do. So did Father. There are three papyri from the Eighteenth Dynasty that tell how she was secretly buried to prevent the jealous queen from defiling her grave and stealing the riches Pharaoh had surrounded her with. And Herodotus himself wrote of the treasure of Hatiri."

"The old Greek mentions a lot of things; some of them are even true." He took her in his arms. "But there are no undisturbed royal tombs in the Valley of Amun waiting to be discovered. Your father worked there for decades. Don't you think he would have found such a tomb? And if not him, then surely his intrepid daughter."

"You're laughing at me."

"Just a little." He kissed the top of her head. "But you'd

as well search for Atlantis as the treasure of Princess Hatiri."

"Now you sound like Ian," she muttered.

He stiffened. The last thing he wanted was to be grouped with the martyred Mr. Fairchild. "Sorry to hear that. I only met him once, but I didn't think we had anything in common." *Aside from you,* he thought with dismay.

She sat up. "You've no reason to resent Ian. It's you I love. The funny thing is, if you'd had the chance, I think the two of you might have gotten along. He was half Welsh, you know."

"What!" That was too much for Dylan. He flung himself out of bed, feeling suddenly agitated. "That's impossible. His name was Fairchild."

"Fairchild was his father's name, but he did have a mother. And his mother was Welsh. I believe the family comes from Aberystwith. He spoke Welsh too—probably not as well as you—but he was just as proud of his heritage. In fact, when he was a boy, he sometimes took part in the *Eisteddfod.*"

"I don't want to hear any more."

He began searching for his shoes. Anything to distract him from the unpleasant news that Ian Fairchild and he shared not only a love for archaeology and Charlotte, but a Welsh background as well. And to hear that he participated in the Welsh bardic festival of *Eisteddfod* sent the blood rushing to his head. So Fairchild had a taste for poetry too.

Damn it all, but perhaps Charlotte only loved him because he reminded her of her late husband. Some part of him suspected that was the real reason she refused to become Mrs. Dylan Pierce. No matter how much she claimed to love him, Fairchild had come first. And he always would.

"You're working yourself up into a temper for nothing," she said softly. "I love you, Dylan. Ian is dead and gone. Don't let him or his memory come between us."

Taking a deep breath, he turned around. Charlotte lay naked on the bed, her hand outstretched. Only a man of stone could resist, and he had always been made of far-too-willing flesh. In a moment, he was on the bed beside her, pressing her against him.

"I won't mention Ian again," she whispered.

"You can speak of whomever you like, lass. I'll just have to learn not to be a jealous fool."

Jealous *and* guilty, he thought as he held her close. Like Charlotte, he too felt responsible for Fairchild's death in the cave-in. If he hadn't been so ill and feverish that day in the desert when Charlotte came riding out to stop him, maybe Fairchild would still be alive. But malaria, Charlotte's tearful pleas, and the prospect of sailing down the Nile with that Frenchwoman—all had combined to turn him into the irresponsible rogue once more. Yet he gladly accepted the guilt. For if Fairchild hadn't died, then he wouldn't be here now clutching a naked and very willing Charlotte.

She sat back, her mysterious gray eyes gazing into his. He only wished he could read her as easily as he read ancient Persian or Greek.

"I've never loved anyone as much as I love you," she said quietly.

"I'll try to remember that."

"No." She shook her head. "Try to *believe* it."

He smoothed back her hair. "I worked undercover for the Service too long, I'm afraid. It's not easy for me to believe— or trust—anything."

"Why did you quit, darling?" She stroked his cheek. "Was it because of the Cairo fire?"

He nodded. "It was one thing to put my own life at risk, or the lives of looters and criminals, but not innocent bystanders. Not children. My undercover activities had goaded someone into trying to kill me once. I was certain they would try again. And I couldn't let any more innocent people be harmed.

"Then too, I was tired of watching my back, tired of pretending to be someone I wasn't. After a decade spent in the company of greedy, unethical men, you get worried that maybe you don't know how to behave decently. I was proud of the work I did, but if I spent my whole lifetime trying to stop the smuggling, it wouldn't begin to be enough." He hugged her close again, burying his face in her fragrant white-gold hair. "All I wanted was to dig in the earth once more. I wanted to have my life back. I wanted to *have* a life."

They remained quiet, she tucked against him, her naked body feeling like satin.

"I've never told another woman this before," he said finally. "I've been responsible for exposing more than one smuggling ring. I have powerful enemies."

"I won't breathe a word." She kissed his forehead.

"I suspect you may have an enemy or two as well."

She gave a startled laugh. "Me?"

"Someone stole Nefer. They may not have harmed her, but I think it was a warning."

"That was probably just Ahmed being his usual disagreeable self. Besides, what would they be warning me against?"

"Working with me, perhaps." He thought a moment. "Or working on the Valley of Amun exhibit."

She shrugged. "I can't see why."

"How do you explain the scorpions?"

"They most likely crawled into the crates back in Africa. It happens all the time."

"Yes, yes, it does." But someone had been watching him last night. The person who returned Nefer? Or someone who meant him serious harm?

"Still, I feel like I'm back in the desert again, on my guard, trying to outwit the smugglers and thieves."

She held his face in her hands, looking searchingly into his eyes. "We have to stop letting the past affect the future. *Our* future."

He kissed her. "And how do you propose we do that?"

She pulled off his shirt once more. "This is a good way to start."

Then she proceeded to show Dylan that even though he had the scandalous reputation, her wildness more than matched his.

Charlotte brushed her hair, wanting to shake a finger at her reflection in the mirror. She'd never admit it, she was disappointed that the man she loved so deeply was not the legendary rogue called the Lion. Of course, she knew most of the stories about him were embroidered, more fiction than fact. Still there was something exciting about being in the company of such a dangerous, daring fellow.

She peeked at Dylan in the mirror. He was attempting to get dressed for the second time this morning, although from the sound of the fruit vendors and newspaper boys shouting from the square, it must be past noon.

Heavens, but she was a silly goose. Why, she could never respect him if he had been such a thieving rogue. And he did admit that most of those wild sexual escapades were true. Certainly he seemed to know more ways to please a woman than she had ever dreamed existed. She would have to read *The Songs of Rajya* as soon as possible, if for no other reason than to keep up with him.

She smiled at his reflection, enjoying his masculine smell, his clothes scattered among her things, although she feared Nefer had swallowed one of his cufflinks. No, the reality of Dylan Pierce was better than any fantasy concocted about the Lion. And he would always be *her* lion: strong and un-afraid.

Humming to herself, she pulled her hair back and fastened a bronze filigree pin about it to keep it in place. She wanted to let her hair fall down her back, like a young, unmarried girl. Since putting aside her widow's weeds, she felt as though she were coming out in society once more. Emerging into the world for the first time. She fluffed out the lavender ruffles that ran down her blouse, wondering how she had remained in somber black all these years.

He came to stand behind her, resting his hands on her shoulder. "I'd best be off. I promised Samson I'd meet with him later this afternoon, and I have to go home and shave. From the looks of your red cheeks, my bristly mug has scraped you raw."

She tipped back her head. "You should see what that scratchy face of yours has done to my thighs."

"If I had the time or the strength, lass, I would." His grin faded. "I hope I haven't dashed all your fancies, but I can't go on pretending to be the Lion any longer. It's just too blasted idiotic."

"I must confess to being a tiny bit disappointed, like learning there's no Santa Claus."

"I didn't say there was no Lion. I said that I didn't know who he was."

She turned around. "So how did you come to be called the Lion?"

He pulled her into his arms. "I'd been in Egypt about five years when I heard about a man involved in the black market who was called the Lion. That's not unusual. Smugglers and thieves often go by names other than their own. There was a smuggler in Upper Egypt who was known as the Falcon, until he was killed trying to escape over the cataracts."

"But why were you thought to be the Lion?"

"My own stupid fault. I had a mistress at the time, a demanding little belly dancer from Giza. Ayanna fell ill one day. She probably ate a chicken that had hung too long in the market. But she was convinced she was dying and accused my former mistress of trying to poison her."

"I'm not certain I want to hear this story." Charlotte raised an eyebrow.

He shrugged. "There's nothing much left to tell. Ayanna worked her cousins into such a lather, they were ready to bury the other poor woman alive. Wouldn't listen to a word

I said until I finally told them I was the Lion. That shut them up proper."

"Why did you do that?"

"These were men who earned their living from looting the sites. So I warned that if they harmed this other woman, I would see to it that no one involved in the smuggling would buy a single stolen artifact from them again."

"They believed you?"

"I already had a reputation in the black market, so it made sense to them. And to me too. As soon as I saw how impressed they were by my revelation, I decided to use it to my advantage. By pretending to be the Lion, I suddenly acquired all the cachet and influence that went with the real smuggler. It gave me entree into the most unsavory circles."

"But weren't you afraid the real Lion would track you down?"

"I think he did. It's very possible that the man who tried to have me killed in Cairo *was* the Lion. After all, I'd stolen his identity and was gathering secret information because of it."

Indeed, Dylan suspected that the Lion had something to do with the scorpions at the museum. Such a man not only wielded a great deal of power but possessed the gold to corrupt any number of Englishmen to carry out his orders.

"What a shame you could never capture him."

"I wish I had. I would have been able to close off one of the most lucrative black market routes. But he was too clever to take the bait. Since he was so successful at siphoning off many of the shipments intended for the Cairo Museum, I assume he has strong contacts with otherwise reputable archaeologists."

Although he looked pointedly at her wedding ring, she didn't notice. "But why was he called the Lion?"

He shook his head. "Never found that out. But last year, a gold Apis bull disappeared while in transit from Cairo to Alexandria. I'm certain the Lion was responsible."

"Even though we never found anything like a golden bull in the Valley of Amun, do you think we have something the Lion wants?"

"Perhaps. If so, I've not been able to discover what it is." Dylan gestured toward the closed door. "You know, we should get downstairs before the sun sets. Randall and the other servants will think I've ravished you a dozen times over."

She stepped back, adjusting the hem of her velvet skirt. "Nonsense. They'll be more proper than you realize and ask politely if we're done reading monographs, or some such thing."

Dylan only snorted in response.

"How odd," she said with a sigh. "All these years I thought the Lion was simply an arrogant, ambitious rogue called Dylan Pierce. I had no idea he was this master criminal you've painted."

"Are you content to learn I'm only arrogant, ambitious, and wild?"

"Oh, you're far more than that." She pulled his head down for a kiss but was interrupted by a rap on the door.

The door swung open and Lorrie peeked in. Her eyes twinkled with amusement. "Randall says that if the two of you are finished ravishing each other, he'll have Cook lay out breakfast downstairs."

Lorrie left as quickly as she appeared.

"I told you," Dylan muttered to a giggling Charlotte. "You know, I wouldn't be surprised to learn that footman of yours is the Lion. He's certainly brash enough."

Outside, a carriage stood motionless. Rain fell in a steady, dreary downpour, a brisk wind rustling the trees and bringing a chill that was unmistakably autumn. In such weather, passersby rushed past, clutching umbrellas, paying no mind to the brougham nor to the lone man inside it. As for the man in the carriage, his attention was fixed on the upper-story window of the stuccoed Belgravia mansion.

A while ago, he had glimpsed a figure move past. Someone with white-gold hair. He knew who that was—and he also knew she was naked. Damned harlot. Hadn't she caused enough trouble? But here she was, parading her flesh for all the world to see. And, of course, she wasn't alone. She hadn't been alone for weeks now, not since she met up with that drunken Welshman.

Dylan Pierce. The name had an ugly sound to it. He'd always thought so. Now he saw that the scoundrel had an ugly, dishonest nature as well. Bedding a grieving widow in broad daylight and with the fool servants aware of every disgusting move.

He'd seen her mother and siblings leave at dawn, not that he imagined their presence would have prevented those two from copulating under the same roof. All of London knew the Graingers were eccentric, shameless, troublesome creatures. If it weren't for Lady Margaret's blue blood and Sir Reginald's knighthood, the entire motley household would have been shunned and, possibly, exiled.

Charlotte moved before the window again. His eyes narrowed when he saw that she was wearing purple. He shook his head. A few hours playing the whore with Pierce and she had thrown off her mourning. Of course, it was obvious that Charlotte hadn't honestly mourned in a long time. He doubted she ever had. When had he ever known Sir Reginald's daughter to be anything but selfish, headstrong, and irritating? But even he did not imagine she would take up with Dylan Pierce so openly—and under the eyes of the servants as well.

It was all he could do not to burst into the mansion and surprise them both. But neither of them was worth the price of discovery.

What *was* priceless was his safety, and the safety of the material sent from the Valley of Amun. If those two buffoons thought they were going to ruin his plans again, they were in for a brutal awakening. But they had taken him by surprise.

How could he have foreseen that the two of them would meet up in London and take such a fancy to each other? Fancy indeed. He snorted at the thought. They were no better than rutting dogs.

He sat back and rapped on the roof of the carriage. With a loud slap of reins, the brougham driver set the horse to moving. Yes, that's what they were: dogs. Stupid, dirty, and exasperating.

Nothing he couldn't handle, nothing he hadn't handled expertly for many years. They were only dogs, after all.

But he was the Lion.

Chapter Fourteen

Samson Pope pointed toward a shadowy corner of the restaurant. "I've heard there's a secret entrance back there."

Dylan turned about in his seat, a forkful of grouse raised to his lips. "What about it?"

"The story is that the door was built so the Prince of Wales and Lillie Langtry could enter without being observed."

Samson pushed away his plate, his braised woodcock and rice untouched. He ate one meal a day, late in the evening; anything else, aside from biscuits and India tea, he considered unnecessary. And a dulling influence on his mental processes.

Dylan shrugged. "Don't see why the prince's shenanigans should interest me *or* an inspector of Scotland Yard, unless you've been hired by the Princess to keep an eye on the old goat."

"It just serves to remind me that deception is everywhere: in a restaurant on Maiden Lane, a clerk's office at the London Stock Exchange." He paused. "Or the Mayfair home of a retired scholar."

His friend looked up from eating. "You've found something on Sir Thomas?"

"Nothing out of the ordinary. Actually, my investigations revealed that his wife is the more interesting character. One might almost say tragic." He lowered his voice. "I fear she's a morphine addict."

"Lady Havers?" Dylan dropped his fork with a clatter. "I'd heard she had a fondness for alcohol. I saw her drink several glasses of sherry when I was there yesterday, but morphine?"

"Remember when she rang for her maid and demanded her medication?"

Dylan nodded.

"When Sir Thomas poured it out, I noted that it was a bluish syrup identical to liquid morphine. Immediately upon taking her 'medicine,' she became blissfully relaxed, almost unconscious. Alcohol, you know, intensifies the effects of morphine."

Dylan sat back in his chair. "My sympathies to the lady, then. I had a great-aunt who was given morphine after she broke her hip. She spent the last years of her life in a wretched state."

"I don't know how often Lady Havers drugs herself, but I will tell you that she seems to be the dominant personality in that household. There isn't a drapery or figurine in the mansion that hasn't been chosen by her, I warrant. Or didn't you notice?"

"I was too busy yelling at Sir Thomas. I just remember an awful lot of pink things in that room."

"Well, there were an awful lot of statues of naked men in that parlor as well, all depicted in a state of obvious arousal."

"What? The woman is close to sixty years old." Dylan shook his head. "Maybe Sir Thomas is to blame. It's possible that he shares Mr. Wilde's predilection for his own sex."

"I've been looking into the backgrounds of the individuals on your list, and Sir Thomas has no alarming vices, no sexual skeletons in the closet. Unlike his wife." Samson frowned. "It seems that Lady Havers is having an illicit liaison with Barnabas Hughes."

Dylan looked stunned. "That little old lady and Hughes?"

"She's a handsome woman, even if she is a bit mature for Hughes."

"I feel dirty about this. I don't care to invade the privacy of people who haven't done me any harm. Besides, I didn't ask for Thomas's wife to be investigated." He gestured to the waiter to bring the bill. "I'd rather not hear any more about the lady."

"I don't understand your sudden delicacy." He heard his own voice grow hard. "After all, you asked me to investigate both the woman you claim to love *and* her dead father."

Dylan flushed red. "That was before. Things have changed since then. In fact, I was going to tell you today that I wanted you to call off your investigation, at least the part relating to Charlotte and Sir Reginald."

Samson tried to contain his own irritation. He had just spent a number of hours investigating the people on Dylan's list; he hated to waste his time. And with the Waterloo Road murderer still at large, his professional talents could have been better spent.

"I can see you're in a conscience-stricken mood at the moment, so I won't continue. But your natural curiosity may soon return. If it does, you'll want this." Samson handed over a leather folder tied securely. "Everything we've learned about the people on your list is in there. Names, dates, a year-by-year account of their lives."

Dylan took the folder from him. "It's an unpleasant profession you're engaged in, my friend."

"How so? I uncover the past in order to prevent a future crime. Similar to what you did as an agent for the Antiquities Service, or didn't you need information on your enemies?"

Dylan stood up. "I had too many enemies. I still do. Now I'm afraid that Charlotte does as well."

"At least Nefer has been returned, and I believe we have Lady Havers to thank for it."

"Why do you think that?"

"Her parlor is littered with feline images, and she seemed alarmed to learn that Charlotte's cat had been stolen. She turned right upon Sir Thomas, demanding to know what this was all about."

"So she assumed he knew?"

"I'm sure he did. She made quite a point of saying how terrible a thing it was to do to a cat, how she hoped no harm befell the creature. And that night the cat turned up in your bedroom. Mere coincidence? I think not." Samson buttoned his sack coat. "Policemen do not believe in coincidence."

"Then it *is* Sir Thomas who works against us." A distracted Dylan handed over a fistful of bills to the waiter.

"Perhaps. All I do know is that despite her morphine addiction and drinking, Lady Havers rules the household *and* Sir Thomas. Make of that what you will." He stood up. "By the way, their mansion may be decorated in bad taste, but it's very expensive bad taste. I don't believe there is anything in either of the Haverses' background to explain this display of wealth."

"Thank you for the work you've done. Despite my bad temper, I do appreciate it."

"You scholar poets are too damned sensitive for your own good. It's a wonder you didn't get yourself killed in Egypt."

Dylan smiled at last. "The trick is not to get myself killed in London."

The two men walked out onto Maiden Lane, turning up their collars at the drizzling rain and chill.

Dylan debated as to whether he should head for the museum or return home. He desperately wanted to look over the material Samson had given him. Every impulse told him to read the report as soon as possible, but it was nearly five o'clock. Charlotte would be waiting for him at the museum. Even if two policemen had been assigned to patrol the galleries, he wouldn't breathe easy until she was by his side.

He briefly thought of dropping off the documents at his house, but he planned to bring Charlotte back to Russell Square tonight. Now that they'd become lovers, he couldn't bear the idea of spending even one night away from her. Their first time together had been wonderful, but this evening he wanted to make love to her in his own home, not beneath her family's roof, even if Lady Margaret and the others were out of town. And he dared not leave the material lying around his rooms where she might happen upon it.

The leather folder felt heavy in his hands. Samson had done a thorough job in his investigations, perhaps too thorough. After he had the chance to read the report, he knew he would have to share whatever he learned with Charlotte. Their life together couldn't begin with deception. Too much of his life had already been marked by lies, even if for a noble cause. He prayed that Charlotte's father was as blameless and ethical as his reputation indicated.

"I've got a mountain of paperwork back at the office, so I'll head for the Underground station." Samson went a few steps, then stopped. "Oh, I thought you might like to know that Ian Fairchild was a Welshman. Funny, isn't it? It seems the two of you have more in common than just the widow."

Dylan frowned. "He was only half Welsh."

"One more thing about Fairchild . . ."

"What now?"

"It was my understanding that the man died in a cave-in."

"He did. In a newly excavated tomb."

Samson pointed to the folder that Dylan had tucked under his arm. "Overcome your scruples and look over the material relating to Fairchild."

"Why?"

"It appears that the man was trained as an engineer, not

an Egyptologist. In fact, before he started working in Egypt, he spent three years building bridges."

"An engineer?" Dylan felt his breath quicken. "Then he, above all men, would have known how to secure the walls of the tomb."

"Exactly." Samson took a deep breath of the cold air. "Unless someone sabotaged the excavation without his knowledge."

"But who? And why?"

He shrugged. "The sands of Egypt are your territory, not mine. I only speculate that Mrs. Fairchild's husband was murdered. Unless you wish to believe it was mere coincidence that Fairchild died in a cave-in that an engineer could easily have prevented."

"No." Dylan looked down at the leather folder, his hand clenched tight about it. "Like you policemen, I don't believe in coincidence either."

He hated her. Charlotte imagined she could feel his hatred like an icy rain against her neck. She glanced over her shoulder quickly. Barnabas Hughes sat a few feet away, glaring at her instead of the papers spread out before him on the table.

With a sigh, she turned back to her notes. She refused to let Hughes's resentment mar this otherwise wonderful day. First, Nefer had been returned, safe and sound, with even her ruby collar intact. Then she and Dylan had become lovers.

She shut her eyes, remembering how it felt to have his strong body moving within her. How exciting, yet comforting, it was to lie next to him in bed, drowsy and tender from lovemaking. She had missed such intimacy since Ian died, missed it more than she knew. And now, after so long a time, Dylan Pierce had entered her life and her heart. She couldn't believe her good fortune. And to think that she would be returning to Egypt with him in November. Not even the angels could know such bliss.

She felt that bitter, accusing gaze once more. This time she turned around with an angry stare of her own.

"Is something wrong, Mr. Hughes?"

He looked down his large, sharp nose at her. Hughes was a man of middle years, but exceedingly robust and muscular. If she hadn't already been witness to his vast knowledge of Egyptology, she might have taken him for a dockworker.

"I didn't expect to see you here today." His voice always reminded her of falling gravel. "It's Sunday."

"I sometimes work on Sunday."

Indeed, she enjoyed being at the Collection on Sundays, when only Dylan and one or two other curators chose to work in the silent galleries. Today, however, she would have preferred the bustle and shouts of Covent Garden to sharing the museum with Hughes.

Nefer, who was curled in Charlotte's lap, let out a soft meow. No doubt she sensed her mistress's tense mood.

Hughes's grim expression darkened even more. "I see that the famous cat has returned. Aren't we the fortunate ones?"

"If you have an objection to either my cat or me, I would prefer you voice it straight out and not resort to these petty insults you're so fond of."

He sat back with a mocking smile. "And have you go running to Mr. Pierce, who would then have me sacked, or at the very least transferred to one of the Colvilles' lesser museums in Glasgow or York?"

"I am quite capable of handling you without running to Mr. Pierce."

"All right, then." He nodded. "I don't hold with uneducated females coming to the Collection and having the run of the place. I've worked in archaeology for twenty years and studied the classics when I was at Oxford. So explain to me why everything in the upcoming exhibit has to pass through your dainty hands first?"

"That's not true. I haven't taken so much as a peek at the mummies that arrived."

"Only because you've been too busy rummaging through the crates like a lady looking for a favorite ribbon among her hatboxes."

Charlotte cursed silently to herself. He'd love for her to fly into a temper. "I worked in the Valley of Amun alongside my father and then my husband for many years. I know this material a thousand times better than you can ever hope to."

He snorted.

"And as for uneducated, I've met dozens of fellows who bought or slept their way through university, so I'm hardly awed by your attendance at Oxford."

"Sir Thomas was right about you." He turned his attention back to his papers. "You've more arrogance than the Emperor Napoleon."

She stood up, cradling Nefer in her arms. The cat purred loudly. "You seem to possess an imperial amount of arrogance yourself. As for Sir Thomas, he knows less about the Valley of Amun—and me—than even you do."

"Clearly we both know you far less than our dashing Mr. Pierce does. But then, Sir Thomas and I haven't spent our youth bedding every female on two continents. I can see that such expertise has done much to reawaken your interest in Egyptology."

It was all she could do to prevent herself from commanding Nefer to attack him. The cat's claws would have made fine work of Hughes's wiry graying hair.

"And I see that your resentment of both of us stems entirely from jealousy."

"Jealous? Of a drunken, whoring Welshman and a brash widow?" His contemptuous gaze took in her frilly lavender blouse and purple velvet skirt. "Although it is evident that your mourning period is decidedly over."

Rarely had anyone wished her this much ill, at least not openly. For the first time, she wondered if Hughes had

217

played a role in both Nefer's theft and the appearance of the scorpions in the gallery. She fought back the impulse to question him about both occurrences; it wasn't wise to prod such a man too far, especially when there was no one else around.

"As much as I'd love to stay here and trade insults, I have to check something in the upstairs exhibition hall."

"I'll miss you dreadfully." He smirked. "Do hurry back."

She grabbed a sheaf of papers. As she walked past his table, she flung them down. "I read over your comments regarding the pigments used on the statues from the site. As you can see, I've made the necessary corrections."

His face grew red with anger. "*You* are correcting *my* notes?"

"Someone has to. For example, the medium that binds the pigments on the paint is gum arabic, a resin derived from the Egyptian acacia tree. You wrote that the medium was unknown." She paused. "Perhaps it is to those who spent too many years reading the classics at Oxford."

"You insufferable witch!" He stared at her with open loathing.

"And you might like to write down that Middle Kingdom red paint was composed of iron oxide and arsenic." She shook her head. "I've found that a working knowledge of chemistry is far more useful than Virgil."

"Take care, Mrs. Fairchild. Or whoever took your cat might decide to steal you away as well."

She felt a shiver of fear but only shrugged in response.

"Well, if they do, I suggest you read a paper on dynastic wall paintings that I collaborated on seven years ago with my father. It will prevent you from erroneously listing the ingredients of the plaster." She opened the door to the work-room. "Those ingredients are gypsum, anhydrite, crushed limestone, and Nile silt. I'll write that down for you, if you like."

As she closed the door, she heard him shout after her. And this time he called her something far worse than a witch.

Charlotte heard Dylan enter the museum before she saw him, his deep voice calling out a greeting to one of the policemen. Nefer ran to meet him; her purrs and delighted howls echoed down the empty galleries.

When she turned the corner, she smiled to see that he was carrying the cat in one arm, like an oversized baby.

"You spoil her more than I do," she said when she finally caught up to them at the door to Dylan's office.

"I thought you would be downstairs in the workrooms." Dylan let Nefer jump to the ground, then leaned over to embrace her.

She hugged him. "There's no one here but the policemen and Hughes. And you know what bad company Hughes is."

Dylan pulled back. "He's not said anything to upset you, has he? I swear, I've held my temper this long because I know he expected to be named director of this exhibition rather than me. I understand that his pride has been hurt. But I'll only tolerate his foul moods so long, especially where you're concerned."

"I can handle his moods, but I worry about his resentment of us. It runs deeper than I suspected. In fact, I wouldn't be surprised to learn that it's taken a treacherous turn."

"Do you think he had something to do with the scorpions?" Dylan asked.

Someone cleared his throat nearby. Hughes leaned against the wall, watching them.

"I was wondering where you'd run off to, Mrs. Fairchild."

Charlotte stepped back, uneasy at being found talking about him with Dylan. The man's mocking smile told her that she'd behaved exactly as he expected.

"What do you want, Hughes?" Dylan didn't bother to conceal his irritation.

Hughes pushed himself away from the wall. "A message

has just been delivered for Mrs. Fairchild." He held out a letter. "The policeman at the rear entrance accepted it for her. Seems the boy went first to Belgravia, then was sent here."

"For me?" She hurried to take it from him. "I hope nothing's wrong with Mother or Catherine."

"It's an invitation to dinner at the Colvilles." Although Hughes spoke to Charlotte, his eyes were on Dylan. "Dinner tonight, by the way, which seems peremptory even for them." He held up two more pieces of paper. "You received one as well. As did I."

"Seems an interesting guest list," Dylan said.

Something in his tone made Charlotte glance over at him. "Why are we receiving dinner invitations at such short notice?"

"It *seems* like a royal command." Hughes laughed. "Of course, for those of us who work with antiquities in Britain, the Colvilles *are* royal. At least their coffers are."

"Well, why don't we just wait and see what the Colvilles want." Dylan kicked his office door open.

Charlotte walked over to him. "I wonder if Aunt Hazel has been invited. If not, I think I'd do well to bring her along."

Dylan shook his head. "Let's leave palm readers out of this."

Hughes cleared his throat again, making a show of looking at his pocket watch. "Seems we have very little time to prepare for the Colville dinner. And they do hate to be kept waiting."

"That's true. We'll barely have time to change as it is." She noticed that Dylan held a leather folder under his arm. She touched it. "What's this?"

"Nothing. I'll show you later. Wait here a moment." He disappeared into his office, leaving Charlotte in the corridor with Hughes, who was now whistling.

When Dylan reappeared, the folder was gone. He took out

his keys and locked the office door, pulling on it twice to make certain it was secured.

She moved closer to him, taking comfort in his presence. Let Hughes spit out venom all he liked. Together, she and Dylan could take on Hughes, Ahmed, Sir Thomas, and the Lion too, if he were in England. She was tired of the disapproval of these men, their resentment, their need to judge her every move. And now she bristled at such disapproval even more because it was also directed at Dylan.

Well, she didn't give a damn what any of them had to say, not even Mr. and Mrs. Colville. Although she had to admit that she was nervous about the sudden invitation.

She curled her hand about Dylan's arm as the two of them walked down the corridor.

"What do you think the Colvilles want?" she asked in a low voice, mindful of the watchful Hughes.

"A lively and unpredictable evening," Hughes piped up as they passed. "And, by heaven, I'm going to see that they get it."

Chapter Fifteen

Dylan had a bad feeling about this dinner invitation.

The Colvilles rarely entertained in the summer or autumn; something about the planets not being favorably aligned until after the winter solstice. So why did they suddenly decide to throw a small soiree in September—and with only three hours' notice?

He gave his hat to the butler, who ushered him into the marble foyer of the Colvilles' Mayfair mansion.

"Is Sir Thomas Havers here?" He wanted to verify his suspicion that the old man had been invited. In fact, he suspected that Havers had somehow orchestrated this evening's get-together.

"Sir Thomas arrived earlier." The butler pointed toward the French doors at the other end of the foyer. "I believe he's taking in the air with the other gentleman, sir."

"And who would that gentleman be?"

"Mr. Barnabas Hughes. Excuse me while I inform Mrs. Colville that you're here."

Those two men chatting together definitely did not bode well. Dylan now had no doubt that the old man had instigated this dinner, and for no good purpose. No doubt he'd been whispering in the receptive ears of Mr. and Mrs. Colville, and this unexpected invitation was the result.

Dylan was certain that both Sir Thomas and Hughes intended to discredit him. It seemed he was to have no choice but to play Caesar to their Cassius and Brutus. He was surprised at how much he disliked the prospect of losing his position at the Colville Collection. Was he so ambitious, then? Apparently he was.

Initially, he had asked to oversee the Valley of Amun exhibit as a way of assuaging his guilt over the death of Ian Fairchild. But the longer he worked on the exhibit, the more he wanted his tenure at the Colville Collection to go well. Being sponsored by one of the two greatest museums in Britain would do much to restore his reputation. More important, it would pay for many years of excavation in Egypt. But with both Sir Thomas and Hughes working against him, he suspected that responsibility for the exhibit was about to be taken away from him. That sank any hope of his one day being appointed director of the Colville Collection itself.

If he'd been in a better mood, he might have laughed at himself. Ever since Lord Barrington died three years earlier, the post of director of the Colville Collection had remained vacant. Dozens of distinguished and ambitious scholars had applied for the position, yet the Colvilles had not yet appointed an overall director. He'd been a fool to imagine that his work on the Valley of Amun exhibit would convince them that he was the best man to lead the museum into the twentieth century. It seemed he would be heading back to Africa sooner than expected. At least that would make Charlotte happy.

Where was she anyway?

She had insisted they arrive separately tonight. Perhaps she thought to give the lie to any rumors of a tryst between

223

them; she might have even reverted to her widow's weeds for the occasion. After what they'd shared in the early morning hours, if she had retreated once more behind those black dresses, it would deepen his already dark mood.

He hadn't gone two steps before Charlotte peeked her head out of a side parlor.

"I thought I heard your voice," she said. "Sir Thomas and Hughes are outside, smoking cigars and acting far too satisfied with themselves. I believe a nasty little plot is being hatched. Thankfully, Mrs. Colville hasn't come downstairs yet."

"Where's Mr. Colville and Lady Havers?"

"Lady Havers was indisposed, and Mr. Colville is in here." She gestured to the room behind her. "He's having his palm read."

"Don't tell me you brought Aunt Hazel."

"Keep your voice down." With a quick look behind her, Charlotte shut the parlor door.

He was glad to see that she looked as bright and warm as the Egyptian sun in a gown of yellow satin, amber beads about her neck and two yellow plumes bobbing in her upswept hair.

"Of course I brought Aunt Hazel. Her opinion weighs heavily with the Colvilles. After all, I doubt they invited us tonight because they want us to sample their kidney pudding."

"I'm sure that Sir Thomas is going to try to engineer my dismissal from the Collection."

"Exactly. That's why Aunt Hazel is here. If need be, she'll even use her crystal ball. I told her to bring it."

"Crystal ball? Lass, I need to answer any objections Sir Thomas brings against me with cold, hard facts. No crystal balls, no tea-leaf reading, no hocus-pocus."

"If you believe the Colvilles give a whit about cold, hard facts, then you're crazier than Uncle Louis." Shaking her head, Charlotte ducked back into the parlor.

"Uncle Louis must be as mad as a hatter," Dylan said to himself.

A loud meow echoed in agreement. He turned around to see Nefer stretched out on a plush divan by the stairway, looking as regal as Nefertiti.

"Naturally she brought you along," he replied as the cat resumed her grooming.

Well, he'd cast his fortunes with the lovely widow, and that meant his life now included not only Charlotte but her eccentric family *and* her cat. He must love the woman to distraction to allow himself to get involved with such a tribe.

So this was romantic love. It shook him as badly as malarial fever; it made him feel vulnerable, yet somehow enervated. Before this morning, he'd wondered if making love to her would cause him to view their relationship differently. Maybe what he had been feeling all this time was lust, not love. What did he know of a deep love between a man and a woman, or heartfelt romance? The only romance that had ever been real to him was the romance of the desert, of the undiscovered and the unexplored. Everything else was sentiment and hunger. Until Charlotte.

Now here she was, gazing into crystal balls with Aunt Hazel, while he was left to stare at the row of baroque bronzes that ringed the foyer. Since he had no intention of joining Hughes and Sir Thomas on the veranda, he might as well give himself a tour of the private art treasures of the Colvilles. Rumor had it that somewhere in their mansion hung two self-portraits of da Vinci.

He had barely inspected three bronzes when he heard footsteps on the winding marble staircase.

"Mr. Pierce, how delightful that you were able to make it this evening." Mrs. Colville raised her jewel-encrusted fan in greeting.

He'd always thought her one of the most elegant women he'd ever seen: tall, erect, silver-haired, with a profile that

225

was positively Roman. In an earlier age, she would have made an impressive Vestal Virgin.

"I'm honored to be invited, madame. I've seen the artwork at your Richmond residence but only heard dazzling hints of what you have here in Mayfair."

If he wasn't mistaken, part of that art collection was decorating her at that moment. Her gold earbobs were sixth-century Greek, while the glittering brooch pinned to her burgundy lace gown surely had once graced a Byzantine empress.

She held out her hand, and he bowed over it. "I fear that as time goes on, these treasures have become burdensome. I know now that some objects are cursed, or bear the ill luck of their former owners. Twenty years ago my husband sold everything at all connected with Marie Antoinette and the doomed Capets. Looking back, we were reckless to even touch such accursed objects, let alone acquire them."

"I would welcome the opportunity to see some of these treasures, ill-starred or otherwise."

"Oh, I fear that the lateness of the hour precludes a lengthy tour. And anything more cursory would not do the collection justice." She linked her hand about his arm, pulling him gently toward her. "I want you to know beforehand that I believe you are a noteworthy scholar, Mr. Pierce, even if you did translate those unsuitable poems. And I am certain that your professional future will not be at all impugned by whatever accusations are directed at you this evening."

He frowned. "Excuse me, Mrs. Colville, but if you're taking the Valley of Amun exhibit away from me, I'd rather be informed as soon as possible."

"Later, Mr. Pierce." She patted his arm.

The butler entered, bowing low. "Dinner, madame."

At the same moment, the parlor door banged open. A woman in flowing robes stood at the entrance.

"We are finished here, my dear Edwina," she announced in a tremulous voice. "You should be comforted to know that Soames's health will improve by the fifteenth of October. And by Christmas, your youngest daughter will give birth to a healthy son. Only take care that the infant sleeps in a room that faces west."

Mrs. Colville clasped her hands together. "What marvelous news you bring us, my dear Mrs. Dunsmore."

This had to be Aunt Hazel. Dylan stared at the woman who now moved into the foyer. She had blond hair nearly as white as Charlotte's, and light-colored eyes as well. Obviously this was the branch of the family that Charlotte most resembled, but he hoped the resemblance stretched only to physical appearance.

The older woman's golden-white hair was not respectably pinned up, but spilled out in a wild mass of curls that fell to her waist. And over what appeared to be an ordinary blue gown, Aunt Hazel wore a coat of silvery, shimmering material, with enormous flowing sleeves. When she stepped under the light from the chandelier, he noticed that she held a crystal ball in one hand, and that every one of her fingers boasted a large ring, each of the gemstones a different vibrant color. Despite her dramatic appearance, he had to admit that Aunt Hazel was not unattractive. Rather, she looked like a lovely, lunatic fairy.

Charlotte entered the foyer with Mr. Colville by her side,

"I presume this is your aunt, Mrs. Hazel Dunsmore?" Dylan asked.

"Of course I'm her aunt." Aunt Hazel turned her gray-eyed gaze upon him. "Anyone can see she is the daughter of my beloved brother, who even now watches over us all from the Great Beyond."

He bowed his head. "I am honored to finally meet you. I've heard a great deal about you and your husband Louis. Allow me to introduce myself. I'm—"

"Stop." She raised her crystal ball so that it nearly touched her nose. "I see exactly who and what you are, young man." She squinted at the ball. "You are not what you seem, even

227

to those who love you. You are a true Celt, stubborn and suspicious. Your name is Dylan, which means 'born by the sea,' but it is not the sea that draws you, it is the desert, and—and—"

How could anyone, even the gullible Colvilles, fall for this claptrap?

"And?" he asked, ignoring a warning look from Charlotte.

Aunt Hazel looked up with a wide grin. "And you had carnal relations with a woman on top of the Great Pyramid!"

Mrs. Colville clapped in approval. "Mrs. Dunsmore is unbelievable, isn't she, Mr. Pierce?"

Dylan could only shake his head. "Utterly unbelievable."

As impossible as it seemed, the evening got worse.

Sir Thomas and Hughes dominated the dinner conversation. They boasted of every antiquity they had stumbled across until one would think they had discovered not only the ancient Lost Ark, but the still breathing body of Noah.

Aunt Hazel occasionally interrupted with some strange pronouncement that had nothing to do with reality as he knew it. Her last comment was, "Watch well the marsupials at the zoo, for winter touches them first with her deadly frost."

The Colvilles nodded gravely after everything she said, so that Dylan began to wonder if they spoke in a secret code.

The one bright note about the dinner was that he had been seated next to Charlotte. When the conversation became too bizarre, he had only to turn in her direction, feel her arm brush against his, smell the enchanting fragrance that was Charlotte, or look into her lively eyes, and know that she at least was real, beautiful and wondrous.

Just now she was dabbing at her mouth with a linen napkin. "Don't make so many faces every time Aunt Hazel says anything," she said under her breath. "The Colvilles won't like it."

He pretended to retrieve his own napkin. "It's not your

aunt," he whispered. "It's this swill we're being forced to eat."

The Colvilles obviously spent all their wealth on art treasures and none of it on food. He imagined he could rummage up a more edible meal from a Whitechapel dustbin.

"And you said that you ate a monkey in the Congo." She peeked over at him, her eyes bright with amusement.

He leaned closer to her. "I did, and it tasted a far sight better than this."

She giggled. "Don't let Aunt Hazel hear you. She's already upset about the marsupials at the zoo."

"Probably because we're eating some of them right now."

Charlotte burst into laughter, hurriedly covering her mouth with a napkin.

"I see that we're boring the lady and gentleman across the table with our dreary talk of lost temples." Sir Thomas drummed his fingers along his bowl of kidney pudding which, like most of the meal, had gone untouched.

"Not at all," Dylan said. "I always did love tall tales. Why don't you relate the one where you stumble upon a stone tablet bearing the Ten Commandments? The two of you seem to have found everything else."

"Arrogant bastard," Hughes spat at him, then seemed to remember where he was. "Oh, please forgive me, Mrs. Colville, Mr. Colville. It's just that this wastrel here is living up to his vulgar reputation. I marvel he dares call himself an archaeologist at all."

"Vulgarity didn't stop me from finding the lost city of Beni Alaan six years ago." Dylan sat back, arms crossed across his chest.

"Sheer luck was responsible for your discovery of the city of Beni Alaan." Sir Thomas flung his napkin onto the table.

"Luck? So says every mediocre man about his better." Dylan smiled wider. He assumed he had already lost the position. Hughes and Havers were acting far too sure of themselves. From this point on, it mattered little what he said or did.

"It's a shame that neither you nor Hughes managed to excavate a site that you were also responsible for finding," he went on. "Always riding on the coattails of others. Never being the true discoverer, never being first."

"Dylan, I don't think this is the tack to take," Charlotte murmured.

"Better to be second than to be cursed." Hughes pointed a beefy finger at him. "It's just as we reported, Mr. Colville. Dylan Pierce has brought ill fortune wherever he's gone. Why, the scoundrel almost burned Cairo to the ground four years ago."

As always, Dylan grew tense at any mention of the Cairo fire. He was grateful for Charlotte's sympathetic smile.

"Not that again. Soon you'll hold me responsible for masterminding the Great Train Robbery."

"You haven't the brains for masterminding anything; you're simply a man who brings bad luck wherever he goes." Sir Thomas nodded toward Charlotte. "As does Mrs. Fairchild."

"Is that your scholarly assessment, Sir Thomas?" she asked.

"This doesn't require a scholar, Mrs. Fairchild. Did your father not die of a mysterious fever? Was your first foreman not killed by a scorpion?" His expression grew more bitter. "And did you not prevent your husband from leaving Egypt—with Pierce's assistance, by the way—resulting in his tragic death?"

Dylan heard Charlotte's sharp intake of breath. He reached out and took her hand. "We've heard enough, old man."

"I don't think Mr. and Mrs. Colville have." Hughes leaned forward. "Ever since you were appointed director of the Valley of Amun exhibit, the museum has received threatening letters."

Charlotte and Dylan looked at each other in surprise. "We've heard nothing about that," she said.

"I'm afraid that it's true." Mr. Colville sighed. "My wife and I received a number of anonymous notes over the summer. All written by the same hand apparently, and all warning us of dire tragedy if the exhibit opens."

"It's probably Ahmed," she murmured to Dylan.

"We didn't want to trouble you with this, Mr. Pierce." Mrs. Colville gave a gracious wave of her fan. "You were so busy, and Mrs. Dunsmore assured us that the stars were favorable for the exhibit."

Aunt Hazel thumped the table with one hand. "The spirits of the desert have a song to sing. Let them sing it in two days."

While everyone stared at her in silence, she turned her attention once more to the shriveled asparagus.

"Well, I believe that the stars have changed their alignment." Sir Thomas cast a wary eye in Aunt Hazel's direction. "First we have Mrs. Fairchild's Egyptian cat being stolen."

"But she was returned," Charlotte broke in.

"Yes, and to the very bedchamber of Mr. Pierce, here," Hughes said in a grim voice. "Very suspicious."

"And then there are the scorpions." Sir Thomas exchanged glances with Mr. Colville.

Mr. Colville sighed. "I must admit I was troubled when Sir Thomas informed me this morning that three live scorpions were found in the Valley of Amun gallery. *Three* of them."

"Most unlucky, most unlucky indeed." Mrs. Colville shivered.

"Exactly." Sir Thomas looked triumphant. "Moreover, they appeared just as Mrs. Fairchild and Mr. Pierce entered the gallery. Almost as if the creatures were waiting for them."

"Oh, come now, Sir Thomas." Dylan reached for his goblet and swallowed the bitter claret in one gulp. Hang his malaria. He felt like getting drunk tonight. "You'll have us believing in fairies and dragons next."

Sir Thomas ignored him. "Even now, your museum is crawling with policemen—"

"Only two," Charlotte protested.

"One policeman would be too much. Why is Scotland Yard there, anyway? I'll tell you. Because even the metropolitan police believe something dangerous is about to happen at the Colville Collection." Sir Thomas lifted both hands as if in supplication. "Is it any wonder that I advise barring both of these people from the museum? And, of course, canceling the Valley of Amun exhibit."

"Cancel the exhibit?" Charlotte squeezed Dylan's hand so tight, he winced. "For three years, everything recovered from the Valley has lain forgotten, hidden away in crates. Gathering dust until Mr. and Mrs. Colville graciously requested the Cairo Museum release the artifacts to the Collection. In two months, the world will finally see how nobly my father spent the last years of his life. Do you really imagine that I will allow you to keep my father's work from receiving the proper recognition just because you blame me for Ian's death?"

"You *are* to blame," the old man shot back. "Look, I've done what I can to warn you, Mr. and Mrs. Colville. If these people continue at the Collection, I cannot vouch for anyone's safety."

"Is that a threat, Sir Thomas?" Dylan asked. "You'd do better to go back to stealing cats."

"How dare you accuse me of taking that filthy cat," Sir Thomas said. "You drunken whoremonger."

"Fit only for drinking and bedding the ladies," Hughes added.

"It is just as our Mrs. Dunsmore has foretold," Mrs. Colville said mournfully to her husband, who sat shaking his head. "There is an ancient animosity among these men that cannot be remedied."

"I agree." Mr. Colville turned to Hughes. "That is why we must dismiss you from our service. I'm sorry to have to let you go, Mr. Hughes, especially after you've worked for us these past ten years. But I fear you leave us no choice."

"What?" Hughes's jaw dropped open. "You're dismissing *me?*"

"Sir Thomas, we also request that you do not attempt to enter the museum any longer, even as a paid visitor," Mr. Colville added.

"I—I don't understand," Sir Thomas said in a shaky voice. "Why in the world are you doing this?"

"After a lengthy discussion of the events both in Egypt and here, we have concluded that it is the two of you who are causing the problems." Mrs. Colville pointed to Aunt Hazel, who gave her niece a quick smile. "Our astute Mrs. Dunsmore has helped us to see where the real curse lies."

"What does that mean?" Hughes shouted.

"It lies in your ambition and jealousy, gentlemen." Mr. Colville closed his eyes, as if trying to shut out the angry stares of both men. "You have done little else except rail against Mrs. Fairchild and Mr. Pierce. So much negative energy might soon make my poor wife swoon. Most unpleasant."

"The two of you are consumed with resentment and envy, and that attracts unhappy spirits quicker than any Egyptian curse." Mrs. Colville smiled at Dylan. "Mr. Pierce is at least young enough to learn to curb his ambition."

Dylan didn't know what to say. He was as stunned as Sir Thomas and Hughes.

"I'll try," he said finally.

Mrs. Colville tapped him on the shoulder with her fan. "In addition, your obvious gift for linguistics is clear proof that you have lived many times before, an excellent asset for a museum director to possess."

Aunt Hazel waved a bejewelled finger at him. "My spirit

233

guide tells me that you were once chief scribe under Pharaoh Seti."

"You see?" Mrs. Colville said solemnly. "What more could we ask for?"

"I don't believe this." Hughes pounded the table with his fist, causing the cruet of vinegar to topple over.

Mr. Colville ignored him. "That is why we have decided to offer Mr. Pierce the position of director of the Colville Collection."

Dylan looked at Charlotte, who seemed as flabbergasted as he was.

Hughes swore under his breath, but Sir Thomas, oddly enough, just sat back and watched Dylan through steepled fingers.

Something wasn't quite right. Despite his elation at being offered the position, Dylan's enthusiasm was tempered. "I would be honored to serve as director. However, you may wish to postpone your decision until I have mounted the Valley of Amun exhibit. After all, you might not like the results."

"No need for that. Mrs. Dunsmore looked into her crystal ball months before you arrived and said the Valley of Amun exhibit would be an astounding success." Mr. Colville rose from his chair, his tall, gaunt frame slowly straightening.

"You dismiss me—after ten years' faithful service—then turn around and give some drunken looter the run of the place!" Hughes stood up, kicking his chair so that the heavy carved wood landed with a crash on the floor. "You deserve whatever happens to the lot of you—and your infernal museum!"

Dylan pushed back his own chair. "You brought this on yourself, Hughes."

"Look at you." Hughes laughed, his gravelly voice making the sound hurtful to the ears. "You did nothing but lie and steal back in Egypt, and now you're playing the gentleman. You think you've won. Think you've got the Collection in one hand and the pretty widow in the other, don't you?"

"Take care, Hughes," He warned.

"We really cannot have any more of this quarreling," Mrs. Colville said. "Unless you desist, I will have you escorted from the house, Mr. Hughes. You jar the very ether with your rage."

"Before you escort Mr. Hughes from the premises, I hope you will let him—and me—make our final case to you." Sir Thomas held up his hand to silence the protests that rose from the Colvilles and Dylan. "All I ask is that you let me read a single piece of paper."

"What's this?" Dylan asked, not liking the expression on Sir Thomas's face.

"Please, Mr. and Mrs. Colville," Sir Thomas continued. "One last request from a colleague who has worked with you for many decades. Out of respect for my dear wife, if nothing else."

The Colvilles nodded to each other. "Very well." Mr. Colville sat down again, while Sir Thomas left the dining room.

Charlotte turned to Dylan. "What is he talking about?"

He shook his head. Hughes sat down as well, still radiating anger, but calmer now, almost smug.

When Sir Thomas returned to the dining room, he held a leather folder in his hands.

"Where in blazes did you get that?" Dylan felt a rush of anger. And dread.

"Isn't that the folder you left in your office this afternoon?" Charlotte asked.

"Yes, it is." Hughes smiled at him. "I needed something in your office after you and Mrs. Fairchild left. Needed it desperately. I fear I had to resort to breaking the lock."

"So you broke into my office and stole my papers." Dylan wanted to pummel the fellow. "You've no right to them."

"Everything that is in the museum belongs rightfully to the Colvilles." Sir Thomas calmly pulled the sheaf of papers from the folder.

His stomach turned over. "You're both deceitful pigs."

"Dylan, what is this all about?" Charlotte tugged at his arm. "Tell me."

He took a deep breath before facing her. "Charlotte, I was going to show you those papers. I swear it on my life. Please remember that." He grabbed her hand. "And remember how much I love you."

For the first time since he'd known her, she looked frightened. "Is it so awful?" she whispered.

He felt as if his world was about to crash in on him. "Yes."

Charlotte suddenly wanted to get up and run from the dining room. Something dreadful was going to happen. And not even Dylan seemed able to prevent it.

"Awful?" Sir Thomas echoed. "Well, that depends on whether you mind having your entire life investigated by Scotland Yard."

"Scotland Yard?" Mrs. Colville asked. "This is not going to lead to unfortunate publicity for the museum, is it?"

"It might. Detective Inspector Samson Pope was recently asked to investigate certain individuals associated with the Colville Collection. He did a thorough job of uncovering episodes in some people's lives that decent men would have left private." Sir Thomas stared at Dylan.

"I'm sorry about Lady Havers," he said quietly. "She wasn't supposed to be part of this."

"At least you admit to responsibility for this investigation. Although if you hadn't, I could have proven it with a list made out in your handwriting." He pulled out the damning piece of paper.

"But why would Mr. Pierce have Lady Havers investigated by Scotland Yard?" Mr. Colville reached for his claret.

"Let me read what Inspector Pope wrote in his report." Sir Thomas cleared his throat. " 'Dylan, here is the result of our investigation into the individuals you included on your list. I have tried to be as thorough as you asked and, as you can see, some of these people indeed deserve your suspicion. If I discover anything further, one or more of these individuals may face criminal charges.' "

"Who is on this list?" Charlotte asked Dylan.

But he refused to meet her gaze, and only stared at the center of the table. She felt her hands grow icy with dread.

Hughes looked positively beatific. "Why don't you read the list aloud, Sir Thomas?"

"First he asks that I be investigated." Sir Thomas sighed. "After all, everyone knows what a reprobate life I have led these sixty-six years."

"Please continue," Mrs. Colville said.

"Let's see." He cleared his throat and recited the names. "Sir Thomas Havers, Barnabas Hughes, Ahmed Vartan." He paused. "Soames and Edwina Colville—"

"What?" Mr. Colville choked on his claret.

"You wanted Scotland Yard to investigate the Colvilles?" Charlotte turned to Dylan, who was grim and white-faced. "That's ridiculous. Why would you do that?"

"Let me continue, please." Sir Thomas looked up at Charlotte. "The next name on the list is your late husband, Ian Fairchild."

The room began to whirl about her. "You asked the police to investigate Ian?"

He finally turned to her. "I'll explain later. Please, Charlotte."

"I don't understand how you could do such a thing. The poor man is dead and you have the insensitivity to—"

"I'm not done," Sir Thomas said sternly. "Where was I? Oh, yes. Ian Fairchild, Sir Reginald Grainger—"

Charlotte's mouth fell open. "My father?"

She stood up and looked about for something to throw at him.

He tried to grab her, but she pushed him away.

"Please let me explain."

"My father! You asked the police to investigate the most ethical, honest man who ever lived! How dare you! You arrogant, lying, hypocritical—" The Queen's English wasn't enough, so she began cursing him in Arabic.

"Hear, hear." Hughes raised his glass of claret in salute.

"I will never forgive you for this. Never, do you hear? It's terrible enough that you keep accusing poor Ian of being a thief!"

"What's this?" Sir Thomas looked alarmed.

"He told me that Ian stole my wedding ring from the Sekkara site." She held out her hand, the gold ring gleaming in the candlelight.

"You *are* a dangerous man, Pierce," Sir Thomas said quietly. "I think you're the one who should be investigated by the police."

"I told you that I had suspicions about your husband, Charlotte," Dylan said.

"And did you suspect my father of theft as well? Good heaven, Father had no personal wealth whatsoever. We live in Belgravia because my mother is the daughter of an earl, not because my father sold antiquities on the black market. Where do you find the gall to cast aspersions on such a fine, decent man?"

"I am not done." Sir Thomas tapped on the table with a spoon.

Aunt Hazel covered her eyes with her hand, her rings sparkling. "I don't want to hear this."

"Our final name on Mr. Pierce's list of rogues is—"

"You're enjoying this, you bastard." Dylan swept his hand through his hair.

"—Charlotte Fairchild," Sir Thomas said with great relish.

"Me?" She could barely croak out the words. "You told Scotland Yard to investigate *me?*"

She felt as if someone had just kicked her in the stomach. For a moment, she couldn't breathe.

Dylan grabbed her by the shoulders. "Charlotte, I didn't

really believe that you were part of a smuggling ring, but I wasn't certain, not completely. And because I love you so, I had to know the truth. Don't you understand? I had to find out all I could about you, and everyone associated with you. I had to know the truth!"

"The truth?" She threw off his hands. "I'll tell you the truth. The truth is that you are incapable of trusting anyone! If Scotland Yard reported that all of us were as blameless as the angels, you would still look for some reason to doubt, some reason to think that we were liars. And that's because you're such a foul liar yourself!"

"You know that's not true!"

"Do I? You told me that you went to Scotland Yard to ask them to find Nefer."

"So I did. I just didn't want to tell you about the list I gave them, not yet. But I would have."

"When? After you'd bedded me a few more times?" Charlotte heard Mrs. Colville gasp.

"I knew it," Hughes said with a crude laugh.

"Well, I'm done playing the fool." Charlotte took a deep, shaky breath, not even knowing how she was getting the words out. "I'm done taking you into my confidence, my home, *and* my bed!"

From underneath the table came the sound of Nefer growling.

He grabbed her arm. "Don't, Charlotte. Let me explain."

"Take your hands off me," she warned.

Aunt Hazel cleared her throat. "I'd do as she says, young man. My niece is a Scorpio, you know."

But he just gripped her tighter. "At least go with me into the other room so we can talk alone. Give me one moment to state my case."

"You've stated your case far too well." Her voice grew harder. "You believe Ian and my father were liars and thieves. *And* you believe the same of me. Yes, you've explained things very well. Now let me go!"

Nefer peeked over the top of the table, fangs bared.

"You will hear me first." He pulled her toward him.

"And I say no!"

Nefer leaped into the air like a charging lion, claws extended.

Mrs. Colville screamed, and Charlotte reached out to prevent any violence. But it was too late.

With a blood-chilling growl, the desert cat attacked Dylan.

Chapter Sixteen

Dylan would have to be trampled by water buffalo to feel any worse than he did now.

He had spent the past two days in considerable pain, both emotional and physical. But he didn't know which hurt more: the injuries from the attack by Nefer or the memory of the betrayed look on Charlotte's face when she'd learned he'd asked the police to investigate her.

"Are you sure a rogue lion didn't maul you?" Samson winced as he watched Dylan apply more salve to one of the scratches. "No one would think it was simply the work of a house cat."

"House cat? Nefer has claws that would scare off Jack the Ripper." The cuts on his face ached like the devil every time he tried to smile, not that he had much cause to smile.

Samson walked over to a nearby wing chair, taking care not to step on the piles of books and papers scattered about Dylan's front parlor. "The London ladies will go into a frenzy when they see you. A few scars alongside that famous profile of yours and they'll be calling you a 'pirate poet' next."

"Hang London and her ladies." Dylan lay down on his sofa, waiting for the salve to take effect. He felt wretched. "As soon as I mend, I'm heading back to Egypt."

"Alone?"

Dylan opened one eye and looked at his friend. "Somehow I don't see Charlotte accompanying me."

"A lovers' quarrel," Samson said as he lit his pipe. "You'll make up."

"And what would you know of lovers' quarrels? You've less fondness for the fairer sex than your fictional counterpart Sherlock Holmes."

Samson frowned. "Please don't insult me by mentioning that arrogant creation known as Holmes. As though Conan Doyle has the slightest idea of how a real police investigation is conducted."

"I didn't know you inspectors had time for reading penny mysteries."

"We don't, nor do we have time for making afternoon calls on friends who've been attacked by cats." He puffed contentedly on his pipe for a few moments. "Lucky for you, we've got a new lead on the Waterloo Road murders, so I can allow myself an hour to see how you're doing."

"How do you think I'm doing? A cat tore my face off at dinner the other night. I had all of two minutes to savor my appointment as director of the Colville Collection before it was snatched away." He put a damp cloth over his eyes, which burned from the fumes from the salve. "Oh, yes, I managed to upset the woman I love so much that she refuses to ever see me again."

"Have you tried?"

"I went to the museum yesterday, but the Colvilles gave orders to bar me from the premises. So it seems I'm now an outcast like Sir Thomas and Hughes."

"Did you try calling on her at home?"

"Don't remind me. I sat on her doorstep last night from dusk till near ten o'clock. It was the giant footman who finally took pity on me. Randall came out and put clean gauze over some of these cuts, then called for a carriage." He lifted up the cloth. "I think my right cheek is infected."

"Maybe it would help if I spoke with her. Explained that you wanted to take her name off that list, and Sir Reginald's too."

"It wouldn't matter. The fact that I asked you to investigate them at all is damning enough in her eyes. Mine too." He balled up the cloth in his hands and flung it across the room. "I don't blame her for hating me. What in bloody hell was I thinking of?"

"You were thinking like a man who cares about tracking down criminals."

Dylan only snorted. "So speaks a policeman."

"You were a policeman of sorts for ten years. Infiltrating smuggling rings, trying to put a stop to illegal activities. From all accounts, your Egyptian exploits were not only scandalous but extremely effective. If you ever lose your taste for mummies and pyramids, the Yard has a place for you."

"Thank you for the offer, but I'm done chasing after criminals." He sat up, his head swimming both from the medication and the whiskey he'd drunk these past two days. "Although I fear that ten years of police work has left its mark."

"How so?"

"You know very well. I don't trust anyone, Samson. I don't even think I'm capable of it anymore."

"That's understandable. You spent ten years never knowing who to trust. Why do you think I live alone?" Samson puffed on his pipe, his eyes growing darker. "I've seen too much of a brutish, inhumane world to believe in any other."

Dylan rubbed at his head. Even though his friend meant

well by coming here this afternoon, he had only succeeded in making him feel worse.

"To be honest, I think the one person I don't trust is myself."

"You're just tired, and worried about your lady. You'll feel differently as soon as those cuts heal."

But Dylan feared that they wouldn't heal, at least not the wounds to his heart and spirit. He'd gone through thirty-three years alone, claiming to revel in it, boasting of his ability to need only the desert and his own company. Trysts with ladies were as easy to come by as papyrus reeds along the Nile; only occasionally had he felt a yearning for something more, a hope that life wouldn't always be so rootless, so solitary. Aside from Egypt and her glories, he had never found anyone or anything to give his life meaning. But that was before he met a woman with hair the color of moonlight.

Now he had ruined his one chance at a life with her.

"Even if she hates me now, I still have to let her know how Fairchild died."

"We don't know for a fact that the cave-in was deliberate."

Dylan stared back at him.

Samson shrugged. "So it very likely was murder. But that was over two and a half years ago, and on another continent. This is what the Yard calls a 'cold trail'."

"I think whoever killed Fairchild is here in London. I think he's responsible for stealing Nefer and planting the scorpions." He paused, remembering how fiercely Sir Thomas and Hughes had campaigned to get rid of both him and Charlotte. "No, the reason Fairchild was murdered lies somewhere in the Collection. I need to go back to the museum and inspect every artifact that was unearthed from the Valley of Amun."

"But you've been refused entry."

"As though I couldn't get past the museum guards and a few policemen. I know of a window or two that would allow easy access with the right crowbar."

"I'd rather you wouldn't tell me you're about to break the law."

Dylan slowly stood up. His joints ached, and he suspected he was running a fever. He hoped he wasn't about to have another malarial attack.

"I'm only going to bend it a bit. Besides, I have to keep an eye on Charlotte."

"Will she let you get close enough to do that?"

"I'm not going to give her much choice."

Samson got to his feet as well. "I suggest you wait until tomorrow before you break into the museum. In your present condition, even my half-blind grandmother could spot you crawling through a window."

"Very funny. Look, do you think you can get me a copy of your report? Hughes stole the one you gave me, and I never had a chance to read it over. Sir Thomas has it now. I would have taken it from him at the Colvilles, but then Nefer jumped on my face and I could barely see, what with all the blood."

Samson shrugged into his raincoat. "I'm so pleased that I went to all that trouble just to provide Sir Thomas with reading material. I'm sure the old man loved the part about his wife's dalliance with Hughes."

"Well, I never told you to investigate Lady Havers." Dylan felt guilty once more. Damn that wretched investigation he'd put into motion. "That could be why she wasn't at the Colville dinner the other night. Maybe he's beaten her—or worse."

"I sent one of my men to Mayfair yesterday to check on things, but both Sir Thomas and Lady Havers were out. Or at least that's what they instructed the servants to say." He frowned. "On second thought, maybe I'll pay them a visit. I don't like that the report fell into Sir Thomas's hands. Or Hughes's either."

"Yes. Apparently I'm the only person in London who hasn't read the bloody thing." Dylan frowned. "If both men read the report, why were they as thick as thieves at dinner? Sir Thomas can't have been pleased to learn his wife was unfaithful."

"Maybe the three of them have what the French call 'an understanding.' Immoral louts, those Frenchmen." Samson shook out his still wet umbrella. "As for a copy of the report, I'm sure I can get one to you."

"In the meantime, I have to try to see Charlotte again, no matter how much she may hate me. Someone has to inform her that her husband was very likely murdered."

"Restrain yourself at least for a day or two." Samson walked up the steps to the foyer. "I advise you to stay home; no breaking and entering for at least twenty-four hours. The rain has assumed typhoon proportions, and you look like you've already been through a shipwreck."

"It's my malaria. Too much alcohol brings on an attack, and I've been nipping whiskey these past two days. I've run out of quinine, too."

"Malaria, murder, *and* love." He opened the front door, and a blast of cold, furious rain poured into the foyer. "No wonder you're feeling so sick. At least I only have murder to worry about."

After he was gone, Dylan sank back down on the sofa. If only his detective friend knew, he thought.

Love was far more dangerous than murder.

A man lay dead on the ground. His murderer stood behind him, his sword still upraised.

"Treachery is everywhere," Charlotte murmured as she examined the papyrus that bore the painted figures of Pharaoh Kotep and his assassin.

Treachery threatened whether one was a young pharaoh or a foolish woman who gave her heart and her trust to a deceitful Welshman.

Nefer skittered past her feet, chasing after a small pile of packing straw.

Grateful to be distracted, Charlotte turned away from the papyrus and watched her cat play for a few moments. She didn't know whether she should reward Nefer for attacking Dylan or shake her by the tail.

"I fear you made sad work of his lovely face," she said aloud.

The cat looked up and gave a soft meow.

She hoped none of the wounds were too serious, not that he deserved any consideration. Randall was concerned enough yesterday to bring out fresh gauze to Dylan, who remained on her doorstep for hours. No doubt some of the scratches had become infected.

"It's his own fault," she muttered. "Lying to me all this time, going behind my back to the police, suspecting Father and me of smuggling."

She'd been so shocked to learn that Dylan had asked Scotland Yard to investigate her and her father that she hadn't paid attention to Nefer's warning growls beneath the table. Too late she remembered how fiercely protective the cat was.

Well, sometimes treachery got exactly what it deserved. In this case, a bloody good mauling. Indeed, the more she thought about Dylan, the angrier—and sadder—she became. After two and a half years, she had finally allowed herself to hope once more, to love, to dream. She should have known such sudden, wild bliss was not to be trusted. Any more than a handsome Welshman with a gift for poetry could be trusted.

She bent back to her notes, but her concentration faltered. Every time she looked at the display of canopic jars, or read over the list of artifacts sent from Cairo, she despaired. How could Dylan believe her capable of smuggling antiquities? Did he know her so little, and trust her even less?

But even if she forgave him for mistrusting her, which was hurtful enough, she didn't think she could forgive him for suspecting Father.

Reginald Grainger was the only child of a Salisbury minister and a church choir mistress. He'd worked his way through school and university, outshining young men with far more advantages. Before he died, he was universally acknowledged as the foremost Egyptologist of his day, knighted by Queen Victoria, respected by scholars on three continents. Not a single word of gossip or criticism had ever been directed his way—until Dylan asked the police to investigate him.

The thought of Scotland Yard prying into her father's past sent her blood boiling. How dare he give the police permission to rummage about in her father's life! The very fact that Sir Reginald was under investigation would indicate that someone suspected him of nefarious activities. She could scratch Dylan's eyes out herself.

She only wished she could tear at her own heart as well. The pain of what Dylan had done was worse than a dozen scratches, and the loss of what they could have shared sent a wave of grief over her. Heaven help her, she had hoped to be done grieving over men, at least for awhile. But Dylan's suspicions had ruined everything.

Taking a deep breath, she raised her head and scanned the exhibit hall that held the material from the Valley of Amun.

Painted sarcophagi lined the shadowy back wall, each bearing a royal or priestly mummy within. Canopic jars, *ushapti* figurines, and alabaster tableware filled the numerous glass shelves. The heads of dozens of faience figurines and basalt statues stared back at her, awe-inspiring even without the torchlight that would be used for the exhibition itself.

But most impressive of all was the polished limestone tomb that stood in the center of the room. Dylan had worked as hard as the Old Kingdom pyramid builders to ensure that reconstruction of the tomb was completed in time. Here it was—a month before the exhibit was due to open—and the tomb stood nearly ready. All that remained was for the workers to lay in metal rods in order to support it properly.

A chill ran through Charlotte. For a moment the dark entrance to the crypt looked exactly like the one Ian had disappeared through.

Nonsense, she thought. Almost three years had passed since the accident, and she refused to let those sad memories ruin what little happiness she now found in the present. Besides, the reconstructed tomb was certain to draw thousands of visitors. Dylan's plans for the exhibit were innovative and exciting. He was an artist as well as a scholar.

She could almost pity him for losing his chance at directing the Collection itself. For as soon as the Colvilles learned that Dylan had asked the police to investigate them, they had withdrawn their offer of the directorship and barred him from the Collection. If she weren't so angry at him, she might have even worked up some indignation at his unfair treatment.

Yet one man's poison is another man's meat. Or woman, in this case. Upon Aunt Hazel's recommendation, she had been given the responsibility of mounting the Valley of Amun exhibit. And no matter how much her heart ached, she was going to do the Valley—and her father—justice.

She heard footsteps behind her. One of the museum guards stood at the entrance, obviously hesitant to enter the gallery. She supposed it did look ominous and forbidding, especially with the storm clouds rolling above the skylight.

"Mr. Pierce is here again, Mrs. Fairchild."

She stiffened at the sound of Dylan's name. "Please send him away. The Colvilles have given express orders that he is not to be allowed inside."

"I'm afraid the gentleman is already inside." He seemed embarrassed about turning away the person who had been giving him orders these past few months. "He's a hard man to keep out, ma'am."

"Then have one of the policemen escort him out."

"They're trying to, but there's all this broken glass. And one of the Bobbies cut his hand—"

"What are you talking about?"

"Mr. Pierce, ma'am. He got hold of a crowbar and broke a window in the Assyrian gallery."

"He what?"

"It made no end of noise. The sound brought us all running, just as he was trying to crawl through."

She cursed under her breath. "Is anyone seriously hurt?"

"Just a few scratches on the policeman, ma'am. But we need to get that window covered up quick. The rain's coming through in buckets."

"Where is Mr. Pierce now?" She flung her notebook down.

"Still in the Assyrian gallery. I don't think he'll get into any more trouble. The gentleman don't look well."

"I'll see to him. This won't take long, but I'd appreciate it if you would stay and keep an eye on Nefer." She nodded toward the cat, who was now tearing the packing straw to shreds. "I'm afraid she might attack Mr. Pierce again."

"Yes, ma'am."

But she noticed that the museum guard remained by the entrance, in case a quick escape was necessary.

"Stay here, Nefer, and be nice to the man," she instructed the cat in Arabic. "I don't want to come back and see you've frightened him."

A playful growl was the only response.

She patted the guard on the shoulder as she left.

As soon as she entered the Assyrian gallery, she was met by blustery wind and the sight of furious rain pouring inside. Luckily the only thing getting wet was a stone winged bull.

"Go to the workrooms and bring back the lids to the packing crates," she instructed the two policemen, one of whom had a cloth wrapped about his wrist. "We'll use them to board up the window until I can get a glazier in here."

The two men hurried past. A quick glance told her no patrons were in the gallery. She had the bad weather to thank for the sparse attendance. The last thing she or the Collection needed was for an innocent museum visitor to get hit by flying glass.

She wondered where Dylan had gotten to. Honestly, the man was more trouble than a dozen desert cats. She did spy the crowbar, however, lying forgotten beneath a glazed brick panel from the palace of Artaxerxes.

"Where are you, Dylan?" Her voice echoed in the high-ceilinged room. "I wouldn't try to explore the museum if I were you. Nefer is running free."

"Charlotte?" someone said from behind the glazed brick panel.

She didn't like the weak, hoarse sound of that familiar voice. "Dylan, what's wrong? Why don't you come out?"

She stalked over, prepared to give him a lecture the likes of which he hadn't heard since he was in knee pants. But the sight of Dylan sitting on the marble floor, shivering, left her speechless.

He raised his head. "I don't quite trust my legs, lass."

Although Dylan wore a raincoat, he was soaking wet. And beneath his dripping hat she could clearly spy those terrible scratches.

She winced at the angry red marks along his cheeks, one perilously close to his left eye.

"I didn't know Nefer had hurt you so badly. Two nights ago, all I could see was the blood."

The aftermath of Nefer's attack had been a wild blur. Mrs. Colville screaming, Hughes and Sir Thomas cursing, Dylan knocking into the table, plates flying. And Nefer scratching like a tiger until Charlotte pulled her off. Charlotte had been so upset that she left almost immediately. She hadn't seen the results of Nefer's attack until now. In some perverse way she felt as guilty as if she had raked him with her own nails.

"You're drenched." She knelt down beside him. He was soaked to the bone, and his shoes were covered in mud.

"It's raining," he said in a hoarse voice.

"I can see that. And it's as cold as Boxing Day out there.

251

Why in the world are you out in this weather? More to the point, why are you breaking into the museum?"

"I had to see you. And I knew you wouldn't let me in."

"So you decided to smash a window or two."

He shook his head. "I only meant to pry away the window frame, but I lost my balance. Next thing I knew, the window shattered and I was inside."

She took off her thick woolen shawl and gently dried his face with it. Despite a flinch or two, he seemed curiously unresponsive.

"You're shivering." Charlotte sighed. Even if he had betrayed her and her father, she couldn't help but be concerned. "Take off your coat before you catch your death."

He attempted to remove it but was trembling too badly. She pulled the coat off herself.

She bit her lip when she saw the scratches close up. "Oh, I'm so sorry about your face. I had no idea Nefer was going to attack you."

His teeth chattered. "D-d-doesn't matter."

"Of course it matters. It's a wonder she didn't scratch your eyes out. She's never done anything quite like this before." Charlotte wrapped her shawl about his neck. "It's just that she thought you were hurting me. If you had simply let go of my arm when I asked you to, this wouldn't have happened."

He grabbed her arm now, but very gently. "It's not Nefer's fault. I'm to blame for everything."

Now that he was touching her, she could feel how terribly he was shaking.

She laid a hand against his forehead. Even wet from the cold rain, it burned to the touch. "You're running a fever."

Charlotte cursed silently. The scratches were probably infected. She'd never forgive herself if he became seriously ill. As angry and hurt as she was by his suspicion, Dylan didn't deserve to suffer like this. That cat was going to get a stern lecture tonight.

252

The Lady and the Lion

"Let's go out in the hallway where it's warmer."

With great effort, she pulled him to his feet. With his arm slung over her shoulders, she slowly walked him over to one of the marble benches in the corridor.

He sat down with a weary sigh. "It's not the scratches making me ill. It's malaria."

"You shouldn't be running about London with malarial fever! What in the world am I going to do with you?"

She tried to feel his forehead again, but he grabbed her hand.

"You can forgive me." He shook so hard, it was a wonder he remained upright.

The tears that filled her eyes threatened to spill down her cheeks. "Dylan, I don't think this is the time to talk about everything that's happened. You're ill and—"

He squeezed her fingers. His skin felt frightfully hot. "I didn't mean to hurt you. I swear it. It's just that your wedding ring was stolen from my site. I couldn't help but be suspicious after that."

"Not the ring again."

"Maybe your husband didn't steal the ring," he said hoarsely. "Maybe he did buy it from a native in Luxor, but that ring was stolen from Sekkara." He stopped for moment while he shivered uncontrollably. "It was stolen from me."

She sighed. He couldn't help being who he was: a man who'd worked undercover for the Antiquities Service for ten years, a man who trusted no one. Not even her. It broke her heart to realize that, but her heart also ached to see him so ill, so weak.

"None of that is important now. I'm going to call a carriage and take you home. Then I'm going to send for the doctor."

"I just need more quinine." He gripped both her hands in his. "I wanted to tell you how sorry I am. I love you, Charlotte. I didn't mean to hurt you."

Her chest felt tight, and she couldn't meet his eyes. She

looked away from his injured face, focusing her attention on the the marble busts of Greek philosophers lining the hallway. Anything not to see his pain.

"I know you didn't mean to hurt me," she said finally. "But you did."

"I—I want to trust people." The sound of his chattering teeth made her tears come faster. "I need to trust. I need to trust you. It's just so difficult for me."

She forced herself to face him once more. God help her, she shouldn't love him this much, not after he all but accused her of theft. And Father too. Of course, he had never really known her father. If he had, he would realize such a thing was impossible to believe. Yet he had claimed to love her, then went right ahead and told the police to investigate her.

But even if he thought *she* had stolen the wedding ring, at this moment she couldn't work up any rage against him. Not when he was burning with fever.

"Don't worry about that now. Just sit here. I'm going to call for a carriage."

But when she tried to stand up, he pulled her down again. "Tell me that you forgive me first. I need to hear that, lass."

"You're ill. You need to be in bed. This is no time to talk."

He shook his head, the tremors getting stronger. "But I have to talk. I have to tell you about the Valley of Amun. The accident was not an accident."

"You're delirious." She looked about for a museum guard or policeman, someone to call a carriage for them.

He grabbed her chin in his trembling hand, forcing her to look at him. "You're in danger. Just like him."

"What are you talking about?"

"He was murdered. I think he was murdered."

"Who was murdered?" she asked, alarmed that he was babbling so.

But Dylan's only response was to collapse unconscious at her feet.

Chapter Seventeen

Dylan lay on a sand dune. Each labored breath seared his chest with fire. Every inch of his body felt raw, as if hot shards of glass were being ground into his skin. He felt exposed, unprotected. Where was his tent? His blasted camel? His head pounded, and he feared he'd gone into the desert without even a hat to shield him. His face burned to the touch, and when he tried to sit up, he realized he was naked.

He gave a cry and fell back. He'd been waylaid by desert brigands. That must be what happened. Stripped of his valuables and left to die naked and alone on the desert. So many times he dreaded such a thing might happen. He was always in the company of treacherous men, never knowing if he had told one lie too many, or misjudged the lies of another. Now he had met his fate. He tried to touch his burning face, but something prevented him. He didn't have the strength for another effort. Better to surrender to his bleak destiny. All men died, and he at least would die in the desert he loved. But dying so alone was sad, desolate. If only he could see

Charlotte one last time. There was something he had to tell her, but now it was too late.

"Charlotte," he said between painful, blistered lips.

"Shhh. Don't try to talk."

The tender words were obviously the last stages of a deathly delirium brought on by exposure to the sun. He felt something wet and cool touch his face, soothing beside the heat and pain. Groaning, he surrendered to the fever and to the mirage that spoke to him in a soft voice, a mirage that had tender hands and made him think of fragrant jasmine. There were worse ways to die. Too bad he had not made a better job of living.

"Father never had attacks as bad as this," his mirage said.

"The infection from the cuts on his face has worsened the situation," a gruff voice replied from a distance. "And I don't think he's been dosing himself with enough quinine lately."

An awful shuddering overtook him so that the whole world seemed to quake. He wondered if a sandstorm raged about him.

Again a coolness pressed against his forehead. "He feels like he's on fire, Doctor. His temperature must be at least a hundred and five."

Dylan leaned against that coolness, weary and pained.

"Probably higher. I knew a Dutch sea captain once . . ."

The voices faded. It no longer mattered what his mirages were saying. He surrendered to the heat, and to the scent of jasmine that perfumed the blistering *khamseen* wind. It made him think of Charlotte, his brave lady with the white-gold hair. If he opened his eyes, he imagined he saw her gray eyes staring back at him, their hue more unearthly than ever.

He couldn't look too long, however. His eyes hurt, and too many other images erupted around him so that he grew confused, agitated. One moment he was staring at his beloved Charlotte, the next moment a pyramid shimmered before him. He shook his head, but the strange sights continued to appear: a crystal ball held by a hand glittering with rings, the enraged face of Barnabas Hughes, a singing pirate who brandished a sword, growling cats.

It was too confusing. He would grow mad if these visions did not cease. Scorpions climbed over his naked body, and a woman with orange plumes in her hair laughed and laughed, the sound as brittle as chalk. He flung up his hands as a great lion loomed over him, its hungry jaws wide open. He was dying. And he had so many regrets, but none he regretted more than Charlotte.

"Forgive me, Charlotte," he said hoarsely. "I love you."

Then he gave himself over to his fate, a fate that—tragically—he knew he had earned.

The years in Africa prepared her for this. Charlotte wasn't frightened by Dylan's malarial attack. Her own father had suffered from malaria, and she knew well the disease's insidious effects: chills, headache, raging fever, myalgia, fearsome paroxysms. In fact, during the three days she tended Dylan, she quickly realized that she was more knowledgeable about malaria than the family physician, who was more accustomed to treating gout and dyspepsia than tropical diseases.

Yet, despite the other malarial attacks she had witnessed and tended to, this was worse. Worse because poor Dylan was suffering not only from malaria but from an infection caused by those terrible scratches. She didn't blame Nefer; how could she? The fiercely loyal cat was only trying to protect her, and Charlotte had been enraged enough that evening to have attacked him herself.

Caring for Dylan these past few days, however, had slowly made the anger go away. It was difficult to be angry with a man who called out for her in his delirium, who begged forgiveness, who proclaimed his love in pitiful whispers.

She did try to hold on to her resentment. She had never been deceived so cruelly, and by a man she loved. His stubborn belief that Ian was guilty of theft and smuggling was at least understandable. Where Ian was concerned, Dylan let his jealousy cloud his judgment. But suspecting her father and her of such crimes was inexplicable. Especially after all that they had shared.

"I love him as I love Egypt," she said aloud.

For she forgave Egypt all the trials and difficulties that her years in the desert had visited upon her. What she felt for Egypt was unconditional and unchanging. It shook her to realize that her love for Dylan ran as deep.

This morning he looked better, sleeping peacefully for the first time since she had him brought to her home in Belgrave Square. His forehead was blessedly cool, and she noticed with relief that the sweating and tremors were gone. She thanked heaven once again for the miracle of quinine.

She felt so relieved by Dylan's improved appearance, she planned to return to work at the Collection. There was so much left to be done if the exhibit was to be ready in four weeks, and she felt even more responsible for its success since the Colvilles had put her in charge. She'd sent messages to the museum these past few days, but she could not continue to do that much longer. There was a great deal that required her actual presence.

Randall and Lorrie could take turns watching over Dylan today. Charlotte had already given orders that the house was to be aired. The morning was bright and clear, without a hint of rain. Fresh air and sunshine would do wonders for everyone's spirits after the storms of the past few days.

Although she was dressed and ready to leave, Charlotte sat beside Dylan's bed, still wincing at the cuts that at last were beginning to fade. While in his delirium, he had clutched at her hand, calling out her name. A thousand conscious heartfelt apologies wouldn't have touched her as deeply as his fever-ridden guilt and regret.

She heard the door creak open behind her.

"Nefer, I told you to stay out."

The cat sat on her haunches, her amber eyes shining innocently.

"You know you're to leave Dylan alone."

But Nefer only gave a plaintive meow, looking toward the sleeping patient. As if to prove she meant the Welshman no further harm, the cat leaped upon the bed before Charlotte could stop her.

"Don't you dare," Charlotte warned, ready to grab the feline.

The cat raised a paw, now sheathed, and gently touched Dylan's arm. With a rumbling purr, she circled once, then plopped down beside Dylan, nestling close to his side.

Although Charlotte was glad to see that Nefer wanted to make amends, she worried that Dylan might become agitated if he woke to find the cat on top of him again.

"You can only stay a few minutes." Charlotte walked over to the armoire. She picked up her hat, pulling out the jeweled pin stuck in its green velvet. "Then you and I must leave for the museum. I've a lot of work to catch up on."

"Charlotte? Is that you?"

She spun around. Dylan was awake, and although he looked pale and exhausted, his eyes didn't shine with fever.

"Dylan, finally." She dropped the hat and hurried over to him.

"Where am I?" He stared at the cricket bat hanging on the wall opposite him.

"In Belgrave Square." She felt his neck, which was damp but cool. "We put you in Michael's bedroom. You've had a nasty attack of malaria."

"By thunder, it's the cat!" His startled gaze rested on Nefer, half lying on his chest.

"It's all right. She won't hurt you now." Lifting the cat off the bed, Charlotte cradled the purring Nefer. "In fact, I believe she came in to say she was sorry."

She whispered in the animal's ear. Nefer gave a last look at Dylan before jumping down and trotting out of the room.

He struggled to sit up. Charlotte rushed to prop up the pillows behind him.

"So she wanted to apologize, did she?" he said in a tired, hoarse voice.

"I think she does regret attacking you. Her appetite has been off these past few days. Even muffins won't tempt her."

Charlotte sat beside him on the bed. Now that he was awake, she felt suddenly uncomfortable.

He looked at Charlotte, his eyes searching hers. "It's not just the cat who wants to apologize." He reached for her hand. "I am sorry, lass. I should never have gone to Scotland Yard. I was mad to have asked them to investigate you or your father."

She looked down at his hand holding hers. "We've been very worried about you these past three days. I had you brought here straight from the museum. Your fever was nearly a hundred and six. Luckily you responded to the quinine."

He pulled on her hand. "Look at me."

After a slight hesitation, she did.

"I can't do anything more than beg your forgiveness. You don't have to give it, but you'll break my heart if you don't."

She swallowed hard. "I fear you've already broken mine."

"I admit I'm a suspicious, bloody fool who has to learn to trust people. Especially people I love. And I do love you." He struggled to sit up but fell back on the pillows. "Blast it all, Charlotte, I swear I'll never doubt you again. I swear it."

"I wish it were that easy." She tore herself away from his gaze. His eyes were filled with so much fear—and hope.

"But I love you."

"And I love you."

She felt him relax beside her.

"Then let's try to put this behind us, lass. We'll make a new start." He reached out, pulling her into his arms. "No more secrets between us, no more deception. Marry me or don't marry me—as you will—but you and I shall be together from this point on. And when I'm better, we'll go back to Egypt. Back to the Valley of Amun, or to another site if you wish." He kissed her hair. "It doesn't matter as long as we're together."

She allowed herself to lean against him for a brief instant, grateful to feel that the fever was gone, his heart was beating steadily, his body no longer shivering. He was alive and well, and she loved him. But it didn't matter.

With great effort, she pulled away. She got up from the bed and went back to the mirror. Forcing her hands not to tremble, she straightened the collar of her jacket.

"You're still angry with me." He sounded like a little boy whose mother has refused him his favorite dessert.

Dropping her hands, she stared into the mirror. She could see Dylan reflected behind her. "I'm not angry, not anymore."

"Then what's wrong? I swear I'll never mistrust you again."

She turned around to face him. "The problem is that I no longer trust you."

"Ah, I see." He looked as if she had just slapped him.

"If I don't trust you, how can we have a future together?"

"Bloody hell, Charlotte, I told you why I went to Scotland Yard. Your wedding ring was stolen from my site. It was only natural that I try to find out everything about you and Fairchild."

"Maybe it was natural, at least for a man who once worked to uncover smugglers. What I find unnatural, however, is how you lied to me, telling me you went to see Detective Pope because of Nefer. What I find unnatural is that three days after you went to the police to ask them to investigate me, you took me to bed. And told me that you loved me."

"I do!"

"All this time the police have been looking into my past, mine and Father's. All because you believed me capable of robbing the land and people I love so much." She stared at him for a long moment. "What would you have done if the police *had* turned up something suspicious?"

"I don't know," he said softly.

She was finding it hard to breathe. "That's another lie you've told me. You do know. You would have turned me over to the police. You would have ruined my father's memory. Would you have let them send me to prison, too?"

"That's nonsense. I realize now that you and your father could never have engaged in smuggling."

She tried to laugh but couldn't. "That wasn't what I asked."

His expression grew hard. "I would have seen that as little harm came to your father's memory—and to you—as possible. That's one reason I went to Samson. As a friend, I knew I could rely on his discretion. Had you been guilty, Sam and I could have worked out a more lenient sentence for you."

"Thank you. That makes me feel better."

"You're asking too much of me, Charlotte. I told you how I lived in Egypt. My entire existence was a lie; it had to be if I was to survive. These past three years, I've done what I can to live a normal, respectable life. It hasn't been easy. There are times when I simply want to chuck it all and sail back to Egypt. Back to the danger, the excitement, even the deception."

She nodded. "Well, you've not left the deception completely behind you."

He fumbled for the water pitcher beside his bed, pouring himself a glass of water. His hand trembled. Charlotte forced herself not to come to his aid.

He took several gulps of water before setting the glass down with a clatter. "Forgive me my many faults. I keep forgetting that your husband was a paragon of virtue."

"I never said that."

"You don't have to. It's clear you loved the man. No matter what you tell me, I don't believe that you stayed in black bombazine all this time simply out of guilt."

She stiffened. "I thought you were going to try to believe me from now on."

"Of course I believe you. I just don't think you're being completely honest with me."

She refused to quarrel. He was still too weak, and it would do no good besides.

"Ian was not a paragon of virtue; he was an ordinary man. And at the end, I fear he kept things from me just as you have."

Dylan shot her an injured look.

"I didn't know that he'd been appointed director of the Colville Collection until he was set to pack," she went on. "Sir Thomas and Lady Havers simply arrived in the Valley one morning, announcing that you were on the way to take over my site. I was the only one who didn't know that we were sailing back to England in two weeks. I learned later that even Ahmed had been informed first."

The memory of that day still pained her. After all this time she could still feel the shock—the sense of betrayal—at learning that Ian was giving up the Valley of Amun. Giving up her past and her future, allowing her no say in the momentous decision. She sighed. Perhaps men couldn't help being arrogant and selfish. They'd been taught their whole lives that the world revolved around their work, their needs, their responsibilities. It hadn't occurred to Ian to take her feelings into consideration. Any more than Dylan had when he went to Scotland Yard.

Only the desert, it seemed, was constant and true.

She smoothed down her jacket, busying herself with fastening one of the agate buttons. Anything to avoid Dylan's stricken expression.

"You loved him, didn't you?" His voice sounded as weak as he looked. "You loved him very much, even if he did decide to leave Egypt."

No use pretending any longer. She would leave it to men to pretend.

"I never loved Ian," she said quietly.

He shook his head. "Why would you feel so guilty about a man you didn't love?"

"I feel guilty *because* I never loved him. Oh, I told myself at the time that I loved him. And he was kind to me during the weeks following Father's death. The kindest and gentlest I ever saw him. But I realize now I only married him in order to stay in Egypt."

"I don't understand."

"As a young, unmarried woman, I couldn't remain in the Valley, unchaperoned, surrounded by native workers and an attractive English bachelor. My mother may be unconventional but she's not mad. She would have sent Randall to drag me back home. So I could either leave Egypt or marry. When the Colvilles learned of our marriage, they asked Ian if he would take over the site. He agreed, and the *firman* was transferred to him."

Dylan fell back against his pillows. "But I remember your mother talking about how you fell in love with him; she said it was like a desert whirlwind."

"I certainly wasn't going to tell Mother that I was marrying Ian simply so I could continue to work in the desert."

"So you cared nothing for him at all?" She heard a note of hopefulness in his voice.

"I'm not such a cold monster as that. I enjoyed Ian's company, and he'd been working with Father and me for over a year. We got along famously." Indeed, it was only after they married that they began quarreling. "I liked him well enough, more than any man I'd met up to that time. Without him, I would have been desolate after Father died. He was attentive, amusing." She paused. "And he had the most beautiful brown eyes."

Dylan's own eyes darkened. "I only met Fairchild once, but I guess he was a pretty enough fellow."

Charlotte took a deep breath, It hurt to speak about Ian, to remember her late husband as a handsome, vital young man. "He was far more than pretty, and he deserved to marry a woman who truly loved him. Instead, he ended up with someone who cared more for the desert than for him."

"You're making yourself out to be the villainess in this."

"I am." She yanked on her gloves. "I take no pride in admitting such a thing. Heaven help me, I would have married the mummy of Thutmose the Third if it meant I could remain in Egypt."

"But you won't marry me."

"No, I won't." A familiar pain rose in her chest. Guilt, remorse. And a bitter awareness that she was not destined for happiness in love.

"I married a man I trusted but didn't love. It ended in disaster. I won't make the same mistake again by marrying a man I love but don't trust."

"Charlotte, I told you how sorry—"

"I know. And I'm sorry too. I'm sorry I didn't meet you years ago, when Father was still alive. We might have made a good match then, before all the guilt and suspicion." She swallowed hard, fearing she was going to cry.

"I've made a right mess of everything." Dylan swept back his damp hair, looking every bit as wretched as she felt.

"We both have. Let's not make matters worse." She moved over to the doorway. "Those scratches still look raw. Before I leave, I'll tell Lorrie to apply more salve on your face."

"Leave? Where are you going?"

"I've been looking after you for three days, Dylan. I have to start working at the museum again or the Colvilles will cancel the exhibit."

"You can't go to the museum without me." With obvious effort, he flung back the bedclothes. He stared amazed at his bare legs and feet. "What the devil do I have on?"

"One of Michael's nightshirts. I know it's much too short,

265

but it was all we had." Charlotte heard someone clear his throat behind her. She turned to see the faithful footman standing in the doorway. "Good, Randall, you're here."

Dylan tried to stand up, but his knees buckled.

Charlotte gestured for Randall to help him back to bed. "You're in no shape to go downstairs, let alone to the museum."

"I'll need my clothes, Randall." Dylan pushed the footman aside and staggered a few more steps. The small activity was too much however, and he was forced to rest his weight against the tall four-poster. "I'll be accompanying your mistress to the Collection."

Charlotte sighed. "As you can see, Mr. Pierce needs to rest today. Have breakfast sent up, and take care that he doesn't exert himself too much."

"Yes, madame." Randall gave a last concerned glance at Dylan before leaving the room.

"You'll have a relapse, Dylan. Please stay in bed."

"But you can't go yet. We have too much to talk about." Dylan sat down on the bed. With his bare legs dangling from the too short nightshirt, he looked helpless and vulnerable.

She should never have agreed to work with him at the Collection, and she certainly should never have become his lover. Worst of all, she had fallen in love with him and tragically, caused him to love her as well. It seemed she was fated to bring pain to any man who loved her: first Ian and now Dylan. She swore that only Egypt would have her heart from now on.

"He was an engineer. Did you know that?" Dylan asked, out of breath from his brief attempt at walking.

"Ian? Of course I knew he was an engineer." She eased him back onto the pillows. "His father was an engineer in the army, and he wanted Ian to follow in his footsteps. He never liked it, though. That's why he turned to Egyptology."

"Don't you see? If he was an engineer, how could he not see that the walls of the tomb weren't secured?"

She stepped back. "It was an accident. They happen every season in archaeology. I won't have you blaming him again."

"I don't blame him. But an engineer would have seen that the tomb was not braced properly."

"What are you trying to say?"

"I'm saying that someone sabotaged the tomb before he went in for the last time." Dylan wiped his damp forehead with the back of his hand. "Someone killed him."

Tears rose to her eyes, and she began to shake. She thought she was done reliving Ian's death, hearing once more the terrible sound of the tomb crashing down on him again. She thought she had reconciled herself to his death— and her own selfish part in it.

"It was an accident," she said brokenly. "An accident."

Dylan tried to reach for her, but she pushed him away.

"Can't you let the poor man rest in peace?" A sob escaped her. "First you have to dig up Father's memory, trying to find something dirty, something dishonest. Now it's Ian's grave you're disturbing with your suspicions."

"Charlotte, please. I'm only trying to protect you. I think whoever killed Ian is still alive."

"Yes." She backed up toward the door. "I'm responsible for Ian's death, and I'm still alive! Don't you think I know that?"

"That's not what I mean!"

But Charlotte would not wait to hear more. With Dylan shouting after her, she ran out into the hallway—where only Nefer could see her cry.

Chapter Eighteen

As soon as she caught sight of the marble columns of the Colville Collection, Charlotte let out a sigh of relief. At least for the next few hours, she wouldn't have to think about Ian's death or Dylan's lies. Work, as always, was her most reliable pleasure.

Dylan had so upset her that she'd refused to take a hansom cab or carriage to the museum. Instead, she'd walked the two miles, needing the brisk morning air and sunlight, the presence of jostling people who knew nothing of either her, Ian, or that infernal Welshman. Nefer also welcomed the exercise, her large paws scuffling through the leaves that had already started to fall.

Charlotte stopped beneath a beech tree, one of many that shaded the small park surrounding the museum. Looking skyward, she let herself be dazzled by the orange and gold canopy overhead. The only thing to rival an Egyptian winter in the Delta was an English autumn, ablaze with color and burnished light. She was thankful too for the breeze that cooled her cheeks and dried her tears.

What was the matter with her? Bursting into tears like an ingenue in a bad melodrama. The only thing worth crying over was death—and she had cried more than her share over Father and Ian.

But after all that had happened these past few days, the last thing she needed was for Dylan to remind her of Ian's death. How foolish to think she could ever leave that behind her, as though she could neatly wrap up her guilt and put it away, like a housekeeper packs away the Christmas silver.

No, she would carry the blame for Ian's death for a long time. When she saw Dylan later this evening, she must remain calm, no matter how upsetting their conversation. With luck, he'd be on his feet in a day or two and could be sent home to Russell Square. The sooner they put distance between them, the quicker both of them would learn that their relationship was over.

"Over," she murmured, cringing at the finality of that word.

She would never allow herself to feel such love and need for another person again. As soon as the exhibit opened, she intended to sail back to Egypt. If the exhibit was a success, perhaps she could convince the Colvilles to sponsor a field season. If they refused, maybe Mother knew an antiquities-minded lady with the necessary gold to be her patroness. No matter what, she would stake out a claim in Egypt and spend the rest of her days digging in the sand. She was an archae-ologist. She would never let anyone—least of all herself—forget it again.

Nefer gave a low growl. Alerted, Charlotte turned around. Standing ten feet away was a stocky man wearing a fez.

"Ahmed, what are you doing here?"

"You should not be out alone, Mrs. Fairchild." He pointed to the cat, who sat at her feet like a watchful sentry. "Even if you do have the cat to protect you. It is not fitting that you should walk the streets of London unchaperoned. No wonder you find yourself in so many calamitous situations."

"Ahmed, you scold me more often than my old Scottish nanny did. Did you come to remind me again of ancient curses?"

His large black eyes looked more mournful than ever. "The Valley of Amun *is* cursed, but not by the dead pharaohs, may Allah grant peace to their departed souls."

"Cursed by whom then?" She smiled. "Sacrilegious Egyptologists?"

"No. By those who loot and rob."

She was as startled by his answer as by his worried expression. "*Have* there been looters in the Valley since I left?"

He nodded. "They were there long before you left."

"I don't understand. Are you saying that the site was being robbed while I was still working there?"

"Much happened in your Valley and still does. I had only my suspicions years ago. It is only now that I know for certain. Only now do I realize that the thieves and murderers have taken the Valley for their own."

Her stomach rolled, and she felt a wave of nausea. "Murderers? Who was murdered?" She suddenly dreaded the answer, fearing he would name her husband.

"Samir Jahel."

"Our first foreman? But—but he died of a scorpion bite."

"That is true, but who planted the scorpion?"

The memory of the three scorpions in the museum came rushing back to her. "Why would someone want to kill Samir? He was an honest man, a fine worker. He had no enemies."

Ahmed frowned. "Honest men always have enemies. It is why he was killed. He learned of the treasure, Mrs. Fairchild, and of the plans to smuggle it out of Egypt."

She felt as if she must be suffering from malarial fever herself, so dizzy was this conversation making her. "You know that we never found any real treasure. Funerary goods, mummies, papyri, but nothing valuable enough to warrant anyone being murdered."

"It is as the legend said." He stepped closer and lowered his voice. "In the Valley of Amun lies the gold of a royal concubine, a vast treasure hidden at the command of the greatest of the Ramessid kings."

She gasped. "Princess Hatiri's treasure? Someone found Princess Hatiri's treasure in my valley?"

He waved his hands. "Keep your voice down, Mrs. Fairchild. We should not even be speaking in the open like this. You are being watched."

She looked about but saw only rustling trees and an apple seller on the corner. "Watched by whom?"

"The police." He paused. "And the men who smuggled the treasure out of Egypt. That is why I had to warn you. If they think you will come between them and the treasure, you will be the next to suffer the curse."

He had moved too near and set Nefer to growling. Ahmed quickly stepped back.

Charlotte bent down and stroked Nefer until she quieted. "Was it you who stole Nefer? To warn me?"

He looked offended. "Of course not. It is unlucky to anger a cat descended from the time of the pharaohs. But whoever did steal her surely meant it as a warning."

She stood up, leaning toward him so that she imagined they looked a proper pair of conspirators. "Does Sir Thomas know that Hatiri's treasure was found in the Valley of Amun?"

He nodded. "The old fox knows everything. As does the man called Hughes."

The memory of the Havers's visit to the Valley of Amun came flooding back. Sir Thomas had seemed so eager for Ian to leave Egypt and take over the directorship of the Colville Collection. Was it because he knew a royal ransom in gold lay hidden beneath the sands, and he wanted her and

Ian out of the way? But if so, why did he ask Dylan to take over? Unless he thought they could buy him off. After all, only she and the Antiquities Service knew that Dylan was not an unscrupulous treasure hunter.

She shivered, suddenly feeling as cold as a grave. "Ahmed, was my husband's death an accident?"

His expression grew even more forbidding. "No."

The world seemed to sway and rock for a terrible moment. "So someone wanted him dead," she said in a trembling voice. "As they wanted poor Samir dead."

Ahmed seemed even more distressed than she did. She had never seen him so agitated.

"I should not have said anything. It will only bring you more unhappiness. But you must understand the danger you are in."

"I don't care about the danger! Don't you understand? All this time I believed that I was responsible for Ian's death!" She wasn't certain if it was relief or horror she felt. Perhaps both. "How could you keep this from me? Why didn't you say anything years ago, right after he died?"

"I thought it was an accident. It was only recently that I suspected the truth. And it is a terrible truth, Mrs. Fairchild, but one I should have foreseen. That is why I have sought you out, to warn you to stay away from anything to do with the Valley of Amun."

"You must tell me who wanted my husband dead." She forced herself to remain calm. "Was it Sir Thomas? Hughes?"

He took her by the elbow, startling her. Ahmed had never touched her during all the years they worked together in Egypt. Nefer gave a warning growl again.

"It is not just you who is in danger, it is myself as well. I have been wanting to speak with you these past weeks, but your house is being watched."

She lowered her voice to a whisper. "We'll have to go to the police."

"And are you so certain they can be trusted? Sir Thomas is not without influence, as are the wealthy patrons who buy the antiquities from him. And London police are as easily bribed as policemen in Cairo or Constantinople."

"Perhaps we can go to Mr. Pierce." Despite everything, she could think of no one else to turn to. "He may know what to do."

Ahmed scowled. "Pierce is a looter, the greediest one of them all. You cannot tell him. He will only try to steal the treasure for himself."

She was about to say that Dylan had worked to expose smugglers, yet what right had she to reveal his secrets? Dylan told her he had made powerful enemies when he was a clandestine agent. An unwise confidence to Ahmed might endanger Dylan.

Then again, what proof did she have that Dylan had told her the truth? What if he had lied to her about working for the Antiquities Service? What if he had been deceiving her all along? What if he really was the Lion?

"I shall go mad in another moment," she murmured.

"What did you say?" Even though she didn't think it possible, Ahmed now looked even more worried.

"No, you're right, Ahmed. Until we know who to trust, we should say nothing."

"We must both leave England as quickly as possible, Mrs. Fairchild. Let the treasure go. It is more important that we live."

"I'm not leaving until I know what is going on."

"Yes, what exactly *is* going on?"

They both jumped. Samson Pope stood a few feet away, watching them with narrowed eyes.

Ahmed turned to her. "You should not work at the museum any longer," he said in Arabic. "I believe the treasure lies hidden within. They will want to get it out—and soon."

"But where?" she replied in Arabic. "I've searched all of

the crates that arrived from the Valley of Amun. I found nothing unusual."

"Speak English," Samson ordered.

"The treasure must be there," Ahmed continued in Arabic. "I wouldn't be surprised if most of the staff are involved, as well as those policemen who now patrol the museum. Do not look for it. You would be wise to go home and stay there until the treasure is gone. Only then will we be safe."

"Safe from whom?"

"The less you know, the easier you will sleep. I only warn you because you are the daughter of a great man and I would not see you harmed, if Allah allows me to prevent it."

Samson grabbed Charlotte by the arm and pulled her away from Ahmed. "I said to speak English. Now what's going on?"

She shook off his grip. "You have no right to tell us to speak English or anything else, Inspector Pope."

"I have the right to question suspicious characters, Mrs. Fairchild."

"Really? And is it me or Mr. Vartan who qualifies as a suspicious character?"

"Both of you. It seems that Sir Thomas has disappeared."

Ahmed murmured a plea to Allah.

"Stop that gibberish."

"It is not gibberish," she said. "He is speaking Arabic, an elegant and noble language, which you would know if you weren't so proud of being ignorant."

Charlotte and Samson glared at each other. A moment later, his face creased unexpectedly into a grin.

"No wonder Dylan is besotted. You'll keep him on his toes for the next fifty years and he'll love every minute of it."

"I have no intention of caring about Dylan or his toes for the next fifty minutes, let alone fifty years. What I do care about is being manhandled by Scotland Yard in broad daylight."

"Perhaps you haven't heard what I said. Sir Thomas has disappeared. Lady Havers is extremely upset. It seems he left yesterday morning for an appointment with his banker and never returned." He paused. "We can't find Hughes either."

Although she was disturbed by the news, she refused to show it. Detective Pope had investigated her and her father, all the while pretending to be her friend. She no longer trusted him.

"Very interesting, but what has any of this to do with me?"

"Perhaps nothing. But anyone who knew Sir Thomas and Barnabas Hughes, especially anyone who had reason to dislike them, is under suspicion. I'm afraid that includes you, Mrs. Fairchild."

"Are you taking me in for questioning?" Charlotte asked primly, giving a tug to her kid gloves.

"No, but I think it would be best if you returned home and stayed there, at least until we find out what happened to these men."

"No doubt Dylan would prefer me to stay locked up as well."

"We're only thinking of your safety."

"Well, while you're both thinking of my safety, I must think of the upcoming exhibit." She waved him aside. "So if you will find another innocent Londoner to harass, I would be much obliged."

Samson did not look pleased but had no choice but to take a step back.

Ahmed took the opportunity to whisper to her in Arabic, "I must speak with you again."

"And I wouldn't advise moving out of your rooms in Chelsea, Mr. Vartan," Samson said loudly. "I may wish to question you as well."

Ahmed ignored him. "Please be careful, Mrs. Fairchild. If Sir Thomas and Hughes are gone, that is a very bad sign. It means they are ready to act. I can no longer prevent them from stealing the treasure, but at least I can try to keep you from harm."

"Again in Arabic?" Samson put his hands on his hips. "What sort of secrets are the two of you trading?"

Charlotte turned her back to Pope. "Come to the museum tonight," she replied in Arabic. "An hour after closing."

"Not in the museum," he protested. "It is too dangerous."

She thought a moment. "Then meet me at the St. James Restaurant in Piccadilly. Seven o'clock."

Ahmed gave a curt bow of the head.

Only after he had disappeared around the corner did Charlotte turn her attention to Samson Pope.

"Why are you following me?"

"I'm not. I came to the Collection this morning to order my men to conduct another search of the museum. Perhaps there is something in Hughes's papers or in one of the offices that will indicate where either he or Sir Thomas have gotten to." He shook his head. "I certainly did not expect to see you here. I thought you were home nursing Dylan."

"He's much better. There was no need for me to stay. Now, if this interrogation is over, I must ask you to leave me alone so I can get on with my work. I've had quite enough of Scotland Yard interfering in my life."

Giving a tug to Nefer's leash, she began walking along the crushed stone path leading to the museum.

To her dismay, Samson fell into step beside her. Her thoughts and emotions were in turmoil and she needed desperately to be alone. She didn't know what she was going to do with the information Ahmed had just given her, if indeed there was anything she could do. But she certainly couldn't think clearly with Samson Pope's suspicious gaze turned her way.

"What were you and the Turk talking about?"

"It's private."

"People who guard their privacy so fiercely usually have something to hide."

"Some of us prefer to keep at least one corner of our lives from being sullied by the police."

He whistled under his breath. "I *have* offended you."

She hurried, her heels making crunching noises on the rocks. He easily kept pace.

"I fear I must risk offending you further."

Something in his voice made her stop. "What is it now?"

"As you know, I did a thorough job of looking into the background of you and your husband."

"And my father," she said tartly.

He nodded. "Mrs. Fairchild, it is my professional opinion that your husband was involved in the illegal trafficking of antiquities."

"What! Where is your proof?"

"Call it circumstantial evidence. And I trust Dylan's judgment. If he says the ring was stolen from Sekkara, then it was."

"Assuming that's true, did it ever occur to you that when Ian bought the ring, he was unaware of its provenance?"

"That's possible, but unlikely."

"How about me?" she asked in an icy voice. "Do you suspect me of smuggling too?"

"That too is unlikely, but . . ." He finally had the grace to look uncomfortable.

"But?"

"But not impossible."

"I see." She took a moment to calm her breathing. So both Dylan and Samson harbored doubts about her. She wasn't certain if it was anger she felt or sadness.

"I'm only trying to do my job, Mrs. Fairchild," he said, in a voice that sounded almost apologetic.

"I have no interest in you or your job, Inspector. All that matters is that you don't interfere with me doing mine."

But as she swept into the museum, she heard Samson give

orders for two policemen to stand guard at both the front and back entrances, with another policeman assigned to accompany her if she stepped foot outside the museum.

No wonder he and Dylan were such fast friends. Both were as wary and unwelcome as jackals in the desert.

He was of no use to anyone. Dylan wondered how he had ever maneuvered his way through the smuggling rings and looters of Egypt for ten years. A slight mauling by an overgrown house cat, an attack of malarial fever, and here he was flat on his back like a victim of the Crimean War. How could anyone have ever believed him to be the infamous Lion?

"This is ridiculous. I'm perfectly fine."

He scowled at the maid, who was perched on the corner rocker.

"There's no need to keep watching me like I'm a lunatic about to tear up the asylum. I've slept the better part of the day, and when I'm awake, either you or Randall are stuffing toast and broth down my throat."

"Mrs. Fairchild says we're to keep an eye on you." Lorrie put aside the linen napkin she was mending. "If you're not hungry or tired, I'll put a little more salve on those scratches."

"Don't you dare. You slather on one more coat of that stuff, and my skin will peel like a banana." He frowned, which made his scratched cheeks burn. "I won't have people watching me every moment. If you don't give me some privacy, I'll walk out of this house in Michael's nightshirt, if I must."

Her big brown eyes scrutinized him for a long moment before she finally allowed herself a tiny grin. "All right, sir. I must say you do seem livelier than you were this morning." She picked up her sewing. "But make sure to ring the bell in case you need anything. And don't you worry about the cat. She's at the museum with Mrs. Fairchild."

278

"I'm not worried about the cat. It's your mistress I'm worried about."

Lorrie had apparently heard this once too often today. "Well, you won't have to worry much longer, sir. It's nearly dusk. She should be home soon. And I'd best help Cook with supper."

After the maidservant left, he felt more restless than ever. At least when Randall and Lorrie were in the room, he could complain about how foolish they'd all been to let Charlotte leave the house with only the cat for protection. Alone, he could only rail at himself.

He leaned back against the pillow and stared at the column of toy soldiers lined along Michael's top bookshelf. He wished everyone would stop reassuring him that the cat wasn't home. Did they think he went in terror of Nefer now that he had a few scratches on his face? He'd best get back to Egypt before his reputation went from being a scoundrel and a womanizer to a sniveling coward.

Anyway, it wasn't Nefer and her claws that concerned him, it was Charlotte. She shouldn't be at the museum without him. Who knew what the next nasty surprise might be? Scorpions last time, perhaps poisonous snakes the next. Although she was capable enough to handle a poisonous viper or two.

He threw back the covers. The naps had left him clear-headed and his joints less sore. He gingerly put one foot on the floor, then the other. His legs felt only a little shaky. If he could discover where they'd hidden his clothes, he might even get dressed and take a carriage down to the museum.

Five minutes later he found his clothes—cleaned and pressed—hanging in Michael's armoire. But as he was about to pull off his nightshirt, a wave of dizziness swept over him. He made it to the rocker just before his knees buckled.

"Bloody hell," he muttered.

He couldn't recall when he'd had such a serious attack of malaria. It had to be the strain he'd been under lately, the lack of quinine, the whiskey he'd been drinking. It was as he always suspected: Egypt was far better for his constitution than England. Even malarial fever was milder there.

Suddenly exhausted, he closed his eyes. He felt as tired as Methuselah and twice as old. And to make matters worse, Charlotte hadn't forgiven him. What if she never did? What if she refused to return to Egypt with him?

He'd go back to excavating, of course, back to the work that he loved. But without Charlotte, the years spread before him like a decaying scroll. Nothing but his righteous suspicions to keep him company as he grew old. Nothing but belly dancers and fickle actresses to warm his bed, but never his heart. Charlotte would always have his heart.

But Charlotte said he'd broken her heart.

It pained him to think that he'd hurt her so, yet it seemed anything he said or did upset her now. This morning he was only trying to tell her of his belief that Ian had been murdered. Instead, his statement churned up her old guilt, her stubborn belief that she was responsible for her husband's death. No wonder she wouldn't forgive him. He couldn't even forgive himself.

Opening his eyes, he spied the leather case lying atop the armoire. Another reminder of his folly. Samson had dropped the report off this morning. He'd read it quickly and found himself even more depressed afterward. For there was nothing in the detailed report to point suspicion at Charlotte, the Colvilles, or her father. Why had he included them on that list?

Because he didn't know how to trust anyone or anything, he thought to himself. Not even his own feelings.

Maybe he should reread it before Charlotte returned. Earlier Samson had informed him that Hughes and Sir Thomas were missing. Perhaps the report held some clue to their disappearances. He had read the thing through so fast, a detail or two might have escaped him. Especially with his pounding head and dizziness.

For something about the report *had* bothered him. His head was clearer now; he might be able to figure out what it was.

Hoping his legs were steadier, he slowly stood up and retrieved the papers.

The pages of the report fell open to the section about Charlotte. No, he wouldn't insult her by looking at it again. She was innocent. Even though Samson had told him that he found her deep in conversation with Ahmed that morning—a conversation conducted in Arabic. His detective friend thought they were hiding something. Well, if they were, Dylan knew it was nothing criminal. He trusted Charlotte—he'd just realized it a damn sight too late. He cursed himself again.

He turned next to the sections concerning Ian Fairchild, Sir Thomas, Ahmed Vartan, and Barnabas Hughes. He sat up suddenly. At last he saw what had been troubling him ever since he looked over the report earlier that day.

It was so clear, so bloody clear!

Damn his malaria. Weak or not, he had to see Charlotte immediately. He had to tell her.

After all this time, he had finally discovered the identity of the Lion.

Chapter Nineteen

Charlotte feared that Scotland Yard would drive her completely mad.

The Yard had been underfoot all day. None of the museum staff were able to work uninterrupted for more than ten minutes before a policeman burst in, demanding keys to a closet or asking for assistance in moving priceless exhibits. Two Bobbies had actually knocked over a Doric statue of Apollo, chipping part of the marble. Charlotte flew into such a temper that Nefer had to be restrained from attacking the clumsy policemen.

Unable to bear the sight of the broken statue, she finally stalked off, taking refuge in the Valley of Amun exhibit hall.

"And what did they think they were going to find beneath the statue?" Charlotte asked aloud, her voice echoing in the cavernous gallery.

She restlessly circled the reconstructed tomb.

"Did they think there were clues scrawled on the underside of Apollo, or papers hidden inside the Roman helmets?

Philistines! Brutes! They'll destroy half the museum at this rate."

Nefer meowed as she kept pace with her mistress.

She looked down at her beloved cat. "As though it's not bad enough that they chased away all the visitors, now they're banging about the museum like rampaging Vandals. If they don't find something soon, they'll end up tearing down the very walls."

"It's not so bad as that, ma'am," a voice said.

She spun about, but the gallery was empty.

"We're almost done in here," the voice continued from inside the tomb.

"Get out of there right now," she ordered.

A moment later, two policemen crawled out of the tomb's narrow entrance. Their blue uniforms and stovepipe hats were covered in dust.

She pushed past them and did a quick inspection of the crypt's interior. When she reemerged, she gasped to see the limestone posts and lintel wobbling precariously.

"Don't touch that," she hissed at the policeman who was running his hands over one of the stone posts. "The lintel was just cemented to the posts. It's not yet dry. You'll send it crashing down on your head."

He looked up at the heavy inscribed block. "Well, this looks blooming dangerous. Any one of your museum visitors could brush against it and get their skull bashed in."

She counted to ten in Arabic *and* English. "As I explained earlier, the exhibits in this gallery are not ready for the public. They won't be for another month. That is why it is roped off. And that is why we've posted warnings every ten feet."

With a weary sigh, she laid her hand on the sign placed directly in front of the posts and lintel. "Now if you gentlemen are done, I would appreciate it if you would leave this gallery and let me get back to work."

It was a marvel she was able to speak in a calm voice. "And please do not enter the tomb again. That too is not yet properly supported." She forced herself to smile. "I wouldn't want the museum blamed for any injury that might befall the London police."

The younger of the policemen colored slightly. "Sorry, ma'am, but we have our orders from Detective Pope. He'd have our heads if we didn't do a thorough job of searching the premises."

She took a deep breath. "Since you've been searching the Collection for the better part of eight hours, may I safely assume you are done?"

"Have to get inside those cases first," his partner said.

Her heart stopped. "Cases? What cases?"

Both men pointed to the sarcophagi that lined the back wall of the gallery. "Over there."

"You can't be serious. The only thing inside the sarcophagi are mummies!"

The policemen looked alarmed by this revelation. "You mean the mummies of them dead pharaohs that the curse talks about?"

"Yes, that's right. They're cursed." She pointed to the hieroglyphics inscribed on the lintel. "Do you know what that is? It's a warning to anyone foolish enough to disturb the ancient dead. It promises all manner of vile and terrible punishments to those who do."

They looked properly taken aback. "Maybe we don't need to open all of them up. But Inspector Pope will want to know we looked in one or two of them."

"Gentlemen, please. *We* haven't even opened up most of the sarcophagi. They're sealed tight with five-thousand-year-old resin. And when we do open them up, the procedure is immensely time-consuming. One must be very careful not to—"

"We found just the thing!"

Charlotte bit back a scream. Three more policemen entered the gallery, one of them waving a crowbar.

"You can't destroy these priceless artifacts!" She thought

wildly for some way to stop them. "Think of the curse!"

But it seemed that Scotland Yard was impervious to ancient threats. And all she could do was cringe as the London police mercilessly ripped open the painted coffins.

"I don't care who you are. You can't come in." The policeman rapped his knuckles against the engraved sign beside the museum entrance. "This says the Collection closed an hour ago."

"But I didn't come to visit the Collection." Even though Dylan had ridden a carriage here, he felt as exhausted as if he had walked a hundred miles. If he didn't sit down soon, his knees were sure to buckle.

"I need to see Mrs. Fairchild," he went on. "She's in charge of the new Egyptian exhibit. If you could just tell her that Dylan Pierce wishes to see her." He braced his arm against a nearby column. "I have information that she must hear as soon as possible. Urgent information."

"Sorry, Mr. Pierce, but Mrs. Fairchild is very busy. She gave orders that she was not to be disturbed." The policeman stepped back into the shadows of the entrance.

Dylan pushed himself away from the column. "Look here, I insist you let me in. Mrs. Fairchild will want to hear what I have to say. I'm not leaving until I see her." Overcome by a wave of dizziness, he stumbled and nearly fell.

"Go sleep it off, mate." The policeman's voice now dripped with scorn. "Mrs. Fairchild's not the sort of woman who needs to be bothered by the likes of you."

Dylan flung himself at the heavy door as it began to swing shut. In his weakened condition, however, he was no match for the tall policeman on the other side who was pushing it shut.

"Let me in!" Only a small crack in the entrance remained, and Dylan let fly a string of Welsh curses.

"No need for that kind of language," the policeman replied in Welsh. A second later, the door slammed in Dylan's face.

Stunned and out of breath, Dylan could only lean weakly against the door. Then he began pounding on the heavy bronze as though his life depended on it.

He knew now—with chilling certainty—that Charlotte's life did.

Charlotte sat with her head in her hands. It had taken only thirty minutes for the policemen to open up and rifle through two of the sarcophagi, but it seemed to last an eternity. She couldn't bear to watch. Instead she sat on the floor, waiting silently for the barbarians to finish their willful destruction.

"We're done in here, ma'am."

She looked up to see the young policeman standing over her.

"I trust you found nothing of interest," she said.

"You were right." He gave a sheepish shrug. "There were just some more little coffins inside, until we got to the mummy. Sorry we busted up the boxes so bad, though."

She gathered up her courage and looked. Lids and wooden fragments lay scattered over the floor. The other policemen filed past, avoiding her accusing gaze.

"Are you quite finished in here? After all, you only destroyed two of them. There are at least twenty more for you to tear apart."

"No, ma'am. We don't see any reason to open the rest of them up. Besides, them boxes are sealed tighter than a cement house."

"You mean they *were* sealed tighter."

He took a step back. "In fact, we're done with the search. The three Bobbies assigned to patrol the museum tonight should be here already. Soon as we gather all our men, we'll be on our way."

"Thank merciful heaven." She dropped her head back in her hands. "Please get out of here. Go home, and take the crowbar with you."

"I—I feel a bit bad about all this mess, ma'am. Would

286

you like a few of us to stay and help clean up?"

She stood up quickly.

"No! I don't want any of you to touch a single thing in this gallery ever again. *I* will clean up. Please just go."

But long after the Metropolitan Police left, Charlotte could only stare at the wreckage they had left behind. They were worse than looters, destroying the past not for gold but because their superior ordered them to. The next time she saw Detective Pope, she'd set Nefer on him. She swore that she would.

When she finally brought herself to peer into one of the broken coffins, the destruction was so great that she screamed.

Her cries brought no one running, however. She was grateful. That must mean that the police were at last gone, except for the two or three who were patrolling the cavernous corridors and galleries.

Confident that no one could hear her, she began railing in Arabic at the idiots who had bashed in the ancient coffins. They'd even ripped at the linen strips that bound the mummies, tearing off the sacred amulets, only to leave them scattered about the ground.

"Bloody hell!" she yelled again.

Nefer sat watching with wide eyes. Even her cat seemed afraid to approach her in her present mood.

Getting down on her hands and knees, she began to carefully pick up the amulets. They were originally meant to bless the deceased, to protect him or her from harm. Now they'd been carelessly flung about as if they were little more than river pebbles.

"Here, now. What's this?"

She sat back, running her fingers over the green faience amulet. It was an amulet fashioned in the shape of a lioness, the goddess Sekhmet. Her breathing grew short. Years ago she had found just such an amulet while digging in the Valley of Amun. It became her good-luck charm.

287

She held it up to the gaslight and looked closely at it. She had never taken it off, save for the day she draped it about Ian's neck.

Her hands began to tremble. Nonsense. There must be more than one green faience amulet of Sekhmet. After all, the last time she saw her amulet, Ian was wearing it. And Ian was dead and buried in the Fairchild family cemetery in Lincolnshire.

"I see you've found your good-luck amulet, Charlotte," a voice said. "Pity it won't do you any good."

With a shocked cry, she swiveled about. A policeman stood watching her from beneath the darkened skylight.

It was Ian Fairchild.

Chapter Twenty

"Ian?" The lioness amulet dropped from her suddenly lifeless hands.

He took a step closer. In the flickering gaslight, her gaze took in his blond hair, the scar on his forehead, his clean-shaven face. She almost collapsed with relief. Ian had jet-black hair, ruddy skin unmarked by a scar, and always favored a goatee. This was simply a man who sounded like her late husband.

"Who—who are you?"

"I know it's been nearly three years, my love, but I hoped you hadn't completely forgotten me." He laughed, and the room spun madly about her. She clapped her hands over her mouth, trying to keep back a horrified scream.

He pointed to the amulet on the floor. "I knew I should have supervised the packing of the sarcophagi. Everything of value was supposed to be inside the mummy wrappings. But my men were too greedy, throwing in every amulet and scarab just in case we could sell them as well. I should have crushed *your* amulet under my heel, to be safe."

"This can't be!"

He glanced over at the growling cat. "That infernal animal remembers me."

"This is impossible," she said, her voice coming out in gasps. "This is impossible."

"Only you have ever proved impossible, Charlotte."

"You're dead! You died in the cave-in. I was there." She swallowed hard as the painful memory came flooding back. "I was there. No man could have survived it."

He shrugged. "Perhaps you're talking to a ghost, then."

But he was no ghost. He stood only fifteen feet away, and Charlotte could see that he was flesh and blood. Now that he was so near, she recognized those all-too-familiar features. Certainly she would have known that voice anywhere. It had been haunting her dreams ever since his death.

But he hadn't died. He was alive—and the years of regret and guilt were for nothing. Nothing!

"It took three months for the workers to retrieve your body." She tried to breathe normally, tried to make sense of all this. "They wrote me when they at last dug through. Whose body did they dig out if not yours?"

"There was no body to recover. I simply decided three months was a reasonable time to remove the rubble and rock. After all, I was trying to convince you and the world that I was dead." He ran a finger over his scarred forehead. "Although I did sustain a scratch or two."

"What are you saying?" She felt hysterical laughter rising up. "A coffin was shipped from Egypt with your body in it! Who in heaven's name is buried in that Lincolnshire graveyard?"

"The coffin was weighted with other material."

Charlotte tried to get to her feet but fell back. In another moment she'd lose consciousness.

She suddenly understood. "Treasure! The coffin was weighted with treasure, wasn't it?"

"Very good, Charlotte." His expression was almost approving, as though she were a slow pupil who had surprised him with the right answer.

"The treasure of Hatiri," she continued.

His eyes narrowed. "Who told you about the treasure of Hatiri?"

"I did." Ahmed appeared at the door to the gallery.

Charlotte let out a cry of relief.

"Oh, thank heaven you're here, Ahmed!" This time she did struggle to her feet, clutching Nefer in her arms. "Ian is alive!"

Both men looked at her with scorn, and something akin to pity.

Ian turned back to Ahmed. "I should have known. You persist in trying to spare this maddening woman. I swear, you should have been the one to marry her."

Her relief at seeing Ahmed quickly disappeared.

The Turk moved farther into the gallery. "I hoped telling you part of the truth would convince you to stay away, Mrs. Fairchild. When you didn't meet me tonight at the restaurant in Piccadilly, I knew I had failed." His dark eyes seemed genuinely sad. "I am sorry. For once I wish you had taken my advice."

Ian laughed. "The man has a soft spot for you, my dear. I told him that you could not stay away from all this." He nodded toward the mummies and the statues of Amun-Ra. "These dead relics are irresistible to you, more irresistible than any lover, any mere mortal. I told him that we couldn't scare you away either."

"So it was you who planted the scorpions."

"Mr. Hughes was entrusted with that task," Ahmed said.

She clutched Nefer closer. "And you stole Nefer."

"That was Sir Thomas's idea." Ian voice dripped with contempt. "One of his more asinine ideas, I might add. When his wife found out about it, she made him take the silly beast back straightaway. I told him it was a ridiculous notion. We could have kidnapped your whole family and you would still have come here every day to play about with your amulets and scarabs."

"Ian, I'm trying to understand all this." But she felt so confused and upset, she feared she never would.

"I thought Ahmed told you." Ian shrugged. "Perhaps he left out the best part."

She took a step back and bumped against the edge of the shattered sarcophagus. "The best part? He said the treasure of Hatiri was found in the Valley. I—I assume you were the one to find it. If it's as rich as legend promises—"

"Richer," Ian said softly. "A mountain of gold, my dear. A veritable mountain. It's taken us nearly three years to dig it all out."

Both men slowly moved toward her, like an animal they had cornered. If she somehow could get on the other side of the tomb, she might have a chance to run past them.

"I can understand how finding such a treasure might tempt a man." She inched her way along the sarcophagus. "Even a man of principle."

"Please stand still," Ian said. "I've no intention of letting you leave this room."

"But—but that's no reason to go completely mad," she continued. "No reason to throw away your life's work. No reason to become a looter and a thief."

"Are you really so obtuse, Charlotte? From the moment I began calling myself an archaeologist, I've never been anything *but* a thief."

"Your husband is far more than that," Ahmed protested. "In Egypt, we called him the Lion."

This time her legs did give out. She sank to the floor.

"*You're* the Lion?"

"You don't still imagine that drunkard Pierce was the Lion?" Ian sounded insulted by the idea. "Although I admit it suited my purpose when people began to mistakenly attribute my exploits to him. But there was an agent working for the Antiquities Service who was getting far too close to discovering my identity. I dared not remain in Egypt for the completion of that last field season, not without risking capture."

Charlotte looked up in alarm. Had Dylan been so close to capturing Ian? If only he had. So much pain and heartache might have been avoided.

"That's why I wanted Pierce to take over the Valley of Amun. I would have been safe in London, overseeing the Colville Collection, and he would have had only a few months to putter about the site before I had him killed. The world would have believed the Lion was dead, and I would be safe." He laughed. "I tried to get rid of him the year before in Cairo. I arranged a meeting with Pierce and one of my men. But the fool never showed up. We ended up burning down half of Cairo for nothing."

Merciful heaven, what sort of monster was she married to?

"I see the very idea of his death distresses you." Ian's voice grew bitter. "I'm sure you would have truly mourned Pierce's death, and not pretended to grieve as you did for me."

"Pretend? What do you know about how I have felt these past two and a half years!"

"Yes, no doubt you wept buckets of tears every time he made love to you."

She felt herself flush red.

"If you'd been a proper wife," Ian went on, "a proper *woman,* I might have confided in you. Despite your contrary nature, I did harbor feelings for you. We could have been together these past few years. I've been living like a pasha in North Africa. Under an assumed name, of course. You've no idea how profitable the smuggling has been. And once this greatest treasure is sold off, I shall be richer than most crowned heads of Europe."

"Dylan was right. He was right all along. He said that you

had stolen my ring from Sekkara. I wouldn't believe him."

All this time she had accused Dylan of not trusting her when *she* hadn't trusted him. She'd refused to believe him when he claimed the ring was stolen, refused to believe him even after learning that he worked for the Antiquities Service. She was such a hypocrite to turn him away because of his suspicions, when she held so many of her own. She didn't deserve his trust, nor his love either.

"I should have believed him," she moaned again.

Ian shook his head. "I'm surprised he did recognize the ring. I'd always heard Pierce drank so much, he could barely stand upright, let alone identify dynastic jewelry. Certainly he could never have found the treasure of Hatiri."

He removed his policeman's hat and flung it to the floor. Now she could see how oddly discolored his hair was.

"Imagine, Charlotte, you and your father excavated over a decade in the Valley of Amun. Both of you digging like little dogs, trying to find the tomb of Hatiri. And the first month I was on the site, *I* found it."

"Where?" Despite her fear, she was desperate to know.

"Hidden behind a previously excavated tomb, one bearing the remains of an ordinary priest of Amun. In fact, it was your first foreman who found the secret tunnel. Poor wretch came running to me with the information, not quite sure what the tunnel indicated. But I knew. You would have known too." He paused. "As would your father."

She dropped the cat as a terrible realization hit her. "You killed Father, didn't you? It wasn't just the foreman Samir. You killed Father too!"

Ian's expression hardened further. "We had no choice."

She let out a horrendous wail.

"He was an ethical man," Ian went on. "He would have turned over the entire treasure to the Cairo Museum, and what would have been the use then of all our work? All that gold recovered only to lay moldering in some bloody museum hall."

Sobs shuddered through her.

"Mr. Fairchild wanted to arrange for you to die of a fever as well," Ahmed added. "Or what looked like a fever. But I convinced him that you were more use to us alive."

She stared in horror at both men. All these years she had been surrounded by lies, treachery.

"The Colvilles always were fond of your family, especially that crazy Aunt Hazel. I correctly guessed that they would ask the Cairo Museum to turn over your father's permit to me." Ian gave a mocking bow. "If I became your devoted husband."

"I could kill you myself," she spat at him.

"Now that's the Charlotte I remember." He chuckled.

"I wish now you had died in the cave-in!"

"Did you really think that I would enter a tomb that wasn't properly braced and supported? Really, my dear, you knew I was once an engineer. I worried that the scheme wouldn't work precisely because of that, but we fooled you." Ian nodded in obvious satisfaction. "We fooled everybody."

"I held myself responsible for your death." She felt sick with shock and despair. And rage. "What a fool. I blamed myself."

"You *were* to blame. If you hadn't interfered, I would have been in London overseeing the Collection. But you had to run to Pierce and convince him to turn down the site. You spoiled all our plans and necessitated my premature—and quite dramatic—death." He nodded at Ahmed, who rushed toward her.

"Stay away!" She pressed herself against the sarcophagus.

Nefer arched her back and hissed.

The Turk stopped, his eyes widening at the sight of the angry cat.

"Bloody beast," Ian said with disgust. "I should have drowned it that day in Egypt. I told Ahmed to find a cat and claim he discovered it lying at the entrance to the tomb. I knew it would scare off the superstitious workers from entering the tomb with me." He laughed. "Instead, he had the good fortune to actually find a kitten already asleep in the tomb entrance. And what does he do? Convinces himself that the animal is a real omen from the gods."

"She has been sent by the Goddess Bastet." Ahmed wiped at his damp forehead with his sleeve. "If we harm her, we will know nothing but bad fortune."

Ian pointed at Charlotte. "My wife has brought us more bad fortune than a dozen cats."

"How have I done that?" she asked, desperate to keep Ian talking.

"I needed to smuggle the material out of Egypt. For years I had been sending stolen antiquities to Hughes and Sir Thomas here at the Collection." He picked up a funerary urn. "Once it was safely stowed away in the basement storerooms, it could be broken up and sold to private collectors, other museums. But then Lord Barrington got an attack of conscience."

Her mind was in a whirl. "Lord Barrington? The previous director of the Collection?"

"Yes. He turned coward on us, began moaning that he'd get sent to prison for sure if this kept up. We certainly couldn't entrust the treasure of Hatiri to that old sod. So Hughes and Sir Thomas arranged a little accident. Once he was dead, who better to take over the Collection than me?"

He lifted up the urn and aimed it at the cat. "Then you went and ruined everything. As always."

Ian threw the urn at Nefer. Charlotte screamed. The artifact shattered an inch from Nefer's face, scaring the cat so that she leaped upon the nearest sarcophagus.

Once the cat no longer barred his way, Ahmed grabbed Charlotte and pinned her arms behind her back. She struggled, shouting at the top of her lungs as he yanked her to her feet.

"There's no one to hear, Charlotte. The other policemen patrolling the museum tonight belong to me, as do the two guards." Ian pulled a handkerchief from his jacket. "But just in case . . ." He stuffed the cloth so far down her throat, she gagged.

"In the tomb," he said to Ahmed, who began dragging her. "Ironic, isn't it? You believed that I died in an ancient tomb, but now you'll be the one buried alive in this one." He patted the limestone blocks as they passed. "Imagine how your death will add to the curse of the Valley of Amun."

She kicked Ahmed's shin. He only gripped her tighter.

"We need something to tie your arms with." Ian scanned the gallery.

"I tried to warn you, Mrs. Fairchild," Ahmed whispered. "I told you to stay away until the treasure was gone. Just one more day. If only you had listened to me this once. We would have been gone with the riches, and you would have your life." He sighed. "Now I will have another death on my conscience."

She lashed out at him again with her foot, but no matter how she twisted and kicked, he did not let her go. Instead, he began pulling her toward the entrance to the tomb. She looked up at the heavy carved blocks. Did they mean to tie her up and throw her inside? All Ian had to do was exert the right pressure and these unsupported stones would crush her as surely as she once thought they had crushed him.

If only she could see Dylan one more time. If only he could know that she was sorry, that she believed him, that she would have trusted him with her life from this point on. But now she would have no life. And he would always think she died not trusting him. Not believing in his love for her.

"No!" she screamed behind the gag, and threw herself against Ahmed.

Startled, he lost his balance and fell. She landed on top of him.

"Can't you hold on to that woman?" Ian shouted.

Her hands were free now and she pulled the gag off. Gasping for air, she tried to pry his hands off her, but Ahmed was too strong. Cursing under his breath, he dragged her to the entrance of the tomb.

She sunk her teeth into his hand. He howled in pain and released her.

Charlotte got to her knees, determined to throw herself on top of him with fists flying. But then she saw his eyes go wide with dread.

From behind her came an ominous growl.

"Keep the cat away!" Ahmed shouted, but Nefer had already pounced.

For a second, Charlotte felt as though she were reliving Nefer's attack on Dylan, but this was much worse. Nefer's fangs sliced open Ahmed's cheek. Her front claws slashed across both of the Turk's eyes, so that blood streamed down his face. His screams filled the cavernous gallery as he tried to pull the furious animal off him.

Ian appeared suddenly, kicking her out of the way.

Charlotte flung herself at Ian and knocked him to the ground. Out of the corner of her eye, she saw Ahmed finally wrestle the cat off him. Bleeding and terrified, he crawled backwards into the crypt. The growling cat disappeared after him.

Ian pushed her away. "I'm going to kill that cat! And you!"

But he never got the chance.

A deafening crash sounded overhead. Both Ian and Charlotte looked up. Broken glass rained down upon them, and she quickly covered her face.

The skylight had inexplicably shattered. Charlotte felt the sting of what seemed like tiny balls of ice pelting her skin and clothing, and it sounded as though they had been caught in a hail storm.

When the noise subsided, she dared to lift her head again and get her bearings.

"What the hell is going on?" Ian cursed beside her. "Who the devil did that?"

A familiar face peered down at them through the hole in the roof. Charlotte wanted to weep with relief and joy.

"Dylan!" she cried.

The drop looked longer than he had anticipated, but he had no choice. He could see Charlotte sprawled on the ground beside the Welsh-speaking policeman who had barred him from entering the museum. Except he was no policeman; it was Fairchild—it had to be. Ian didn't look like Dylan remembered, but all the pieces fit together.

Fairchild was half Welsh, according to Charlotte and the Scotland Yard report. Moreover, Charlotte claimed her husband had been as proud of his Welsh heritage as Dylan was. Small wonder that he had taken the alias the Lion. For the report stated that while Ian's father was Joshua Fairchild, his mother was born Elizabeth Llew.

And, as any decent Welshman or linguist knew, *Llew* was Welsh for *lion*.

"I'm coming down, Charlotte!" He looked for a safe place to jump. There wasn't one.

He would simply have to let go and hope to land on top of the tomb. Since the structure wasn't braced yet, he'd probably send it crashing to the ground. But he had no choice. He needed something to break his fall.

With luck, he would only shatter a dozen bones.

"Dylan, don't jump!" Charlotte struggled to her feet.

The policeman made a grab for her, but she moved out of reach. And sight.

"You'll kill yourself!" she shouted from some unseen corner of the gallery.

"Stay there! I'm coming." He eased himself over the side, cutting his hands on the jagged ridges of glass along the edges of the skylight. For a heart-stopping moment, he let himself dangle in the air.

Below, he saw Fairchild get to his feet. He had to jump. Now.

In the moment before he let go, he heard Charlotte scream for Nefer. Then he was falling like Alice through the rabbit hole. His descent seemed endless, the statues whirling below him. Again he heard Charlotte call out. His legs hit the top of the tomb, and blinding pain shot through him.

His body shuddered so, he feared his bones would shake loose from his flesh. He struggled for air, the breath knocked out of him. Even through his suffering, he was dimly aware that the tomb had not collapsed as expected.

"Charlotte," he whispered.

Then he felt a trembling underneath his back. As though in a dream, he heard one stone block crash to the floor, then another. The roof shifted beneath him as the tomb began to fall apart in slow motion.

Unable to move, Dylan could only lie there at the whim of the construction falling apart beneath him. One of the stone blocks hit his arm, and he moaned in pain. He thought he detected a muffled scream, but the roar of destruction quickly drowned it out.

At last, it was over.

It was a miracle he was still alive, but he couldn't move. How many bones *had* he broken?

He heard nothing for a long moment and feared that Charlotte had somehow gotten crushed by the falling rock.

Then he heard shouts from another part of the museum.

That didn't matter. He had to find out if Charlotte was still alive. He forced himself to raise his head. The pain shot through him like fire, but he ignored it.

"Charlotte, are you all right?"

Merciful heaven, where was she?

"I'm here, Dylan. I got knocked down by one of the posts." Her voice sounded nearly as weak as his did. A moment later, Charlotte herself appeared, covered in dust. A rivulet of blood ran down her face.

She smiled, although he could see the tears in her eyes as

well. "Never mind about me, my brave darling. Are you badly hurt?"

Dylan tried to move, but his legs felt as if they'd been sawn in half. As long as Charlotte was alive, however, it didn't matter what happened to him.

He suddenly remembered Fairchild. In another moment he was going to pass out from the pain. He struggled to remain awake.

"Where's Ian?" he asked hoarsely.

"The lintel fell on him."

He wasn't certain if he understood. He feared he was hallucinating. Somewhere in the distance, he registered other voices, loud, excited. And he could have sworn one of them belonged to Samson Pope.

Dylan lay back, exhausted. He felt the cold night air but was too dizzy to see the stars shining above the broken skylight. He was losing consciousness. He didn't mind that or the pain. As long as Charlotte was safe.

"Well, Mrs. Fairchild," he heard Samson say loudly, "it looks as if you're a widow. Again."

Dylan laid his head back with a sigh of relief. Then everything went black.

"He's the bravest man in the world," Charlotte sobbed. "The bravest."

Samson watched as his men carefully laid the unconscious Dylan on a stretcher. "He's certainly the luckiest. That fall should have killed him."

One thing Dylan's fall from the skylight—and the collapse of the tomb—did do was destroy at least a quarter of the exhibit. Dozens of artifacts lay smashed about the floor, as did several black, ominous statues.

Charlotte seemed oblivious to the destruction. Instead she knelt down beside Dylan and gently kissed his face. Samson was only grateful that he'd gone back to Charlotte's house that evening with his latest news. As soon as he discovered that both Charlotte and the malaria-stricken Dylan were at the museum, he'd rushed over here.

Not that they needed his help. The lovesick fool had jumped through a skylight! He'd never heard of such a thing. And the resulting collapse of the tomb had led to Ian Fairchild being crushed to death beneath one of the falling stones.

Dylan moaned. Samson guessed that both legs were broken, along with one of his arms, a few ribs, and probably his shoulder. Imagine loving someone so much that you'd take such an insane risk. For the first time in his life, the police inspector envied that absurd specimen known as a man in love.

"I assume Mr. Vartan is somewhere under all that." Samson pointed at the rubble that was once the tomb.

Charlotte nodded, not bothering to look up. "I believe he's dead."

He bit back a chuckle. "Yes, he probably is."

"Dylan *will* be all right, won't he?"

"He'll be fine. Although I don't think these broken bones will do his malaria much good."

Charlotte looked up at him, her lovely eyes filled with wonder and admiration. "Can you imagine? He came here to rescue me when he was still weak from malaria."

"I guess you'll just have to take very good care of him."

She nodded. "As soon as he can walk, I'm taking him back to Egypt. He needs the heat and the sun."

And you, he thought wryly.

"Oh, Inspector, I think you should know. There's a great treasure hidden here in the museum."

"Yes." He gestured toward the sarcophagi lined along the walls of the gallery. "The gold is hidden inside the mummies. Or what is made to look like a mummy."

"How do you know that?"

"Lady Havers." Samson frowned to recall how hopeless the older woman had seemed. As though she had just lost

302

everything she had banked her life on, which indeed she had. "Fairchild unwisely decided to eliminate Sir Thomas and Hughes. We found them this afternoon, floating in the river."

Charlotte shuddered.

"When we informed Lady Havers of these deaths, she realized at once who was responsible. And told us everything." He cleared his throat. "It seems she was exceedingly fond of *both* men."

"But from what Ian said, Hughes and Sir Thomas were working with him. Why would he kill them?"

"Greed, I suspect. Lady Havers claims that Fairchild had been confiding less in her husband and Hughes and relying instead on Ahmed. The men quarreled, and Sir Thomas and Hughes decided to appropriate some of the treasure for themselves. Fairchild must have learned of their plan and killed them, which explains their disappearance two days ago."

He knelt down beside Ian's lifeless body, still covered by fragments of the ancient stone. "What do the hieroglyphics on this stone say? One of my men told me it was a curse."

"It is a curse," Charlotte said solemnly. " 'Beware to the greedy man who trespasses upon the priestly dead. Let the crocodile chase him on the waters, and the serpent pursue him on the land. A thousand tortures he will suffer before his spirit is crushed beneath his iniquity and guilt.' " She paused. " 'And his doomed spirit will forever be denied the blessings of Amun-Ra.' "

He nodded. "The Egyptians knew a thing or two about curses. Like me, you traffick in a dark and dangerous world, madame."

"Actually, the Egyptians cursed very few objects, Inspector." She pointed to the small, shiny treasures scattered about the floor.

"Those are protective amulets. The green-glazed frog was worn by women wishing to become pregnant; the alabaster grasshopper was thought to bestow riches and prosperity." She smiled. "And that little amethyst monkey served as a love charm. Whoever wore that amulet believed their sexual powers would increase, and love would come into their lives."

"I see." Samson looked with renewed interest at the artifacts.

A policeman appeared at the entrance to the gallery. "The ambulance wagon is here, sir."

"Be careful with him," Charlotte warned as six policemen lifted up Dylan's stretcher.

"One moment, Mrs. Fairchild," he called out as she started after them.

She paused, obviously eager to be with Dylan.

"We learned from Sir Thomas's wife that quite a few staff members were involved with the smuggling. In particular, those who worked with Hughes on the mummies. Apparently every mummy that was shipped to the Collection was in fact little more than a linen-wrapped treasure chest. I hope you won't be too upset if we arrest half your staff."

"They're the Colvilles' staff, not mine. And I certainly wish to see justice meted out to everyone involved in the smuggling." She cast a furtive look at her dead husband. "I can't believe I was such a fool all those years. Never to have guessed what was going on."

"Dylan never guessed either. Of course, he surprised them just as much. Lady Havers said her husband was outraged when the Colvilles agreed to let Dylan mount the Valley of Amun exhibit. They had every reason to believe Hughes would be selected. Then, when you joined the staff, everyone panicked. Fairchild was certain you would stumble upon their secret, especially given your obsession—sorry, I meant your familiarity—with these artifacts."

She shook her head. "You were right the first time. I have been obsessed with them. And it blinded me to the truth."

"Maybe something else was distracting you." Samson grinned.

To his relief, she smiled back. Even with her hair tumbling from its pins, her dress torn and covered with dust, and her face cut from the glass, the woman looked enchanting. He wasn't surprised that his friend was throwing himself through skylights.

"Dylan is quite a distraction," she said. "I fear I'll have a devil of a time trying to divide my attention fairly between him and Egypt."

The desert feline, limping slightly, walked over to her mistress. With a soft meow, she jumped into Charlotte's arms.

Charlotte hugged her close. "And I mustn't forget Nefer."

She murmured to her in Arabic. The cat closed her eyes and purred.

He laughed. "Keeping secrets again?"

But Charlotte only gazed at him over the top of Nefer's head. For a mesmerizing moment, she looked as regal and untouchable as an Egyptian queen.

"I must go," she said softly.

Then she turned and swept out of the gallery.

Samson sniffed. The air smelled of jasmine. It smelled of Charlotte. He was glad Dylan had found love with such a woman. He was happy for him. He was. But, hang it all, if Dylan Pierce was not a good friend, he'd chase after the gray-eyed lady himself. He'd find some way to woo and win her, some way to—

He stopped, amazed.

"Bloody fool, that's what I am," he said aloud, startling the other policemen who were prying open the sarcophagi along the back wall.

Best to get back to work and forget about the woman with hair the color of moonlight. Women only confused the thinking. Women broke your heart and sometimes your spirit. Women had no place in his life. Neither did romance or love.

But even as he tried to convince himself that he believed these statements, he searched through the rubble, lifting up

305

amulets and scarabs until he found the one he wanted.

Making certain no one was watching, Detective Inspector Samson Pope clutched the small amethyst monkey in his fist.

Then he closed his eyes and whispered, "Bring me love."

Epilogue

If not for the sandstorm, they would have been married by now.

Then there was that rogue leopard that terrorized the region for nearly two months. This part of Egypt hadn't seen a leopard in almost a century; Dylan and Charlotte had been so worried by the jungle cat's appearance that they'd postponed the digging for four weeks. But the leopard had been killed, and an Egyptian winter was safely upon them with no threat of dust storms until March.

There was no better time for a family visit. And Charlotte insisted on having her family with her when she married. Her first wedding had been a hasty, impersonal ceremony. If she married again—and Dylan had spent the past sixteen months trying to convince her to do just that—then the Graingers must be gathered about her.

Charlotte suggested they wait until they returned to London in May, but by then she would have given birth. No matter how scandalous his past, Dylan Pierce refused to let his first child be born out of wedlock, even if he had to import every blood relative she had.

Dylan squinted into the sun. The Nile glittered like blue diamonds in the distance, but he was more interested in the eight camels making their way over the sand dunes. To get a better look, he climbed onto the pedestal of a granite statue of Thoth. When he jumped down, he narrowly missed one of Nefer's kittens.

Isis pounced upon his bootlace.

"Can't you find a desert mouse to occupy you, little one?"

She gave a tiny meow, then ran off to chase a dung beetle.

Dust rose up all around him as he walked across the excavation site. Everywhere he looked, there were native workers, teams of surveyors, young Egyptologists fresh from university. He was extremely impressed by Mr. and Mrs. Colville's largesse. And by his own good fortune. Not only had the Colvilles reinstated him as director of the Collection, but they'd agreed to fund the site of Dar Fayem for as long as he and Charlotte wished.

Charlotte seemed to share his happiness with their new location, and he happily deduced they would be digging here well into the new century. He was grateful she had not asked to return to the Valley of Amun. Even he had begun to regard it as cursed, but fortunately Charlotte felt her father's memory was vindicated by the discovery of the treasure of Hatiri. The exhibit had finally opened to great acclaim, and she had rarely mentioned the Valley since, except in the tones of a person recalling a dearly departed friend.

Now if he could only find her before the camel train arrived . . .

He stood on a mound of rubble. "Charlotte!"

Her head popped up from a nearby excavation pit, a pith helmet sitting prettily on that marvelous white-gold hair.

He made his way down to her. "Darling, I just counted eight camels. That's more than expected."

"One of them will be a native guide." Even with the pith helmet, her elegant nose was peeling from the January sun. "You can't expect Mother, Catherine, and Michael to navigate the desert on their own. And I asked them to bring a minister to perform the ceremony."

"That still leaves three camels unaccounted for." He jumped down into the pit and wrapped his arms about her. He hadn't touched her in at least an hour, and that was an hour too long.

She nestled against his chest, taking care to keep her trowel from poking him. "You're hardly limping at all anymore, sweetheart. The bones in your leg must finally be healed."

"About time. It's been well over a year." Dylan gave her a long, lingering kiss. Her lips tasted of the tamarind juice she'd drunk for breakfast.

When he finally relinquished her mouth, she peeked up at him. "We don't have to get married, Dylan. I love you and promise to stay with you until I die. There's no need for a ceremony."

"Not that again."

"Just remember I didn't make a very dutiful or obedient wife the first time." Her lovely eyes turned dark and serious.

"It's not a dutiful and obedient wife I want, lass. I want *you,* and I want our child to be born with my name." He kissed her again. "And your eyes."

Camel bells sounded from the far end of the site. Nefer leaped out of the pit and went running off in that direction.

Charlotte peeked over his shoulder. "Our guests have arrived."

"I don't believe it." Dylan shaded his eyes from the sun. "That footman of your mother's is here. And Samson!"

"Randall *and* Samson? How extraordinary."

Dylan climbed out of the pit. Even more extraordinary

309

was the sight of a blond woman in a purple caftan. "Is that Aunt Hazel?"

"I wouldn't be surprised. She always wanted to perform her sun dance in the desert."

"I think she's already started." As soon as she got off her camel, Aunt Hazel ran over to the temple ruins and began darting about the sandstone pillars. All he could see now was a billowing purple caftan and Aunt Hazel waving her arms about as if she'd been bitten by a spider.

"Good lord," he muttered as he started off for their guests.

"Dylan, wait," Charlotte called after him. "I think I've found something down here."

But he was too amazed by the unexpected appearance of Samson Pope, who looked for all the world like an archaeologist: canvas boots, visored cap, work shirt with sleeves rolled up showing his already sunburnt arms. And he looked more relaxed and happy than Dylan had ever seen him.

"Sam, you rogue. What are you doing here?"

"Don't begrudge me a little fun. I haven't had a holiday in eight years." Samson clapped him on the shoulder. "And when I learned that you and Charlotte were at last getting married, I figured this was the perfect time to see the Pyramids."

"Dylan, look at me!" Michael waved his wide-brimmed hat in the air like a cowboy. "This is my first time on a camel. What fun! I could ride all the way to Sinai."

Lady Margaret kissed Dylan on the cheek. "We'll never get him off that animal. He was just like that with his first pony."

Randall appeared instantly at her side, offering her a drink from a canvas bag of water. "I don't know why the wedding couldn't be performed in Cairo, sir," he said with a disapproving sniff.

Dylan laughed. "Nice to see you too, Randall."

Lady Margaret pushed away the water. "Nonsense, Randall. Charlotte married Mr. Fairchild in Cairo. It would be bad

310

luck to marry there again. Besides, I found sailing on the *felucca* quite invigorating."

"Like mother, like daughter," Dylan said with a smile.

"Where is my daughter, by the way?" Lady Margaret gazed out over the vast site filled with workers, half-buried statues, and golden sand. "Unearthing some royal mummy?"

Catherine dismounted from her camel. Although Samson tried to assist her, she refused. However, she did take his friend's arm once she was on solid ground. For two people admittedly wary of the opposite sex, Dylan thought they seemed quite companionable.

"Yes, where is Charlotte?" Catherine gave him a quick hug. With her dark hair and tanned skin, the young woman looked positively Egyptian. "She wrote to us of her condition. I do hope she's not unwell."

"Charlotte is *never* unwell in Egypt." He gestured to where Charlotte was working. "Perhaps you can convince her to stop digging. I rarely have any luck. If nothing else works, tell her we're having *torshi* at our midday meal."

"Torshi?" Lady Margaret asked.

"Pickled turnips and limes." He lowered his voice. "She and the baby seem to crave it."

With a grin, Lady Margaret held out her hand so Randall could assist her over the uneven ground. Samson and Catherine sauntered off arm in arm, as if they were taking a stroll along Tottenham Court Road. Nefer ran after them, meowing until Catherine picked her up. Even over the din of the workers, Dylan could hear her sneeze.

He glanced over at the temple ruins where Aunt Hazel still danced among the pillars. As exhausting as they were, he was relieved the Graingers were so unconventional. Very few English families would sail all the way to Egypt to attend a wedding in the middle of a desert—and with the bride five months pregnant too. He only hoped the minister they brought was as liberal-minded.

"Where's the minister, Michael?" he asked the schoolboy as he trotted by on his camel.

"There!" He pointed to two men talking beside their camels.

Both men wore Arab headdresses and hooded ankle-length robes known as *jallabahs*. Dylan frowned. From this distance, neither fellow looked like a Protestant minister. Did they think to have an Islamic wedding?

Dylan decided to discuss this with the others first. It seemed that everyone had somehow managed to squeeze into the small excavation pit with Charlotte. When he got closer, he could hear shouts, and excited laughter.

"What's going on here?" He jumped into the unit and pushed his way to where Charlotte was kneeling.

He crouched beside her. "Charlotte, it's too close in here with all these people. Come out of the pit before you faint."

"Faint? Don't be silly. But you may faint when you see this."

She pointed with her trowel to the hieroglyphics barely discernible through the dirt. He silently read the inscription.

"Is it very important?" her younger sister asked.

He sat back, amazed. Charlotte hugged him.

"Isn't it glorious!" she said. "We're sitting atop the palace complex of Pharaoh Mehmet."

She stood up. Everyone gathered about as she began to relate the story of Mehmet, a powerful and rich Middle Kingdom pharaoh. And of the palace that was believed to have been destroyed. But Charlotte had found it again beneath the desert sands. Dylan began to laugh at the wonder of it. Lost and buried for thousands of years, the palace of Mehmet would be brought to life again—just as Charlotte's love had brought him to life.

"We must send straightaway to Cairo for more workers," Charlotte was saying. "Maspero at the Cairo Museum will have to be informed, and we must send a telegram to the Colvilles. Perhaps the boats haven't left yet. If we hurry, maybe we'll have time to sail back to Giza. I'd love to tell Maspero this in person."

Dylan stood up, no easy feat in a pit crowded with six adults and one large cat. "Charlotte, we're getting married."

She looked distracted. "Yes. Of course, Dylan."

"We're getting married today." He pulled her into his arms. "You've given me excuses for over a year."

"A few more days won't matter. This is such an important find and . . ." Her voice faded. She flushed under his gaze.

"You promised to marry me, lass. You've been my mistress long enough." He raised his eyebrow. "I've always grown tired of my mistresses. A wife, however, is a different matter."

"You've no reason not to marry Dylan," Lady Margaret said.

"And a very important reason *to* marry," added Catherine. "Think of the baby. Besides, even Mrs. Pankhurst married, and if marriage is good enough for her . . ."

"Do you love me, lass?" Dylan asked.

"You know I do," she said quietly.

"As much as this?" He nodded toward the surrounding pillars and statues—and the newfound discovery beneath them.

She gazed into his eyes so intently, he thought for a second that at least part of the mystery that was Charlotte had been revealed. "Maybe more," she whispered. "I may love you even more."

As they kissed, he heard Samson say, "About time."

"I'll fetch the minister." Randall climbed out of the pit.

Dylan pulled Charlotte into another tight embrace. "I didn't see anyone who looked like a man of the cloth."

"Oh, we brought a minister," said Catherine.

"Yes, he entertained us all the way from London." Samson sounded amused. "Better than five circus acts, let me tell you."

Dylan caught sight of Randall and another man striding

toward them. The other fellow suddenly flung off his *jalla-bah* and headdress. He indeed was wearing a clerical collar—as well as white knee breeches, sandals, and a bright yellow shirt with gold flowers embroidered on it. He turned his head once and Dylan saw that the man's thick brown hair was pulled back and tied with colored twine. His ponytail hung halfway down his back.

And when he smiled, his mouth glittered! It took Dylan a moment to realize that the minister had diamonds drilled into his front teeth.

"Who in the world is that?" Dylan said, stunned by the sight.

"Uncle Louis!" Charlotte clapped her hands in delight. "What a marvelous surprise."

Uncle Louis responded by jumping into the pit, nearly knocking everyone else down. He embraced his niece.

"As soon as I heard you needed someone to marry you, I got on the first boat leaving Iceland."

"Iceland?" Dylan asked. "What were you doing in Iceland?"

Instead of answering, Uncle Louis grabbed him in a bear hug. "So this is the man who jumped through a skylight for my niece. I have to admire such mad and foolhardy bravery. Yes, I do!"

"Come, Hazel, they're getting married." Lady Margaret waved her arms in the direction of the temple.

"Right this moment? I thought we'd have the ceremony after lunch." Dylan felt Nefer climb over his feet. "At the very least, we should get out of the excavation pit."

Charlotte put her hands on her hips, no small accomplishment amid the press of people. "Now who's looking for a way to delay our marriage?"

He kissed her once more. "Start the service, Reverend Louis."

Later on, he'd try to find out which denomination Uncle

Louis belonged to; he wouldn't be surprised if it was some congregation that met on Mars.

"We are blissfully gathered here today in the sight of—"

"Not yet!" Aunt Hazel arrived in a flurry of purple silk. Everyone groaned as she squeezed into the pit. Catherine put her arms about Samson's neck in order to make room.

Uncle Louis beamed at his niece, who was the prettiest bride Dylan had ever seen. Even if she wore a pith helmet for a veil and carried a trowel instead of a bouquet.

"We are gathered here together in the sight of God and—"

"Wait!"

Michael came running over, followed by all of Nefer's kittens. The boy had more sense than any of them and just stood along the edge of the hole, fanning his face with his cap. The kittens, however, leaped into the crowd, which sent Catherine into a fit of sneezing.

Charlotte laughed and gave Dylan a quick kiss on the cheek.

"Are we ready now?" Uncle Louis grinned. His teeth glittered in the sun.

But before he could begin again, Nefer jumped into Charlotte's arms. The desert cat rubbed her head against first Charlotte, then Dylan. Nestling against her mistress, Nefer finally settled back with a string of delighted purrs.

Dylan smiled. "*Now* we're ready."

Aphrodite's Kiss
Julie Kenner

Crazy as it sounds, on her twenty-fifth birthday Zoe has the chance to become a superhero. But x-ray vision and the ability to fly are only two things to consider. There is also her newfound heightened sensitivity. If she can hardly eat a chocolate bar without convulsing in ecstasy, how is she to give herself the birthday gift she's really set her heart on—George Taylor? The handsome P.I.'s dark exterior hides a truly sweet center, and Zoe feels certain that his mere touch will send her spiraling into oblivion. But the man is looking for an average Jane no matter what he claims. He can never love a superhero-to-be—can he? Zoe has to know. With her super powers, she can only see through his clothing; to strip bare the workings of his heart, she'll have to rely on something a little more potent.

___52438-4 $5.99 US/$6.99 CAN

Dorchester Publishing Co., Inc.
P.O. Box 6640
Wayne, PA 19087-8640

Alicia's Song

SUSAN PLUNKETT

For Alicia James, something is missing. Her childhood romance hadn't ended the way she dreamed, and she is wary of trying again. Still, she finds solace in her sisters and in the fact that her career is inspiring. And together with those sisters, Alicia finds a magic in song that seems almost able to carry away her woes.

In fact, singing carries Alicia away—from her home in modern-day Wyoming to Alaska, a century before her own. There she finds a sexy, dark-haired gentleman with an angelic child just crying out for guidance. And Alicia is everything this pair desperately needs. Suddenly it seems as if life is reaching out and giving Alicia the chance to create a beautiful music she's never been able to make with her sisters—all she needs is the courage to sing her part.

___52434-1 $4.99 US/$5.99 CAN

➤ the
Mermaid of Penperro
LISA CACH

Konstanze never imagined that singing could land someone in such trouble. The disrepute of the stage is nothing compared to the danger of playing a seductress of the sea— or the reckless abandon she feels while doing so. She has come to Penperro to escape her past, to find anonymity among the people of Cornwall, and her inhibitions melt away as she does. But the Cornish are less simple than she expected, and the role she is forced to play is harder. For one thing, her siren song lures to her not only the agent of the crown she's been paid to perplex, but the smuggler who hired her. And in his strong arms she finds everything she's been missing. Suddenly, Konstanze sees the true peril of her situation—not that of losing her honor, but her heart.

___52437-6 $5.50 US/$6.50 CAN

Dorchester Publishing Co., Inc.
P.O. Box 6640
Wayne, PA 19087-8640

WICKED ANGEL SHIRL HENKE

A gawky preacher's daughter, Jocelyn Angelica Woodbridge is hardly the type to incite street brawls, much less two in one day. "Holy Hannah," as those of the *ton* call her, would much rather nurse the sick or reform the fallen. Yet ever since a dashing American saved her from an angry mob, Joss's thoughts have turned most impure.

The son of an American Indian and an English aristocrat, Alexander Blackthorne has been sent to England for some "civilizing." But the only lessons he cares to learn are those offered by taverns and trollops. When a marriage of convenience forces Jocelyn and Alex together, Joss knows she will need more than prayer to make a loving husband of her . . . wicked angel.

___4854-X $5.99 US/$6.99CAN

BLACKHEART
TAMARA LEIGH

Desperate to put an end to the humiliating rumors surrounding his lack of an heir, Lord Bernart Kinthorpe orders his virgin wife to the bed of his sworn enemy, Lord Gabriel de Vere. Though Juliana expects to feel revulsion and pain in the arms of the blackheart responsible for her husband's impotence, she discovers a man of passion and honor.

When Gabriel de Vere learns that the sensual lover who had come to him in darkness is the wife of his enemy, he vows to take back the child stolen from him. Yet something about the woman he abducts turns him from vengeance. But the flower of their love will have to be carefully nurtured if they are to triumph over Lord Bernart and raise the child of their love as fate has intended.

____4855-8 $5.99 US/$6.99 CAN

. . . and coming
May 2001
from. . .

A Passionate Magic

Flora Speer

Sent as an offering of peace between two feuding families, Lady Emma is prepared to perform her wifely duties. But when she first lifts her gaze to the turquoise eyes of her lord, she senses that he is the man she has seen in her most intimate visions. Dain of Penruan has lived an austere life in his Cornish castle on the cliffs, and he doesn't intend to cease doing so, regardless of this arranged marriage to the daughter of his father's hated rival. But though he attempts to disdain Lady Emma, the lusty lord can not ignore her lush curves, or the strange amethyst light sparkling from the depths of her chestnut eyes. Perched upon the precipice of a feeling as mysterious and poignant as silvery moonlight on the sea, Lady and Lord plunge into a love that can only have been conjured by . . . a passionate magic.

___52439-2 $5.50 US/$6.50 CAN

Always a Princess

Alice Chambers

The woman is a fraud if ever Philip Rosemont has seen one. And not only is she masquerading as an aristocrat, the dark-haired beauty is posing as the Princess of Valdastok—a tiny country that has been a dukedom for years! Yet though this impostor can hardly be a noblewoman, Philip has good cause to believe he will find her anything but common.

Eve Stanhope despises the aristocracy: a gaggle of scoundrels that are noble in name alone. She has few scruples about stealing their jewels. But ripping off rubies is harder than she expected, especially when she is cornered by a man who knows too much. And if kisses are illicit, the viscount is an arch-criminal.

___4867-1 $4.99 US/$5.99 CAN